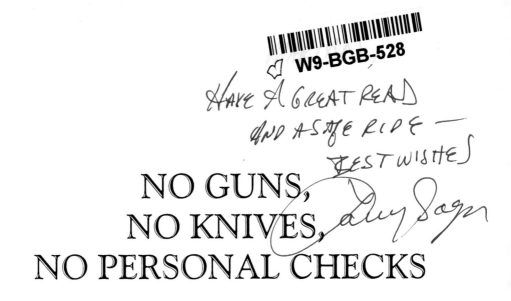
Have A Great Read and a Safe Ride — Best Wishes Larry Sager

NO GUNS,
NO KNIVES,
NO PERSONAL CHECKS

The Tales of a San Francisco Cab Driver

Larry Sager

All illustrations by Shanon Essex except for illustration
on page 181 by Emil

Printing by

Falcon Books, San Ramon, California

ISBN 10: 0-9785751-0-5
ISBN 13: 978-0-9785751-0-6

Published by
EVERETT MADISON PUBLISHING
41 Sutter Street, Suite 1557
San Francisco 94104
www.everettmadison.com
www.nogunsnoknives.com

This book is presented as a work of fiction. Any resemblance to persons living or
dead is entirely no coincidence. Names have usually been changed to obscure
the identities of those guilty, blameworthy, or otherwise at fault.

PRINTED IN THE UNITED STATES OF AMERICA

TABLE of CONTENTS

"What's your best cab story?"

"Ever pick-up any weirdos ?"

"Has a drunk ever puked?"

"Anyone ever have sex in your cab?"

"What happens when a guy won't pay?"

"Anyone ever try to kill you?"

"Do you get traffic tickets?"

"Can you refuse to give someone a ride?"

"Anyone ever die on you?"

"Are you ever scared?"

"Can't you catch diseases from sick passengers?"

"Ever kick someone out?"

"Are there other drivers who speak English?"

"What's your real job?"

These questions are all answered in this book.

—Larry Sager

INTRODUCTION

I think of San Francisco as a small, big city. Friendly neighborhoods from North Beach to the Castro contribute to the town's intimate cosmopolitan character.

There are traffic jams and homeless people. There are robberies and murders—of cab drivers.

Driving a cab has been rated the most dangerous job in the United States, surpassing the risk of being a police officer. At the same time, it is most entertaining. The cab driver transforms from driver to psychologist to whipping boy to public servant, all in a night's work. Especially in San Francisco, cab passengers are from diverse and contrasting walks of life: the rich and the poor, the sorry and the psychotic—drug dealers, gang members, French tourists, hookers, derelicts, celebrities, transvestites, policemen, muggers, churchgoers, pets and even other cab drivers. People sit in the back seat and share predicaments, a snippet of their lives. Sometimes a snippet is too much.

FOREWORD!
FROM THERE TO HERE

A combination of circumstances led to my applying for work at Yellow Cab Co-op, intended as a temporary fix for a temporary financial downturn. Although enjoying decent money working as a professional musician, I had grown tired of its hassles and hustles.

A long-time somewhat-friend and guitarist suggested cab driving as a solution. Long ago, he became more committed to IT than to his arpeggios, though he still characterized his driving as a temporary fix. He added a dire warning that the ease of the job leads to complacency, sometimes followed by depression and despondency, not necessarily in that order. I did note this "temporary fix" of his was now going on thirteen plus years.

Could I become **TRAPPED** by this job? Completely depressed? Despondent? Suicidal? I imagined it possible.

My virtuoso friend introduced me to yet another musical talent. They had grown up together, cohorts from a well-to-do burb in Ohio. His name was Bruce and he was anything but despondent and depressed.

In fact, Bruce was pleasantly upbeat, offering a personal demonstration of his latest original bass riffs, fed into his midi-powered digital recorder. After nine and one-half years of driving cab, he had dramatically cut back his hours, able to make more time for his musical pursuits, all while maintaining his standard of living at his abode located at 14th & Mission Streets (amidst one of the roughest couple of blocks in town). He also mentioned, in passing, that a newly-blossoming business was providing a supplement to his income: he was selling crack to everyone in the neighborhood. The challenge, of course, was making sure the local junkies didn't make off with his state-of-the-art musical recording equipment.

Might I wind up in a drab studio apartment, yellow-stained curtains and steel bars blocking the alleyway's morning sun, with some strange woman sprawled on the bathroom floor howling for more drugs? Possibly, but I couldn't entirely see that happening.

The driving part seemed a little more dangerous than my two anxious advocates would admit. Bruce advised that my apprehension about navigating through certain "dangerous areas" of the city was unfounded, fed by rumor and fear-mongering.

"The dealers on the street aren't interested in shooting people," Bruce explained. "They're interested in sales, making a profit. They don't want trouble." It sounded logical. I figured his advice came from first-hand experience.

Driving sounded flexible, even profitable. Working at night would free me to attend classes by day. The cab would simply be a vehicle to get me where I needed to go. Requirements of the job: a driver's license that is not suspended, knowledge of the city's few main streets, and no outstanding warrants. My driver's license was in good standing; I knew every city street north of Army (or Cesar Chavez, as some insist on calling it); and a few months of community service had expunged an outstanding assault charge stemming from a street confrontation with a guy who owed me money.

I applied for the job at the yard.

Completing my first Saturday day-shift—after 10 hours of driving; after paying the gate and gas; after tipping the cashier, the dispatcher, and the backroom radio guy (the only way to "pull an airport")—I netted a whopping $22.45 profit. When I was seven years old, I made more money selling Kool-Aid. Making some adjustments and seeking friendly advice, my bottom line quickly strengthened. Most helpful was luck. At the company's lottery, with the names of one hundred drivers on scraps of paper in a hat, my name was chosen. I was the owner of a coveted night shift.

And I was on my way.

CAT WOMAN

ow, she's quite something! Look over there, quick!"

"It's a guy."

"No. No way."

"Yep."

"She's beautiful. That's not a guy."

"Believe me," I tell them, "it's a guy."

"I'm talkin' about the one in black."

"So am I. It's a guy."

"Not the fat one," specifies the front seat passenger. "The skinny one."

"Yeah," I nod, "the good-looking one. It's a guy."

"How can you tell?"

"Well, I can't necessarily, except, on this street, any woman dressed like that is a guy."

It's Cat Woman. I first saw him/her a few weeks back, thought it was a one-time deal but, apparently, he's attempting to develop a specialized clientele. She's fully attired in a black leather miniskirt, black nylons, knee-high black leather boots and a low-cut bra showing plenty of cleavage. It's staggering. I don't know if it's makeup, transplants, hormones or what. She's swinging a whip and slithering up and down a silver lamppost, alternately wrapping one leg and then another around the pole—all this at the busy intersection of Bush and Larkin Streets. My two very heterosexual, blond, blue-eyed passengers salivate mentally from the front and back seats.

"Look at THOSE two," says the guy sitting next to me. "Now, *they* are women."

"No, they are men." I flip on my turn signal.

He's pointing at two transvestites walking along on the sidewalk. One brunette, and one with streaked blond hair, both dressed in tight stylish clothing, high heels and every hair on their heads neatly in place. I don't know if these guys wear wigs or just grow it long. Their hair looks great—shiny, full and healthy, right out of a shampoo commercial on TV.

"No way," argues the disbeliever, seated in the back. "Dude. I'm in love. Yes!"

"They're guys," I repeat.

"Let's just get out," excitedly advocates Back Seat Dude. His friend seated in the front has become a little less sure.

"Now that one over there," I say pointing, "walking in front of the two good-looking ones? She's a woman."

"No, no," says Back Seat Dude. "They're all women over there."

"The two good-looking ones are guys."

"No way," insists Back Seat Dude. "Let us out, *here*."

I figure these two as airheads from Los Angeles, but they're guys—"himbos," as Seinfeld would say. "You sure you wanna get out?" I ask. My only interest at this point is that they remain in the cab long enough for the meter to click off a few more dollars. That they might be confronted with a surprise package from one of these folks on the street doesn't matter to me, but I don't make money if they're out doing research on the difference between a male and a female.

"How can anyone tell?" asks Front Seat Dude.

"The closer you get," I slow the cab, "it becomes…clearer."

"Wowww. It *is* a guy. That's amazing, dude."

"Don't tell me that," says his back seat friend.

"On this side of Hyde Street, all the good-looking women are men."

"They're not men," the back seat surfer disagrees.

On the other hand, Front Seat Dude has now seen the light. "He's right." He turns to his friend. "Dude, she has gigantic hands. Look at her Adam's apple."

We drive another block down only to get stopped at another red light. Traffic is backed up from people stopping to ogle and negotiate with the transvestites. There's a guy dressed in a red sequined cocktail dress, matching long red nails and, of course, again with the perfect hair.

"Oh God, I'm in love," says Back Seat Dude. "Look at her. She's gorgeous."

I hear him shifting around in the seat.

"That's another guy," I tell him.

"Nooo. No way. I'm in love. Dude!"

"It's a man," says Front Seat Dude. "I'm gonna have to watch you."

The cab computer buzzes with a message on the screen: *ANYONE SEE CAB #294 TELL HIM HIS SHIFT IS OVER.*

"Where you guys from?" I ask.

"Santa Cruz. We're staying on Leavenworth. That's one scary place, dude."

I knew it. Surfers. "There's better and there's worse." I'm referring to the Leavenworth motel.

"The guy there gave us these clubs to check out. He was kind of … swishy or something."

"Yeah, we're not sure if we trust him. He was wearing make-up."

"Dude, he was not."

"Yes he was. You can't tell the difference between a man and a woman anyway."

I don't want them fighting with each other. A peaceful ride translates into a larger tip. "Where did he suggest?" I ask.

"The Triangle. Are there real women at the Triangle?"

"Yeah, the ones over there are real." We're at a standstill, stuck in heavy traffic.

"He also told us, um…the End Place?" He pulls out a folded piece of paper from the back pocket of his blue jeans.

"The End Up?" I clarify.

"Yeah, that's it. Is that place all right?"

"That's south of Market. They have lesbian night once in a while. Most of the time it's straight, I think. It's a popular place."

"Yeah, but we want to meet chicks who aren't dudes."

"Well, it's a possibility."

"What about the Pleasure Dome?"

"I don't go in these places, I just drop people off." Although I'm suspecting this guy back at their motel may have been jerking their chains.

Wowww. It is a guy. That's amazing, dude.

"How do you know which night it is?" asks worried Front Seat Dude, looking back at his friend with a newfound lack of trust.

"I'm not sure about the list," says Back Seat Dude. "The Triangle has lots of women, right?"

"I can't guarantee you numbers." A white pickup pulls up behind us and starts honking.

"What kinds of people go there?"

"You won't run into many guys dressed as women, unless it's Halloween." I slowly inch the cab forward. "You guys will like it there." I swerve out around a line of four cars and accelerate across Polk Street.

"Wait," says Front Seat Dude. "How much to get there?"

"How much ya got?" I ask.

"Dude, he's messin' with us."

"Six bucks or so," I volunteer.

"Fuckin' 'a,' dude! We're there."

I slam on the brakes as a disheveled ruffian wearing a black-stained, light grey jacket jaywalks in front of the cab. He tugs at his long matted brown hair while carrying a five-foot-long brown pole in his right hand, which he methodically hits on the ground as he walks. I tap the horn at him. He turns and gives me the finger, slows his pace, hits the pole against the ground once again, this time more violently, releases his hand and then catches the stick as it bounces up into the air. Nolan Ryan would admire his form. Maybe the guy is a former Olympic javelin thrower? They say the backgrounds of some homeless people are remarkable. Other than a shot at the Wheaties box, what career choice presents itself after a champion spear throwing stint? Harpoon fishing in Alaska? Cab driving? How far do those things travel? As a cab driver it could be a deadly deterrent for those pesky deadbeats who run off without paying. *The fare was up to $9.00 and he ran off, but I got him in the foot with my javelin.*

The light has turned red, against us. As it turns green, we continue across Van Ness and make a right onto Franklin Street. My speedometer indicates that we are gaining speed. We are headed slightly down hill, although tourists usually don't think of it as "slightly." Front Seat Dude has grabbed a tight hold on the armrest. Maybe they're not surfers.

"You ever scared, drivin' a cab?" he puffs, as he thinks to buckle his seat belt.

"Sometimes. More on my guard than scared." I tap the accelerator for more gas, just enough to make it through the timed green light on Franklin Street. The rear bumper scrapes the road as we gently bottom out at the foot of the hill.

"Really? Is it that dangerous?"

"A driver got murdered in Richmond. That was five months ago. Another driver was just found dead in his cab, over in San Mateo, two weeks ago."

"You don't have those shields. In L.A., they all got 'em."

"They're starting to require them," I affirm. "Supposedly, it's going to become mandatory."

"You don't want one?"

"I don't know. This last driver—they shot him through the front windshield—one bullet grazed his face, another bullet in his shoulder.

A shield wouldn't have done him much good, except to jam his knees into the dashboard while he's driving for ten hours."

"I guess you're careful who you pick up?" says one of the dudes.

"I try to be."

"Can you refuse people?"

"Yeah, if you think someone wants something other than a ride, like to kill you or rob you. But, well, the kids who shot the one driver—they weren't even his passengers. He was dropping someone off. Someone standing around on the street pulled a gun and shot him."

"Damn." Front Seat Dude nervously tugs at his seat belt. "I wouldn't drive a cab."

"That driver just came back to work, too. I saw him a few nights ago."

We make a left on Broadway.

"How did he look?"

"Not that dramatic, big bandage on his cheek…he lost a lot of weight; bunch of guys asking him questions. They looked like the paparazzi."

"Wow. Radical, man."

"I'd think he'd give it up." Now I make a nervous adjustment to the side view mirror.

"Maybe he figures he won't get shot again," offers Back Seat Dude. "Like earthquakes, they don't strike the same place twice."

"Dude. That's lightning," corrects his traveling partner. "Lightning doesn't hit twice."

"Whatever." He pulls a piece of gum from his jacket pocket.

"Well, don't worry," assures Front Seat Dude. "We're not gonna shoot you."

"Good, I was worried about that."

A guy pulled out a knife a couple of weeks ago, wanting a free ride down Mission Street. I'm not comfortable telling people those details. I didn't even tell my girlfriend. She already wants me to quit.

I turn right on Fillmore Street overlooking the Golden Gate Bridge and Alcatraz. We descend the steep hill. This one is actually a REAL hill, the one they've loaded with snow for that summer skiing event. We cross Union Street to Filbert. It's a busy night at Pierce Street Annex, music blasting. We stop.

"It's happening. Thanks, bro'," says Front Seat Dude. "We really appreciate this."

"Careful where you stick it," I advise. "Keep some rubbing alcohol on hand."

"Right, dude!" He hands me a ten-dollar bill. "How much is it?"

"$6.80." I hand him three dollars.

He gives it back to me. "Keep it, dude."

"Thanks." I pocket the cash. Turning off the meter to make me eligible for another fare, I book-in on the computer, pressing the "book" button—"five"—"three"—"send." The computer beeps twice and I'm logged into Zone 53—the Marina District. The computer beeps again—setting off the car alarm of a red convertible parked across the street. The alarm completely startles a couple of romantics, no longer holding hands, who were walking on the sidewalk next to the once undisturbed car. They turn their heads and veer away from the shiny red vehicle, as if to avoid being found guilty of a violation. Meanwhile, Back Seat Dude is still trying to get out of the cab.

"What's up with that?" he asks.

"The computer sets off car alarms," I tell him. "Some car alarms."

"Radical!" He sticks his hand out at me and we do a version of the hip-dude-surfer-handshake.

"Hey," he says, "can you come back in a couple hours to pick us up?"

"If I'm in the neighborhood, I'll honk."

"That's cool. What's your cab number?"

"It's 490. It's on the side of the cab."

"Can we call and request you?"

"Dispatch won't do that."

"Dude, do you have a cell phone? We could call you when we're done."

"Sorry, no cell phone," I inform them.

"Oh, you should get one, dooo-ood. We're gonna look for you."

The computer beeps again: ZONE 53—PLACE 3. In Zone 53, I'm third in line, back on the road. I drive empty all the way to downtown. At Powell and Market Streets, two women flag me down. They're both smoking cigarettes, walking stiffly, wearing leather jackets and sporting tough-looking hair.

"Is it okay if we smoke?"

Besides being deathly allergic to it, there's nothing I hate more than breathing cigarette smoke—second to inhaling exhaust fumes. And I'm getting plenty of those already.

"It's a no-smoking cab," I pronounce. "Sorry."

"That's okay," says the skinny one with barely a figure. Her larger companion does not look as agreeable. They request a few extra moments before having to bid their final farewells.

"Take your time," I tell them.

Both take hard James Dean drags, blow out the smoke and throw down their butts. The larger woman glares back, as though she'd prefer stomping me into the curb rather than her barely smoked cig. The possibility of a good tip has likely been extinguished as well. No one elicits less sympathy from smokers than a non-smoker—a non-smoker telling them not to smoke.

"We're going to Clay and Polk, please," says the skinny woman, politely.

"Right by the donut shop," demands the bigger, tougher-looking woman. "Geez, I'm so fuckin' tired."

They sit side-by-side in the back seat. A billow of residual cigarette smoke fills the cab. I roll my window down several inches.

"We'll get home, watch some television—crash out," adds the skinny one, petite and feminine despite her dirt-stained baseball cap.

In contrast, her friend is about forty-five pounds overweight, has a five o'clock shadow and a permanent scowl on her face. Ditching the cigarettes is not going to improve her mood. It seems an unusually high percentage of people who ride cabs smoke cigarettes, at least those flagging my cab. If they're out drinking, they're also usually smoking. Over the last few weeks I've tried a new anti-smoking approach that has enjoyed limited success as well as relieved some of the tensions created by separating these poor souls from their tobacco sticks.

"Sorry about the cigarettes," I apologize. "I just quit, sort of."

"That's okay," says the skinny one.

"I'm on a patch," I tell them.

"Oh yeah?" says the bigger one, nodding. "That's hardcore."

I glance back and catch sight of her sparkling green eyes, thick blond eyebrows, large teeth, and the military dog tag attached to a thick silver chain hanging around her neck. She looks like she could tear me limb from limb.

"Good luck," says the petite one.

"What?"

"On the smoking, good luck."

"Oh, thanks. I need it." Rare is the smoker who hasn't tried to give up the habit (several times).

"Does that shit work?" questions the tough one. "How many milligrams you takin'?" She has a hoarse resonating voice, a bad temperament and asks too many questions.

"Ummm," I stall, not knowing the answer. Milligrams aren't very big, could be twenty, fifty, a thousand? It's something I should know if I'm taking them. "Not enough to keep me from wanting a cigarette," I reply.

They both chuckle. The tough one seems nice enough. She imparts the impression that she doesn't take crap from anybody.

"Here," she says to me. "Have a cigarette."

"Don't offer him a cigarette," scolds her friend. "It's hard enough trying to quit." She's attractive in her own way; a cute little nose and a soft soothing voice, except two of her teeth are missing. If she grew her hair out a little, that would help. Shopping in the women's department might not hurt either.

"I'll take a cigarette." I humor them and hold out my hand.

"No, you won't," says the cute one. "You're gonna make it. You gotta think positive."

"I'm thinking positive." I take a right on Larkin. "I'm positive I'm going to start smokin' again."

"You can't think that way."

The cab computer buzzes once again: *CAB #294 YOUR SHIFT IS OVER. DONE. BRING IN THE CAB. NOW!*

"Disgusting. It's a disgusting fuckin' habit," says the tough one. "I wish I could quit. But I gotta have a cigarette with my morning coffee."

"And after sex," pokes her friend. "Beth was on a patch. She's smoking again."

"Yeah," says the fatter one. "If you smoke a cigarette while you're on that, you can have a heart attack."

She actually had me on the road to feeling guilty about my feigned withdrawal symptoms from a non-existent habit. This woman knows all about this stuff: patches, milligrams, heart attacks… She's trying to kill me.

"My doctor warned me about that," I nod.

"I hope you make it," says the cute one. "I heard it takes ten tries for a smoker to finally really quit."

"Well, it's only my seventh time." I turn on the rear window defroster.

"Fuck, it's easier to give up heroin than cigarettes."

"I feel like I'm cheating with this patch," I confess.

"Shit," says the tough one. "Whatever it takes; wish I could quit."

"Yeah," I acknowledge, tapping my fingers on the steering wheel, creating an odd polyrhythm. "If you don't smoke, don't start." I lightly continue the finger tapping, as if I've developed a permanent nervous tic. "And if you smoke, don't quit."

If she knew the truth, she'd be body slamming me on the pavement.

Instead of going over to Polk, I purposely stay on Larkin to see if Cat Woman is still doing her gymnastics. We get stopped at the light on Bush. Cat Woman is still there, slowly caressing the street pole up and down with her long, silk-stocking-covered leg.

"Boy," says the cute one. "Look at her."

Cat Woman points his whip and blows us a kiss. "Hey Mr. Cab Man, aren't you lonely?" he asks.

My window is still rolled down from when the dynamic duo got into the cab accompanied by a cloud of smoke.

"She was here about twenty minutes ago," I remark. "Two Santa Cruz surfers fell in love with her."

They both laugh. I wonder if they actually condemn this scene as some male chauvinist, sexist portrayal of women. We drive a couple of blocks to California Street and make a left turn. At Polk Street, we make a right.

"Would you mind stopping at that store?" requests the tougher one. "Over there, next to the burger place. You want anything, driver?" she asks.

"Yeah," I answer, "a pack of cigarettes."

"You're not gettin' no cigarettes," says the cute one, giving her friend a scolding look. "You're gonna quit."

"Okay, no cigarettes. Thanks for asking, though." I'm suddenly worried about making the big tough one jealous—this banter between her mate and me is getting a little flirtatious. Maybe that's why she's trying to kill me. I'm gonna shut up. We drive a few more blocks. I pull into a bus stop and the fat one gets out.

"Don't forget my beer," says the skinny woman, remaining in the cab. "You have enough for a six-pack?"

"Yeah," says her friend as she shuts the cab door.

At the risk of being offensive, obtrusive, and losing my tip, I'm curious about her reaction to Cat Woman—wondering how two women who have rejected their stereotypical sexual roles view this man aspiring to present himself as a female sex object. Even if she doesn't like the question, she's much less likely to smack me than her friend.

"What did you think of Cat Woman back there?" I ask.

"San Francisco has some strange, confused people. I guess it's part of what makes the city interesting. I used to go to the movies a lot, before I moved here. Now I spend more time just walking around town."

The cab computer buzzes. The message reads: *BEWARE GREENWICH BETWEEN BRODERICK/DIVISADERO—FLYING ORANGES.*

Her friend returns with a large shopping bag and I drop the two of them off at their apartment, where they will cap off their evening with cigarettes, beer and television.

It's back on the road for me, looking for customers. Driving back through the Tenderloin, I notice a commotion on the street up ahead: screeching horns, shrieking voices and red taillights. It's a young teenage female in distress, a prostitute as best I can tell, weaving in and out of traffic, on foot, screaming at the passing cars for both sympathy and a ride, desperately trying to get a cab, or anyone, to stop and help her. In one hand, she looks to be carrying a black object. I notice two other taxi drivers who refuse to let her into their cabs. She is approaching me from the middle lane, the sole cause of a backup now stretching halfway down the block, due both to her actual obstruction while straddling traffic lanes and an essentially see-through loose-fitting pink blouse revealing an almost equally see-through lace bra. She's *at best* 18 years old, appears rather sympathetic, to me, not particularly dangerous, and seems to have a painfully severe limp. I pull over to the right, through two lanes of traffic, contributing further to the ruckus, honking and gridlock.

"Fuuuu-uck," she screams. "Why don't you stop?"

"I'm stopped," I say to her.

"Son-of-a-bitch." She gets into the back seat, out of breath, fumbling with her purse in one hand and a black high-heeled shoe in the other. "Shit!" She slams the door shut.

I look back at her. A trickle of blood flows from her left nostril. The bridge of her nose looks black and blue, a sharp contrast to her creamy light complexion. Her white leather miniskirt has a noticeable black smudge of dirt or grime. It's also riding up on her and she was already showing plenty of leg.

"Are you okay?" I ask.

"No! Get me to the fucking hospital."

"Which one?"

"Stupid asshole, I don't give a shit. What the fuck is wrong with you?"

"There's Hyde and Bush?"

"Shit, the closest one. Just go!"

"Okay." I want to ask if she has money. She's going through her purse and applying tissues to her face. She's definitely a working girl. I assume she can come up with a few bucks for the ride. Once she stepped into the cab, traffic seemed to immediately calm down and start moving smoothly.

"Are you all right? Do you want me to call for the police?"

"No, I don't want the police."

I drive down Geary and take a right onto Leavenworth.

"Where the fuck are you going?" she accuses.

"Hyde and Bush. That's the closest hospital, isn't it?"

"How the fuck should I know? You're the cab driver. I'm not from this fucking town."

"It's right down this street."

"You don't know where the fucking hospital is?"

"We're two minutes away."

"Shit. Never mind, just take me home."

"Okay. Where is home?"

"O'Farrell and Taylor."

It's in the opposite direction. I go around the block, doubling back to where we came from.

"Where the fuck are you taking me, now?"

"Look, you want O'Farrell and Taylor, right?"

"Can't you see I'm hurt?"

"Do you want the hospital?"

"Just fucking get me to 1140 Post Street, the fastest way."

"1140 Post," I repeat. I'm feeling highly suspicious of whether she has money. The fare hits $2.90.

"Shit," she comments while going through her purse again. "That son-of-a-bitch."

"What's wrong?"

"Nothing. Can't you fuckin' drive faster?"

"Listen, I'm nice enough to pick you up and you're just fucking rude." I pull the cab to a stop. "Get out."

"You're right," she apologizes, wipes her nose with a finger and sniffs. "I'm sorry. I was ripped off."

"Oh," I answer. "Ripped off" could mean any number of things: her pimp took her money, a john didn't pay, someone on the street attacked her—maybe she wasn't ripped off at all. Someone *did* hit her in the face. I gently hit the gas. We continue in silence until we arrive at 1140 Post, a large apartment building. I double-park in front. I turn to collect the fare as she closes her purse and dashes out of the cab—without paying.

"Hey!" I quickly get out and follow her. "That's $3.50."

She runs up the marble steps of the apartment building and grabs the phone hanging at the side of the door. I'm right behind her.

"The fare is $3.50," I calmly recite, watching her every move. If she had wanted some help for a few minutes, I would have been fine with that. I don't like her attitude; I want the three-fifty.

"Leave me alone," she growls. "The guy stole my money."

"Go to the bank," I suggest. "I'm not a free public service."

She hesitates, then dials #303 on the silver intercom. If ever there was a favorite prostitute's line to a john, it would be "*Let's go to the bank machine*," always said in a very innocent, sincere tone of voice—like it was the first time it ever occurred to them. "*I'm coming, I'm coming*" is another expression of sincerity, reserved for later in the evening.

"Are you going to pay me? The fare is $3.50."

"Man, I told you." She impatiently taps her foot. "I was ripped off."

"That's not my problem."

"Fuck you."

"If you don't have money, don't take a cab."

"I told you. I got fuckin' ripped off."

"So you're gonna rip me off?"

"It's me," she barks into the phone.

"I want the money," I tell her.

She slams the phone back on the receiver. The door buzzes, she runs in.

As the door begins to close, I put my foot on the sash to keep it open as she hurries through the apartment corridor. "Pay," I repeat, "or I'll call the police."

"What is fucking wrong with you?" She runs back to the door, unsuccessfully trying to close it on my foot. She gives up, then runs down the hallway.

Should I follow her? The cab is still running on the street. I grab a yellowing newspaper lying outside on the porch, prop the door open, go back to the cab and turn the engine off. The meter reads $4.10. I walk back up the white marble stairs, pick up the phone and dial #303, apartment number twelve. It rings twice.

A woman answers. "Hello?"

"Hello. Your friend just took a cab and didn't pay the fare. She owes four dollars and ten cents."

"I don't know anything about it."

CLICK.

I dial again: pound—three—zero—three.

"Hello?" It's the same woman.

"Listen, apartment twelve, this is the cab driver again…"

She hangs up. Fighting over a few dollars is ridiculous. It's simply the principle. I redial. This time, a man answers.

"I'm calling the police," I tell him, "unless someone gets out here and pays the cab fare, right now."

"I didn't take a cab."

"Well, your friend did."

"It's not my friend."

"I don't care who it was. Pay it, or deal with the cops." There's no way I'm going to call the cops—to recover four dollars? It could be hours until they show up, if at all.

"Quit calling us."

"They might be interested in your little prostitution ring."

"What? There aren't any prostitutes here."

"Tell it to the police, pal."

There's a pause.

"How much is it?" he asks.

"It's $4.70."

"Okay, I'll pay it." He hangs up.

I wait three minutes and still no one appears at the door. I call again.

"Hello?" It's the same man.

"The police are on the way."

"She's coming down to pay you."

As I'm debating what to say next, a woman appears in the hallway and walks toward me. I hang up.

"How much is it?" she asks.

"Five dollars and thirty cents."

"I thought it was four-something."

"The meter runs until I get paid." *My Cab Policy.*

"Here." She hands me six dollars.

I reach into my pocket for change as she turns and walks away. I return to the cab and book into Zone 26. The computer beeps: *Zone 26—Place 1.* I drive down Post, circle around Union Square and head back down Geary to Polk Street. I'm starting to be sorry I didn't short-shift earlier, when I had the opportunity. At Polk and Bush, I pick up two guys on a flag.

"We're going to Pleasure Dome at Second and Townsend."

I hit the meter.

"Could you shut that window?" pleads his fashionable companion, dressed in a bright-orange jacket, red-orange and black striped slacks, black gloves and oversized black horn-rimmed glâsses. If he's striving for that Halloween pumpkin effect, he has succeeded.

I roll the window up most of the way. Pumpkin Man's friend reeks from some awful perfume. Yes, it's patchouli. It's a close call whether I'd prefer smelling that or ripe body odor. The computer buzzes with a message: *THERE IS NO EXCUSE FOR REAR ENDING ANOTHER.*

"What's that noise?" inquires Pumpkin Man.

"It's the computer, a message from headquarters," I explain. "Actually, the radio room." Pumpkin Man rests his arm on the front passenger seat headrest and leans over to view the computer communication. Within the last fourteen hours, I estimate that he has consumed a meal heavily spiced with garlic. He reads aloud: "There is no excuse for rear ending another."

"Another what?" blurts out his perfumed friend.

"I think it's a typo," says Pumpkin Man.

"Another car," I volunteer, taking a left on Townsend as we violently hit a large pothole.

"How 'bout, there's no excuse for hitting another rear end?" quips the perfumed Prince of Skunk, adjusting his bluish-gray sport coat, which covers a white shirt buttoned stylishly to the top.

"That would work," says Pumpkin Man, leaning back into his seat.

Crossing Third Street, we arrive at the club. I pull ahead of two other cabs at the entrance, which is pulsating from blazing, loud, monotonous music. A line of people awaits their chance to crowd into the club. The meter reads $5.60. I'm handed a defiled and pungent twenty-dollar bill and told to "make it seven." My sinuses are reduced to involuntary convulsions from the particle bombardment of the powerful and odious cologne that has now penetrated almost every molecule of the cab's interior. I hit the button for the automatic window. It swiftly rolls down all the way, as I hand Skunk Prince his thirteen dollars.

"Thanks," I say. "Have a good night."

"You, too." They get out and walk to the back of the line.

"Keep your friend away from any open flames." The remaining windows roll down in unison, as I turn the heater to full blast, causing my windshield to fog. I make a slow U-turn on Townsend, hoping for a fare off the computer. Not one for where I am, but where I intend to be in about eight minutes. As my windshield clears, I book-in on the computer. It beeps twice. There's a pause, and it beeps again. I'm fourth in line for Zone 26, essentially the Western Addition. It's a slow night, getting slower. That zone usually has only one cab—mine.

I take a right on Third Street, drive past the Moscone Center and turn left on Howard. At Fifth Street, two guys with bad haircuts wildly wave their arms at me. It's marginal gang territory, not a good area to be walking the streets at this time of the night. Most people out on the street are either dealing, hustling, drunk, on drugs, or passed out. When business is slow and you've barely made enough to pay the gate, you can get into trouble by picking up someone you wouldn't normally stop for. Generally speaking, if I see someone flagging in this area, I lock the doors and keep driving. Even if the person flagging appears an acceptable risk, there could be someone else standing in a doorway armed with a knife, gun, or glass bottle (just for kicks), ready to trash you or your cab.

I slow down to get a better view of these two haircut-challenged gentlemen. They don't look dangerous, just goofy and probably lost. If it wasn't for their white jackets and white shoes, they might pass as businessmen. Maybe they're evangelists. Do evangelists tip well? I doubt it, but stop the cab anyway to make a closer assessment, hoping not to appear suspicious of them—which can also cause repercussions. Someone might take it out on you because they thought you thought they were suspicious looking—reasoning similar to the "what are you looking at" syndrome, both of which are excellent reasons to beat someone to within an inch of his life.

"Can you take us?" asks the taller haircut of the two.

"Where are you going?"

He steps closer toward the cab window. "Away from this area, please."

Sounds reasonable. I'd request the same. "Okay." I wave them forward. I unlock the doors, they get in, and we proceed toward Market Street as the windows roll closed.

"It is our last night in town. My brother and I want a special place. What do you recommend?"

Tourists. "What are you looking for?"

"We want a good place."

"Do you want dancing, beer, a full bar, a local place, live music?"

I still smell the residue from the Prince of Skunk's nauseating perfume. The brothers converse in an odd language—not as hard and curt as German, not quite the easy ebb and flow of Swedish.

"Where we can meet women."

I need more information. "Where are you from?"

"We are from Finland," he proudly announces.

The closest to Finnish I know are a few words in Swedish, mostly having to do with calling people "farmer-devils." In Sweden, the worst form of an insult is to call someone a farmer. In Japan, farmers are held in the highest regard. I don't know about Finland.

"Do you ever get to Sweden?" I ask.

"We have cousins in Stockholm," says the shorter haircut. Like I'm going to know his cousins. Now I'm going to disappoint them. I just want to know if they are familiar with any farmer-devils.

It's good to say a few words to foreign tourists in their native language; it makes them a little more comfortable. But, still, they figure if you're driving a cab they're going to be taken to their destination using the most circuitous route possible. (I know it when I'm a tourist in a strange city.) Although San Francisco tourists are in strange surroundings, you can tell by the expressions on their faces they're excited to be here. At the same time they're worried about dealing with "the unknown" of a city—and an American city at that—especially for Europeans who have been watching too many cowboy and mobster movies, or who still think it's the Wild West. So they go to Fisherman's Wharf, The Hard Rock Cafe, maybe hop on a tour bus, then it's back to the hotel. A low-risk agenda, plus they get some T-shirts out of the deal.

The brothers converse again in Finnish. I imagine what they're saying: *Why does this taxi stink so, my brother? American cab drivers cannot afford to bathe with hot water. Disgusting. They are like Swedish farmers.*

"Finland is a beautiful country, isn't it?"

"It's very cold."

"It gets cold here, too."

"San Francisco is warm compared to Finland."

I try to think of an area where these two guys would have some choice of things to do, and still make the ride worth my while.

"Have you been to North Beach? That's Broadway and Columbus—the strip places, naked women—between Fisherman's Wharf and Chinatown."

"We have seen this, how do you say, but we have not gone."

"There are lots of bars, good music, restaurants. Tourists miss it by going to Fisherman's Wharf and the Hard Rock Cafe."

"We will go there, as you say."

Sold. We cross Market, zigzag past the major downtown hotels, pass several cable cars on Powell Street, wind our way to Kearny Street, and turn left on Columbus.

"That's a jazz bar." I point to the right.

We pass the former location of the Carol Doda neon sign on the corner of Broadway and Columbus. Next door, there's an adult bookstore with a red, black and white neon sign flashing: "*Will Work for*

Sex." My passengers express interest in the neon sign on the opposite side of the street reading: *"Live Sex Acts.*" On Columbus we pass an establishment promising *"Talk To a Naked Girl for a Dollar."*

The brothers converse excitedly in Finnish.

"Grant Street has a couple of blues bars, a rock 'n' roll place, some cafes."

"We want some quiet. Not many people. We want to sit with women and conversation. Do you understand?"

"There's naked-girls-for-a-dollar," I offer.

"This is not what my brother and I have in our mind."

"There are some very good restaurants here." I'm happy to drive them around in circles. "This area is not as much a tourist trap as it looks."

"We don't want the tourists trap."

They're a couple of wild and crazy guys.

"Have you been to Union Street?"

"No, what is on the Union Street?"

"Bars, restaurants; the stores are kind of…international. It's safe to walk around," I add. The brothers discuss their options. "Take us there."

The computer beeps with a message: *ANYBODY FIND A WALLET?* It sets off the alarm on a pickup truck parked next to us.

The two brothers crane their necks to see what or who has caused the alarm to go off, hoping to catch a glimpse of an authentic American burglar. Alas, there is no one on the street, let alone someone burglarizing the truck. The one brother makes a quiet but serious inquiry to the other brother, in Finnish. I make a left onto Stockton Street.

"It is dangerous in this area?" asks the brother.

"It's pretty safe here," I say, as the whooping car alarm fades in the distance. "That's Coit Tower." I point. "Lit up over there. On a clear night it has the best view in the city."

"Can you drive us for different areas of the city?" asks the brother.

"Sure, it's up to you."

"You do not mind?"

We enter the Broadway Tunnel.

"I drive in circles all night. Not a problem."

"We want to see the homosexual people. Do you know them?"

"Well…" I restrain my laughter, "There's Castro Street, if that's what you mean."

"We have heard of these areas to look. Is that all right?"

"That's fine, but there's really nothing there. Have you heard of the Mother Lode?"

"No."

"It's, ahh…it's a transvestite bar. Men dressed as women. We could drive by there."

"Yes. We do not want to go in, but we will look, only to look."

"That's fine."

"We are not the homosexuals. Do you understand?"

"Yeah, yeah, I understand."

Meanwhile, there's a line of seven cabs in front of the upscale pickup joint on the corner of Broadway and Polk. Although the windows are tinted very dark, two female patrons can be seen dancing on the bar countertop. I turn left down Polk Street.

We're headed back toward Cat Woman's turf and the transvestite prostitute scene. Turning left on Post to Larkin, we stop at the entrance of the MOTHER LODE. The bar is moderately crowded. Repetitive dance music blares out from the inside. A security guard watches us from the doorway.

"You see the women in that bar?" I ask them.

"Yes."

"They're all men."

"No!"

There's a row of parked cars between us and the entrance to the popular establishment. The brothers are craning their necks from the back seat to look inside the bar. There's a customer with shoulder-length blond hair, wearing a blue and red formal evening gown with matching long gloves, dancing and mouthing the words to resounding dance music from atop the elevated stage next to the dance floor. We continue to observe as a shapely young man with slender legs, wearing a shiny two-piece leather outfit, walks into the bar.

"These all men?" asks the brother.

"All men."

From inside the bar, a group of people notices the brothers and me vying for position to get a better look at the clientele. They crane their necks back at us in an exaggerated manner, returning our stares. I decide to leave before someone gets upset with us. As we pull away, two young cuties wearing tight mini-dresses, low-cut blouses and glossy boots strut and wiggle, walking alongside the cab. One waves at us and winks.

"Hi, boys," says the second one, blowing a kiss in our direction.

My passengers' eyes are fixed on them.

"Those two there?" I say to them. "Men."

The one brother explains the "situation" to his brother.

"These are men?" he asks, for some reason, astonished.

"All guys," I comment.

"How do you know this?"

"In this area, the men dress like women."

"Something is *very* wrong with these people."

"Well, I don't know. If it's not one thing, it's something else."

"We don't have this thing in Finland. In Finland we are, how do you say—NORMAL."

Right. This stuff probably originated there.

"You don't have any of this—over there?" I ask.

"No. In Finland, we have the mother and the father together. Do you understand? My English is not good."

"You mean families?"

"Yes, families."

We get to the corner of Bush Street. I look to the right and there's Cat Woman, still writhing and wrapping her legs around the light pole. She bats her eyelashes at our yellow vehicle, lowers her leg from the pole, turns and juts out her breasts toward the three of us.

"Hey, Mr. Cab Man," Cat Woman seductively shouts, staring us up and down. "Aren't you hungry?"

"She is quite something," says the brother.

"That's a man, too," I tell them.

The brothers converse.

"We must leave here, right away. It is very upsetting to my brother. Do you understand? We have seen enough."

"I understand." They truly seem a bit bent out of shape. We continue up Larkin toward California Street. "Where would you like to go now?"

"You know," says the brother, "some things in America are not good."

31

I offer an abbreviated chuckle and raise my hand in the air to surrender.

"We would like to go to the Union Street," he says.

"Sure."

Four minutes later, at Union and Octavia Streets, I point left. "That place usually has some good jazz bands. You guys want to look?"

"Would you wait?" asks the brother.

"I'll wait." I stop the car. Both get out, go into the bar, and come right back.

"It is too noisy," says one brother. "Too many people."

"Okay. There are more places down the block."

"Yes, please."

I stop at a second place.

"There are not enough people there," one of them whines.

They're actually getting on my nerves now. We stop at a third bar.

"Too young," says the shorter haircut, as if he had just conducted a comprehensively profound scientific analysis. "We want to meet three women; to sit and talk."

Maybe they want me to set up some blind dates? Is that what taxi drivers in Finland do? And how do they come up with three? I drive down Fillmore Street past two solid blocks of bars and restaurants. They don't like any of them. They're looking for a group of women with a sign saying:

```
┌──────────────────────────────────┐
│   WELCOME TWO BROTHERS           │
│      FROM FINLAND—               │
│      WE DESIRE YOU.              │
└──────────────────────────────────┘
```

"I don't know anywhere else to take you."

They then host another intercontinental Finnish conference.

"Do you know where we find prostitute?"

"Prostitutes? Umm, yes, but, you know, that's illegal here."

"We would like women for sex. Please understand us."

"The prostitutes are downtown, the better-looking ones."

"Take us downtown."

Traffic is thinning out. We make a couple of passes downtown. The girls are out in full force: three on the corner of Taylor and Post, five on Mason at Geary, four more over on Powell.

"Are they clean?"

Clean?

"They're prostitutes. You take your chances," I warn. Once again I try not to laugh. Maybe there are government controls in Finland. Regardless, it's probably too cold for any type of bacteria to be able to survive. But they seem to understand.

Altogether, I've been driving them for forty-five minutes. The taller brother informs me that, since they must be up early in the morning, they have decided to go back to their hotel on Post Street. Maybe they don't like what they see; maybe they don't like what I told them. Maybe they now realize that, on the streets of San Francisco, commodities are offered "as is" and it's "buyer beware."

We drive down Sutter to Van Ness and back to Post. The fare is $23.30. They get out of the cab. The taller haircut turns to address my services.

"You are the best cab driver."

"Thank you." Many European tourists don't tip—most of them don't. I have a good feeling about these guys.

"This night we will have in our memory."

"Good, I'm glad. Sorry we couldn't find a place you liked."

"No, please. It was a good tour. We appreciate much; very much."

Big tip—unless they tip like Germans.

"We write a letter to your boss and tell him."

A letter? Maybe drivers in Finland get a salary, I don't. But, putting in a good word can't hurt. "Here." I hand him a yellow receipt. "You can call them at this number."

The meter goes to $23.60 as they say their goodbyes. He hands me a twenty and a five.

"Keep the change for you," says the brother proudly. Letters, phone calls—how about a real tip? They trudge into their hotel, white coats, haircuts and all.

Driving down Post, I turn right on Powell, pass the front entrance of the St. Francis, and make a right on Geary. Besides the prostitutes and a police car, there's one panhandler on the street, another guy in a sleeping bag tucked away in an art gallery's doorway, and a woman yelling obscenities at a brick wall as one of her breasts hangs out of her flannel shirt. I drive past the American Conservatory Theater and several more four and five-star hotels. Nothing. Circling around to North Beach by way of Johnny Love's joint might lead to some business, especially traveling on Polk Street. Caught at the stoplight on Larkin, I change my mind, wondering how Cat Woman's doing. I turn right and pass the MOTHER LODE. On the sidewalk several male prostitutes continue to strut and pose in their miniskirts and nylons, baring their cleavage and various protrusions. I drive two blocks to Bush Street. Cat Woman's gone; her pole—vacant. Maybe he got a customer, maybe he just went home. I wonder if his night has been more profitable than mine.

The light turns green. And I step on the gas.

OLD AGE

A woman and a small boy about three years old are riding in the back seat. His mom has strapped him down with the seat belt.

Out of nowhere, he asks me a question: "How old are you?"

"That's not polite to ask," says his mother. "And give me that."

"How old do you think I am?" I playfully ask.

He ponders the question for a moment. "Eight years old?" he asks in a serious, contemplative tone.

"Actually, I'm a little older than that. Eight years old must seem pretty old to you."

"Yeah." He nods his head in the affirmative as we look into each other's eyes in my rear-view mirror.

How cute.

"Give it to me!" says the mother. "Give me that milkshake," she demands.

I didn't see a milkshake. And at about that point, this eight-year-old future Bob Feller slash Roger Clemens throws the milkshake—somehow making its way over the front seat head-rest, exploding upon impact against the front passenger-side closed window—turning the jet black interior to a milky vanilla-white.

THE OLD TIMER

Read the published reports of the United Taxicab Workers (UTW) union. Robberies happen constantly. March 3, *robbery with a gun*; March 15, *robbery with a gun*; March 21, *attempted armed robbery with a screwdriver*; March 22, *robbery: "Driver picked up two men at Tenth & Mission on a flag. They told him to drive to Lincoln High School. The man riding in the front seat pointed a gun at the driver; the other passenger grabbed him in a chokehold from the back seat. They took the driver's money, his cellular phone, and then locked him in the trunk..."*

In the screwdriver attempt, after the assailant warned, "Don't do anything stupid," the driver grabbed the screwdriver and the suspect fled. The same bandit gave up the screwdriver routine soon afterward, going on to successfully rob eight cab drivers in three weeks by the tried and true method of holding a pistol to the driver's head. Finally, after a week of nightly warnings to all cabs, and an All Points Bulletin (APB), the police apprehended him.

The UTW posts their literature at the airport garage, where drivers wait in line for up to three hours for a fare. From there, if your cab gets into the terminal area within an hour, the airport is said to be "moving." But you may never get a fare at all, staying parked in the garage for hours. That's when the airport is "not moving." There's not much reading material at the airport garage so, inevitably, drivers (those who can read) end up reading these gruesome robbery accounts. The robbery bulletins describe the suspects, date, time and location of the robbery.

Currently, there are three young white kids on a robbing spree in the Haight-Ashbury area, carrying with them a sawed-off shotgun. Wouldn't you notice someone getting into the cab with a shotgun?

Well, I'm not sure, but I don't want to find out either. You try to picture the perpetrators, but the descriptions are vague, ambiguous. You try to see a pattern in the robberies—common locations, common language, a tattoo, some article of clothing—anything you can grasp to avoid being the next victim or fatality, to avoid becoming a faded memory, a blurb on a list. Drivers recite various commitments and personal guidelines: "I'll avoid that street," or "I won't go over there after 10 o'clock." Maybe there's an apartment complex in ill repute for that month. Many incidents occur near housing projects, but many of them don't. Many occur late at night...but not all of them.

It's 2:30 in the morning. Usually, I would have turned in the cab by this time and be home eating Rice Chex, maybe checking out the TV—winding down from my adrenalin peaking out, and resting my eyes from the strain of the 4,000 pairs of headlights that came at me throughout the night. But, instead, I've still got a solid 35 minutes until the cab is due back at the yard. My waybill is time-stamped 5:05 pm, just the perfect time to hit the peak of rush hour. But that was more than nine hours ago, and it seems an even longer time. It was numerous rides ago, traversing traffic, and people—some having good days and some having bad.

This evening was one of those biting, chilly San Francisco nights, perfect for those tourists who packed only three pairs of Bermuda shorts, their favorite baseball caps, and a slew of short-sleeved tee shirts. It's a bit foggy at the Wharf, and just plain cold, as I drive down Van Ness Avenue, my window cracked open, the heater at half-blast. I covered my gate pretty early, kept a good pace despite the late start. It's only Wednesday, and it's my third ten-hour shift of the week. I'm tempted to stop just up the street a bit and grab a fast food burger when I see a guy flagging me at Geary. He looks to be in his late fifties, probably in his sixties, shabbily dressed in an untucked grey shirt that clashes with his dark but faded pants. He gets into the front seat. I never like that—no matter what time of the night or day. It's an invasion of my space, and it just feels less safe, although it's probably not. He's drinking out of a bottle wrapped in a small brown paper bag. I don't like that either. Of course, I wonder why he's out so late, and if he has any cash left to pay the fare.

"I'm going to work," he says, claiming to be a cab driver, and directs me toward the location of a rival taxi company yard in a bad area of town. Well, they're all located in bad areas of town, or else the owners of the properties would build condominiums.

"Makin' any money ta-night?" he asks, with a hint of a high-strung Northeastern accent.

"Nahwww," I lie. "It's been pretty quiet." He could use a shave. Looks as though it's been at least three or four days since his last one.

"How long you been driving?" he asks.

"A few months or so." It's none of his business. "About nine," I add, actually surprised that it has been that long already.

"Shit, I've been drivin' twenty-five years."

"Oh." I try to sound impressed.

"Yeah." He pauses. "Phhhh." He pauses once more, seemingly doing some kind of calculation not necessarily involving math. "Twenty-five," he grunts proudly, "years."

I'm not sure I believe him. That's a long time to be doing this.

"Another cold one," he says.

I think he's talking about the weather.

"Seems like to me," he says and takes a sip from his bottle, "it's been a pretty fuckin' busy night," he slowly drawls. "Couldn't even get me a fuckin' cab." His voice sounds hoarse, and impatiently challenging to my assessment of the night's business.

I would feel safer if I could verify that he was actually a cab driver. Maybe I should ask him if he started his 25-year driving career as a *temporary fix*. He doesn't strike me as a bass player. He's too short. Maybe he's an aspiring writer? He probably thinks writing is a waste of time. Apparently, tucking in a shirt, shaving, and removing taco stains from his pants are also wastes of time. His demeanor has oddly provoked me; I'm feeling hostile and defensive. It's late and I'm tired. I glance over at the little bottle on his lap, then at him, attempting to strategize an appropriate conversational direction. I should chill out. Asking about the "temporary fix" would be an obnoxious thing to say—risking not only my tip, but maybe a sideswipe from the bottle in his bag. Meanwhile, I'm disturbed that he has an additional 24 years on me? Is this some side effect of the job that I've been warned about? I really need to get an earlier start out of the yard.

The bag makes a crinkling sound as he takes another sip from the bottle. I'd like to know what he's drinking. Perhaps his driving career began one night, just waiting for the sun to rise and sobriety to set in, apparently never able to coordinate the two.

"Ya gotta go with yer gut, doin' this fuckin' job," he crackles.

"Yeah," I agree. "Really."

He's making me nervous. Taking my eyes off the road momentarily, I try again to glimpse the bottle peeking out of the wrinkled bag, but he has it securely concealed, braced against his protruding stomach. He's holding it steady, creating a crease in his belly. By the time I direct my eyes back, the brake lights of the car in front of us brighten. I hit the brakes and stiffen my back. The cab jolts slightly to a stop. He doesn't seem to notice, or care, the bottle in the bag still holding steady.

"Had two guys riding around with me the other night." He drinks from the bag and wipes his mouth with his sleeve. "I was getting a bad fuckin' feelin' about 'em, ya know?"

"Yeah, I know the feeling." Like the one I'm having right now.

"Can't take that too lightly," he nods. "Folla yer instinct. Yep. Folla yer instinct and these two fuckin' guys were up to no good."

"So, what did ya do?" I ask, trying again to sound both interested and impressed. Actually, I'm feeling sorry I picked him up at all. I'm not only regretting my late start from the yard but also feeling the increasing weight of fatigue on my shoulders that generally sets in between the eighth and ninth hours of driving the city streets.

"Thought they might be the fuckin' assholes who been robbin' drivers. You heard about 'em?"

"I don't know." I lie again.

Talking about the weather, Midwestern tourists, or Cat Woman are fine ways to pass a few minutes. But I don't like discussions about my personal night's cash flow. I don't like talking about cab robberies. I don't necessarily like discussing the dangers of picking up suspicious strangers in the middle of the night, especially when one is sitting right next to me. He takes another nip of his drink. I consider the bottle a potential weapon, particularly once he empties its contents. Regardless, it is not going to add any redeeming quality to the ride. If he is drinking hard liquor he might get more belligerent. Worst case scenario: he pukes. If it was 2:30 in the afternoon, the bottle would not be bothering me. But at 2:30 in the morning, I just don't like it.

"These two bastards," he continues, "I could tell they was trouble. Picked 'em up on O'Farrell, and hell, you know, first they wanna go over here, then over there, kept changing their minds. The fare was up, hell, 'bout seven dollars. I don't give a shit. Seven bucks ain't worth no bullet in the face. So I pretend I'm feelin' sick."

"Left at Army?" I ask.

"Yeah," he says. "You should lock your doors around here."

I don't like his persistence about the subject matter. My forehead suddenly seems very warm and I can feel sweat forming, probably visibly above my upper lip. Maybe it's the heater. I'm trying to think of a way to change the subject. Am I in some kind of denial about the dangers of the job? Or the opposite, steeped in paranoia? I do notice that I've become increasingly superstitious, for lack of a better description, specifically regarding discussions having to do with people getting stabbed and choked—cab drivers being stabbed and choked. I don't want a bad experience preceded by what could be described (in hindsight) as ironic conversation. I don't need or want that kind of irony anywhere in my life.

"It's a bad area," repeats my unshaven passenger. He turns his head away from me, reaches over and locks the back door.

This strikes me as somewhat odd. I quietly unbuckle my seat belt.

"Yeah," he continues with his story. "I tell these two guys: '*Hey man, I'm really fuckin' sick. I been pounding down the pink liquid, but man, I think I'm gonna fuckin' puke. I gotta get home.*' So I stop the cab and tell them I'm sorry, that I won't charge them for the ride."

"Let 'em go without paying, huh?" I comment, feigning both admiration and respect for his supremely perceptive sensibilities and impeccable common sense approach.

"Oh yeah. That's the way ya do it. And I kept apologizing. Got 'em the fuck out and sped off."

"That was last night?" I ask.

"Three nights ago," he says, taking another swig from the bag. "They're still lookin' for 'em; gotta watch yer ass out here."

Perhaps this guy is vying for a free ride. That's what his jabbering is all about.

"You call the cops?" I ask.

"Naw," he shakes his head. "I mean, wasn't sure it was them. What could I say?"

We're getting close to the yard. It's the warehouse district off Army Street by Evans—remote, dark and deserted at three in the morning. I spot the rival cab company's sign off to the left, just down the street less than a couple of hundred feet.

"Don't go all the way in," he says abruptly. "Stop right here. Shit, I don't want no one seein' me in a Yellow Cab."

"Sure." I slow down and pull off to the side. I turn away from him, looking out my window to check where I'm parking. There's no curb, just dirt and potholes.

"I've got this," he says.

I turn back around to face him and see a gun, six inches from my face, a large silver gun barrel with a black and brown handle. Startled, I involuntarily jerk from my seat.

"I pull this out when there's trouble," he says.

The gun isn't pointed directly at me, but he's got it in my face, waving it in the air. I take a quiet deep breath through my nostrils—eyes wide-open, focused on the gun. I can grab it, I can run—maybe I can talk him down.

"Things get fuckin' rough in this city, ya know?" He looks off to his right and then back at me, shaking his head up and down.

"Yeah, I know."

"It's just insurance." He's still waving the silver gun barrel in my face.

I slowly glance to my left. For safety, when we went through the Mission, I locked my door. Tonight I'm driving one of the few remaining cabs without automatic door locks. Or, under this circumstance should I say, automatic door UN-locks. I'd have to reach over my shoulder to unlock the door. Not very subtle. However, there's a black tire iron wedged between the driver's side door and my seat. I think. Or was that the other night?

"That's great." I slowly reach over and stop the meter, partly to test his reaction to my movement.

"Comes in handy once in a while," he says, cocking his head to the side.

"I'm sure," I nod, giving him a quick hard look. He's got a flattened nose with visible red blood vessels, dark eyes and a receding hairline. He looks as though he might have been a boxer in his earlier years or a real hard drinker. I look out ahead into the darkness of the night. Is that the last thing I'll see? (That and a flash of light from the gun?) There's no reason he should shoot; "cooperate, cooperate," that's what you're supposed to do when confronted with a weapon—cab company guidelines, police guidelines. Or maybe it's those television crime shows—the forensics channel or something. I don't know.

The outside seems more quiet than usual. Suddenly, it does not seem like such a noisy, busy city. There's a stillness; no foot traffic, no cars. I wonder how much a gunshot would reverberate, as I ease back into my seat, dropping my left arm down to the side of the seat, feeling for the black metal tire jack. It's at a perfect distance for my reach.

"Keeps people from fuckin' with me," he says.

"Absolutely." I reach into my pocket for my cash with my right hand, while positioning myself lower in the seat. I lean slightly to the left to pull out a small wad of money from the right front pocket of my jeans and meanwhile, grab the tire iron with my left hand. If I'm going to bash his head, I've got to make a complete follow-through, not just some little doink to his head.

"I always carry it around with me," he says proudly.

The cab computer connected to the dash next to the meter, buzzes with a message on its narrow two-inch-high screen, and startles us both: *PULLING AWAY FROM THE CURB? ALWAYS USE EXTRA CAUTION.*

"How do you like those computers?"

"They're okay," I shrug.

"Lotta drivers quit when they installed those." He points the gun at the screen. "It took jobs from people."

"You're right," I nod, while slowly raising the tire iron up from the floor. "They're always sending these stupid messages."

"I don't like people FUCKIN' with me and I don't like FUCKIN' computers!" he snarls, redirecting and pushing the muzzle of the gun against the computer's tiny read-out. So he's gonna shoot the computer and then me?

He squeezes the trigger.

The gun makes a loud click. I flinch and jerk back. He squeezes the trigger again. Another click. He looks at me, and points at the gun. "It's not real," he cackles. "It's a cap gun. Can't ya see?"

"Uhhh…yeah." I can *kind of* see it isn't real, but I am not consoled. I imagine whacking his head anyway and think about what a mess that would be—blood all over the seats and everything.

"You never seen one of these before?"

"When I was a kid, I guess."

"Pretty convincing, eh?"

He's crazy. If you're going to carry a gun, shouldn't it shoot bullets? Real bullets? He puts the gun back in his coat and scratches his chin with the edge of his brown paper bag.

"Yeah," he lets out a sigh, "carryin' it makes me feel better."

I guess I still look doubtful.

"I feel safe with it. Ya know what I mean?"

NO! "I know what you mean," I tell him.

"Here's eleven bucks. Keep the change."

A three dollar tip. I release my grip on the tire iron. It clunks to the floor. He *must* have heard that.

"Good luck," I tell him.

"There's some crazy people out there." He slams the door and walks into the night.

"Yeah…" I turn the meter off, and book into a zone across town.

BAMBALONE

"Oral is my specialty."

"Forty dollars."

"I don't do nothin' for less than sixty, honey."

"I give you forty."

The hooker walks away from the cab. She has long brown hair, dark red lips, a shapely figure, clear complexion, great legs—she's one of the better-looking ones on the street tonight.

"They're not big on negotiation," I explain.

"I vant HER," he says.

"Maybe on a regular Monday or Tuesday night, forty dollars. There's a doctors' convention in town. They raise their prices."

"I must have-a her."

"Well, sixty dollars and she's yours."

•

"Where is a disco with many women?" is this international hipster's initial question when I pick him up at two in the morning from a local bar, which was closing up a few minutes early on a slow night. He speaks English with a heavy accent. It takes me a little extra time to figure out what he says. He repeats himself a lot, making the deciphering a little easier. He's clean-shaven, tall and skinny. His face has hard features, high cheekbones and a flattened forehead. His medium-length dark hair is slicked back with grease with a little flip-up at the front. He's a good-looking guy. I'm surprised he's not wearing sunglasses.

"The city pretty much closes down after 2 a.m.," I tell him.

"Take me to discotheque."

He resembles a cliché from a '70s television show. A thick, gaudy gold chain around his neck protrudes from his chest as it rests on a thick bed of dark hair. I imagine him wearing a white suit practicing his "moves" to the beat of some hacker coverband's rendition of the Bee Gees' Greatest Hits.

"You're a couple decades late for an actual discotheque. You want an after-hours dance place?"

"Yes, with many women."

"I can't guarantee that."

"Where are the most women?"

Business has slowed considerably. Against my policy, I've spent fifteen minutes parked in front of this bar waiting for a fare, ending up with Mr. Aimless.

"There's South of Market. Have you been there?"

"No, how far is there?"

"A few miles."

"How much?"

"Seven, eight dollars."

"There are many ah-women?"

"I can't tell you how many women are there."

"I want the best for women."

Somehow I doubt that. "On a Tuesday," I tell him, "there's not much happening." I smell sulfur and smoke. He has lit a cigarette. "Sorry, it's a no-smoking cab."

"I cannot-ah smoke?" he asks in disbelief.

No destination and now he's gonna blow smoke in my face? Go back to Europe.

"Sorry, I just quit smoking," I calmly explain.

"I will open window."

"I'm on a nicotine patch. I can't breathe smoke." I don't think he'll be asking me about milligrams.

"Ohh, yes?" he says sympathetically.

"My doctor told me: I breathe smoke—heart attack. Something to do with, uh, you know, an overdose of nicotine." He probably has no clue what I'm talking about; a little smoke is going to suddenly cause a heart attack? Ridiculous. Well, I can claim I'm not really sure what the doctor told me, but I'll insist on my interpretation. Or maybe my doctor is just an idiot, but that's what he said.

I check my passenger's reaction in the mirror. He seems to be considering it. "It would be very, very bad for me," I continue. "That's what my doctor says. Me, personally, I would like to have a cigarette." I'm hoping he gets it, and stays seated in the cab. It's getting near quitting time and I don't have time to scrounge the streets for another fifteen minutes looking for one last passenger.

"I will put it out," he says, and from the corner of my eye I see him flick it out the opened window.

"I've got nicotine gum, too. You want some gum?" I hold up the blue package that was lying on the dashboard—it's like driving around with a plastic Jesus, an icon to make believers out of those sinners who doubt my "I quit smoking" routine. Who would have a pack of this crap unless desparately needed?

"No, thank you," he says.

Good decision. It's some of the most putrid stuff I have ever tasted. "It's good stuff," I tell him, balancing it back in place on the dashboard. I purchased the gum as a prop the night before. It's expensive, but I'm very proud that it has already become useful, definitely worth the investment. Hopefully, no one will ask me to chew it.

"South of Market is good-a-place?"

"There's no alcohol after 2 a.m. But there's dancing, and you can smoke." After all, if you can't smoke, why dance?

"Okay, good." He likes my idea.

I turn right on Polk Street and head south.

"San Francisco is very beautiful city." He still has his window down.

"Where are you from?" I ask.

"Italy."

"That's a beautiful place, too."

"Have you been there?"

"No. I would like to go."

We drive about six blocks.

"How much further?" he asks.

"About eight minutes."

"Take me to home, Apred-aherick-kah Street."

"You don't want a night club?"

"I am at A-pred-aherick-kah Street."

"In the Haight?" I don't understand the street name.

"Apred-aherickerah Street."

"Do you know the cross street?"

"Apred-aherick-ah," he says.

Great. I turn right on Geary. Apredahericka? I hope he means Frederick.

"Do you know where—women for sesso?" he asks.

"Sex?"

"I will pay for sex. Do you understand-ah?"

"A prostitute?"

"Yes, putan-ah. Can you take me to prostituta?"

"They're mostly downtown. It's the other direction."

"This is what I want."

"I can, but you know, prostitutes are illegal."

"How far away?"

"Close, a mile," I estimate.

"Please go there. Is that all right?"

"That's fine with me. I don't have any other plans."

"How much is prostitute?" he asks me.

"It depends on what you want."

"For sex."

"You discuss the details with them."

"Thirty dollars?"

"I don't think you'll get very far on thirty dollars."

"More?"

"Maybe...forty, fifty, sixty...it depends, I can't really say."

The computer beeps with a message: *WHO HAD THE TRIP FROM SFO TO LOMBARD/JONES JUST NOW?*

We're on Post Street. At Larkin, we see a beauty on our right: bright red lipstick, long perfectly-conditioned black hair, nylon stockings and boots, curvaceous figure, provocative pose. "I must have *her*," he says, like I'm the one he needs to convince.

"That's a man," I tell him.

"A man?"

"A man dressed as a woman."

He closely studies her, while mumbling in Italian.

"How do you know?"

"On this block, the women are men."

He exclaims something: "...*Mama mia!*"

"The women-women are a few blocks away," I tell him.

"I do not want a man." There is a definite trace of panic in his voice. "Please, do you understand-ah?"

"I understand."

The next woman we pass has short blond hair and long legs. She's wearing a thin, white, mostly-see-through tube top and blouse.

"A woman?" he asks.

"That's a woman," I confirm.

"I am in love. Her, how much?"

"I don't know. She's not working for me." I pull the cab to the curb. "Ask her."

She walks up to the cab. "Ya wanna date?" She has stunning dark blue eyes, small ears, and perfect teeth.

"How much?" asks the Italian.

"Sixty dollahs," she says in a nasal twang. "For a *good time.*"

"Too much."

She raises her shoulders and frowns.

"Drive again," he says.

I lightly step on the gas.

"She looks-ah better from far away," he says.

Next, we pass a short curvy brunette wearing a tight miniskirt.

"I must have-a her." He points, "There."

She sees us, stops, and waves at my passenger. I pull over.

"How much?" he asks.

"Sixty," she says. "Ya wanna date?"

"Forty," he counters.

She seems lucid, quick and business-like. She has a smooth, clear complexion. I doubt she's a drug abuser.

"Sixty or nothin'," she says. "You wanna do it or not?" She has tall black boots, ending below her knees. I love boots. Her miniskirt has no wrinkles, and her low-cut bikini top reveals a lot of cleavage, very firm cleavage. They're probably fake. I'm actually feeling a little jealous, hoping he is unable to consummate the deal. I turn and look back at him.

"What is she saying?" he asks me.

"Sixty dollars," I tell him.

He holds up two twenties. "Two of these?"

"No," I tell him, "she wants three of those."

"Too much, too much."

She lights a cigarette. It's such a shame to watch a young beautiful woman smoking a cigarette. All the prostitutes smoke.

"Sixty, honey, ca-peesh?"

She blows the smoke out of the corner of her mouth, holds up three fingers, stands back from the cab, makes an abrupt turn and slowly walks away.

We're back driving in circles. The only people left on the streets are the hookers. He falls in love every other block.

"Where will I take a girl?" he asks me.

"Anywhere. Here, if you want."

"Noooo; right here?" He laughs. "In the car?"

"Sure, right here. I don't care."

Driving around with him having sex in the back seat should be an easy additional six bucks. Plus a small surcharge added to the fare—it would be cheaper than getting a room and there wouldn't be as many cockroaches. Add the trip back to the Haight when he's done—now, that's a good ride.

"I want girl to suck-ah my dick-ah. Do you-ah understand-ah?"

"I understand. But you have to *be quick about it*. This is NOT legal."

"I know."

"The police will put you in jail. You AND me."

"I like her." He points to a blonde. "We will do it here? She will do it?" He is now sitting on the very edge of his seat, talking into my ear, like I'm deaf. I smell the garlic on his breath.

"I don't know." But "*Sit back down*" I want to tell him.

"Here?" He laughs again. "You will stop the car and we do sex?"

"I would keep driving."

"Driving while sex? This is okay?"

"If you want; I can't park. Or you can ask if she has a place to go."

"Her." He points. "To the left."

I turn onto Mason. The woman turns around. She looked better from behind.

"Never mind," he says. "Keep driving."

"Look, we can't keep doing this. We can go to jail. "

"I will get girl to come."

"It's the police who are going to be coming."

"Don't worry. It's okay."

"I can't keep driving in circles any longer."

49

Sixty, honey, ca-peesh?

"Blowupjob," he says. "Blowupjob."

"I know, but you have to be fast about it."

"Don't worry," he says. "You speak *Italiano*?"

"My Italian is not too happening."

"*Parla Italiano*? You speak *Italiano*?"

"No *Italiano*."

This guy seems to go in and out from consciousness of understanding the English. I'm not sure he understands as little as he says.

"Bam-ba-lonay," he says. "You know-a bam-ba-lonay?"

"No, I don't know."

"Bam-ba-lonay."

"*Bambalone*?"

"Blowupjob—in Italian. Bam-ba-lonay. You understand-ah?"

"Yes, yes, I understand."

We drive around in one more circle. He falls in love—I pull over. None of these girls will give him the time of day because he won't pay sixty bucks. Apparently tonight, they have a fixed price. They think they're OPEC.

"You know," I break him the news, "I have to take you home."

"I must have her." He points to another woman with dyed blond hair and red high heels. I pull to the curb. She's staring straight ahead, not paying attention to us, leisurely walking on the sidewalk.

"Hello, can we talk?" I ask.

She swaggers over to the cab and leans over. Her blond hair falls touching the window. Her cleavage screams for attention.

"Ya wanna date?" she asks, raising her plucked eyebrows.

"This guy doesn't speak English," I tell her. "He wants a blow-job for forty dollars."

"Sixty," she says impatiently. "You wanna pay sixty?"

"I give you," he holds up two twenties and a ten, "this."

"That's fifty dollars," I tell him. "She wants sixty."

"Yes," he says.

I shake my head and sigh. The woman walks away. In the rear-view mirror, I see a police car two blocks away. We drive down the street one block and make a left turn. "To suck-ah my dickie?" he says. "Here?"

"Yes, here, but it's gonna cost sixty dollars."

"Okay, this." He holds up two twenty dollar bills.

"You're back to forty now? Three." I hold up three fingers. "Three twenties."

I hear a siren. I look in the rear-view mirror. A police car is tailgating us, red lights flashing. I pull over.

An officer gets out and swaggers over. He bends over at the passenger-side window, belly hanging over his belt, and coldly stares my tourist between the eyes. "Hey there! I'm going to give you a warning this time, but the next time, your passenger will get a ticket." He looks back at me. "And you. It's a three-hundred-dollar fine."

"Sorry," I apologize.

"I don't want to see you doin' this ever again." He rubs the handle of his gun and bites the inside of his lip.

"No problem," I tell him. "We're out of here. Thank you."

He struts back to the patrol car.

"We have to leave," I tell my passenger, while directing our vehicle west toward Van Ness Avenue.

"Prostitute, prostitute. Bam-ba-lonay."

Perhaps he thought this was some kind of a police escort; a special city service for horny Italian men.

"Nope. Sorry. No *bambalone* tonight."

"One more, just one more girl."

He doesn't get it. His pronounciation has also suddenly improved.

"The police warned us to stop doing this."

"Bam-ba-lonay," he whines. "Bam-ba-lonay."

"Illegal. Jail, police, handcuffs. Understand-ahh?"

"One time only."

"Time to go home, sorry."

"I must have bam-ba-lonay."

"I can take you to a club."

"No. Take me to Apred-aherick-ah Street."

I drive down Sutter, turn left on Gough and right on Hayes Street. We're close to the projects on Buchanan. Two women about sixty years old are standing on the corner at Octavia. They're overweight, drooping bloodshot eyes, and drugged out looking. It's not their age; they're just ugly—missing teeth, matted hair. If they were thirty years old they wouldn't be attractive. They do have that "Hey, you wanna have sex?" gleam in their eyes. I'm sure they're good at what they do, if you can overlook a few particulars.

"This area is less expensive," I emphasize. "Cheaper."

"Bam-ba-lonay?"

"Yes, *bambalone*. You see the woman over there?"

"Yes. Prostitute?"

"Fifteen dollars—*bambalone*." Taking a closer look, I see she's been collecting Social Security for several years. This night time work provides a small non-taxable income supplement.

"No, no. Take-a me home," he requests. We're a mile from Frederick Street. "Other places for prostitute?"

"Call on the phone," I suggest. "Massage."

"I am staying at my friends' house."

"There's nothing we can do tonight. Try tomorrow."

"I am with my friends tomorrow."

"*Bambalone* with your friends."

"My friends do not like this thing."

"Well, I can't drive you anymore."

"Is there another place?"

"My shift is ending. I have to return the cab."

"Please," he whimpers, "I will pay extra."

"I'm sorry. I've got to go. My shift is over."

We drive two blocks down Frederick before he recognizes his friends' house. I stop the cab. He doesn't get out.

"That's $22.40." I stop the meter. I'm hearing heavy breathing from the back seat. I don't think I want to see this. There are various advantages to having a shield separating the driver from the passenger. Unfortunately, this cab doesn't have one. I look back at him for the fare. He's crying.

"Are you okay?"

"I am sorry. Thank you very much."

He wipes his eyes and pulls out his wallet. I get out and open the door for him. He hands me a twenty and a five.

"Just give me two dollars," he says.

A sixty cent tip. I'll finally have enough to get that roll of two-ply toilet paper I've had my eye on, adding it to the $1.40 from the Finland brothers in my pink plastic piggy bank at home.

Mr. Bambalone shuffles about and finally dislodges himself from the back seat. I consider giving him a lecture about tipping; these Europeans have got to learn. I hold out his two dollars. He clumsily stuffs them into his pocket. For some reason I look at his shoes. They are scuffed-looking and worn.

"You take care," I tell him.

"*Arrivederci.*" He sadly makes his way past me and up the driveway of the large converted Victorian apartment building.

"Bomba-derci-lonay," I mumble, and half-wave goodbye with my hand as he ascends the steps—out of my line of sight.

REAL MEN WEAR BLACK

Jimi Hendrix. I pick up an otherwise unremarkable passenger who gets into the cab and starts talking about Jimi Hendrix, maybe because Hendrix is playing on the radio. I know there is a full moon.

"You know," he says to me, "Jimi Hendrix died walking in outer space."

"I thought they faked all that outer space stuff." I gently apply the brakes as a streetcar stops up ahead. He does not pickup on my sarcasm. It only further excites his advocacy.

"They didn't fake it. They were EXPERIMENTING on him!"

"Oh. Well, that's not very good. Do, uhhh…do you have enough to pay the fare?"

"I got enough. Don't worry, here, look, I got it."

He pulls out a crumpled ten-dollar bill.

"Okay." I jerk to a stop, this time for a jaywalking pedestrian crossing Market Street. I apologize to my passenger, offering a detailed justification for my financial inquiry: "Cabs are, ya know, very expensive for many people. More money than some people realize. And that's really terrible about Jimi. I didn't know that."

He doesn't seem concerned about my question regarding his financial wherewithal. He remains focused on the outer space thing. "Even with the regular astronauts, man," he says, "you gotta wait three days before ya go on a space walk. So you don't choke on your vomit, man. They were negligent…Jimi walkin' out there right away…"

"Right away? Right away after eating?"

"Yeah, man, and in outer space—NEGLIGENT!"

"It sounds that way," I agree. "I've heard you don't go swimming after eating, I didn't know about walking in space. That's a good thing to know," I conclude, as if "walk in outer space" was on my to-do list for next week.

"Oh yeah, in outer space, man, everything is multiplied by one hundred. And that's how he died. Those people at NASA, man, they messed up bad. Jimi's dad is suing the government."

"I didn't know that...that's very interesting. Did you want Market or Octavia?"

"Just on the corner."

He gets out, pays the fare and space walks into the liquor store. I proceed to drive down Market and take a left on Castro Street. I've noticed only a few cabs out on Market Street tonight. Hopefully, that will increase my chances of picking up a decent fare on this otherwise quiet evening. Pulling to the corner at Eighteenth Street, I decide to park and wait in front of the Walgreen's for a passing customer. A dauntingly muscular black man approaches the window.

"Are you available, sir?" He's wearing a Raider's shirt saying: **REAL MEN WEAR BLACK.** It's an unusual spot to be picking up a guy wearing football paraphernalia. First thought: he's big, he's black, and he's dangerous. Second thought: he's a lost tourist, maybe sightseeing in the gay section. I'm in the heart of the Castro and, whatever the case, there's a 60-89% chance that it's safe to pick him up. He gets into the cab.

"I'm not sure where I wanna go. How about, how about Sixteenth and Noe?"

"That's fine." I pull into traffic and start the meter. A customer "not sure" where they want to go is not a good sign. You don't hop into a cab when you're meandering around the town. Chances are, they know exactly where they're going—just putting it off until they either get their nerve, you're off your guard or the time feels right to clunk you on the head and empty your pockets.

"Would you make that Sanchez, sir, THE JACKHAMMER BAR, over on Sixteenth or something? Sorry for the short ride."

"You gotta go where you gotta go." So he's *not* a tourist nor, with that destination likely to be a robber. It's a small local bar, tough to stumble upon unless you know about it. I really don't mind the short distance. Drivers will get nasty with a customer going a short distance.

They figure that $58 ride to Palo Alto or the airport was on the next block but, because of this $4.00 ride, they're going to miss that once in a lifetime fare. Chalk me up as an unbeliever—some days you're going to score that airport and some days you're going to get the fare going from the Sheraton to the Hilton—that one schlub standing in line between the well-dressed couple going to the airport and the guy going home to the secluded Marin County hills (even a better ride than the airport). It's not unusual that someone will make up the short ride with a nice tip unless, of course, they're European tourists. The exception is the gay European tourist who has obviously been briefed about the practice by his American counterpart. Even gays from Canada give good tips.

"I might go on from there. Is that all right, driver?"

"Sure. So, you're a Raiders fan?"

"Well, yeah," he says. "A football fan."

"So, what's the quarterback deal this year?"

"I don't know. I've just been following who's been signing contracts and who isn't with the 49ers."

"Oh."

"Are you straight?" he asks.

I pause. I hate that question. I dislike the "Are you a homosexual?" question just as much, maybe because I don't have a snappy comeback for it. What would that be anyway? The old "I'm a lesbian in a man's body"? Or the equally mold-ridden "I was until I met you." Besides, I don't need to encourage pain-in-the-ass behavior. I generally treat the question in a business-like manner.

"Yeah," I answer.

And why are they always asking me? I never know what to expect next, but it is not unusual for these questions to lead to situations. Maybe these guys make overtures because they want to "turn me," thinking I'm a challenge. How do women deal with it constantly—men and their questions?

A gay hairdresser told me a story one night about a woman trying to "turn" him. She was convinced he just "hadn't met the right woman." She purchased round trip tickets to Paris and offered to buy him a vintage motorcycle if he would sleep with her. He turned her down!

"I can't tell you how lucky you are. It's a bunch of bullshit," says my REAL MEN WEAR BLACK passenger. "A bunch of crap. If I could take a pill, or get something that changes—changes your psychological disposition, I'd do it."

"Sounds like you're having trouble tonight."

"No. Trouble *all the time.*"

"Well, you know," I attempt to console, "women are no picnic. Then again, if the alternatives are men, that doesn't sound too great either."

"Believe me, men are a lot worse."

"If it's not one thing, it's something else, isn't it?" A very reliable fall-back cliché for those in the service industry dealing with unfamiliar subject matter, or simply used as a stalling mechanism hoping the topic of conversation will change.

"I guess so," he says.

We get to The JACKHAMMER and it looks quiet.

"Geez, I don't know," he says. "Doesn't look like anyone's in there."

"If you wanna look, I'll wait." There's barely a soul on the street, the computer is quiet; it's a dead night, about to get even worse.

"You don't mind?"

"No problem." I look at the blank computer screen. "It's slow tonight," I concede, figuring there's no harm telling him that. He seems like a nice guy; a thought is to suggest that if he's having relationship problems, perhaps a bar isn't exactly the place to work them out. On the other hand, the bars south of Market are much busier this time of night, and that's a ten-dollar cab ride—again, not a solution for relationship problems, but good for business. Perhaps I'll suggest south of Market as a better spot to trade in his old troubles for some new ones.

He gets out and goes in. There are about six people in there, best I can tell. He comes right back to the cab. That's a good sign.

"I'm gonna stay."

"Okay. Well, good luck."

"Thanks." He hands me a five. "Just give me a dollar."

I was so sure he wouldn't stay at the bar. We could have kept cruising and it would have been the ride of the evening, making a dent in my gate fee for the night. Maybe the bartender was cute.

I drive back to Market Street and hear tires screeching. There's a red Camaro taking a turn up a hill. The car doesn't appear to be going that fast but it spins out and slides sideways up the hill into oncoming traffic. Somehow he manages not to smash into anything. Taking a left on Market, I circle back to Castro and 18th Street where I first encountered Mr. **REAL MEN WEAR BLACK** seemingly just moments earlier. I pull into the bus stop and wait. I usually drive around with the windows open for air circulation (when there are no passengers in the car). Unfortunately, people are always coming up and talking to me, like I'm a complimentary and obligatory government service, there to assist anyone changing flat tires, donating spare change, or unloading "lukewarm" merchandise.

A scrawny guy wearing an unkempt plaid hunting shirt scurries up to the passenger side window. He doesn't look dangerous, but I can tell he's going to pester me about something. I pretend I don't see him.

"Hey. Hey, look what I got." He's pointing. "Hey man, hey."

I poke my head up to where I can see the sidewalk. A dozen gay men's magazines are laid out on the cement. Apparently, he set up shop between the time I picked up my last fare and returned to the spot.

"A-buck-a-piece," he says.

"No, I don't think so."

He grabs a few to show me. "Come on, a-buck-a-piece, a-buck-a-piece."

He opens one up. It's two naked guys, spread-eagle.

"I'm not interested," I quip.

Now he's holding up one page of naked guys after another. I would like him to go away. "I don't want any. Really, you're wasting your time."

"Come on. A-buck-a-piece, a-buck-a-piece—they cost ya seven or eight bucks at a store!"

"I'm working. Don't bother me, please." How am I gonna get a fare with this nut-case blocking the way? I figure if I tell him to get lost, he'll never leave. It might be worth a buck to get rid of him. Maybe that's even a part of his business plan.

"Three, for two bucks!" He holds up three magazines.

"No, that's okay. No."

Thankfully, he finally wanders off, trying to sell them to one of the other few people walking up and down this uncharacteristically quiet street.

The computer buzzes with a message: *POLICE ACTION AT EDDY/LEAVENWORTH.* I'll try to remember to steer clear of the Tenderloin.

A minute later, the magazine guy is back at my window. "Come on, there's only nine left. A-buck-a-piece, come on."

"No!"

"Hey, if you don't want them, maybe some of your friends will want them."

"None of my friends want them." Maybe my girlfriend would want one. It's only a dollar. What am I thinking? I'm NOT buying one of those magazines.

"Take me to Church and Market," offers Magazineman, "and you can have all of them for three bucks."

"I don't want any. Go away."

A man steps past him and the magazines, asking if I'm available to drive him home.

"Absolutely," I tell him. He gets in, and I hit the meter. As we pull away from the curb, I can still hear the magazine man calling out to a passerby.

"Buck-a-piece, buck-a-piece. Only a few left; buck-a-piece."

CALL MOM

Noe Valley at Diamond and Jersey Streets. I get out and ring the doorbell. A man of average height, about fifteen pounds overweight, in his late forties (maybe early fifties) comes out of the house. He's casually dressed in a sport coat and slacks, his hair tentatively greased.

"I'm going out to Twenty-Sixth Avenue and Fulton," he informs.

We both descend the steep stairs leading from his porch and walk to the curb. I open the cab door for him. He gets into the back seat. I close the door, go around the car and get into the driver's seat, buckle my seat belt, turn on the meter, and head up the hill.

"How's your night been?" I ask.

"She kicked me out," he says. "We got into a big argument."

"Oh. I'm sorry about that."

"Put eight thousand into fixing that place and she throws me out."

"Your wife?" I ask.

"Oh, no; girlfriend. So I'm a little drunk, big deal."

"She kicked you out of your own place?"

"That's her place."

"You put eight thousand dollars into her house?"

"Yeah, it's a bitch. I put a lotta time in the god-damned place."

"How serious of a throwing-out is this?"

"Uhh, I'm going back later tonight."

A dark green car has stopped at the intersection directly in front of us. The driver seems to have fallen asleep. I blast him. His head and shoulders jerk up to attention; he looks to the left and proceeds. However, by this time, a grey and black Jeep coming from the right has already begun to cross into the intersection. The Jeep jerks to a stop to avoid hitting the green car. The driver of the Jeep blasts his horn and shakes his fist. Once the two vehicles clear the intersection, we move forward. The green car is still traveling up ahead.

"What did you have done to the place?" I've done some Victorian renovation work myself, once upon a time.

"Ripping shit out—painting, woodwork, custom tile, you name it. So I don't need a bunch of crap 'cuz I have a couple drinks. Geeez."

"Yeah." I glance back at him. "Well…"

"So, how's YOUR night going?" he asks in a stern serious tone.

"Not too bad." We cross Market and make a left onto Seventeenth Street, the green car once again impeding our path.

"My meter is having some trouble." I point.

"How's that?" He sounds genuinely interested.

"We've driven almost a mile," I indicate. "The meter reads $2.60. It should be $3.50."

"Has it been doing that all night?"

"I don't know. I've had short rides most of the night, it's possible. I just noticed it."

"That can crimp your profits," he says.

We start out tailgating the green slow-mobile as we ascend the steep grade of the Seventeenth Street hill. My cab begins to lug heavily, bang and chug as our speed decreases from 25 mph to 20 mph. Giving it more gas is to no avail. The engine coughs and lugs the remaining distance up the hill. Once atop Seventeenth, even the green car is long gone. It's all downhill to Stanyan Street. The cab motor sighs with relief.

"Time for a new transmission," he says. "Can I smoke?"

"It's a no-smoking cab. Sorry." I'm sensing that the "I just quit smoking" routine would not go well with this guy. I'm not even going to bother.

"O thou weed, who art so lovely fair and smell'st so sweet," he cants.

"Pardon?" I'm hoping he's not coming on to me.

"Shakespeare, it's Shakespeare. Look, I really want a cigarette. How about if I open the window and blow the smoke out of the car?"

"I guess," I cringe.

"You won't even know I'm smoking," he says cheerily. "Does it really bother you that much?"

"Well, yes. I'm deathly allergic." The truth of the matter.

"I just need three puffs. That's all. Then I'll put it out."

"If you need it that badly," I sigh unhappily. Being reasonably sincere and very polite makes points with me.

"Hey, never mind. I won't smoke," he says with determined commitment. "If you told me it *wasn't* all right, I was gonna smoke. Since you said I could—I won't."

I think I called it right. The "I just quit smoking" routine would not have gone smoothly. "I've been getting headaches the last few weeks, I suspect from exhaust leaking into the cab all night." The other possibilities are my late night apple juice or the take-out *Pad Thai*. The last culprit I discovered was miso soup—MSG and fish.

"Well, that's good to know," he says sarcastically. "Exhaust fumes?"

"I guess I shouldn't tell that to the clientele, hmm?" We pass the Golden Gate Park panhandle and turn left onto Fulton.

"How long you been driving?" he asks.

"Ever? Tonight?"

"Tonight."

"I'm going on nine hours, one more to go."

"You started at what, 4:30? That's a long shift."

I hear a squeak as the rear window rolls down.

"At least there's no traffic for the last few hours, or else I'd go crazy."

"You seem really calm for a cab driver," he compliments.

"You should see me as a civilian. It evens out, believe me."

"Last driver picked me up—drove like a fuckin' maniac."

"Oh, I know that guy."

"Yeah?" he laughs. "He spoke English, too."

I smell smoke. Not a lot, but I smell it just the same—can smell a cigarette a block away. My mother would say the same thing when I was a kid. I thought she imagined it. And now I've apparently developed that same talent, or curse. Over my shoulder I can see that he has set fire to his fair and lovely weed and, basically, his head is out the window. He is blowing most of the smoke outside, but a good deal of it is blowing back into the cab despite this uniquely contorted pseudo-yoga position. It's a sincerely valiant effort. So much for his "I will if you say I can't—and won't if you say I can" psychobabble. He has actually placed his body in potential jeopardy of a too-close encounter with opposing traffic or a close-passing truck. I'm still getting smoke in my face, but I appreciate his well-intentioned attempt. I crack my own window and slide a few inches to my left to get a better mix of fresh air.

"Twenty-Sixth Avenue, about halfway down on the left. Do you mind waiting for me when we get there?" he asks, as if this idea has just occurred to him.

"How long are you going to be?"

"Just a few minutes. I'll be right out. I promise."

The meter reads $5.60.

"It's just that my meter is screwed up." He takes a last puff on his cigarette, throws the half-finished butt out the window and blows the smoke out.

"Look," he says. "How much should the fare be?"

"I don't really know. About double what the meter shows."

"Figure it out and I'll pay it, if you wait for me. Fair enough?"

"Sure." I push the voice button on the computer and hit send. "I'll call in to check for the fare." The computer beeps. My message has been sent. We keep driving.

A few minutes and more than a mile later, the meter reads $6.80. The computer beeps again. The readout says: *GO TO CHANNEL TWO FOR VOICE*.

I hit Channel Two and pick up the microphone off the hook attachment on the lower part of the dash next to the glove compartment.

"The white house," he points, "with the puke color Volvo."

I park in front and hit the trip odometer on the dash so that it reads 0000. It should be easy enough to multiply the number of miles we drive times $1.80. Hopefully the trip odometer is accurate.

"Five minutes," he says. "Don't worry about the meter." He dashes out of the car.

"Six-six-one?" says the dispatcher coming over the radio. He has the art of sounding irritated, right down to being able to put someone on the defensive with a three-syllable number.

"Yeah, how ya' doin'?" I answer, expecting very little sympathy, but hoping to at least get some hard numbers for the next negotiation. "I'm having trouble with my meter. How much should the fare be from Diamond and Jersey to Fulton and Twenty-Sixth Avenue? Over."

"About thirteen dollars, driver. What does your meter read?"

I sit and glare at the L.E.D. readout. Damn. Has it been doing this all night long and I'm just now noticing it?

"Six-six-one, what does your meter read?" repeats the dispatcher impatiently.

"Six dollars and ten cents. Over."

"Sounds a little slow."

"Yeah, I noticed that. Over."

"Yeah."

"Can I charge him the $13.00? Over."

"No," he says. "And you don't have to keep saying 'over'."

"Oh. Can I keep track of the miles and charge him by the odometer? Ov..." I stop myself just short of another "over."

"You gotta go by the meter, six-six-one," he says as if he's my second grade teacher leading the Dick and Jane reading session. He pauses. "Or you can work it out with the passenger. Why don't you just bring the cab back in and exchange it?"

"My shift finishes at two-thirty. It's not really worth it."

"That's up to you, six-six-one."

"I'll try and work it out with the passenger. Thanks."

The computer buzzes. It reads: *GO BACK TO DATA CHANNEL*.

"Piece of crap," I mumble at the sluggish meter. The meter responds by changing to $6.40. I hit the "clear" button on the computer and the numeric readout reappears. A man in a sparkling new gold Mercedes pulls into the driveway next door. Meanwhile, there is no sign of my passenger. I hit the "destination" button, then "two one." That's downtown. When I do shut down the meter after the ride, the computer will book me into Zone 21, where I'm expecting to drop my passenger. The Mercedes guy has now walked up the driveway to the porch of his house and is slowly unlocking the front door.

I press the "send" button. The computer beeps and the Mercedes' car alarm sounds off. It's one of those whirring alarms with five different obnoxious sounds. The man jerks to attention, fumbles for his key ring and turns the alarm off while craning his neck toward the seemingly undisturbed vehicle. The computer beeps: *TEMPORARY ZONE*. The man resumes unlocking his front door. As he enters his home, I hit the "send" button again. The computer beeps. His car alarm goes off. He yanks the keys out of the front door lock, fumbles with them, turns the alarm off with the remote on his key chain, walks down the three steps from his porch over to his gold car, circles the vehicle, straightens his tie and shakes his head.

Six minutes later, the meter has been advancing as slowly as ever. My passenger reappears and gets into the back. Meanwhile, the neighboring Mercedes owner has retreated into his house.

"Head back into town," he says. "Thanks for waiting," he adds, changing the topic.

"No problem."

Developing an appreciation for the amusing aspects of one's working conditions is important. I hit the "send" button. The car alarm on the Mercedes goes off again, whirring, buzzing and beeping.

"Man, that's irritating," says my passenger.

"Yeah," I nod. "The guy should get that fixed."

I turn the cab around and head back to Fulton Street while checking the Mercedes in the rearview mirror. The gold car's owner comes running out of his house, turns off the alarm, scratches his head, tugs on his pants, bends over toward the cement driveway and tries to peer underneath his troubled car and, at the same time, avoid putting his knee to the ground and mussing the pant leg of his wool suit.

"You figure out the meter thing?" asks my passenger.

"Well, if it was working properly, it would be about thirteen dollars."

"Like I said, just tell me the amount and I'll pay it."

"I appreciate that. Thank you."

"Okay," he says happily. "Go back down Fulton and let's hear some music."

"What do ya wanna hear?" I ask my passenger.

"Oh, I don't care. How 'bout some classical? Would that bother you?"

"No, not at all; 102.1?"

"You listen to classical?" he asks.

"Actually, I've been known to play it."

"What do you play?"

"Classically trained on the piano; made a living playing the guitar for a long time." I turn the radio on, find his station, and adjust the balance between the front and back speakers to a comfortable volume (for him). Comfortable to me would be deafening for others. I've spent a lot of time on stage, posing in front of crash cymbals.

"Where's a good place to find some hookers?" he queries.

"The best looking ones are downtown. Mason Street's a popular spot." I pause. "There's O'Farrell and Taylor. The cops have been pushing them around lately. It varies night to night. There's always Hayes and Octavia."

"What do *you* recommend?" he asks.

"It depends what you're looking for. There's a couple of three-hundred and fifty-pounders who hang out in front of this bar on Geary."

"I don't think so. O'Farrell and Mason, let's go there," he decides.

"The thing is, the police don't appreciate cab drivers soliciting prostitutes. I've been personally warned."

"Oh, I understand. I'll be quick and discreet. If you see the cops, keep driving and we'll leave the area."

"There's not enough real crime to keep the cops busy, ya know?"

"And you can't walk two blocks in this town without people hitting you up for money," he adds.

"Yeah. A 'spare change' guy busted out my cab window while I was getting gas a couple weeks ago."

"How come?"

"I wouldn't give him a quarter. Well, actually, I suggested he get a job and he didn't like that."

"Well, that's a novel thought."

"And I might have told him to go fuck himself, too."

"I see. One of the homeless?" he asks.

"No, one of the criminal. It was three in the morning, the end of my shift—I turned my back to fill up, he smashed the window and ran. It cost me a hundred bucks."

"So I guess you should have just given him the god-damn twenty-five cents. These guys seem to have their personal territories staked out."

"Yeah," I nod. Proceeding at a good clip on Fulton, the windows are still open from when he was smoking his cigarette. It's getting a bit chilly, so I turn on the heat.

"You know any open liquor stores?" he asks.

"There should be some downtown."

"I know one on Van Ness," he says. "Can we stop on Van Ness?"

"Sure."

A minute later, I hear faint "snorting" from the back seat.

"Damn," he curses, "I can't see anything."

Sounds as though he's having a bit of trouble with something; hopefully, he's not crying. That should wait until *after* we fail to consummate a deal. I reluctantly turn around to look. He has a packet in his left hand, a tightly rolled bill as a straw in his right hand, and white powder covering his sport coat and the front of his shirt.

"Would you like me to put the light on?" I ask.

"Uhh, yeah. That would be great."

"Here." I turn off the heat and hit the automatic window control to shut the windows. "You probably don't want that stuff blowing around."

"No, I don't," he says. "Thank you."

He completes his toot. "You can shut the light off now. That helped." He's leaned back in the seat, relaxed, eyes closed. We drive for several blocks as the music plays—Mozart's *Requiem* (very beautiful, but a little on the depressing side).

"That is excellent," he comments. "Mozart." He pauses. "Ya know, if you'll excuse me saying so, Dostoevski said you judge the level of a civilized society by the conditions of its prisons. I think you judge a society by its encouragement of art, respect for culture. Frankly, that disturbs me about our country."

"Music and art are not exactly priorities these days."

"Money worship," he reflects. "That's all some people relate to."

We pull to a stop at the light on Ninth Avenue; Golden Gate Park is on our right. Loud, distorted thumping bass accosts us from the car speakers of a shiny white Camaro on our left, quite the contrast to our *Symphony in D Minor*. The light turns green. Our neighboring driver guns the powerful eight-cylinder engine and lays a patch, leaving us behind. Up ahead, as we continue down Fulton, looms City Hall, a conventionally majestic domed marble building.

The computer beeps with a message: **ANYONE FIND A BRIEFCASE?**

"Once you go left on Van Ness," he directs, "there's a liquor store down by Jackson or something. Then I can smoke another cigarette, too."

We make a left on Franklin and a right onto Bush Street, in close proximity to Cat Woman's territory. I don't get the impression he would be interested in her wares. At Van Ness the light is red. It turns green and as I step on the gas, a fellow Yellow Cab comes speeding through the intersection against the (very) red light. I slam my foot on the brake while noting the black embossed number on the side of the cab—it's number 294. I also notice the silhouette of Cab 294's lone passenger bouncing from side to side in the back seat as the cab careens around a bus. Sparks fly from the bottom of the vehicle after scraping the pavement while bottoming out in the intersection a short city block away. It makes a sharp screeching right turn and disappears around the corner. Late at night, barely an auto in sight, and two cabs nearly smash into each other.

"Nice driving," remarks my passenger.

"Yeah. Very impressive."

Two older Japanese businessmen wearing suits and ties driving a Honda sedan with a rental sticker on the fender are stopped next to us at the intersection, excitedly conversing and pointing in the direction of the wild cab that almost sliced into both our vehicles. For some reason, Cab 294 seems familiar to me. Maybe I was recently assigned that medallion for a night. I jot down the cab number on my waybill, the time and location of the supersonic incident, make the left turn and drive past a few more streets to a liquor store sporting a large burned-out neon sign. As requested by my benefactor seated behind me, I park out in front.

"I'll just be a minute. Here." He gets out and pulls a cell phone from his coat. "Make a phone call while ya wait. Call anywhere."

"That's okay," I refuse.

"Make a call. I'm gettin' free long distance."

"I really don't have anyone to call," I tell him. Maybe that will get him off my back.

"Go ahead." He's jabbing at me with the phone. "Hit this button for a dial tone."

"Okay, all right." I accept the shiny-silver folded apparatus from him. "Thanks."

He hurries into the liquor store. I lay the phone down on the seat next to me. Four minutes later, he's back, toting a tall paper bag containing at least two bottles of something.

"All set. Let's head downtown." He jumps in and shuts the door. "You make a call?"

"Well, actually…no." We continue down Van Ness.

"Make a call, c'mon. Where are you from?"

"Detroit."

"Call some people in Detroit."

"It's 4:30 in the morning there."

"C'monnnnn, call 'em. Don't wimp out on me."

"I don't have any phone numbers with me."

"Give me a name."

"They're all asleep." I make a right turn onto Pacific.

"I know you can give me a name."

"Marty Liebman."

"What's the area code?"

"3-1-3."

He buttons on the phone. "Operator," he says, "the number for a Marty Leafman in Detroit. L-E-A-F-M-A-N."

"I don't think he's listed," I tell him. And, he spelled it wrong.

"How do you spell that?" he asks me.

"You got it." I turn right on Polk Street.

"Operator," he pauses. "I'm calling from San Francisco; hold on just a minute."

"He's not listed," he says to me. "Give me another name."

"Uhhh, Lori Shumann. She's gonna be pissed."

"She'll get over it."

I swerve left as a parked car pulls out, nearly sideswiping us. Four cars on the road and every one of them is trying to ram us.

"Thank you, operator," he says. "What's your name?"

"You talkin' ta me?" I ask, in my semi-DeNiro. "Or to the operator?"

"I'm talkin' ta you," he says.

"Larry."

"Take the phone, Larry. I dialed the number for you."

"Thanks, I think."

I listen for a moment. "It's the machine," I tell him. I hold the phone out in front of me hitting one button and then another. I can still hear her voice on the answering machine. "How do you hang this thing up?" I hand the phone back to him. He listens to the end of the message.

"I'll leave a message," he says.

I figure there's no use arguing about it.

"This is Bob Grambling, NBA basketball coach. We've won the series and I flew in here to San Francisco to celebrate winning the title. Larry's showing me around; we're having a great time. Wish you were here." He lowers the phone. "You want to say anything?"

"Only that I had nothing to do with this." I take the phone from him. "Sorry, it's kind of late to be calling, just thought I'd say hello. Ummm, talk to ya later."

He takes back the phone. "All right, who else do ya wanna call?"

"No one, really."

"You gotta have someone to call. Any relatives?"

"My relatives would be asleep." He doesn't seem to get it.

"Turn down Post," he says, disappointed.

"The cops have been cracking down on cruising."

"I won't get you in trouble. One pass, that's it."

The computer beeps with a message: *101 NORTH IS A PARKING LOT - ACCIDENT AT 280 CUT-OFF.*

We turn left on Post Street. At Larkin, we stop at the light next to a corner bar. Two transvestites in short skirts, blouses with low-cut necklines exposing their cleavage, sway their hips as they cross the street in front of the cab, awkwardly wobbling in their extra-high heels. They turn and see me watching them.

"Hi, honey," says one of them. Both wave.

I wave back. The light turns green. We drive another four blocks to a welcoming gathering of three hookers. I slow down.

"Oh god," he says. "Keep going."

Farther down the street we come to an anorexic-looking pale-skinned blonde suffering a red rouge overdose, hair in a pouf, black hot pants showing off her long legs. A slow leisurely stroll accentuates her long-sleeved fire-red silky blouse, and a thin belt squeezes her petite waist. No police cars in sight. Her arms look too thin for her to be a cop.

"Yes," he points. "Yes. Get her in the car."

I pull to the curb next to her, step on the brake and roll down the window.

"Hi," she says, "You wanna date?"

"Hop in," I offer, and she quickly scoots inside, next to Bob.

"How are you tonight?" she asks, seeming relaxed and comfortable, like we've all known each other for years.

"Good," says my passenger. "It's a beautiful night, isn't it?"

"*Freezin',*" she says.

"What's your name?"

"Tracy. What's yours?" She possibly has a touch of a southern accent or maybe she's fakin' it.

"Bob," he says. "You have a lovely voice, Tracy. Where are you from?"

"Southern California."

Not quite exactly the *South* I had in mind.

"Just drive around for a few minutes," Bob directs, "around the block a couple of times."

The computer beeps with a message: *ZONE 68, A WOMAN WHO IS PREGNANT AND COLD WANTS TO GET TO ZONE 76. ANYBODY?*

"Listen," Bob tells her in confidence, "I want you to get a friend, and then we'll all go to my place and have a good time." Bob chooses his language with precision.

"Okay," she agrees, not missing a beat.

"A hundred for you, a hundred for your friend; how's that?"

"That's good," she says showing very little enthusiasm, like she's doing him a favor accepting this insulting cut rate. She doesn't fool me and she doesn't fool Bob. A hundred is good money. He seems quite aware of the fact himself. His negotiation skills are at least equal to hers.

"We'll go to my place near the Castro," he says. "Is that okay with you?"

"Yeah," she answers.

"Good," says Bob. "First, I want you to make a phone call."

"What?"

He's waving the phone in his hand again. "Make a phone call," he says. "Call anywhere."

"Yeah?"

"Call your mother. I'm gettin' free calls."

I look back because I have *got* to see her expression. She looks a little baffled. I raise my eyebrows and then smile. She smiles back.

"Call anywhere," encourages Bob. "Talk long as you want."

"Anywhere?"

I can tell her mind is racing or, okay, going at least as fast as it can. I figure she's trying to think of someone to call in Europe or Argentina. Maybe she has some hooker friends in Bangkok.

"Where does your mother live?" asks Bob.

"San Diego," she says.

"Call San Diego," says enthusiastic Bob. "Call her up."

Too bad, way too close. Let's make some *REAL* long distance calls here.

"Give me the phone," she laughs.

"What's the number?" He pauses. "I'll dial for you."

She doesn't say anything. Stalemate.

"Here," says Bob, handing her the phone. "Okay. You dial."

I quickly look back again. She doesn't appear so anorexic close-up. Despite the layers of makeup, she's actually attractive, in a plain kind of way. They would card her going into a bar. She could be twenty-five; she could be eighteen. With all this, I've forgotten about my challenged meter not working properly.

"Thanks," she says.

"Let me talk to her when you're done," he says.

"You want to talk to her?" says Tracy.

I'm sure Tracy has seen and heard many things, far beyond most young ladies her age. Apparently Bob's got a first on this one. And I can just imagine the conversation: "Hi Mom. It's Bob. Do you know anything regarding your daughter's history of contagious or infectious sexual diseases?"

Bob explains the phone's features. "You hit this button to dial out."

"Yeah, yeah," Tracy scoffs. "I know."

She dials. "Hi, Mom…fine. Nothing."

It's not her mom. She's obviously faking it. They fake orgasms; this has got to be a lot easier.

"From San Francisco," says Tracy. "Yeah. How's Joe?"

If it's really Mom, doesn't she wonder why her young, naive and attractive daughter isn't at home after midnight on a weekday?

"You are?" says Tracy. "Good…I'm in a cab using this guy's cell phone. Can you hold on? He wants to talk to you." She gives Bob the phone.

"Hi, Mom," says Bob. "I wanted to tell you that you've got a beautiful and lovely daughter, sweet as can be. Yes, you're very lucky; she's a wonderful person. You did a great job with her. We're out on the town and it's a beautiful San Francisco evening. Thanks, you take care. Here's your daughter back."

Tracy takes the phone. "Yeah, Mom, yeah, fine. I'll talk to you later. I love you too. I'll call you on the weekend. Bye, Mom."

I hear the electronic buzz of the phone as she hits one button and then another.

"How do you hang this thing up?" she asks.

"This button," says Bob. "Your mother sounds like a very nice woman."

"We get along good."

"Do you live in San Francisco?"

"Yeah, but I'm not sure for how long."

"So, what about your girlfriend?"

"She's right down the block. Turn on Mason."

We're back on Geary in front of the St. Francis. I drive one block and turn left at Mason. "There she is, over there," she points. "With the long black hair."

"Larry, can you get her in the car?"

"Her name's Gina," says Tracy.

I stop the car, roll down the window and yell, "Gina!" She looks at us and I wave her over.

Gina crosses the street and walks to the cab. Her black leather miniskirt accents her shapely body.

"Hi," says Gina.

"Gina," says Tracy. "Get in."

Gina gets into the back seat next to Tracy. Her cheekbones are not quite as high as her friend's, but her perfume is as sweet as Tracy's.

"How are you?" asks Bob.

"Good," says Gina. "How are you?"

"Great. We're having a great time. Are you Chinese?"

"Three-quarters Chinese."

"You're a very beautiful girl."

"Thank you."

"Go back down Geary," says Bob. "We'll get to know each other a little. I've got to go to a bank and then we'll go to my place. Okay?"

Gina looks at Tracy. Tracy nods her head.

"Okay," says Gina.

"Tracy, I want to give you $120 and I'll give your friend $80. But I've got to go to an ATM."

"Oh no, no. We split even," says Tracy. "We split everything even."

"Well, I've got two hundred bucks. You split it however you want. Two hundred, that's the deal tonight. Where's an ATM?"

"There's one over on Market," says Tracy.

"Let's go there," says Bob.

"On Eighth Street?" I ask.

"Whatever," he says. "Then we're going to Sixteenth Street and Sanchez."

We turn left on Hyde Street, pass United Nations Plaza, and travel to the other side of Market to the bank. Bob leafs through his wallet and pulls out an ATM card.

"Here, sweetheart," he says to Tracy. "Get me a hundred dollars. Take my card. I already got two hundred out tonight. I can only get another hundred."

"I don't want to use your card."

"I'll give you my number."

"No," she says.

"Look," says Bob. "I don't want to get out of the car."

"I don't do that type of thing," she says very seriously.

I turn to watch their exchange.

"C'mon," Bob prods. "Just get me the money."

"I don't want your number."

"What are you going to do? Get my money out some other time because you know my number? Take the damn card—six, nine, seven, zero."

"I don't want it."

"It will take you *one* minute."

"I told you, I don't do that."

"Look. Just put the card in the machine."

"It's your card," she shakes her head. "I'm not touching it."

"I can't believe you," he laughs. He gets out and walks to the machine. The three of us watch.

"Gina," whispers Tracy, "he's gonna have you make a phone call—to call your mother."

"Where?"

"He's got his phone with him. He talked to my MOTHER. Be ready for him to ask you."

"What's with him?"

"He's okay."

"Yeah?" she doubts.

"You know, I'm not going to give him a blow job. I'll pretend to, but I'm not going to. No way."

Bob gets back into the cab.

"All right, we're rollin'," says Bob. "Market and Sanchez."

What commotion would be created by mentioning to Bob what Gina was *not* going to do?

"Gina," says Bob, "that's your name, right?"

"Yes."

"You know anything about these illegals coming into the San Francisco Bay?"

"I heard about it," she says.

"I'll bet you know more than that, or you could find out."

"Are you the police?"

"No," laughs Bob. "I work for a magazine."

"What magazine?"

"That's not important. I'm interested in finding out about these illegals, the poor sons-of-bitches. They pay their life savings, arrive in America crammed into the bottom of a fuckin' fishing boat, get thrown in jail and sent back to Taiwan."

"Why are you so interested?" asks Gina.

"To get the bastards running the operation. They're working out of Hong Kong, makin' millions. It's not right. And it's a great news story."

"What would I have to do?"

"Just get me some names. No one will ever know you were involved. Think about it. You can make some money, maybe ten thousand dollars."

"Can you get the money first?" asks Gina.

"No," says Bob. "That's not how it works."

"Can I smoke in here?" asks Tracy.

"It's a no-smoking cab," says Bob.

Yes, BOB! The computer beeps with a message: *ZONE 68 CALLING BACK. STILL WAITING, STILL COLD, STILL PREGNANT.*

"Gina." Bob hands her the phone. "Make a phone call. I'm getting free calls. Call mom, call your mom."

Gina hesitates, then slowly buttons the phone.

"Mom? It's Gina. How are you? Yeah, yeah…good. Yeah, I saw them yesterday. They might offer me the job. Anyway, I only have a minute; this guy is letting me use his phone. Oh, nothing. I'm just with some friends.… Yeah, Mom. I will. Okay. Bye-bye."

Through the rear-view mirror, I notice a police car following behind us. Sure enough, the siren goes on, blue and red lights flashing. The squad car pulls out with a screech and speeds past us while Gina is still pushing buttons on the cell phone.

"How do you get this to hang up?" asks a frustrated Gina.

I smell cigarette smoke.

"Here," says Bob, "give it to me." He takes the phone from her. "You wanna make any other calls?" he asks.

"Would you call this guy for me?" asks Tracy. "He's a real jerk."

"Sure," says Bob.

"You met Richard," Tracy says to Gina. "He's a lying son-of-a-bitch. I didn't tell you what he did last week."

I wonder what kind of "dispute" Tracy and Richard had—money, drugs, sex? It's a combination of the three, most likely. How many dates does it take to get a working girl to go to bed with you? Maybe the guy is a semi-bona fide boyfriend or maybe even a pimp. Many of the "girls" working the streets work independently. Some don't. If you happen to watch long enough, you can sometimes spot the pimps. While the girls are walking the streets, the pimps might circle the block by car. Sometimes they'll stand on a street corner opposite the hooker, cajoling with other pimp heads of state.

Perhaps the commonality of unlawful professional activities creates camaraderie. You'd think the competition to score business, rack up johns and hook the best-looking girls on the worst drugs would breed contempt or at least mistrust; but, apparently, that's not always the case. The pimps seem to get along with each other better than the drivers of competing cab companies.

"We'll get him good," says confident Bob.

"Tell him I've been in a terrible accident—that I'm all fucked-up in the hospital." She gives him the number. "His name is Richard Nelchowsky. He's a dick."

Bob dials. "What's your last name?"

"Taylor. Tell him I'm in the emergency room; tell him I'm dying."

"Hello, this is Dr. Goodman," says Bob, in a stately authoritative voice. "I'm trying to reach a Richard, Richard Nelchowsky. I'm calling from the San Francisco General Hospital Emergency Room. We have a young woman here, a Tracy Taylor." Bob pauses. Richard must be on the phone. "Do you know her? She's been in a very serious accident," he says, as though very experienced at breaking this type of news to soon-to-be bereaved friends and relatives.

The classical music is still playing faintly on the radio—doesn't exactly set the Emergency Room mood they're trying to create. I turn it off. My window is cracked open. I roll it up to decrease the level of background noise.

"We got your number from her personal effects," continues Bob. "I'm her attending physician, Dr. Goodman." Bob pauses again, perhaps hitting a nerve with this Richard guy. "Yes," says Dr. Bob, "we've got a very, very *critical* situation here. Can you help us in reaching her family? Perhaps her mother, would you know how we can reach Ms. Taylor's mother?"

Tracy excitedly pokes Gina in the ribs. "He's such a fuck," she whispers.

"We can call you back. Any information you could provide would surely be helpful."

"Tell him I'm dead," says Tracy.

"Extremely serious," says Dr. Bob. "I'm due back in surgery. Being able to reach her mother would be of great assistance, thank you, sir. Good-bye." Bob hangs up.

"Did he sound worried?" asks Tracy. "Did he sound worried?"

"He seemed concerned. He's going to try and get your mother's number."

Tracy hoots with joy.

"Can we call him later and tell him I'm dead?"

"We'll call him from my place. Gina," Bob changes the subject, "what do you think about tracking down these scoundrels bringing in the illegals? Maybe you could ask around about these boats coming into the bay."

"Give me the ten thousand now," says Gina.

I quietly smile.

"Sweetheart," Bob says, "this is a long-term proposition."

"I'm interested in the *short-term.* I need to make lots of money, fast. That's what I want to do."

Making money fast. I guess that's how they look at their situation. But do they hang on to any of it? Does it do them any good? Do they get

Oh, nothing. I'm just with some friends....
Yeah, mom. I will. Okay. Bye-bye.

out unscathed, not addicted to drugs, disease-free? The fast track of free-market capitalism. "It's good to have a focus," I mumble, doubting they're paying attention.

"If we find these boat-runners, we can both make lots of money."

"Lots of money," says Gina. "I want to retire."

It sounds like something she has contemplated for some time.

"And these illegals will get money too. I'm serious. No bullshit," guarantees Bob.

"I need the money, *now*."

She reminds me of my friends' two-year-old son when he had a bad case of diarrhea. They had him on a bland diet. Mom is feeding him toast for the third day in a row, when he suddenly spits it out and says, "I want a cookie...and I want it NOW." Almost the kid's first words.

"You'll like my place," Bob says to the two women. "You girls be nice to me. Three minutes; that's how long it's going to take. You can handle it."

We slow for the red light at Market and Sanchez. Thinking about it, Bob's "night of improvisation" has actually been pretty smooth. He started out asking for my recommendations as if he was randomly playing by ear. I think he had the agenda planned before he ever got into the cab: the coke dealer, the liquor store, the prostitutes, and back to his place. As long as I get paid—the girls and I feel the same about our services.

"Make the left on Sanchez," Bob requests. "The light turns green. There's little traffic; we make the turn. "It's that white and yellow apartment building," he says.

I stop the car, get out, and open the rear passenger door. It feels good to stand up, and I get a better look at the girls as they make a quick exit from the cab. Time is money in my business and theirs. Bob lets himself out from the other side. My hobbled meter reads $21.50. Bob hands me two twenties.

"Give me back five, does that cover you?"

"That sounds about right." I get back into the cab. The trip odometer shows we drove eleven miles from where Bob purchased the cocaine or whatever it was. I lay the two twenties down on the seat next to me.

"And give me a receipt," he adds.

This must be research expense for his article. Instead of writing out a receipt, I calculate 11 x $1.80 on my scratch paper clipped to my cab-zone map comes to $19.80, plus the original $13.00 trip to the coke dealer, that's $32.80—what the meter would read if working properly. Thirty-five dollars comes to a two dollar and twenty cent tip. I'm a little disappointed, but it was the longest ride of the night. I hand him a blank receipt. "There ya go." Who knows how much I gypped myself during the first nine hours of the night.

"Thanks a lot," he says.

"Have a good night." I believe he will—until his medical results come back. I pull the wad of cash from my pocket and separate out a five-dollar bill. The two prostitutes have already crossed the street, now waiting at the walkway to Bob's flat. Bob follows closely behind.

"Find someone who'll talk," I hear Bob say. "Serious, Gina. We'll break the case. It's a great opportunity."

I raise my hand with the five (his change). "Um...your," I mutter. Bob has his arm around the blonde. He's not thinking about his five dollars. The blue numbers of the digital clock on the cab's dash indicate 2:18 a.m. I pick up the two twenties from the seat and put them in my pocket along with the five-dollar bill.

Bob unlocks his front door and the trio disappears into the building.

I write our final destination on my waybill and notice at the bottom of the page my scribble of notes about the near-miss with maniac Cab 294. I promise myself to check twice for people running lights, especially on Van Ness, and to pay more attention to whether the meter is working. Picturing Bob in bed with the two women, I scratch out my notes about Cab 294—transforming them into a blackened ink blob. I turn off the meter, shift into drive and step on the gas. It's quittin' time.

MY BABY'S IN THE HOSPITAL

Exactly 11:58 pm the following night. I've been burned. No one's answering the door. It's a well-groomed Victorian flat near the bottom of a hill on Vallejo Street in North Beach. It's a quiet evening. I can hear both the motor running and the taxi's radio from where I'm standing atop the stairs at the front door. I knock again. Nothing; it's a no-show. I retreat down the stairs, back toward my cab. The apartment door opens. Out comes a young white woman in her early twenties carrying a tough businesslike demeanor. She's not unattractive and looks as though she might even smell good. Her clothing is a combination of hippie, beatnik and biker: fringe hanging from the bottom of her jeans, a stylish worn-smooth brown leather jacket, army boots, a French beret on her head and a tiny silver stud in her nose. Without saying a word, she charges down the stairs and passes me by as if I'm invisible.

"Did you call a cab?" I ask.

"Yes, and I'm in a hurry," she says, exasperated.

Catching up to her, I open the back door. She gets in. I close the door behind her and get into the cab. My courtesy does not impress her. I'm wasting time.

"Could we get going?" she says impatiently. "Get me to the hospital."

I imagine she has a tattoo on her bicep: ♥*MOTHER*.

"Which one?" There are several hospitals in this city.

"You don't know? Jeez, the one by the school."

"Near U.S.F.?"

"I don't know."

"Do you know the street name?"

"You don't know where it is?" she abruptly accuses. "How long you been driving a cab?"

I swivel around to meet squinted eyes and a scowling face. Her stiff shoulder-length hair adds to the image of this drill sergeant portrayal, but her petite build makes it a hard sell.

"Do you know a cross street?" I ask.

"It's by the school. Just GO, okay?"

I kick the transmission into drive, depress the accelerator and hope she approves traveling in the direction we're already facing; there will be hell to pay, taking her to the wrong place.

"Do you have a preferred route?"

"Yes, the fastest."

The "I don't know where I'm going, and get me there fast" is a new one for me. Hopefully she wants St. Mary's near U.S.F. (University of San Francisco).

"How's your night?" I miscalculate, attempting to diffuse tension.

"How's my night? Well, not very good. My baby's in the hospital."

"Ohh. What happened?"

"It's none of yer business."

Okay, fine. I wonder how she was separated from her baby in the first place. How did it get to the hospital at midnight without her? We ride in silence for three-quarters of a mile.

Unfortunately, our route brings us to chance encounters with several stop signs, a stop-light and even other traffic. I do my customary "California stop" at two intersections. At the third intersection, I actually come to a *complete* stop—concerned there may be a cop lurking somewhere in the darkness.

"You gotta go faster," she whines.

"What?"

"You're going slow on purpose," she accuses.

"What would you like me to do?"

"You're stopping at every corner."

"If there's another route you want to take, I'll take it."

"You don't have to keep stopping."

"I can't be running every stop sign. This is the fastest direct route I know."

Two blocks later it's another red light. We stop.

"Fucking shit. You're doing this on purpose, aren't you?"

"I don't run red lights. I'm sorry."

Should I admit to personally erecting these obstacles earlier this afternoon, having precisely calculated her evening travel plans? She can jam sharpened poison bamboo slivers under my fingernails; I'm admitting nothing.

"You don't need to intentionally stop," she says.

"I don't know what you're talking about."

"Ya know, I'm gonna complain to your company. I've never seen anyone drive like this. I'm gonna call your boss. You think this is funny?"

Maybe she's high on meth. We come to Pine Street and I make a right. It's one of the fastest streets in the entire city for getting across town. Cruising at 30 mph, we hit three green lights in a row with more just ahead of us. She should be happy now.

"Would you go *faster*?" she says. "You can fucking go faster."

"Look, these lights are timed. There's nothing more I can do."

What she needs is an antidote for her personality—we're talking billions in medical research. Pine Street smoothly curves into Masonic and, to our left, a striking and beautiful panoramic view of the city lights, the Bay Bridge, and the East Bay.

"We should have been there already," she grunts.

"Maybe you should have called an ambulance, not a cab."

"You're GOIN' the wrong way," she screams, smacking her hand down on the fake leather seat interior.

"Listen." I try a more authoritarian approach, *Marine to Marine.* "You want Stanyan, near U.S.F. It is three blocks south, one mile down the road."

"Where are you taking me? Where the hell are you going?"

"To the hospital," returning to sarcasm, "if I recall."

"I want the fastest way."

"If you want a different route, you just tell me."

"YOU'RE GOIN' THE WRONG WAY!" She bobs up and down in my rear-view mirror, perhaps nervous about being dropped at the local asylum.

"Believe me," I say calmly, "it's only a few minutes more."

On Turk, about eight blocks from the hospital drop, she makes her next observation.

"This fare is way more than I thought. I'm not sure I have enough."

Whoooaaaa. I immediately hit the brakes and pull over to the curb by what was formerly Lone Mountain College.

"Shit," she hisses. "What are you doing now? You're stopping. Why are you stopping?"

"Do you have enough money?"

"I can not fucking believe this. You'd better keep driving." She bangs the seat again, arms flailing. "Drive," she screams.

"I'm not driving anywhere. And you can get out right here."

The computer beeps with a message: *WHO EVER JUST DROVE BY 571 BUENA VISTA EAST AND HIT A CAR—GO BACK THERE. NOW!!!*

"What's that?" she asks.

"You've just won the lottery!"

"I'm gonna have you FIRED! I'm gonna call your supervisor!!"

"Call anyone you want. You're out of here if you don't have money."

"Fuck you. You're HISTORY."

"Do you have money to pay the fare?"

"Son-of-a-bitch, that's none of your business."

"It's very much my business."

"I don't have to tell you how much fuckin' money I have—it's none of yer fuckin' business."

"And I don't have to drive you anywhere."

She lights a cigarette.

"It's a no-smoking cab."

"Why's that?"

"'Cause I said so."

"You're gonna be one sorry motherfucker. I have an emergency, asshole. So, GO, you retard freak."

"You brought it up, can you pay the fare?"

"Fuck, I have enough. You just fuckin' start to drive."

"I need to *see* the money. You think this is some free service?"

The fare is eight dollars at this point. She pulls out seven dollars, at most. It's hard to tell. The currency's all crumpled up—some kind of standard procedure with these people who are short or plan to ditch. There's nothing better than catching this before it's too late to do anything about it; hopefully, in a context that makes it extremely inconvenient for them.

"You need more than that. We still have another mile to go."

"I *have* it," she says, hysterical. "Keep driving."

"Show me the money." I always wanted to say that; never thought it would actually fit a true-life situation. If I weren't so pissed off, I'd probably be laughing.

"Oh, you're history," her mantra. "You are sooooo HISTORY."

"That's fine, but I still wanna see the money." I turn and watch her count from a wadded ball of one-dollar bills and loose change; some from her pockets and some from her pocketbook.

"Here. Ya see?" She shakes the money at me. "I've got it. GO!"

If science could harness this raw energy of hers, nuclear power would be obsolete. The Arabs would go broke.

"Okay, fine." I pull into light traffic, trying to stay calm—but slowly losing that battle.

"I'm late, and it's 'cuz of you. You're in big trouble."

"No tip? Is that what you're saying?"

"Fuck you!" she chops with a devilish rasp.

It hasn't been a great night and she's no improvement. I just want to get paid. If this hassle had occurred earlier in the ride I'd have kicked her out. Calculating the time and money invested at this point, kicking her out would do her more good than me. It's only a fifteen-minute walk. We're not in the best neighborhood, but it's not unsafe enough for any vicarious satisfaction. It's not even uphill.

It's a curiously interesting pattern, though: people complaining about *not going fast enough* so often being short of funds. *Hurry up and get there before you find out I can't pay.* I consider the appropriate implementation of a new Cab Policy: when someone complains about not going fast enough, pull over and demand to see the money.

We get to the hospital entrance located inside the parking garage. We both get out of the car. She hands me the permanently creased funds, and stomps toward the emergency room doors. I quickly count the money. She shorted me a buck.

"Uh, wait a minute." I follow her. "You're not going anywhere until you give me the rest of the money."

She stops and turns—goes ballistic (again). Hopefully, her hysterical, obscene screaming, reverberating throughout the garage, will attract a security guard or some hospital personnel in case reinforcements are needed. They should have more experience than I in dealing with nuts like her. Unfortunately, no one seems to be around. If anyone can hear her, the undoubtedly sane thing to do would involve finding a quick and convenient exit and vacating the area.

"You don't even deserve to get paid," she screams. "I'll kick your ass!!"

So, she does have a sense of humor.

"I don't need this." I open my palm to her. "Give me the rest of the money."

"You're lucky to get ANYTHING. This was TERRIBLE service." She turns away and tries to scurry through the hospital doors.

I rush out in front of her, and put my arm out to block her path. She walks forward, bounces off my hand and gets pushed back slightly. My mistake. I can hear it now: ASSAULT AND BATTERY!!

"You got all my money. I don't have any more."

"Yes, you do. I saw it. I'm calling the police." It's bluff vs. bluff, over one dollar.

"You don't know how to drive. You're gonna be one sorry fired asshole."

She doesn't mention me "pushing" her. I'm very relieved.

"It's fine with me," I announce. "The police can settle this."

She gives me a buck. And I've kept the meter running.

"You owe another dollar for the time you've wasted," I inform her.

"I don't believe this." She throws another dollar on the ground. "You're history," she snarls. "I've got your cab number."

"Good. And get my name right." I slowly spell it for her.

She goes into the hospital.

Maybe she *will* report me. I write a brief explanation under "remarks" on my waybill to beat her to it. Likely, she will come across as a lunatic. "Baby" has his or her hands full. But I seriously doubt this woman had a baby. No, I *hope* she doesn't have a baby. Possibly, "baby" is some drug overdosed loser boyfriend. Or maybe hospitalized and suffering from an overdose of her personality. There's no known antidote for that. At least with food poisoning, you can have your stomach pumped. No such straightforward solution here.

Getting back into the cab, I feel an ache in my back and a pounding in my head. I decide to call it an early night and take a leisurely drive back to the yard. Nine hours is enough for tonight.

THE MESSAGE

Two days later and I'm back at the yard for my shift. The first order of business is to fetch my time card from the wall and hand it in to the cab dispatcher, David, at his window. Unlike the dispatchers sending out orders and communicating with drivers on the road via the radio and the computer, David "simply" disperses the few hundred cabs for the start of each driver's ten hours. The order dispatchers' office is a large dark room located in the bowels of the company offices. David's office sits at the front of the sunny yard overlooking the cab parking lot.

I slip my green time card to him under the half-moon window cutout.

"You got a message." He sounds very irritated. But, he always sounds like that.

His voice is amplified by the microphone in the booth. He slips me a wrinkled piece of paper with some chicken scratches on it. He blows out the smoke from the corner of his mouth and takes another hard drag on his cigarette. Wacko-woman from the other night at the hospital is my immediate thought. Telling him about it would only serve as a vent for my nerves; for him, an extremely boring waste of time. An encounter with a psychotic? How surprising; no cab for you today.

If you're looking for sympathy, compassion, empathy, or welcome—you've come to the wrong place, pal. Any wisecrack from a driver will be met with a worldly, sarcastic, lightning response that you will have plenty of time to ponder during the next ten plus hours, after he assigns you a rickety "spare" cab—parked in row six. It will be a vehicle on its last ravaged legs with an odometer well past 300,000 miles and a particular smell emanating from some location that you can't quite pinpoint. Dozens of people have puked on those seats during this taxicab's lengthy life span.

"Thank you," (for the message) I reply. He just looks at me. With him, it's "thank you" no matter what. If you get something good, a nice cab or an early departure from the yard, "thank you" and you shut up. It's as if he doesn't want anyone else to know that he did you a favor. If you get a piece of crap to drive for the night—"thank you"—or you'll get something much worse the next time. He will remember any complaint, disruption or speed bump in his afternoon whether you appear at his window the next day or three weeks later. He's one of those guys who seems like he's not really paying attention, but not a detail escapes his notice. And, again, you will suffer if you raise his ire.

David determines whether you wait 10 minutes for your cab or three hours; it's not unusual on a Friday or Saturday night for some people to give up and go home after hours of waiting. On occasion, I have.

David decides whether you drive a spanking brand new cab with 36,000 miles, or not. The yard has plenty of variety from which he can choose. You can be pre-assigned the nicest car in the yard and a quintessential (prime time) 3:15 p.m. shift; it doesn't mean that you will get it. He has what appears to be total discretion, including veto power. He might say he doesn't have a car available; he might have assigned your cab to someone else; your cab might be headed for the shop. Yes, there are 35 cabs sitting in the lot, and you HAVE been waiting for an hour and forty-five minutes past your assigned shift. A complaint is not going to help you. A ten dollar bill might help, but if there's anything in your style, expression or demeanor that communicates quid pro quo, that you're expecting a certain return for your money, that will piss him off too. You're not at the flea market, no one's holding a bake sale and he's not a mercenary. I'm sure the tip speaks louder at certain times than others, but I have yet to figure out that time schedule and protocol. My practice is to slip him five dollars (seven or eight on a Saturday night), go sit down, and—did I mention? Shut up. Oh yes, and sit somewhere out of his sight. "I WILL CALL YOU WHEN I HAVE A CAB. I DON'T HAVE ANY MEDALLIONS RIGHT NOW."

You need a medallion to go with your cab. The medallion makes you "legal." And yes, he has a dozen medallions sitting out on the front counter in his smoke-filled room—but none of them are for YOU. Not until he says. Don't get it wrong. His "when I feel like it" system is methodical and organized. And if he thinks you're hovering over him, he's going to hit you with another 45 minutes of waiting time.

Occasionally, I'll see a driver tip ten dollars. I've seen drivers give him one dollar. They think they're saving money—but they're going to be spending extra time warming a bench, rather than being out on the road where they can actually make a buck.

There are a couple of other part-time cab dispatchers. Regardless, David works five days a week with two or three hundred cabs going out every night. You don't stand there and ogle, but I notice many drivers tip him five dollars. Do the math—a thousand dollars per night? A little more or a little less? An impressive amount of cash for sitting in a booth, telling guys to shut up and sit down. Perhaps he performs really difficult paperwork? I'm unclear about the required qualifications, but I imagine a long line of envious folks waiting to displace him, if only in their dreams. I'm waiting, but I haven't the slightest idea how to get on that list.

I slink off to a corner where I can decipher the message in private. If I were getting fired or in trouble, wouldn't they be summoning me upstairs and not by means of a crumpled piece of paper? There is a barely legible scribbled phone number with the name "Bob" below it. Speaking of five bucks, if it's Bob from the Tracy and Gina Show, I guess he wants his back. It doesn't say, of course.

I call the number. A man answers. It's Bob. I doubt the girls are still with him.

"All right!" He sounds excited, as usual. "I'm glad you called," he spouts, as if this was something I initiated. "Listen, I've got a proposal for you."

I don't know anything about illegals being smuggled into the country and I also can't keep driving him around looking for prostitutes. It's too risky. I really have to be more careful if I want to keep this job for a bit.

"I have a few projects I'm working on, and I'd like to be able to call you, say, if I'm in a pinch to get a ride. Not a big thing," he reassures. "I just need someone, you know, dependable, trustworthy."

It sounds good, but it sounds bad too. It strikes me as trouble, with his slightly reckless activities and all—the coke, the prostitutes, driving around in a cab....

"Maybe you need a limo," I suggest. "I drive all over the city. I never know where I'm going to be, and I never know when I'm going to get there."

"I can't afford a limo; they won't expense that for me. Plus, that takes too long. Stuff happens fast in my business. I snooze, I lose."

And just what exactly is his business? I think he mentioned writing an article—for some magazine, but which one? I don't think he ever said. He seems more like a salesman than a writer. Then again, a little salesmanship never hurts, usually.

"Look, if you're busy, that's fine. If you're available—you come and get me. Really simple, no strings attached. I'll get you a cell phone—I'll call you if I need you."

Not with the phone again.

"It sounds really good," I pause, "but I'm required to be available to the public." I need some kind of an escape clause with this guy, maybe a couple—and a sanity clause.

I hear David call my name. It's always better to be completely out of his sight. As if I have no expectations.

"I'm getting paged," I excuse. "Can we talk about this later? My cab is ready."

"That's perfect; can you come and pick me up?"

The timing couldn't be much better. To have a fare before I leave the yard? He's only a few minutes away and in the opposite direction of rush hour traffic.

"I need to make a few calls. I'll let you know where I'm going, probably downtown, but I'll let you know for sure when you get here."

Downtown? A great fare to start the night; should be an easy place to make another pickup from there. I don't believe his "no strings attached" part but, for tonight, why not?

"I should be there in, say, fifteen minutes?"

"That's great," he says. "You remember where I live?"

"Sixteenth and Sanchez, right off Market."

"No, no. I'm over at the girlfriend's, Diamond and Jersey." He repeats the street number.

Twelve minutes later, I arrive at his location. He bolts down the stairs and out of the house.

"Chinatown," he announces. "We're going to Chinatown!" He gets into the car. "And here, take this phone." He pulls it out from his pants. "It's yours. I'll expense it."

I start to object. He won't hear it.

"Look, I'm meeting a couple of guys. It's about those illegals coming in, you know, I talked to the girls about it." He slams the door shut. "Hey! And you'll be happy to know, I quit smoking."

"That's great."

"Ahhh, whatever. I'll be smoking again in two weeks. No expectations."

We arrive at the appointed spot, off Waverly Street.

"Just drive around the corner; by the time you get back around I'll be done. This is gonna be real short. Or, if not, you can drive the block again. This really shouldn't take long." He hands me a twenty.

"You don't have to do that."

He drops the bill on the seat. "Take it. I'm coming back. You've got receipts, right?"

"Yes. You know, I might get stuck in traffic or...."

"That's okay, I'll wait. Just keep the meter running; it's not a big deal. These guys have some names for me. So I might have a few more stops after this."

He gets out and slams the door, nods and waves a subtle "hello" to the two men standing inside the doorway of a building one half-block down. There is an old Chinese woman slowly walking the street. She's plainly dressed, looks very modest, about 80 years-old, might be one-hundred. I gently hit the gas and proceed to make my circle. There's the usual amount of backed-up Chinatown traffic. It's about eleven minutes later when I make it back to retrieve Bob. He awkwardly waves. I stop. He walks up, letting himself into the passenger side of the cab.

"Shit." He slams the door.

I only see the old woman on the street. The other guys are gone. I notice that Bob has a black scuff mark on his forehead that I'm fairly certain wasn't there when I first picked him up. It looks like a smudge of woman's makeup. His nose is also bleeding.

"They beat the fuck out of me, fuckin' bastards," he points. "That woman over there, I think she saved my life. She was screaming at them and they stopped."

I'm a bit taken aback. It's the old hunched-over Chinese woman, wearing a withered black and grey winter coat, calmly and quietly staring at us. One of her hands juts out from her body, palm up, as if she's asking for spare change. She's meeting my stare with a much more intense one of her own. I finally look away. She could almost pass for a homeless person.

"They were kicking me; one guy, I think, had a stick or something, he was hitting me in the back, didn't even hurt actually. Then she comes around, starts screaming at them in Chinese, and they run off. I'm tellin' you, she saved my life."

The woman is still staring at us, watching closely. She doesn't look friendly at all. Bob's eye is swelling and closing up. Maybe he can't see that she just doesn't quite pass as the Good Samaritan type, not in my estimation. But, what do I know?

"That one guy," he murgles, "I think a punch loosened a tooth."

"Maybe we should get you to an Emergency Room."

"No, no, I'm fine. Take me home. My side is killin' me." He coughs and clears his throat.

The woman is still staring—relentlessly.

I lock the doors. "You know," I begin, as I drive forward and make a left turn, "you sure she wasn't directing them and not just telling them to stop?"

"No, no. That can't be. She wasn't here when we first started talking. She came walking over after they started in on me. It was…it happened so suddenly. That short guy, he says, 'We got a message for you.' I said, 'Yes, that's why I came down here.' He grabs me by the coat, throws me on the ground—I mean, I don't even know how I got on the ground—I just know they were goin' at me." He sounds short of breath. "You wouldn't have any ice, would you?"

"That woman…." I begin. She's still staring and giving me the creeps. "Anyway, why don't we have someone take a look at you?"

"Take me home, quick, if you don't mind."

I make a turn onto Stockton and head south toward Market Street. Once at his home, he asks me to wait; he goes in and comes back out with his girlfriend in hand. She's very attractive, tall, modestly dressed—a bit stern-looking and worried. I don't ask any questions.

"Just over to UC, driver," Bob requests. We ride in silence, Bob holding an ice pack to his face, his girlfriend attending to some of his wounds with ointment, a towel and some disinfectant-type stuff.

I drop them at the hospital Emergency Room.

"I'll try calling you when we're through here." His voice doesn't sound good.

"Okay," I agree. What am I going to say, "No"?

I check back into traffic, book into the zone to wait for my next fare, and just keep drivin'.

THE PHARMACY

October 31st—Halloween. My favorite holiday. And San Francisco's favorite holiday. Of course some contend that it's Halloween here all year long.

The height of the festivities are over and the evening's winding down when I accept a fare off the computer to pick up a prescription from a 24-hour pharmacy at the corner of Eighteenth Street and Castro. I'm to take the medicine to an address in Diamond Heights. There's nothing better than the dollars clicking off with no passenger in the car. Just turn up the radio, relax and drive.

I flip on the meter and head toward Eighteenth, no longer obstructed by the tens of thousands of folks who were milling through the streets only an hour ago. Still, I can't find a place to park. From about six o'clock, the police blocked off traffic within a four-block radius of Market and Castro Streets. With the crowds dispersed, all that's left is to clean up the trash, but the cops are uncooperative about my choice of a parking space for my medicinal mission.

"You can't park here," says the stern woman officer.

"I'm picking up a prescription one block from here."

"There's no parking on this street."

"I'll only be a minute."

"Keep driving, sir. I'll have to give you a ticket."

"C'mon. Can't I park at the corner for six minutes?"

"No. Keep moving."

I park three blocks away. I run to the pharmacy, get the drugs, walk back to the cab and drive to Diamond Heights. It takes me fifteen minutes.

The wife answers the door on the third ring.

"I have your prescription."

"I don't think it's going to help," she says.

Not help? I stand there thinking of all the time I've wasted.

"I mean, I don't think he needs it anymore. He's gone."

"What?" It took so long that he left the house to go get it himself? Am I gonna get paid?

"Just a minute ago. He's dead. He just died." She pauses and stares.

Shit. I'm wondering if I had parked closer to the drug store instead of almost a half-mile away, if that would have made some kind of a difference. No one said it was an emergency. I don't even know what kind of medicine is in the bag.

"I guess I should pay." She turns, slowly reaching for her purse that's slung on the banister, fumbles with her wallet and hands me the fare. And a two-dollar tip. "Thank you," she says.

SAFE SEX

"**U**m goin' home." He's short and, if he were a woman, I guess you'd say he was petite. He flagged me at Eighteenth and Castro Streets, just after the bars closed up. He has long dark hair and a moustache wearing very tight pants—not the moustache, him.

"Of head a few drinks," he slurs, like I couldn't figure that out.

"That's fine." I start the meter. "Where's home?"

"Up the hill. Corbett," he says in monotone. "Sorry for such a short ride."

"If that's where you live, that's where you live." I make the right turn on Eighteenth, another on Diamond, cross Market and turn left on Seventeenth Street, heading toward Corbett.

"Yer kinda cute," he says, moving over to the middle of the back seat so we can gaze at each other in the rear-view mirror. "Ya wanna come home with me?"

"No, thank you." His squirming all around in the back seat interrupts what would otherwise be a welcome, if somewhat uncomfortable, silence.

"You're sure you don't wanna come home with me?"

"I'm working. I'm sorry, but no."

"Oh come on. Turn on the light; let me look at you."

"The light bothers my eyes." We pull up in front of his address.

"Ohh. Turn on the light," he says. "Lemme see you better."

I figure it's the easiest way to get him out. I turn on the light. He grabs onto my shoulder and squeezes.

"Oooh, you must work out. It's so hard."

I turn off the light.

"You're sure you don't have a few minutes?" He's now massaging my shoulder.

"No, sorry."

"You can go back ta work later."

Things seem to happen in clusters, like they say, in threes (or more). This time around it's squeeze-the-driver's-shoulder-month, in fact, it's been extremely popular in the last couple of weeks. First, there was an alcoholic ashtray-scented barfly with rollers in her hair coming from Pete's Saloon on Mission Street wanting to get to know me better; and then there was this very vivacious but scary looking Irish woman (her boyfriend passed out on the back seat), and now this guy—all grabbing my shoulder. Of course, it's never Claudia Schiffer or Nina Oord (yes, Nina Oord, look her up on the Internet and then you WILL know her).

I turn around and look my current passenger in the eye. Maybe he's suffering from some self-esteem issues. "You're a good-looking guy." I turn back around. "You shouldn't have any trouble out there." In other words, go pick on someone with your own sexual preferences.

"Oh please, you're just bullshitting me now. C'mon, we'll have a good time."

"Thanks, but no."

"You get this all the time?" He slightly changes his tune.

"Occasionally. A four-hundred-pound egg-shaped woman with long sideburns made an offer last week."

"Mrs. Humpty Dumpty," he says. "I *know* her."

"I didn't ask her name."

He has grabbed onto the back of my seat, pretending to have trouble reading the brilliantly lit meter. His face is about three feet away from it. I haven't seen any money yet.

"That's two dollars and ninety cents," I translate for him.

"You're probably straight, huh?" he slurs.

"Yes, I am."

"Well," he leans forward again, now filling the rear-view mirror, "I am a *beautiful* woman." He poufs up his hair and bats his eyes at me. "Sure you don't wanna come with me?"

"I'm very sure."

He sits back down. We're not making progress here.

"I've caused you trouble." He hands me a five. "I'm sorry. Keep the change."

A two dollar tip.

"Thanks." I quickly pocket the five. It's a dollar more than the talk-to-the-naked-girls get on Broadway and I don't have to be naked. So maybe I'm not doing so badly.

He starts to open the door to get out, then abruptly changes direction—essentially pulled back into the cab due to the magnetic attraction between the Corinthian leather seats and his ass. "Come in with me," he says.

"I gotta go."

"Ohhh, come onnnnn," he says.

Maybe he's done the same math as I, and figures I owe him more small talk for the extra dollar. I'm not sure how many minutes you get with the naked girls for one dollar. Regardless, I'm fully clothed and it's going to stay that way.

"I'm sorry," I tell him. "You've got to get out. I have to pay for this cab and it's due back."

"You pay for the cab? How much?"

"It's a hundred a night."

"I could help you," he says still holding the door open.

"It would be plenty of help if you would get out."

He sighs, "Ohhh-kay," but doesn't move.

I hit some buttons on the computer causing it to buzz back at me. "I've got another call."

"I'm just drunk and horny," he says.

"I noticed. I've really *gotta* go."

"It would be a great night if you came in."

"No! Good-bye. You'll have better luck next week."

He lowers his head and moans. "It's always like this."

"You'll be fine," I say. "You gotta get out, please."

He peels himself from the seat, gets up, gets out and shuts the door. I shift out of "PARK" and he watches from the middle of the street as I pull away. I thankfully wave to him, and drive back down the hill.

The computer buzzes with a message: *CAB #294, YOUR DRIVING INSTRUCTOR HAS A MESSAGE FOR YOU: A RED LIGHT MEANS STOP! SLOW DOWN!!!!!!!!*

I think the dispatcher needed one more exclamation mark to make his point. Without it, 294 may misconstrue its importance.

I continue driving in circles without a fare. A half-hour ticks past since dropping the petite guy claiming to be a beautiful woman at his Corbett address. Circling back and forth between a few different South of Market establishments finally turns up some stragglers: three men coming out of a popular gay bar, *THE STUD* on Harrison Street. One guy, who could easily pass as a bouncer, is wearing a bright bleached white tank-top tee shirt emphasizing his steroid-induced muscular build—6'3"and at least 225 pounds. His two companions climb into the back seat. One guy could be a *GQ* model; his partner sports the escaped-convict look—head shaved, beard unshaven, dressed in a Goth black shirt and black pants. And someone, pray tell, has taken several sharp metallic objects and run them straight through his face. It looks painful, but doesn't seem to bother him. Of the group, I spotted him first and I wasn't going to stop. But when GQ playfully grabbed the metal-pierced escaped-convict's buttocks, and both seemed to enjoy the routine, I realized they were together and figured they were a safe pick-up. If anyone looking like Thug is flagging me from a ragged street corner in the Tenderloin, I do *NOT* stop. Admittedly, on Union Street and in the Castro district, I've gambled and picked up some of these guys, at the same time measuring out my willingness to confront them over a few measly bucks. On these occasions, there's an anxiety that rises up in my gut as I wait for these unknowns to utter their first words or anticipate what may transpire when it's time to exchange money for services rendered. Have I picked up a gay guy or a psycho? Will they be producing a five-dollar tip, or asking for donations at gun point? It's all part of the job's intrigue and the very reason I should find another one.

With GQ and Thug comfortably positioned in the rear, belligerent Bouncer attempts to open the locked front door.

"Unlock this door," he yells, agitated and frustrated.

I'm already reaching over, pulling at the handle to unlock it, but the mechanism remains locked in place while he's trying to open the door at the same time.

"Open the fuckin' door!" he howls in a thunderous voice.

I can hear him fine. There's no need to scream. The window is rolled halfway down. He releases his grip on the door and bangs on the cab's roof with his fist. I try the door again, but he again beats me to it, his hand pushing on the latch from the outside.

"Let it go," directs the GQ model from the back seat, "so he can unlock it!"

"Oh," says the bouncer. He raises his hands in the air.

I try again to unlock it as he grabs the handle.

"Shit," he says. "I'll fuckin' do it." Reaching his thick muscular forearm through the window, he unlocks it and gets in.

Having the front seat pulled all the way up gives people sitting in the back more leg room. Ninety-nine point nine percent of passengers sit in the back and I encourage maintaining that statistic. My feeling that my space is invaded when people sit in the front seat has not changed, particularly since the "Old Timer" pulled the gun on me (real gun or not), and from another time when a guy was fiddling with a knife—also in the front. Maybe people are carrying guns and knives in the back seat too but, certainly, what you don't see and never find out doesn't bother you (as much). In addition, cab company guidelines (for robbery prevention) recommend that only the (physically) handicapped sit in the front. (Guidelines regarding the mentally handicapped remain conspicuously unaddressed.) Frankly, I don't care for people sitting in the back either. Until the Halloween incident, my favorite fares were picking things up from various places and delivering them—the radio blasting from four speakers, the meter flipping happily along, no pesky bothersome passengers. Fed-Ex is the next day—but *we* can deliver in fifteen minutes. The bad news: these fares come up about once every three months. So, unfortunately, I've resigned myself to picking up tourists, gays masquerading as thugs, and other strangers in the night.

"Mr. Cab Driver," says the bouncer. "Why was the door fuckin' locked? Don't you let people fucking sit in the front?"

His friends are now giggling—undoubtedly from his sexual double entendre. I'll pretend I missed it.

"It's fine with me," I tell him. "Either way." Like I'm gonna disagree with a guy whose muscles are larger than my head? And there's more giggling from behind me.

"And what the fuck?" Muscleman's knees are jammed into his chest. "You got fuckin' midgets ridin' in here?"

"You can pull the seat back," I point. "The lever is...."

He pulls the lever, slides the seat back and bangs into Pierced Face Man's knees.

"Ahhhhh, SHIT!" wails Thug. "You just busted my kneecaps."

"Shut up," says Muscleman. "I need room over here."

The computer beeps with a message: *FARES WAITING AT PIER 39.*

"What's that?" asks Muscleman.

"It's the computer. They're sending me your rap sheets."

He leans left and reads the screen. "FARTS waiting at Pier 39. Hmphhh. Big farts or little farts?" He grunts and rolls his window all the way up. "I feel one comin' right now, aaarghhhhhhh-uhhhhhrrrreh." He's moaning and groaning, hands tugging at his own behind.

"Spare us," says GQ. "You're not even funny."

"We wanna go eat," says Thug. I notice that he has a trace of bright red lipstick on his lower lip. "What's open?"

"In what part of town?" I ask.

"The hamburger place on Seventeenth," says Muscleman. "That's open all night."

I drive forward and turn on the meter, which I've almost forgotten to do with all the commotion. At Twelfth Street we come to a stop sign. Two young men on the corner to our right are passionately making out.

"Hey look." Muscleman rolls the windows down. "Stop that!" he yells. "Hey fags! You fuckin' homos. You're fucking disgusting!"

The two on the corner pay no attention. Muscleman starts digging through his pockets and twitching around. "Watch what I'm going to do," he says.

Pull down your pants and moon them? Pull something else out? As long as I'm not robbed, no one throws up, and I get paid, I'm relatively happy. However, I don't need to see this either. I accelerate slowly, hoping this does not upset Muscleman and cause him to yank the steering wheel from its attachment to the vehicle's axle.

"You guys should have seen what I was going to do," he says. "Boy, what I was gonna do." We drive along for two more blocks without incident.

"You know any jokes, Mr. Cab Driver?" asks Muscleman.

"I've got a bad memory for jokes, sorry."

"I got a joke." He's very excited. "You wanna hear my joke?"

"Sure," say I. Rather that than have him hanging his ass out the window.

"He don't wanna hear yer joke," says Thug.

"Shut up," says Muscleman.

"Hey, Mr. Cab Man," interrupts Thug, "why don't you come out with us?"

"Shut-the-fuck-up," says Muscleman. "I'm tellin' a joke here."

"How late do you have to work?" asks Thug.

"I get off at ten after three; another half-hour."

"There's this guy collecting wood in the forest...." says Muscleman.

"Oh, pleeeze," sighs GQ, "not *that*."

"Hey Mr. Cab Man, aren't you lonely?" meows Thug.

"...and these two bears in the woods...."

"Mr. Cab Man, come out with us." Thug's voice rises. "Aren't you hungry?"

"Shut up," says Muscleman, "I'm trying to tell a joke."

"We've heard your joke," complains GQ. "It's still not funny."

"Shut up and quit bitchin'. There's this bear in the woods, right?"

"Okay," I agree, accelerating along Duboce Street under the freeway.

"Does a bear take a bigger dump than a gorilla?" asks the inquisitive GQ.

"Hey Mr. Cab Man," says Thug, "are you straight?"

"Yeah," I answer.

"Yeah, straight to the next one, huh?"

There's something strikingly familiar about Thug. I have a terrible, terrible memory for faces. I would never know if I'd seen him before or not. My recognition of voices, though, is excellent. I'm thinking it's just that gay voice inflection thing.

"Oh, fuck you guys," says Muscleman. He pulls out a condom from his wallet. "This thing is too small for me. I gotta start buying the extra extra large." He takes it out of the wrapper. He puts it to his mouth and starts blowing it up like a balloon.

I've never seen that. Condoms can take a lot of air and get pretty damn big. I thought it was going to explode and cause temporary deafness (like when you accidentally explode a firecracker inside the car, the entire family is present, and your mother thinks you have caused her to go deaf in both ears? But, again, it's only temporary). Regardless, the muscleman bouncer continues blowing this thing up and it's growing quite large. By the time we've driven the next block, it's over a foot long with a diameter of at least eight inches. He continues blowing air into it. It's an amazing and rather impressive transformation.

"Stop over there," he muscles to me. "Stop right over there."

"Over there" is a white two-door compact parked on the side of the road next to a police car where a woman is intently conversing with none other than an immaculately uniformed officer. Pulling our bright yellow vehicle to a stop next to the couple so engaged does not seem like a prudent thing to do. I'm clocked in at a job, driving around with big black numbers on the side of my car. These guys are not so traceable. I carefully weigh the potential entertainment value of the situation versus getting yelled at by the cops, handcuffed, and dragged from the cab by the scruff of my neck (not necessarily in that order).

I pull over.

Muscleman most graciously presents this attractive fluorescent-white blown-up condom out the window to the woman. "Here," Muscleman offers.

"What? What is that?" she says taking a step back.

"Here, take it," he says. "It's a party balloon."

She's flattered. "Oh how pretty." She takes it and carefully examines it. "How very beautiful." This thing is not exactly shaped like a *balloon.* She holds it up in the air and admires it.

"Thank you," she smiles.

The policeman steps forward, suspiciously eyeing the white object, sensing something is not quite right but finally nodding his authoritative approval.

"Let's go," encourages Muscleman.

We drive on to the hamburger joint. Even GQ is laughing.

"Mr. Cab Man, Mr. Cab Man," says Thug from the rear, "come and pick us up in an hour. Okay? You know you want to…."

"Sorry, my shift is ending."

The computer buzzes with another message: *DRIVERS WATCH OUT FOR CITY CAB #522 STOLEN AT 17TH AND NOE.*

We pull to a stop in front of the gay burger place.

"More farts?" asks Muscleman. He opens the door and gets out.

"A cab was just stolen, right around the block."

I hear sirens, maybe related to the cab-jacking? I doubt it.

"Come on, honey. Come have a burger," Thug says to me. "And a bun."

"That's okay, but thanks," I decline.

"How much?" asks Muscleman, as he slams the front door and sticks his head back inside through the open passenger-side window.

"$6.80."

He hands me eight dollars.

"So. Are you *coming*?" queries Thug, still anchored to the back seat along with GQ. "Or do we have to WHIP you into shape?"

"I just dropped a guy on Corbett," I say. "He was lonely for some company. I can take you over there."

"Is he cute?" asks GQ.

"Yeah," I tell him. Maybe I could make good money opening a gay dating service, creating a data base using cab passengers and, shortly thereafter, retire from the cab business.

An impatient Muscleman directs his hungry words towards Thug. "Get out of the cab already! I need a burger."

Is Thug concerned that an angry impatient muscle man might pull the metal from his face, piece by piece? Thug pays no attention. Muscleman strides into the restaurant.

Forgetting that my ten hours are about spent, I book into Zone 37 to register my eligibility for a call. This sets off the car alarm of a Jaguar convertible parked in front of the restaurant. A man comes running from his seat at the counter with a steak fry in hand. He inspects the car, looks around, keys the alarm off and calmly returns to his restaurant stool.

The computer buzzes with another message: *DRIVERS, APB ON CITY CAB #522. JUST GIVE LOCATION.*

It's the third APB on a cab in a month and that's just during my shift. I would think it's less conspicuous to car-jack a civilian. Maybe the cab-jacking is only connected with an attempt to make a getaway after a robbery. They don't supply those details over the computer. It does sometimes feel like I'm playing a game of Russian roulette and I should quit while I'm ahead. I've already been attacked twice, not counting the guy who broke out my window at the gas station as he feigned having a gun under his coat. Is another attack inevitable—to round it out to an even three?

"Come in with us." Thug taps at my shoulder, still with the smudge of red on his lips. "I'll buy you a cheeseburger."

I *am* hungry and these guys are fairly entertaining.

"Come on," Thug beckons, now grabbing hold of my shoulder.

It would be trouble; besides, my cab is due in and there's nowhere to park.

"I'll take you to Corbett," I offer, "while I still remember where he lives."

"No," he says releasing hold of my shoulder. "I'll see ya later."

Thug and GQ get out, swagger to the door of the hamburger joint and squeeze by two gigantic fat guys holding hands coming out of the establishment. The computer beeps with a message: *FARES WAITING MARKET/CASTRO.* Not for me. I realize the time, eight minutes to get the cab back to the yard. And soon I'll be home—safe and at home.

SPANK ME

B usiness has slowed. The evening has been dragging, boredom has set in, there are few cars on the road and there's no foot traffic either. The computer beeps with a fare waiting, a request for a pickup at the Grand Central Hot Tubs, an establishment that charges an hourly rate for a private room equipped with a hot tub, sauna, shower, mattress and a small dressing area. It's out of the way for me and it's probably a short four-dollar-and-ten-cent ride for one of the local prostitutes going back to her corner at Taylor and O'Farrell. (Ironically, prostitutes don't tip.)

I accept the call.

Seven minutes later I drive up to the Fell Street entrance. To my dismay, one young woman stands waving at my cab, no miniskirt, no see-through blouse. She's not even wearing tall high-heeled boots. This is *not* a working girl; her hair has barely grown out from a crew-cut, she's wearing a green jacket covering a flannel shirt and a small purse swings from her hand. She quickly seats herself in the back and locks both doors, almost as if being pursued.

"How ya doing?" I can see her eyebrows in the rear-view mirror. She keeps them plucked and confined to a very tight area.

"Not a good night." She has a deep, hardened voice, giving me the impression she definitely does *not* want to talk about it; which, of course, tempts me to pry.

"Go down Van Ness," she says curtly.

"Sure." I make a right and pass the red neon sign of the 24-hour greasy spoon.

Driving to McAllister, we're caught at the traffic light in front of City Hall. She breaks the silence.

"Can I smoke?"

"Sorry." I look into her eyebrows. "It's a no-smoking cab."

"That's all right," she says with disgust.

Prostitute or not, there's going to be no tip on this ride.

I decide to trot out the "I'm trying to quit smoking" routine. Last week, another passenger called me on it. "You said it's a no-smoking cab and now, all of a sudden, you've quit smoking? Well, which is it?" he demanded. I stuck with my story that it was both. I thought it was quite believable. He didn't leave a tip.

With Ms. Eyebrows, I figure there's not much to lose at this point. She was pissed off when she got in and I doubt the denial of nicotine will elevate her mood. "I'm on a patch," I lie. "Not a big deal, but I'm not supposed to breathe smoke." And this time, I've done some research to back my claims—my imaginary patch dispenses 21 milligrams of nicotine. That's what the heavy smokers start with and it gets reduced from there. My phantom portable drug delivery device is hardcore. I left my nicotine gum at home along with Bob's cell phone. So tonight it's the patch story.

The light turns green as a tall man with a hooded winter coat pulled over his head scurries across the street in front of us. He's holding a white styrofoam cup in one hand, a piece of brown cardboard in the other.

"Oh, wow," she says with empathy. "Good luck."

"There's nothin' I want more than a cigarette." I rhythmically tap the black leather steering wheel with three fingers from each hand and bob my head. This is now a permanent addition to my addict-in-recovery dance since its seemingly successful trial run with the two Polk Street lesbians.

"How long ago did you quit?" she asks with compassion.

"Uh…two weeks."

We get stopped at another red light. The cab computer buzzes with a message on the screen: *ATTENTION DRIVERS—APB ON CAB #713. DON'T STOP HIM, JUST GIVE LOCATION.*

Another stolen cab—some joyriders have found a new activity. So not only is it "squeeze the cab driver's shoulder" month, it's now officially "steal a cab" week. The stoplight turns to green as an empty electric bus, white and orange, zooms past.

"So…." I hesitate. "I'm sorry you're having a bad night."

"This guy punched me, like, as hard as he could, motherfucker."

She *is* a working girl. Her eyebrows are still bobbing in the rear-view.

"Assholes who think they're better than you; I expect to be treated like a woman."

"You're right." I agree, glancing back. "You should be."

She's not so bad looking. She could lose the nose stud and the crew cut. Maybe she has a wig in her purse. It would have to be a pretty small wig. She has light features, blond eyelashes, high cheekbones. I don't care for that extreme plucked eyebrow look.

"It's cool when I know up front." I hear her unwrapping something. "He told me what he wanted. I thought there'd be some spanking and stuff. Then he just slugs me."

I look back at her again. "Are you okay?"

"Yeah...I kicked him in the balls, hard as I could." She pops a piece of gum into her mouth. She's not wearing lipstick. "Ya wanna piece of gum?"

I figure if I supposedly quit smoking I can't turn down a piece of gum. "Sure." I accept, calculating the measured enthusiasm of a person who would rather have a cigarette. She hands me a stick. I pop it into my mouth; some kind of sugarless gum. I figure she's on some kind of a health kick. The gum will exit right after she does.

From personal experience, "Kicking a guy in the balls can be a very imprecise science," I tell her. "I was living in Oakland, pulled into the driveway one night and surprised this burglar inside my house. A very ambitious guy. He had all my stereo stuff unhooked and stacked up at the door—ready to go. And that's a lot of stuff."

"Turn right on Post," she says. "What happened?"

"He spotted me coming home, bolted out the front door, tried to run past me. I grabbed him by the face for some reason, and like you, decided to kick him between the legs—absolutely no effect. He hit me, my glasses went flying into the bushes—I felt like an idiot. I ran into the house, grabbed a baseball bat and went after him again with that in hand. Much more dependable."

"Well," she proudly offers, "I think I got him pretty good. He slipped, or fell, or something, and I was gone before he got up."

"Nice work."

"You have your good days and your days that aren't so good. Ya know?" she smiles.

"Yeah, that's certainly true." I drop her off in the Tenderloin. The building has faded paint and the typical gated front entrance. She tips me two dollars on the four-dollar fare.

"Be careful out there."

"You, too," she says.

THE DANCER

Reluctantly, on a busy afternoon, I accept a call for a FARE WAITING at Twenty-First Street between South Van Ness and Folsom, apartment number two. It's a high crime area, not a great part of town for picking up passengers. There's a lot of gang activity, seemingly random shootings, stabbings and muggings. A fare off the computer is usually less risky than a flag off the street. But it's no guarantee.

Arriving at the approximate location, I'm disturbed to find that the buildings on the block are without street numbers. I can't be certain, but I estimate my destination to be a modest flat, three buildings from the middle of the block. I park at the curb and intermittently honk. Trying this approach for several minutes yields mixed results: no one comes out of the building, but no one tosses a bottle at the cab either. Shutting down the engine and getting out of the cab, I walk up the stairs and ring the bell for apartment number two. Nobody stirs. It's looking like a no-show. I ring once more and decide to give it up. Going up and down the block searching out people who think a visible address is optional equipment for their home seems like a sure waste of time. As I retreat down the stairs, a short husky young woman opens the door. Her hair is long, black and spiked on top. A prominent nose ring and a nasty-looking eyebrow stud accentuate a sleeveless undershirt that exposes several tattoos on her arms. She's at least eighteen years old, maybe twenty-one.

"Do you mind waiting?" I can already tell she has an attitude—a lesbian with tattoos and an attitude. "I'll be out in a minute."

Waiting time amounts to $18 an hour gross—less expenses, gate, and gas—as opposed to when you're on the road and moving, when the meter clicks off eighths of a mile which amounts to about $30 an hour. It's looking like a busy night (at least for the moment) and I'd much rather keep moving at the $30 an hour pace. A *minute* is okay, but I've already wasted five minutes calculating addresses and honking my horn up and down the block.

"I'll wait," I tell her. I feel invested in the ride at this point.

The minute goes by, and so do two others. There's no sign of her. Another minute and I flip the meter. Three minutes pass. I turn on the meter. Two more minutes tick away. I'm better off just leaving. I don't want a fight because the meter shows $5.00 before we even go anywhere. The meter hits $2.60 and she finally comes out. She's not so bad looking; again, on the short stocky side but, just the same, she's attractive and has a certain, well, charisma and a pretty face. Her jet-black hair and dark eyebrows compliment her brown eyes; early twenties, I adjust my estimate. She has added a shirt to the sleeveless one and her tattoos are no longer visible.

"Thanks for waiting."

"No problem," I lie, waiting for her to object to the meter having a head start. I'm not going to take any crap from her about it. She can wait for another cab if she's unhappy.

"I've got three stops to make. Is that all right with you?"

"Sure."

"First stop, Market and Seventh."

I turn the cab around in the driveway of another unmarked building and head downtown.

"You're a change from the drivers I've been getting." She doesn't mention the meter. I didn't know I had done anything out of the ordinary.

"Oh yeah?"

"I appreciate that you're not an asshole."

"What's happened to *you?*" I ask.

"I've had the worst experiences with drivers. The last one was swearing at me for making a stop to pick up my clothes. The guy before that was a rude fuck head. I get 'em all."

"Like anything else, there are all kinds of drivers."

"Oh yeah, another guy drove me way out of the way. I mean, I know my way around a little bit. I know when I'm goin' in circles...sorry for the complaining. I'm sure you don't want to hear about it."

"I get the occasional odd passenger—hearing about drivers out of their minds is a good change. I usually just deal with their driving habits."

"After Market Street, can you take me to Larkin and O'Farrell?"

"Sure."

"I'm on my way to work. I'm a dancer."

I don't know if she knows that I know that her destination on Larkin is a strip joint; Fred Astaire, Ginger Rogers, Jerry Rice—dancers. This girl is a stripper. Some folks would make a distinction.

"I've mostly worked in New Orleans and Chicago. I just moved here."

"How do you like working in San Francisco?" I ask.

"I like it here a lot. It's different."

"Oh. What's different?"

"The places here are sleazier. And the women are really different. I can't believe how bad some women look who work in the clubs here. They're overweight, they don't present themselves. Some of 'em can't even dance. I spend a lot on clothes, on outfits."

What a job. She takes the dancing part seriously, probably more so than her customers.

"You must have a very negative view of men."

"Oh no. Not at all."

"I would think you would get...um...abused." Sexually harassed?

"There are some weird customers."

"Yeah? Like what?" She must have had some curious encounters. I want details.

"Oh, all kinds. You don't want to hear about it. I'm sure you get plenty of weirdos yourself."

"Some. I imagine yours must be of a different variety."

"Well, because of the way I look, I get requests for S&M and domination stuff. This one regular thinks I'm gonna come over his house with my whips," she laughs. "That'll be the day. I don't do house calls. Not on him."

I wonder if she's seen Cat Woman. They work in the same neighborhood. Cat Woman would probably welcome a house call.

"You've got to have some great stories." I know she's holding out on me.

"I get lots of men in business suits who wear corsets underneath."

"What? Corsets?"

"Oh yeah, a bunch of 'em."

"Hmmmmm." I don't even know where to take it from there. It doesn't even seem that weird, at first. Why the hell are they wearing corsets? She's trying to sound boring, get me off track. She's obviously more interested in talking about her cab rides from hell.

"You know," she starts, "this cab driver charged me five dollars because I had luggage. Can he do that?"

"No."

"I didn't think so, I wasn't sure, ya know? I just, I just paid him. Who needs the hassle?"

"The crap these guys get away with. You should have reported him."

"It never occurred to me."

"Every cab has a number. The company keeps track of who's driving each car. I'd never get away with something like that. "

It does occur to me that maybe she's really interested in reporting ME for hitting the meter while I waited for her to decide what she's going to wear for the evening. But, actually, it turns into a long ride. After the shopping mall, she has me go to the Burger King drive-thru window. We cross Van Ness, now three blocks away from her final destination. As we pass the corner, a guy and a young woman, both in their early twenties, are flagging desperately from in front of a vacant, dilapidated building while fumbling with several paper shopping bags and two backpacks. From the looks of it, they've figured out they're possibly in a dangerous area, it's getting dark and the ratio of tourists to aggressive panhandlers is taking an unfavorable turn.

"I'll get them after I drop you off," I tell her.

"You don't want to pick them up. French tourists don't tip."

I know obnoxious French tourists don't tip; obnoxious and French, is that redundant? But how could she ever tell they're French just from driving by? Maybe her sense of smell is even more sensitive than mine? "You think they're French tourists?" I ask.

"Absolutely. I can tell by looking at them, by their faces."

Yeah, right. Nevertheless, I compliment her on her astute perceptiveness, dropping her off a few minutes later at the strip joint, I mean, dance theater at Larkin. Happily, upon circling back, the young couple who had been struggling with their numerous belongings are still at the corner on Van Ness, still looking desperate. I pull up in front of them.

"Thanks for stopping," says the woman. She has a thick French accent, I think.

"How long are you here for?" I inquire.

"About a month. We're visiting from Paris."

"I'd love to move to France," I tell them. Yeah, if ever the French pack up and leave the country.

I hit the meter, open up the trunk and the side door, help them with their backpacks, shopping bags and sleeping bundles while calculating the additional BAGGAGE CHARGE that will be added to their fare once they reach their intended destination. *Mahalo.*

MICHELLE

Hostile aggressive biker lesbians. I've had several of them–that is, giving me a hard time, usually while extremely drunk (while *they're* drunk, not while I am). You don't want to piss these women off, especially the ones who are six-feet-two, 269 pounds sporting eight-penny nails through their foreheads.

It's Thursday night. I spot a woman politely flagging while standing at the bus stop, corner of Seventeenth and Castro. She's wearing a smooth-looking skirt, cut at the knee; a blue silk shirt, and a brightly colored scarf. In one hand she's carrying a small yellow backpack and a large red and white department store shopping bag. I'm always wary of flags from a bus stop. Does she have more than a dollar left in her purse? Maybe she spent all her cash shopping? She's very attractive. I stop. She gets in. Her destination is the Lower Haight. Calculating how best to avoid traffic, get across Market and merge onto Divisadero, I turn the cab around and proceed to the highlighted route.

"How's your night been?" I ask.

"Weird. Not very good."

"Sorry to hear that."

"This town can be frustrating."

We ride in quiet for several moments. She breaks the silence.

"You don't mind if I change my blouse do you?"

Definitely not. I look over my shoulder and keep driving.

"Just my blouse," she says. "It's been bothering me all night. I just wanna change."

"That's fine with me."

"Don't look," she adds.

We cross Market and head toward the Haight. "I tried to pick up this woman in a bar tonight," she sadly recounts, "and I messed up."

"Ohh?" I almost look back again, but stop myself just in time.

"She IS the hottest thing this side of Phoenix—want her in the worst way," she continues while doing an excellent job of rustling around in the back seat as we come to a stop sign. "I just gotta have her."

I would never have guessed her a lesbian. She's a light-skinned black woman, maybe part Puerto Rican, bright shiny eyes, a friendly inviting smile, pretty teeth, long carefully styled hair.

"Did you get her phone number?" It's a customary question to ask a guy pursuing a female, but not one that immediately occurred to me in this case. I'm a little flustered. Maybe the rules are different; maybe they have some kind of special procedures.

"It's a long story."

"Well, great," I protest, "now that you've piqued my interest."

"You must hear this crap all night long. You could write a book, I'll bet."

"I'm workin' on that. It doesn't pay much in the meantime."

"Well," she pauses, "I knew her but didn't recognize her. I mean, I didn't remember her, but she remembered me."

"Oh, you can get past that," I encourage. "I never remember people I meet. I'm terrible."

"Yeah, but after I told her I'd like to get to know her better, she asked how much better since we had already SLEPT together."

"Ohhhh, well...*that* might be different. When did you sleep together?"

"'Bout a year ago."

She's still changing the shirt ever so slowly and I'm trying my best not to look, when a pickup truck blasts the horn from my "blind spot." Don't I at least have to check the proximity of my vehicle to theirs? I can't go crashing into things or running people over because there's a naked woman in the back seat and I've made a pact with her not to turn my head. I look. She's pulling a blue tee shirt over her head, soon to conceal a black lace bra with parental guidance cleavage and a belly button in perfect proportion to her flat stomach. She definitely works out. I also manage to check for traffic and pedestrians. It's all clear—as far as external hazards emanating from outside the cab are concerned. I

Don't look.

quickly face forward before she gets the shirt over her head. The truck honks again.

"What in the fuck is he honking at?" She folds the removed shirt and slides it into the bag.

"You, I think." C'mon. I pull to the right preparing to make a turn and the truck pulls along the left side of the cab.

"Hey," yells the passenger in the pickup truck. "Woooo-wooo."

I look at him and then at her.

She waves and then gives him the finger. "In your dreams, buck-o," she says.

I make the right turn.

"Yeah," she says. "I was really drunk."

"Tonight or when you slept with her?"

"When I slept with her. I blew it. I just didn't remember. I want her so bad, and I made an idiot of myself."

"Did you get her phone number?"

"No, I was too embarrassed."

"You know where she hangs out?"

"I know where she works."

"So, I guess you could stop by and say hello," I suggest, as we approach a stop sign on Duboce. "Or would that be stalking?" I look left, right, and then back at her. If she wanted, she could easily attract a man, or a slew of men. She can probably attract the big ugly lesbians, the little ones, the good-looking ones like Miss Phoenix...she's got all kinds of options.

"Was she being friendly?" I ask.

"Oh yeah. She was glad to see me. She is *so* hot."

The computer beeps: *ANYONE SEE CAB #127 TELL HIM I WANT TO TALK TO HIM!* Deciding to punch in my drop-off point on the computer, I press the "destination" button, then "four"—"one"—"send." A car alarm sounds from a four-door sedan, parked adjacent to us.

"I'm such a fool," she says. "I told her I'm extremely perceptive and could tell she was a very special person. I'm sick about it. Of all time, I'm in love with three women. No one can compare, but this woman tonight comes close: Grace Kelly, Ingrid Bergman, and Michelle Pfeiffer. They're tops. Two are dead, so that only leaves Michelle."

"And Miss Phoenix," I remind. "Sounds like a good selection." Only my passenger's eyes appear in the rear-view mirror.

"I love tall shapely women in heels and stockings. Nothing turns me on more—lesbians in heels. God, that gets me hot."

"What about short women? You don't like them?"

"I don't know about short, but there are a lot of gay women who are fat."

She said it, not me.

"And seem damn proud of it," I add.

"No," she says without hesitation. "That's gross. I like shapely feminine sexy women. And I like to be that way too."

"That's not very, uh, very egalitarian of you."

"I don't want no short fat women."

"You're a sexist!"

"Well," she grabs at my shoulder, "I guess I am. How can you stand driving around this city?" she asks, releasing my shoulder. "It would drive me nuts. You have another job?"

"I was playing music."

"I guess you'd rather do that than drive?"

"Well sure but, unfortunately, driving seems to pay more bills."

"Does your girlfriend like you doing this job? I mean, this is dangerous, isn't it?"

Did I mention a girlfriend? I don't think so. Maybe she's just asking whether I have one. Or is she hitting on me? Sounds like she hits on everything. But it's possible I said something in our banter, I'm not really sure. It's been a long night.

"She doesn't really like it. But being around her isn't necessarily less dangerous than picking up strangers in the middle of the night." I let that information slip out—oh, alright, maybe it *was* intentional.

"What does that mean?" queries my passenger. "She have an exploding pussy?"

"No, no." Maybe she *is* hitting on me. "An exploding temper and three ex-husbands. We have a couple of issues."

"It pays more to drive than play music?" She somewhat changes the subject. Maybe she's not hitting on me. I've brought the world of heterosexuality too close to our conversation and she's already in retreat, back to the sensitive, less complicated lives of lesbian lovers. Oh, well.

"It pays almost double, compared to a bar gig."

"The bar scene here is a pain," she says.

"What do you mean?" I ask.

"Smelly obnoxious guys always tryin' to pick up on me, I can't stand that."

"I think I know what you're saying." I've been hit on by men ever since I first moved here—when I'm walking down the street, eating in a restaurant, or just standing on the corner waiting to cross the street. It happens more often when I'm by myself. For gays, San Francisco must be like a candy store. The thing is, if a guy is the slightest bit friendly anywhere in this town, you don't know if he's coming on to you or if he is just making totally innocent, friendly conversation. So, I just don't talk to men. I don't want some guy following me around because he thinks I'm flirting with him. It's not worth the aggravation, so I just do without the small talk and banter—and keep to myself.

"In this town," she continues, "guys wait 'til last call to decide whether they like you or not. Something better might come along—you know, keep their options open."

"You go out with men too?"

"Sometimes. It's not as bad as in L.A. People who live there have trouble putting sentences together."

"Their brains have been fried in the sun."

We arrive at her address on Page Street.

"Five dollars even." I stop the meter. "I like Michelle Pfeiffer too. It could be a problem if she shows up and we're both there."

"Hey." She hands me seven dollars. "She's mine."

"C'mon, you've got Miss Phoenix."

"You'll have a major fight on your hands over Michelle."

"I'll be in training." I get out and open the door for her while she's fiddling with her backpack. She's wearing pointy high-heeled boots.

"I noticed your phone. Do you take phone calls from passengers needing rides?"

"Well, it's not really my phone."

"It's your girlfriend's?"

"No, no. It's not that. It's...." Do I tell her about Bob? Not a good idea. He didn't mention whether or not I should be giving out the number to other passengers. I think the idea is that ONLY I shall be at his beckoning.

"Sure, if you need a ride, give me a call." I scribble the number on the back of a receipt and hand it to her.

"Thanks." She gets out. "I'll only call you if it's an emergency." She smiles, and half-winks at me, I think. "Don't give up your music."

"Thanks." The starving artist thing has gotten a bit old. "Good luck with Miss Phoenix." I have that uncomfortable feeling—the one you get when a date doesn't go that successfully—that she's going to give me a hug. She doesn't.

"Here." She juts her hand forward—very delicate looking, nails neatly manicured. "This is for you. Don't look at it right away. You have to save it for an emergency." She hands me a tiny scrap of paper.

This is flirting, definitely. "Okay," I promise. What did she write? Don't give up your day job? Don't lust after lesbians? And what's all this talk about emergencies?

"Thanks." She definitely winks at me, then makes a sudden stop in the middle of the street, narrowly avoiding an oncoming speeding American sedan with one headlight burned out. It passes by within inches. It's yellow and it's 294. It continues down the street, runs a stop sign, makes a screeching left turn and disappears.

Meanwhile, my ex-passenger has crossed the street and is now walking up the stairs to the front door of a brightly lit Victorian apartment building. I watch her unlock the door and open it. She turns and waves.

I wave, smile, and get back into the cab. Should I have asked for her phone number? I don't even know her name.

She enters her flat and closes the front door behind her. A little late now; I'd have to go up to the door and knock. And what if someone else answers? How embarrassing. What if her girlfriend answers? What if her *boyfriend* answers?

I get back into the cab. The computer beeps twice, registers me fifth in line for Zone 42. Not unusual. Zone 42 is a popular attraction with drivers. That's why I favor Zone 41, usually less backed up. I try Zone 41; the computer beeps, I'm sixth in line. I drive, and try Zone 26, the Tenderloin. The computer beeps twice; fourth in line, an improvement. A few minutes later, the computer starts beeping, almost heaving—I figure it's sending a fare my way. A few more beeps and heaves and a final buzzer. For some reason, it has completely booked me off—some kind of a glitch. I book back into the zone: beep, beep, heave and buzz. I'm sixth in line. It's time for the old-fashioned way of doing business—looking for people off the street.

In my estimation, this amounts to an emergency situation—an excuse to unravel the small piece of paper. Maybe it's her phone number. Nope, high hopes. It's a fortune, a fortune cookie fortune. It reads: "Nothing in the world is accomplished without passion." I'll take it as a compliment, or should I? C'mon, it's a fortune cookie, probably from a take-out place. How personal is that, really?

Well, I hope she calls me. And then what? The computer beeps again; and again, I'm knocked off line. I double back to Haight Street and make a left; not many folks left on the street tonight. At Masonic I turn left and head for downtown. It's gonna be a long night and not one filled with much passion, far as I can tell.

JUST ADD BLEACH

Another Thursday night. Of course, Thursdays are not as busy as Saturdays or Fridays, but are a vast improvement over dead Mondays. A lot of people go out on Thursday nights anxious for the weekend to start. This one has been pretty typical, consecutive rides for the last several hours straight. I had no lunch or breakfast before getting to work and I'm starving. I buy a giant La Cumbre burrito at Sixteenth and Valencia, the heart of the Mission District. I worked a few blocks over on Capp Street for a couple of years when I first moved to the city, doing political work with the Lawyer's Guild. I have a certain fondness for the area but never felt entirely safe walking down the street even though nothing ever happened. It's not as clean as I remember it. There's more broken glass in the streets than there used to be, from bottles and busted out car windows. Apparently, from what out-of-town visitors report, that's the case in most American cities these days. Bruce the crack dealer slash musician slash cab driver, my buddy's buddy who recommended trying this gig in the first place—lives a couple of blocks away.

A good dozen bus lines run through here, along with BART. The gays and young heterosexual whites have been slowly moving in for years, gentrifying a few houses at a time. But essentially it's a commerce, transportation and communication hub for illegal immigrants, the lower-middle working class and the underclass.

And, in keeping with San Francisco tradition, you can never find a place to legally park. There's a lot of *street action*—obvious drug dealing, gang members flashing hand signals, aggressive panhandlers, the down-and-out just hanging, people wearing bad attitudes expressed on their faces and in their eyes, and other folks moving slowly along the sidewalks left behind by a society rapidly moving ahead of their personal predicaments. You try to either be invisible walking in this area or completely avoid it. However, my old-time favorite burrito place is located smack in the middle of it all. The same people are still running it as when I first walked through the door almost twenty years ago. The prices are great, the food is good, it's quick and, most importantly, it has a clean bathroom.

Today, thankfully, there's not much of a line. I order quickly and exit the premises, escorting my huge piping hot beef burrito a short distance to an open-air pay phone anchored to the sidewalk. While methodically removing the aluminum foil to unveil my burrito, I watch my back. Managing a conversation over the electric buses and traffic noise from the busy intersection will also be a challenge. As I pace in half-circles, watching the street action, my pepper spray is close at hand. A Latino woman walks up with a little boy holding her hand. The kid is about 2½ feet tall, looks half Hispanic, half black and has pleading eyes.

"Could I have forty cents to get him some juice?" she asks.

"No," I tell her. "Sorry."

"Oh come on; any spare change?"

"No."

Now the kid is pointing and wiggling his tiny fingers at me. "I want a bite of the burrito," he says.

Cute, but I don't think so.

"Can he have a bite of your burrito?" she asks.

"No."

An older model American car with two unshaven ornery-looking men inside pulls up into another miraculously vacant parking spot. I keep my eye on both of them. The passenger uneasily opens the car door. His face is prematurely lined, wrinkled, and worn from drugs and drinking. He staggers out of the car. The people on the street seem to know him. A lively exchange ensues. They don't seem to notice me at all.

Meanwhile, the kid and the mom are still circling the area, begging for spare change and bites of burritos from passers-by. They're not having much luck.

From my vantage point at the old and withered payphone, I'm keeping watch on the guy in the driver's seat of the vintage mobile. I can only see him from the neck down. He turns and pulls out a bottle of bleach from behind the front seat. There's no Laundromat within walking distance, and I doubt he is about to embark on a clean-up-the-streets campaign. It occurs to me that he's actually going to drink from the container. Still in the driver's seat, he unscrews the cap from the bottle as a police car careens around the corner, its lights blinking but its siren off. I keep watch as I dial a number on the payphone. The street noise seems to be increasing so I hit the "loudness control" button. It raises the volume, but raises the static interference just as much.

My girlfriend answers after two rings. I generally try to keep her informed of my location at least once or twice during my shift—for safety, to alleviate boredom, and in an attempt to maintain what's left of a relationship that's deteriorating in slow motion. Perhaps it's a part of that complacency, depression, and despondent mode that my driver friends warned about? No, it probably has more to do with the bookshelves she pushed over in one of her mad rages, or the time she "pretended" (according to her) to attempt to run me over in her car. Hitting the streets in this innocent yellow vehicle has little connection with that spiral.

"I can barely hear you," she complains.

I hit the volume control again. It doesn't help.

"I forgot to bring Bob's cell phone with me." Although he "gave" it to me, I still refer to it as his.

"I know—it's been ringing for an hour."

"Crap."

"You should give it back to him. He's a wacko."

"I'll be careful." At least he's a wacko who pays.

"Next time—they'll beat you up and him. What's all that screaming?" she asks.

"It's some guys over by the store. I'm on Valencia, getting a burrito."

"I thought you said you're going to stay away from there."

"I just dropped someone off—like, a block away. I drove by and there was a parking space, right in front."

"It sounds like they're screaming at you."

"There's a guy sitting in this car in front of me and I think he's gonna drink bleach."

I look away from the car to more carefully check on the various street activities in progress.

"It's just a couple of guys buying wine at the store. They're ten feet away. It's nothin' to do with me."

I turn back around in time to observe the guy who is seated in the car unzip his pants and struggle to place the wide blue and white bleach bottle between his legs and…yes, begin peeing into it.

"He's peeing in the bottle," I report over the phone.

"What?"

"The guy in the car with the bleach bottle—he's peeing in it."

"Is that why they're screaming?" she inquires. "I don't like all that screaming."

"No, no. It's a different…never mind." San Francisco needs more public toilets.

He finishes relieving himself, screws the top onto the bleach bottle, reaches back and places it in the back seat, apparently for later use. So, how many pees per bottle is he getting? The city could save millions. Instead of installing portable toilets, issue empty bleach bottles to tourists at the airport: *"We need two gross of bleach bottles at Gates 47 and 48."*

The hungry kid and the mom return, slowly walking past me.

"I wanna bite!" He points and stomps his little foot. "I WANTA bite!!" and throws a full-blown tantrum.

Is this totally staged? The kid is out of control. Obviously, the mom coaches him on how to beg for food but, if this is part of the act, it's quite an elaborate accent. I grip the burrito, keeping it an arm's length away from the little bugger and try to resume my conversation.

"What did you say?"

The man in the car has now moved over from the driver's seat, opening the passenger door and emptying the contents of the bleach bottle onto the sidewalk. The mom is headed for the puddle.

"You woke me up again last night—having some dream about running through some neighborhood with people chasing you."

"I don't remember that."

"Well, maybe we should have a tape recorder next to the bed?"

"Okay. I'll set that up. Talk to ya later." I hang up the phone.

I wanna bite! I WANTA bite!!

Actually, I do remember the dream now, and the anxiety. Walking around to my valiantly parked cab, I enjoy the last moments of my great parking space, scan the area for potential pillagers, quickly unlock the door and get in. As I turn the ignition, the engine hesitates at first then loudly turns over. I continue on my way, burrito in hand, heading towards Zone 37, the Castro. And I re-lock the four doors.

TAXI!

Sunday night; there have been slower ones. It's my third time circling the Castro—no flags, nothing off the computer.

"Taxi!" A man frantically hails. "Taxi!"

Across the street, near the 24-hour grocery, a slightly heavy black man about fifty-eight years old, carrying two white plastic bags of consumables in each hand, tries as best he can to flag down a speeding cab. His mouth looks caved in—perhaps he's missing some teeth. He's wearing a white hat—a cross between a baseball cap and a painter's hat. Those damn plastic bags are easier to carry than paper, but you can barely use them for garbage bags and the groceries in them shift around. If you have a loaf of bread in a plastic bag with other groceries in there—forget it. Your bread will never regain its youthful loaf-like shape.

I wave back at him as another cab drives by him in the opposite direction. The other cab doesn't stop either. I think because it has passengers in the back seat, although I'm not sure. Stopping in front of him, I reach over and open the back door for him.

"Thank you for stopping."

"You're welcome."

I help scoot his plastic bags across the back seat so he has room to sit. He looks more like sixty-five or seventy. Black people don't show their age; he could be in his eighties.

"Thank you again so much for picking me up."

"That's okay. I don't have many other plans tonight."

"If you will please, take a left on Diamond and go all the way up to Diamond Heights."

I hit the meter and drive up hill.

"I really appreciate you stopping. A few days ago I got thrown out of a cab after going three blocks."

"You're kidding. By who?"

"Same cab company. A woman told me to get out."

I'm hesitant to ask why. Maybe I'll have to kick him out too. This guy's like a kitten.

"Why did she throw you out?"

"Said she wasn't comfortable and made me get out."

I take another look at him. Maybe I'm missing something. It's the same guy, kind of portly, receding grey hair and pleasant demeanor. He has plenty of energy for a man his age. He's not a gun-wielding, knife-throwing, car-jacking hoodlum. Not that I can see. I shake my head.

"Some drivers won't pick up black people," I say, knowing it's no revelation for him.

"If you're not gonna drive black people to where they goin', then don't pick 'em up. She drove me four blocks away and then dropped me where it's a lot harder to get a cab—there were no cabs at all."

"That's nice of her." From the intonation of his voice, he appears to think this has to do with some universal cab company policy. "What did she look like?"

"Kind of like one of those lesbians. She was kind of...burly."

"Well, I thought I might know her if you describe her. She doesn't sound familiar."

"I didn't get a good look at her. It happened so fast."

"There are a few full-size women drivers."

We get to his address and the fare is five dollars. I get out, open the back door and grab two of the bags. He gets out.

"Is that your doorway?" I point.

"Yes."

"I'll set these down over there for you."

"Why, thank you."

He walks over as I set the groceries down. He opens his wallet and slowly goes through it. He hands me a dollar.

"That's for a tip. Now, I think I have five more."

He counts out three dollars.

"You must be from back east," he says. "People back there help one another."

"I'm from Detroit."

"Is that right? I'm from Ohio," he proudly beams.

"What city?"

"Columbus."

"That's pretty close."

He's still going through his wallet. "I thought I had five singles in here."

I can see more bills in there. He's having some kind of trouble for some reason.

"I don't like to carry much money around," he says.

"These days, you can't carry anything with ya," I join.

"Yeah, I know." He goes into another compartment of his wallet. "Oh, four, five." He hands me two more dollars. "I work at Eighth and Brannan," he says. "You look for me."

"Okay." He actually seems serious.

"I always take a cab. Please, pick me up if you see me."

"Sure. I sure will. I'll look for you."

I get back into the cab, book into a zone and shut off the meter, waiting as he slowly fits the key in the latch and opens his front door. He turns and waves.

"I got it," he says.

I wave goodbye and drive back down the hill.

THE CALL

This night I've remembered to take the cell phone with me. I haven't heard from Bob, nor have I looked forward to hearing from him since I dropped him at the hospital after the Chinese guys beat him up. I expect he will call regarding either his "investigative" or personal pursuits or to at least ask for the return of his phone.

I'm in the Avenues, transporting an elderly Russian couple, when I get the call. The display reads: unknown caller.

I answer.

"Hi." It's a friendly female voice. I figure it's one of Bob's extracurricular acquaintances making the call, or maybe his nurse.

"Hello," I respond.

"It's Michelle—the undressing lesbian. I need to go across town. Are you nearby?"

"I'm in the Avenues. I'm dropping a couple of folks off."

"Oh, okay." And before I can say anything else, the line goes dead. I'm not sure if she has hung up, if I hit a button by accident or the reception simply gave out. Maybe she suddenly became embarrassed? She doesn't seem the type. I put down the phone, hoping Michelle tries again in the next few minutes.

She doesn't call back.

BLOOD, NO GUTS

Drivers are instructed not to smell up the cab by driving around with food. Smelling up the cab is the sole domain of passengers. At the Burger King drive-thru an emaciated teenage girl, anxiety-ridden from a long battle against the proliferation of a facial zit-farm, hands me my cheeseburger-no-mustard-extra-pickles hot from the microwave along with an order of onion rings, the purchase of which and consumption thereof violates my personal guidelines forbidding deep fried "foods" and items masquerading as "edibles" that contain no redeeming social value and doused with saturated fats. Just then, the computer beeps for a pickup at Jones and Turk, right off Market Street. The stop is about five minutes from my burger purchase; plenty of time to wolf down my newly acquired contraband and get to the address. I press the "accept" button and the order is mine.

Taking a quick right turn from Van Ness, hanging a right on Franklin and another right on O'Farrell Street points me to where the prostitutes will be hanging at Polk Street which makes for a more entertaining ride. You start with the transvestite and transsexual prostitutes from Polk to Larkin. From Hyde to Leavenworth you get a mixed crowd: women along with a few men dressed as women. By the time you reach Taylor Street, most all of the prostitutes wearing high heels and skimpy revealing clothing are women who have always been such. Of course, there's no law guaranteeing that a person won't run up against some exception somewhere—some nubile entrepreneur doing business in the city for the first time (and unfamiliar with the lines of demarcation) or maybe someone purposely flaunting the rules.

Imagine that! Hence some rather high-profile "oops" for certain men who fail to recognize the significance of a large Adam's apple here or a bulge there—until it's much too late to avoid the press, an unflattering photo with poorly placed lighting or some other embarrassment suffered within the precinct station walls. The orderly separation of the sexes by street, so to speak, is upset when those overly industrious police officers begin patrolling or busting the women prostitutes at Union Square. This forces the women to move further west, toward the transvestite prostitutes' turf. When that happens, it can get a little more difficult to tell the post-operatives from those actually born with and maintaining original factory-installed parts.

Now five blocks from my onion ring purchase, the Mitchell Brothers' O'Farrell Theater appears on the right. Four conservative-looking men, waving their arms wildly, run into the street in front of my cab.

"Stop, stop!" yelps one guy, white shirt half sticking out of his pants and clashing with his suit and tie.

I've taken two bites of the burger. I take one more, and throw it back in the bag. There's a giant wad of napkins in there. I grab one, wipe the grease off my face, hands, the seat, steering wheel, speedometer and ceiling. They pile into the cab talking and laughing as I swallow the last remnants of a pickle.

"What a great place," says the one guy with a dweeb haircut—possibly rendered by the same barber as the brothers from Finland.

"Yeah," agrees his old fraternity buddy rushing into the front seat. "Shoot your load in there once a year."

"Hey," says the fatter guy removing his glasses, "speak for yourself."

I hope they don't see or smell my bag-o'-grease slop, which I've kicked under the seat.

"Parc 55," says Dweeb. "Eddy and Mason or something."

Perfect; and we're off. Their destination is just around the block from my fare waiting at Jones. In between, I can finish my eats.

After three minutes, Haircut Dweeb comes up with a brilliant proposal: "Let's go hear some music."

"Smells like French fries in here," says the fat guy. "Let's go to that steak place near the hotel."

"Steve, how about North Beach?" says another guy.

I'm always suggesting that people go to North Beach. They usually just go to their hotels instead. And these guys come up with that on their own? It's too far from my destination.

"What about the Fairmont?" asks someone.

"Let's go back to our hotel. We can drink there."

Yeah, the hotel—get drinks there. I've got to get to Turk and Jones within the next six minutes.

"Let's hit the Mark Hopkins."

"It's closed," says another guy. "They're renovating or some shit."

"Hey," says a guy in back. "Who farted?"

"I think that's my onion rings," I confess.

"Let's go to that Thai place," says the fat guy.

"The Fairmont," insists the pushy guy sitting in front.

Damn. And, as the fat guy sits whimpering in the back seat, I take a left on Taylor, the opposite way from my fare at Turk and Jones. At least it's closer than North Beach. I'm intently watching the clock. I finally drop them off.

I'm cutting it close. It's been 12 minutes since I accepted the fare. It should be okay. I smoke down Mason, almost go airborne over the steep hill toward downtown simultaneously wolfing down the remains of the burger and onion rings at a frenzied pace. I'm two blocks away from my fare on Jones. Here comes a guy in the middle of the road wearing a white tee shirt, frantically swinging his jacket in the air.

"Stop! Stop!" I can hear him from down the block.

"Get outofthedamnroad," I mumble.

"Stop," he persists. "Stop!"

It's a bad area of town deep in the Tenderloin. There's no way I'm stopping. But he's zigzagging in the middle of the street making it difficult for me to out-maneuver his unpredictable legwork without sideswiping him.

"Please," he shrieks. "Help me, please."

He's covered with blood—blood everywhere.

"Please stop. Help me."

I slow down. All the doors are locked. If not for the profuse bleeding, I wouldn't even consider slowing down. His one hand's pressing against his head as he walks up to the passenger side window.

"Please help me, man," he says walking alongside the cab as I continue at a five miles per hour pace. "It's an emergency."

Isn't it always? I stop the cab. I don't see anyone else on the street.

"I'm on a call," I say half-heartedly.

"Can you take me to a hospital? This woman attacked me."

I'm looking at the blood.

"Please man, I'm begging you—just to the hospital."

Great. Blood all over the cab, and he probably doesn't have money. Is society to a point where you, literally, can't stop to help someone bleeding in the street?

I unlock the door.

"Okay." I motion him in.

He gets into the back seat.

"Thank you so much," he says. "I really appreciate it."

I get out of the cab to close the door for him—and get a better view of his injury. I don't want him getting blood all over the seat, the handle and everything else. I'm also concerned about the possibility of his transmitting AIDS. He seems to be bleeding *neatly*. The blood is running down from his head to his shirt, a majority of it absorbed by his clothing. It could be worse—him dripping all over. I get a better glimpse of his gash, more than enough for me, a deep-looking crater above his eyebrow. The area around his eye is swollen and puffed up. He looks pretty bad. I'm glad he is relatively calm. I shut the door and get back behind the wheel.

"You're gonna need some stitches in that," I blurt. Why am I telling him that?

"I been hurt before, this ain't so bad."

I resume traveling the route down Jones Street. I can even see the building where I'm supposed to be picking up my passenger on Turk Street, near Market. I don't see anyone waiting outside. I make a right turn heading for the hospital. Maybe this is the guy who called?

"You didn't call a cab, did you?"

"No man, please just take me to the hospital."

"Just checking."

"It don't pay to come down here," he says.

The meter is still going from the four men I dropped off. Turning it off will wipe out the Jones Street address on the computer. It's too late to send the order back; I'll get written up *and* yelled at. I write down the address and apartment number, shut off and start the meter again. "The woman hit me," he describes, as if having been interrupted at some point. "I was just playin' around. Next thing I know, I'm bleeding like crazy."

"Someone you know?"

"We were talkin' and BAM! She hits me with a bottle."

"We'll be at the hospital in a couple minutes."

"You got something to stop the bleeding?"

"I don't think so." I search the glove compartment and the side compartment of the door. There's a stained map of California, some miscellaneous papers and the cab's registration.

"You don't got nothin'?" he asks.

"Sorry."

"Maybe it was a crow bar or somethin'. It's like, pulsing," he complains. "You got any ice?"

"No, sorry."

Ice? Maybe he smells the residual fumes from the burger and onion rings and figures I'm running a mobile restaurant/ambulance/taxi service with an ice machine in the trunk.

"You gotta have something," he whines.

I guess if I were truly dedicated to his rescue, I'd give him my shirt. But I can't go driving around without a shirt on.

"Oh...wait," I say. "I think I got something."

The cheeseburger! Not the actual burger—the napkins. I reach for the take-out bag pulling out the stack of napkins.

"Here," I hand him the wad. I feel so *prepared*. Look both ways, know your emergency codes and carry plenty of napkins for bleeding passengers.

"Great, thank you," he says, gratefully sorting through the napkins. He arranges them, presses them against his head and moans. "I can't believe this."

"Are you okay?"

"I'm okay. Just get me to the hospital."

I make a little-sharper-than-needed right onto Leavenworth.

"Man," he groans, "there's a lot of blood coming out."

"Try to keep pressure on it."

"It don't help."

"Head injuries bleed a lot, it makes them seem worse."

"It won't stop bleeding."

I look back at him and he's examining the bloody napkins.

"You gotta keep pressing on it. Lean your head back."

We're four blocks from the hospital.

"This is really fucked-up," he says. "Ya know?"

"I know. We'll be there in a minute."

"I really wanna find the woman who did this to me."

"That's definitely understandable." I notice a group of three young men in their early twenties, dressed in dark clothing and baggy jackets loitering/casing out a pristine (for the moment) maroon Honda parked in front of a large apartment building.

"I wanna get a good description of her, ya know? Take me back to where you picked me up." His voice rises in pitch. "Yeah, yeah, take me back, just for a minute."

"Let me get you to the hospital."

"No, no. I'll be okay."

I've got my Turk/Jones order. At this point, I'd also like to ask if he has money. Regardless, if I can dump him at the hospital, I can resume my business.

"She gotta be around somewhere," he laments.

"She might be a little hard to find."

"Please, take me back there. We'll circle the block."

I drive back to Jones where I picked him up. *SO CLOSE* to my fare, yet so far. Still, there's nobody out on the street.

"Go back around the block, just once."

We drive in a circle for a second time.

"There's some people," he points.

"Is that them?" I ask him.

"No. Go around one more time. Go to Leavenworth."

We drive around the block as two people wearing bulky black coats marked with white lettering on the backs cross the street heading for a crowd assembled at the corner of Ellis Street.

"Those two!" He jumps from the seat. "That's them."

"That looks like two men."

"Stop, stop," he demands. "We can't let them see us."

"They're not lookin' at us."

"Stop here," he clamors. "Call the cops. Can you call the cops?"

I punch three buttons on the computer requesting voice.

"Go in reverse," he says. "Hurry, back up down the street a little."

Meanwhile, as the two coats join up with the other folks assembled on Ellis, the entire group slowly moves down the street headed opposite our direction.

"Let's follow them," I suggest.

"No, no. They'll see us. I can't let them see me."

"They can't see us this far down the street."

Most of the group turns a corner. A couple of them may even have gone into a building.

"They're getting away," he gestures, bloody napkin in hand.

"I know. Let's drive by—so you can see if it's them."

"No. Stay back. Do you see 'em?"

"I can't see anything."

"Don't move the car," he says excitedly, "stay here."

"I'll just drive by and go around the block."

A few of the crowd seem to move back toward our direction.

"No, I can see them," he insists.

"Fine."

I think there's at least one female in the group. They are more than a block away and it's difficult to make out a face.

"Is that her? Can you see 'em?" he asks me.

"I don't know. I just see a crowd of people." This time the entire crowd takes a quick turn around the block.

"They're gone," he says. "It's your fault."

"Well, let's drive up there." I inch the cab forward. "They won't be able to see you in here."

"Don't you understand?" he screams. "Back-up, man."

"I'm stopped. Just relax."

"No, back-up! Back-up!"

I put the cab in reverse.

"I see 'em," he says. "You can't see 'em?"

"I can't see around a corner. Let's drive up a little."

"No, they'll come after me. Stay back."

The computer makes a long loud beep. It reads: GO TO CHANNEL TWO. I switch channels.

"Yes, five-five-four," says the dispatcher, "come in."

"Requesting police assistance at Leavenworth and Turk."

"What's wrong?"

"I've got a bleeding passenger. The people who attacked him are down the block, a group of about ten people."

Winos, drug dealers and gang members are the usual types hanging around this area. People doing whatever it is they do—midweek at midnight—in the heart of the Tenderloin.

"Do you want an ambulance?" asks the dispatcher.

"No ambulance," says the bloody guy. "I don't want an ambulance."

He should have an ambulance, not a cab; a paramedic, not me.

"Code six on the ambulance," I tell the dispatcher.

"Okay five-five-four," the dispatcher clicks off. I shut down the radio and go back to channel one—computer communications.

"You watch those two down the street," says my passenger leaning forward in the seat. "Don't let them get away."

Either my eyesight is completely failing, or he's imagining people standing on the street. Maybe it's a side-effect of the gash—or being hit in the head. He didn't mention what caliber bottle they used.

"How does my head look now?" He removes the napkins from above his eye.

"Keep applying the pressure," I scold him.

"Turn the light on," he says.

"You don't wanna see it."

"I want you to tell me how it looks."

"Leave it alone 'til someone looks at it."

"Turn on the light!" Rather demanding for a guy initially claiming he's bleeding to death. "See how it looks."

"Let's just get you to the hospital."

"Please. See if it looks bad."

"You should keep it covered."

"Just for a second. I been hurt before; this ain't bad."

I've heard you can tell by looking at a cut if it needs stitches—something about a butterfly. I was never really sure what people were talking about. When I was thirteen, I bit through my cheek, split it open colliding with another kid, Don Holiday, who was trying to hog a pop-up during a gym class baseball game. I never really saw the damage, didn't want to. I was unable to open my mouth very far anyway and initially it was full of blood. From the principal's office I phoned my mother to take me to the hospital, but she wasn't home. So I called my father at work, about five miles away. He picked me up from school and drove me to the hospital, also less than five minutes down the road. He screamed at me the entire time.

"Damn it! You make me come from work just to drive you? Couldn't the school drive you? What about your mother?" He was furious. "Did you call grandma?"

"Mom wasn't home." I mumbled through the wet bloody wad of coarse paper towels I held pressed to my face. Yes, those stiff brown things fetched from the boys' bathroom, first doused with cold water to slow the bleeding. They were no longer cold, but the pressure felt good.

"Where is she? At one of her rehearsals?"

My mother played in the local symphony orchestra. They often fought about it. My father was a bit jealous.

"I don't know where she is." I was unable to say much, being that my cheek was split open. My head tilted back, I mostly stared at the black dotted vinyl ceiling of his brand new Oldsmobile Cutlass. My father loved that car. "It drives like a jet plane," he'd say, ecstatically. As far as I knew he still loved the car. We didn't talk much. Weeks later he would suffer a fatal heart attack assisted by his Kent cigarettes; an untimely death at age forty.

This guy in the cab wants me to look at his head in the light? It's a nasty looking gash in the dark. He's freaked out as it is—and, more importantly, *I* don't want to see it. I look away when I get a TB test.

"Maybe I don't have to go to the hospital," says my bloody passenger.

"Ahhh…no…you should go to the hospital."

"Shit," he says. "Turn on the light."

I don't want to look at it. I don't want HIM looking at it. I ignore his request.

"Turn on the fuckin' light."

"Okay, okay." I turn on the overhead with a switch on the dash and turn around.

"It don't look that bad, right?" He reassures himself. "Whaddaya think?"

It's a butterfly. The skin is totally separated. I'm trying to figure out how to tell him.

"Well, how does it look?" he asks again.

It looks *horrible*. It's a deep, nasty gash—just missed his eye, more of a near miss than I originally noticed. She really tagged him with that bottle.

"Umm, well, it's not too bad. It's not bleeding that much."

"This ain't nothin'. I been hurt before."

I turn back around and turn off the light. Heartbeat normal. No nausea; no sweating. I'll live. I don't like seeing blood—not mine, not anyone else's. He's gonna need stitches. I remember lying face up on the operating table with a white gauze sheet over my head, the silhouette of the surgeon's arm rising up and down, up and then down; eight stitches outside my mouth, fourteen stitches on the inside.

"This ain't no big deal," he mumbles.

"You should keep applying pressure on it." Hopefully, that will keep him from getting blood all over the place.

"Turn the light back on. Let me look again."

"Just relax. The police will be here in a minute."

"Turn it on."

"You don't wanna see it."

"Yes I do," he says, adamant. "I seen a lot worse shit."

"I know. Do *me* a favor. Let's keep the light off."

"C'mon maaa-aaan." He's pissed and he's not applying the napkins.

"It's probably best to keep some pressure on there."

I want him to stay as calm as possible. He has already had a couple of mood swings just in the time it took to go around the block looking for his assailants.

"I wanna see it."

"You should…."

"Just TURN ON THE MOTHERFUCKIN' LIGHT."

I turn the light on. He positions himself in the mirror.

"*OH GOD!*" he squawks. "Call the dispatch! I needs an ambulance. I needs an ambulance."

He doesn't realize I already told them to send an ambulance. "Code six" meant yes, to send the ambulance. I request voice again to humor him and hope he calms down.

"Yes, five-five-four." It's the very annoyed dispatcher.

"Look, we're still here at Leavenworth and Turk. My passenger wants to confirm the ambulance is on the way."

"Tell them I'm hurt," he howls. "I'm hurt real bad."

"They're on the way," says the unbelieving dispatcher.

"This is an emergency!" yells my passenger.

"Thanks, over." I hang up the microphone. "They're coming. Keep applying pressure."

"Man, she really fucked me up. Shit…shit."

"The ambulance will be here in, like, two minutes."

"Listen man," he says. "I need twenty dollars."

"Yeah?"

"Can you give me twenty dollars?"

"No."

"Please, gimme twenty. You know I'm hurt. I need it."

"I can't do that."

"This is gonna cost me," he reasons.

"You don't have any money?" The realization has now hit me too late.

"I'll have money tomorrow. I'll give it back to you."

"Sorry, but no."

"I'll give you my address. You can come and get it. My address is 240 Hyde Street. I work for the hospital."

"Do I look like the National Bank?"

"I *got* the money. I got the money to pay you."

"Get it from a teller machine."

"I can't. The money's at home."

"No."

"Fuck, man, just gimme fifteen dollars."

"Sorry."

"Come by in the morning and I'll give you back the money," he guarantees.

"That doesn't help me."

"I gotta pay the hospital; I gotta pay the cab fare."

"I *am* the cab fare. You owe *me* six dollars."

"I got a situation. Fifteen dollars, you'll get it back. I know you got it."

"You're supposed to be payin' me."

"It's your fault they got away," he accuses.

"What?"

"You were supposed to be watchin' 'em."

"We could have followed 'em. You didn't want to."

"You lost 'em."

"How can I watch someone I can't see?"

"You fucked up, man. You fucked up."

"Are you kiddin' me?"

"Eleven dollars, I'll pay you back, tomorrow morning. Eleven."

"No."

"Just overnight. This is all your fault anyway!"

He's crazy.

"I'm really fucked." He finally blots his head with the napkins. "You can't lend me a little cash?"

I hear a car a short distance behind us. The computer buzzes with a message: *GOLDEN GATE THEATER BREAKING NOW!*

"Damn!" He slams his hand on the seat. "Give me the money."

I look over my shoulder as he's waving his hand at me.

"Give it to me." He juts out his arm.

It's like that Lenny Bruce routine with the guy in the ambulance bleeding to death and he makes a play for the nurse. Never miss an opportunity. I turn off the engine, grab the keys, quickly open my door and get out of the cab. He's a big guy and he's getting way too aggressive. I'm not taking on a guy with a bleeding gash. Meanwhile, the headlights of the car behind us approach closer. There's an advertisement on the roof—it's a cab. I'd prefer an ambulance or the police. I wave at him to stop. I think there's a passenger in the back, but I'm not certain. It speeds by without hesitation and without slowing. One block down, the taxi makes a screeching turn and leaves my sight.

"I need some money," says my passenger who has now gotten out of the cab.

"You're not gettin' it from me."

I've kept the driver's side door open. If he comes after me I can quickly get back into the cab. There's a police siren coming our way. If I can hold him off for one minute the cops should arrive.

He steps toward me.

"I told you I'll pay you back," he yells. "First thing in the morning, ten o'clock."

I walk a circle around the cab and survey the landscape. His one hand is still holding the napkins to his head. He's waving his other arm in the air and taking giant steps pursuing me in a circle around the cab—it's like some Three Stooges routine.

"You owe me," he says with a determined scowl. "It's your fault they got away."

I see red lights flashing up ahead, coming down the street the opposite direction of the one-way street we are on. It's the ambulance.

"Over here." I wave at them.

The ambulance pulls up in front of us.

"Give me nine dollars," says the bloody guy pursuing me one more time around the cab.

"Forget it."

I hurry over to the two paramedics getting out of the ambulance.

"Did you call?" asks the first paramedic.

"Yeah."

"What happened?"

"He has a gash above his eye. He was bleeding real bad."

"That guy over there?" He points to my passenger.

"Yeah. He's getting belligerent. He's hassling me for money."

Here comes my passenger right behind me.

"A woman hit him in the head with a bottle or something," I tell the paramedic.

"In your cab?"

"No, I stopped to help him."

The bloody guy comes up behind me. "Fifteen dollars, can I count on you?" he says.

I walk back toward the cab. He starts to follow me.

"Hey fella!" yells the medic to the bloody guy. "C'mere."

"I was attacked," screams the bloody guy, now pointing at me. "He let them get away!"

"Okay, just calm down," says the paramedic. "Let's get something on your eye there."

The bloody guy walks over to the paramedic. The second paramedic gets out of the ambulance. They start to blot his face and apply a bandage around his head.

Moments later, another siren, more lights; it's the police. They pull up alongside the cab. Two cops get out.

"What happened here?" asks the first cop.

With lightning speed, the paramedics have completed bandaging the guy's head.

"I picked that guy up who was bleeding. He says some woman hit him with a bottle."

The passenger, his head bandaged, walks back over, agitated and still pointing wildly. "She's down the street gettin' away. He could have followed her," he says to the second cop.

I'm shaking my head—no.

"I was attacked," says the bloody guy. "And he saw it. It's his fault."

"Did you see who attacked him?" the first cop asks me.

"No," I tell him.

"He's to blame. Those people, they assaulted me and got away. He let them get away!" yells ex-bloody guy. He steps toward me. "The girl's down the street." He shakes his fist at me. "He knows who she is."

The second cop steps between us.

"Did you see who hit him?" the second cop asks me.

"I didn't see anything."

"He knows who she is," says the bloody guy. "He saw her."

"I didn't see her," I object. "I didn't see anyone."

"He let her get away."

"That's not true at all," say I.

"Come over here," says the first cop to the bloody guy.

They walk over to the other side of the patrol car. The second cop walks me in the other direction while I render "my side of the story."

"You can't identify her?" he asks.

"I only know what he told me."

The first cop returns. "He says you know who she is."

"He was bleeding, so I stopped to pick him up. I only know what he told me."

"We're gonna drive him over and see if he can identify her."

"Look, I would like to go back to work. I was nice enough to try to help this guy, and now I've lost my time and he has no money." I'm beginning to shiver. The cold night air is getting to me a little bit. They probably think that, since my lips are beginning to quiver, I'm lying.

"We'd PREFER if you wait here," says the cop shaking his head. "OKAY?"

"I can't identify anybody. I didn't see anything."

The no longer bloody guy pipes in, "I don't wanna ID her. Make the cab driver do it."

"What?" I throw up my hands. "How do I know who she is? You're the one who said she hit you with a bottle." And she probably had good reason.

"He can do it," the bloody guy nods. "He knows which one she is."

"I never saw anyone's face." I just can't believe this. "I didn't see anyone do anything. All I know is that he pointed to someone in a jacket with writing on it."

"Do you know what kind of writing?" asks the cop.

"It was white writing," I say. "I couldn't see clearly. We were too far away."

"We'll be right back," says the second cop. "Then you can get out of here."

"I'm working. This is taking money out of my pocket."

"It won't take long. Just stay here; we might need you."

Need me? What does he need me for? We're both driving the same make and model vehicle, some key differences: mine has 300,000 more miles, and his has guns.

"I want him to identify the woman," says the bloody guy.

"Can you ID her?" asks the second cop.

"No. If he doesn't know her, how would I?"

"He's lyin' now," says the bloody guy, suddenly calm and matter of fact. "He's lying."

"I'm late to pick up a fare," I tell the cops.

"Just stay here while we take him down the street to identify her. Do you mind waiting here?"

I notice that a crowd has gathered around us. Here we have a police car, an ambulance, a cab and a bloody guy. This is not an area where you want to attract unneeded attention to yourself. Nothing good will come of it.

"Yes, I mind waiting. The neighborhood . . . it's not the safest neighborhood."

"We won't be long," says the cop without emotion. "We're just going down the block and back."

Easy for him to say, Mr. .357 magnum hooked on his pants. I've got a frayed leather belt on mine. If I get into a "situation" I guess I can always threaten someone with the *buckle side.*

"I might drive around the block or something," I tell him.

"That's fine," says the cop. "Just stick around."

I'm very unhappy about this. Back at the cab, the computer is beeping. I get in, it reads: **WHO JUST HAD THE TRIP? A NAKED WOMAN.** I move the cab a little farther down the block, to a liquor store on the corner where I hope to feel a little safer. Taking a keen interest in this late night spectacle, the crowd that assembled moves right along with me—apartment dwellers, customers from the store, vagrants and gang members. I get out of the cab.

"What happened?" asks one guy.

Two guys come out of the liquor store.

"It's going to be hard to pick people up with that blood on yer cab," says a bystander.

"What's that?" I say to him.

"You got blood all over your cab, man."

I walk around to the other side of the cab. The entire passenger side has thick streaks of blood. This is a real problem.

"Can't be picking up people like that, Mr. Cab Driver," says a gang member.

"Shit." I tell him. "I think you're right."

Even though it's dark out, this is obviously not mud or taco sauce. It has a characteristic look. Driving around town with blood smeared across the whole side of the car is just the competitive edge I need.

"Which cab should we take, honey? Oh look, this one has blood on the door. Hurry, let's get in."

I sit back into the cab and call dispatch.

"I've got blood all over my cab."

"You gonna be driving people like that?" surveys a guy standing at the side of the cab peeking his head into the open window. "With blood all over everything."

"I know," I say to him trying to remain patient. "Thanks."

"You can bring it in and take another cab," advises the dispatcher.

By the time I did that, I would lose another hour.

"Can I take the hours on another night?" I ask.

"You gotta ask upstairs."

"Thanks, over."

There are now a noticeable number of Hispanic gang members crowding around the cab. Maybe that's what happened with this guy—a black guy walking on the Latino side of the street or something.

"Is that your blood?" one asks.

"*NO*," I answer.

"Look at all the blood," someone comments.

"*Que' pasa, que' pasa?*" says another kid. "*Hay sangre en tu taxi.*"

"Hey man, whose blood?" asks another guy in a black hooded coat.

"Hey Cab Man, what happened?" pipes another voice from the assembling crowd.

"Did you shoot somebody? Did you shoot somebody?"

"That's your blood?" asks a tough-looking teenager.

"It's not *my* blood," I answer.

That seems to impress him. Maybe if they think I killed somebody they won't bother me.

I get back out of the cab as a guy offers me some paper towels and I attempt to rub out some of the bloodstains. The stuff doesn't come off. Another guy comes out of the liquor store with a bucket of hot water and pours it on the blood. Nothing; it has no effect. My Jones and Turk Street fare flashes through my mind. It's over thirty minutes old. Some guy throws a rag over to me and I try to get the blood off with that. No progress. It won't come off.

"We'll pour this on it." It's some Arabic guys with Clorox who have appeared, probably from the store, pouring the contents on the dried blood. It won't come off.

They keep at it with the Clorox, paper towels and I don't know what else.

I get back on the radio with the dispatcher.

"Is there a carwash around here?"

"I don't know."

"Thanks, anyway; just thought I'd ask."

There's noticeable movement and some excited discussion going on at the front of the car where most of the blood is located, including the people from the liquor store, some supposedly innocent bystanders and the gang members. They're probably stealing the wheels. I once again get back out of the cab trying to seem unconcerned about mine or the car's well-being, to inspect and protect my interest in making sure the tires stay attached to the cab—slowly wind my way around the vehicle as if I don't have a care in the world. Miraculously, the wheels are still in place (I don't think there were hubcaps to begin with). They have cleaned it off completely. No more blood. It's shiny yellow as can be, not even a hint of red.

"Wow, that's fantastic. Thank you very much." I'm not even sure who to thank, so I'm just thanking everybody.

The police arrive back, hocking me again.

"Can you pull up the block to identify this woman?" asks the cop.

"I didn't see anything."

"Just come over there for a minute."

I'm about to get back into the cab when a guy who seems like the gang's head honcho, struts toward me.

"Yer cab is *anporque' de bloodfremm yo cabcho' floo*? Eh bro?"

"What?"

"*Yeca usonque' do blood yo' cabs?*"

"Is it my cab?"

"*Yeca usonque' do blood yera son blood chumasho?*"

He's speaking broken English with some Spanish thrown in, or something. He's slurring words and lisping incoherently.

"I don't understand. I'm sorry."

Now a couple of the young hoodlums in the crowd are snickering.

"*Que'?*" I ask.

There's laughter as he repeats something else in gibberish. He's messing with me. He's not saying anything...possibly.

"Get outta here," I tell him in a *very* good-natured tone. I hope he's just screwing around. He laughs. His friends laugh. They think their pal is real funny.

I again thank some more folks in the crowd, the liquor store guys and the gang members. I don't know who did what, but the car is clean, the windows aren't busted out, and the car still has four tires on the ground. I wave, get into the cab, start the engine, and lock the doors. I drive down the block to where the police have camped. They've got two people wearing Chicago White Sox jackets.

"Are these the people you saw?" asks the cop.

The one woman is shooting me looks that could kill my relatives located in a neighboring state.

"Look, I don't know." I repeat without any emotion. "I didn't see anything. The guy bleeding pointed out some people walking down the block."

"He says he can't identify them," says the cop.

"He told me a woman hit him in the head," I tell him.

"He says YOU can identify her."

How do I convince this guy that I'm not the psychic detective? I try talking more slowly.

"I'm telling you I can't. I only know what he told me." I feel like totally going off on this cop, but I sense that he's giving it his last best effort and is finally going to quit pestering me, whether because he believes me or figures me entrenched in stubbornness—I certainly don't care.

"He says he doesn't know who hit him," the cop replies to me.

I glance back over at the one woman who only moments ago was trying to kill my entire family. She is now sporting a knowing, defiant and victorious smirk. She probably did it.

"If I knew who did it, I would tell you."

"Well then," surrenders the cop, "we can't do anything." As if these magic words are the abracadabra that will change my position.

"I'm sorry," I say. "I can't help you."

"That's okay—happens all the time like this."

"What's that?"

"Victim's scared to make identification 'cause they live in the same neighborhood, or they're doing drugs, whatever."

"Can I go?"

"Yeah, you can go. Leave us your name and phone number."

I write it down for him.

"Could you possibly do me a favor?" I ask. "Could you write a note saying I spent a half-hour with this? The company might let me make up the time."

"Here's the complaint number." The cop hands me the slip of paper and tells me his name. I put the slip in my pocket, get back into the cab, drive over to Jones and head south toward Market. It's been 47 minutes since I got the original call. I pull up to the address. It's a gigantic new building—state of the art low-cost housing. There's an elderly woman with teased hair, wild-eyed, standing inside the lobby. She resembles a stereotypical escapee from *One Flew over the Cuckoo's Nest.*

"What do you want?" she cries from inside the lobby.

"Did you call a cab?"

"What?" She's looking me up and down like she hasn't confronted such a mutant since her narrow escape from extraterrestrial abductors traveling by no coincidence in a banana-shaped craft.

"Did you call a cab?" I point to the giant yellow-colored vehicle in plain view, ten feet away.

She stares at the taxi with a hint of recognition.

I try once more. "Did you call a cab?" Perhaps she suspects my brightly colored yellow vehicle of having some sort of relationship to the dastardly banana-sculpted space probe housing those scoundrels who nearly succeeded in her kidnap.

"What do you want from me?"

I punch in the apartment code: #—6—1—5.

I hear a three-note arpeggio.

A pleasant man's voice comes on the phone: *"We're sorry. You have reached a number that is disconnected or is no longer in service. If you feel you have reached this recording in error, please check the number and try your call again. We're sorry. You have reached a number that is disconnected or is no longer in...."*

I push the number "3" button and get a dial tone. The woman in the lobby is carefully watching me. She's wearing two-piece flannel pajamas with red and blue flowers. Her long thinning white hair accentuates her poised hunchback position, while she leans on her thick aluminum cane. It has a large beige rubber tip at the end where it contacts the floor. She's getting good traction out of the thing.

I walk back to the cab and check the apartment number I previously scribbled on my waybill. It's #516, not #615. I walk back to the intercom, and try the number once more. It rings. Someone picks up the phone. It's the arpeggio again. *"We're sorry. You have reached a number that is disconnected or no longer in..."*

I bang down the receiver and walk back to the cab. The old woman is still watching me with interest. I shouldn't be picking up people who are bleeding—profusely bleeding. I don't know what I was thinking. Oh yeah, I was thinking, I don't want to be one of those people who won't even stop to help a person who is bleeding in the street. Maybe people who don't stop aren't so bad, after all.

The street is quiet. It's a clear night. No fog. If not for the city lights, you could probably see the stars. I take a right on Market Street and head for the Castro.

NO GUNS,
NO KNIVES,
NO PERSONAL CHECKS

Didn't your mom tell you not to pick up strangers?

There are limited guidelines and suggestions advising drivers on dealing with attempted armed robberies. Additionally, the cab yard has signs and bulletins posted everywhere: the walls, lockers and ceiling beams.

Initially, I didn't take the Trust Your Instincts signs seriously. It seemed like a bunch of namby-pamby mumbo-jumbo touchy-feely crap; not really any advice at all. Plus, I had always thought it unfair to make judgments on how someone looks, let alone the manner in which someone holds his body while standing on a corner or even *how* someone flags a cab.

However, as far as surviving this job is concerned, my mindset has changed. Of course, it's "unfair" to make stereotypical judgments, draw conclusions based upon superficial impressions or make a decision without the support of any logical reasoning, but the cab interior is not a courtroom and there are no appeals. As much as the job experience has its social and political aspects, it's not a sociology experiment. Am I going to change the world by letting a bulky jacketed teenager or tattooed miscreant who is possibly the descendent of some psychotic pirate get into the back seat of my cab? If I have a bad feeling about someone from his or her curb-side body language, street mannerisms, or taste in fashion—I take it seriously; I don't stop; I think about it later. I can always circle the block to reconsider my initial decision to pass them by—tell them I was on a call that was cancelled, or I didn't see them, or couldn't stop in time. Despite what I learned in elementary school about not talking to strangers, I might crack the window open, ask where they're going and assess their level of coherency. For those folks I've already allowed into the cab, it's no guarantee that I won't kick them out. It's never too late to stop the cab, get out, and tell them to do the same.

MY CAB POLICY: go with your gut feeling; yes, trust your instinct and listen to that voice telling you what you *really* should do.

Things move fast and happen fast. It's like deciding to make the yellow light. Don't hesitate.

People who smell like urine, thugs, people coughing without covering their mouths, drunks puking—you get them all. You never know what's coming next. If I'm suspicious, I take whatever precaution seems appropriate: unbuckling my seat belt; grabbing my pepper spray; acting friendly; finding a busy, well-lit area to disengage the passenger; calling for the police. What often proves effective is pretending to send messages to the dispatcher over the computer, even though in reality, the computer is simply capable of communicating "yes," "no," or "help."

In retrospect, at times, I'm suspicious of people who turn out to be completely harmless. On the other hand, maybe I prevented something bad from happening by taking some small precaution. You don't know something's going to happen until it does. The thing is, there's no way for me to know I've prevented something from happening, that doesn't happen.

There's not a way that I've figured out to measure the success of my actions. There's just no way to know.

Maybe someone could do an interview show with criminals who have perpetrated crimes against taxi drivers. One should be able to find plenty of them. Statistics indicate the highest number of "workplace" homicide victims are cab drivers. What causes Cab Driver A to become victimized while Cab Driver B skates safely by? The difficulty in finding an answer is that one assumes there's some carefully calculated logic at work here, like when they ask serial killers why they committed their crimes. They're *crazy*, that's why! You want some logic from a guy who eats a human thigh rather than a chicken wing? While some animal rights activists might argue there's no difference, I personally would not expect a reasonable set of guidelines to spring from Jeffrey Dahmer. Did one cab driver have the space alien Zora on his dashboard causing a psychotic to think he'd better find another guy to mess with? And, of course, if you question incarcerated criminals about their professional approaches and ways of reasoning, you have to realize that there's something about their logic that failed—they're in prison!

I read a caption from one study that claimed the majority of robbers "took a highly casual approach" and had done no planning at all. What's even more amusing are the researchers claiming a zero net benefit if a robbery is thwarted—because success in preventing a crime at one location usually results in the perpetration of another one elsewhere. Cab Driver A may be happy—but Cab Driver B is not so fortunate. Is this a good result? Well, just ask Cab Driver B about that. Two additional scenarios: Cab Driver A hands his money over to the robber—cooperating without objection. The next night, the robber successfully hits Cab Driver B, C, D and so on. Scenario two: Cab Driver A puts up a vicious fight, maybe gets killed or injured—but not before he manages to inflict serious bodily harm on the assailant, who after encountering this feisty combatant now decides to get a job at McDonald's and discontinue his plundering. Cab Driver B is thus saved.

So, if you're down at the yard, talking to a bunch of Cab Driver A's, and you figure yourself for a Cab Driver B, you tell them to put up a vicious fight. Of course, meanwhile, if you find yourself out in the field getting hit up by some punks carrying an arsenal of guns, knives, and sawed-off shotguns—and you realize that you are not Cab Driver B, but you are Cab Driver A—you give up the money. Capeesh?

The measure of success is that you make it through the night unscathed and keep a few bucks in your own pocket. You try to be aware of everything happening around you at all times and realize that, frankly, a 100% success rate night after night is not an obtainable goal. But, still, you do your best. You can get sideswiped, swindled, murdered or stabbed. You want to *see* it coming before it does; you want to stay a good couple of car lengths ahead of all potential obstructions. It can be fun. It can be scary. It IS dangerous.

Be careful out there, says the sign. And you try to be.

I TOOK A BULLET

"**M**y favorite aunt just died." He's a scholarly-looking gentleman with tears in his eyes.

"I just had a miscarriage. My baby is dead!" recites another. At first glance, she is a delightful looking, rosy and fair-skinned, almost angelic woman. It seems inconceivable that she ever suffered any sort of trauma, misfortune or even prick of the finger.

The above were received in response to the "How's your day?" question when picking up fares at a hospital. (Not to mention folks like "my baby's in the hospital" trying to find their way TO the hospital). I've implemented a strict Cab Policy: QUIT asking people how they're doing if they're coming from any type of medical facility. Sometimes they catch you off guard by asking how YOU are doing. This is possibly an inadvertent blurtation on their part—an involuntary but ingrained polite social mannerism.

"Fine," I answer. It's entrapment. "And how are you?"

"I've got cancer," followed by uncomfortable silence while I hope to respond with something appropriate that isn't idiotic or trite and at the same time try *not* make a wrong turn first thing out of the hospital driveway.

The strict new **DO NOT ASK** Cab Policy will remain in effect no matter how long silence ensues after the passenger first takes his seat. If he wants to talk—fine. If the passenger asks a question, just answer the question and make no further inquiries, rude as that may seem.

At Haight and Shrader, after dropping a pair of customers who have just satisfied their culinary desires at a fine Italian North Beach restaurant, I accept a fare from UC Medical Center. A casual, confident and distinguished-looking gentleman walks out from the main entrance. He is about forty-five years old, shirt and pants immaculately pressed and thoughtfully manicured hair. He is carrying both himself, and a large manila envelope marked **X-rays,** in an authoritative doctorly manner. I figure him to be one.

"I'm exhausted," he says.

And who wouldn't be, dealing with sick and dying people all day. Maybe he'd like to talk about it? Doctors don't usually get emotionally involved, that's the first focus of their training. I suspend my *DO NOT ASK* policy. What's a rule without an exception, anyway?

"How's your evening been?" I cheerily ask, flipping the meter.

"My wife and I, we're here from Ohio. They've been, well they've been mucking around in her skull. She has a brain tumor."

SILENCE.

The **DO NOT ASK** policy goes back into effect immediately, unconditionally—doctors, nurses, lawyers, funeral directors, it doesn't matter. Don't even wish them a good day. It's not a good day, more likely it's maybe the worst day ever. Hospitals and good days? Forget it.

"She has these screaming fits," he sighs. "Vomiting, grabbing her head. I've been in the hospital room for 24 hours straight—just couldn't take any more. I feel guilty, leaving…but, well the doctor gave me her X-rays and told me to get some rest. She can't even remember that I've been there."

"Is she going to be okay?" I humbly inquire.

"They say the screaming thing's normal. They don't know. No one would do the surgery in Ohio. Nobody; I can't tell you how many hospitals we tried. No one wants the liability."

•

Later that week, there's a fare at San Francisco General Hospital's main entrance, 4:55 in the afternoon. The man and woman who called the cab are actually waiting outside. This is unusual. S.F. General is notorious because of the great number of no-shows. To where do these people disappear? They request a cab as they're coming out of the hospital, I get there quickly, but they're gone. Abducted? Held for observation? I'd like to know. Aren't these people sick, injured and emotionally shattered from dealing with the medical establishment? Despondent over the failure of bodily functions, after the hell they've been through, they take their revenge by ditching a cab?

Apparently these two folks have successfully fought off their potential captors. I consider nominating them for sainthood, but instead hit the door-lock release to allow their entry, vowing to adhere strictly to my **DO NOT ASK** policy.

The woman swings the door open before I can rise from my seat. They're in their mid-twenties, healthy-looking except that he's on crutches.

"We're going to Visitacion Valley. I know some of you guys won't go there; is that okay?" Crutch asks.

On the outskirts of town, Visitacion Valley is the location of a large housing project where several taxi drivers have been robbed, beaten and/or strangled in recent months. Usually these incidents take place at three o'clock in the morning, but not always. I'm not happy about going out to this latest ambush hot spot. Thankfully, at least it's broad daylight and these two seem pleasant and friendly enough.

"Sure," I answer. He's on crutches. How much trouble can he be? I can take the freeway to Bayshore and easily "dead head" to the airport after I drop them. It will be prime time for incoming flights.

"You need help getting in?" I oblige. "You can sit in the front if it's easier," I offer, blatantly disregarding my policy of

NO PASSENGERS IN THE FRONT SEAT.

"That's all right." He struggles to fit into the back seat with his companion and his crutches. "This is fine." He seems glad enough just to be getting out of the hospital. And I'm NOT asking.

He's a big guy, six foot three, 230 plus pounds. We make small talk as I carefully avoid areas regarding medical, mental or personal histories. He directs us through the grid of streets in the "Valley." The neighborhood has its rough spots, and its rougher spots: abandoned housing; dilapidated dwellings with laundry hanging from clothes lines; buildings with windows broken out (some replaced with plywood and some not); pit bulls pacing their territories (sometimes behind a fence and sometimes not); small congregations of people hanging, some on bicycle, some on foot, some consuming refreshments while sprawled on the cement.

The housing projects are one of the few things in San Francisco that remind me of downtown Detroit—or a third world country. And, if this were one, celebrities would be seen on television soliciting money to help the children, rebuild housing and clean up the streets. The only celebrities here are the ones you read about in the UTW newsletter or the obituaries.

We pass two teenagers wearing Raiders jackets and paraphernalia. A few blocks later there's a kid strutting across the street with his pants below his ass, wearing a black and white Chicago White Sox hat (they're considered cool and worn with increasing popularity). I haven't exactly figured out the nuances of the gang colors and stuff. Is there significance whether you wear an item frontward or backward? I don't know. I could ask someone, I guess—maybe the guy with the crutches in the back seat? No. This is just my way of trying to skirt the **DO NOT ASK** policy. I do wonder, especially on occasions such as this, if I could be risking an attack by wearing the wrong colors in the wrong area at the wrong time—get out of the cab wearing a light blue shirt, help someone out the door and a few seconds later it becomes a red shirt. I enjoy a small amount of comforting thought today, as I'm wearing a gray shirt. You'd figure these guys would know it's just a cab driver who happens to be wearing a light blue shirt—not a rival gang member horning in on their drug deals and whores. But some gang members might just be looking for a good laugh, or to test whether their weapon kicks back to the left, right or shoots low. Maybe they need to complete their final qualification for their group's initiation, and if that's the case, my random choice of a fashion statement is not going to save me.

While waiting at the yard one day, I heard a couple of guys talking about a driver navigating a street in Hunter's Point, another potentially rough area of town. The problem was not that he was wearing the wrong colors, but driving opposite the direction indicated. (But officer, I was only *going* one way.) He was pulled out of his car, robbed and beaten. How's that in lieu of a $250 fine?

VIGILANTE TRAFFIC ENFORCEMENT

Perhaps this started as a case of "driver panic" known to the scientific community as survival instinct—being a little too anxious to get out of the area while not paying enough attention to the street signs. Maybe he was taking a shortcut. Maybe he was driving too fast. Maybe he was driving too slowly? Regardless, there was something the local residents (well, the gang members) did not appreciate about his methods. Driving down *their* street as if your nose hairs are on fire conveys a lack of respect. Just *driving* on their street can indicate a lack of respect. It doesn't take much to piss these guys off. One thing leads to another and, before you know it, someone's getting the crap beaten out of them.

"Ain'ts it illegal for you taxi drivers refusin' someone a ride?" queries my female passenger accompanying Crutch. Suddenly she wants to get into it with me? I don't. She's close to home, feeling more comfortable and within walking distance of her bathroom.

"Yes, it is," I simplify. "You should really get their cab number and report them, you know, if that happens."

"Yeah?" she sasses. "Well! It happens. It happens all the time."

Give me a break, lady. I'm giving you a ride. Maybe I'll get paid, maybe not. So far, I've only been ditched at the hospital doors, never actually after the ride. People figure they're traceable just having had an appointment, perhaps treatment and billed $25 for a Tylenol.

Meanwhile, the big man in the back seat, tapping his fingers at the aluminum crutch, directs us with precision to their drop-off spot. There's a vintage white Ford Thunderbird, short one left front tire, with two enthusiastic onlookers at its side. On the other side of the street, three men and a young woman, perhaps of questionable character and more probably than not, engaged on the outskirts of any traditional and/or legal profession, pace and cajole just outside the doors of a liquor store. Numerous folks are hanging. My passengers know several of them. They are barely out of the cab and Crutch is yelling out to people: "I took a bullet in the leg! I took a bullet in the leg!!" People are yelling back at him. Great, get me out of here.

Despite this pleasant homecoming, my nervous system maintains a low threshold for gun play, present tense, past tense, last night, whenever. Hopefully, I'm considered off limits for target practice. I helped him get back home, I'm cool, right? On the other hand, get me out of here. This guy took one bullet from someone with poor aim, who's to say he's not going to take another while I'm sitting there? Maybe someone's waiting for the opportunity to finish off the job—PROPERLY. They pay the fare and add eighty-five cents for a tip. Scanning the rooftops, eyeing the crippled T-bird, my senses on full alert, I check my mirrors and slowly drive away.

I spot a freeway on-ramp but it's northbound, not south. This will lead me back into town instead of toward my initial destination, the airport. The sun is about to set and I decide that an available north bound entrance is more desirable than a later southern exit. I take advantage of the ramp's unexpected appearance. Six minutes later I exit at Mission Street, make a couple of turns and spot three folks—two females and a male—flagging for a ride.

The one woman scoots in back into the middle (hump position). She has a noticeable triple-pierced eyebrow. The other woman and the man get in on opposite sides and file their destination. It's the last I hear from them for several minutes, other than some rustling around and some gurgling noises. I glance back in time to catch the pierced woman making out with *both* of her travel companions. I didn't have the nerve to ask her about it (the piercings, that is).

At Market Street I exchange the cross-kissers for a group of four lesbians headed to a quaint Noe Valley dining establishment. They pile into the cab and get situated, obviously in the midst of an in-depth discussion regarding one of them who had also recently pierced several of her body parts.

What's the deal with these folks with the rings and nails through their cheeks and in their chins? Okay, you're in control of your body...I haven't seen any gang members with sixteen-penny construction nails through their lips. So who *are* the crazy ones?

"Did that one hurt?" asks one woman.

"The upper one did, the lower one here wasn't too bad."

"This one looks like it would be painful," says another.

"Mary had one of those done. She almost passed out."

I didn't have the nerve to see exactly which body parts were being discussed; didn't know if she had her pants pulled down or what. I wasn't going to risk provoking an incident by taking a good hard look. This is about the time I start to wonder why they make rear-view mirrors so small.

The computer makes a five-second-long sustained beep. It reads: *ANYONE SEEING CAB #365—IF HE DOESN'T GO TO VOICE AND EXPLAIN HIS ERRATIC DRIVING—HE'S MAJOR HISTORY!!!*

"I took the ring out of this hole one night. The next day it had already closed up," says the woman. "I had it pierced again, and I'm being more careful this time."

"Oh, I like this one over here," comments her friend. "How can you sleep with that? Aren't you afraid it's going to rip through your skin?"

"I only sleep on my back."

This woman had holes punched everywhere. She rents herself out as a human strainer on weekends. Apparently the piercing of body parts, like gang violence, is on the rise.

Upon arriving at the restaurant the women unload, while a man and a woman approach. I roll down the passenger side window. They inquire if I'm available.

"We ordered a cab," says the man. "The restaurant did."

The woman is dressed in clothing that's a little too tight for both the far and near-sighted onlooker.

"Well, it's not my call, actually," I tell him. "I'll be glad to take you. But you might tell the restaurant that you're canceling, so someone doesn't make a trip for nothing."

"Forget it," he quips. "We've been waiting over twenty minutes. Screw 'em. Is it okay if we just get in? We been going all day—just got here this morning, we just want to get to our hotel and go to sleep." The wife wiggles a gaudy oversized diamond ring at me to accentuate her husband's plea.

"Sure, get in." They're headed for the Hilton. I flip the meter and begin to pull out from the curb when the cab shakes with a loud abrupt THUD. Startled, I pull to a stop, look to my right and check the rear-view mirror. There's another THUD.

Did I run over a strip of nails and my tires are popping? It's an EARTHQUAKE?

"Hey, you! Hey YOU, motherfucker. Fuck you! Fuck YOU!" It's a short, bearded man with a wild look in his dark brown eyes that are piercing through the pane of glass. His face is actually pressed right up against the driver's side window, like we do as kids, contorted against the flat surface. He is seven inches from my face. I can actually see the breath from his nostrils. It would be quite a hilarious view if not for his extremely disconcerting obscenity-ridden tirade and cackling, crackling voice breaking the serene silence of the night.

"Fuck YOU, cabbie. I know who you are. I KNOW who you are. I know WHO you are," he rants and smacks the glass. "And I will get you. I WILL, GET you!"

By now my mouth is gaping open. He flips me the finger and as abruptly as he appeared, peels himself from the side of the cab and walks away into the twilight, leaving a foggy half-a-face imprint, gooey saliva, and what looks like a chunk of partially-chewed food on the

I know who you are. I KNOW who you are.

window. Assuming that my tires are in fact fully inflated and operable, I give the engine gas and we're off to the Hilton (I think they said).

"What in god's name was that?" asks the wife in a combination of fright and disbelief.

"I told ya, honey," volunteers the husband. "There's some crazy people in this town; nuts, just nuts. The men are trying to be women; the women are trying to be men; what the hell's wrong with this place?"

They're coming from a very popular gay and lesbian restaurant. Who knows what they saw in there and I'm just not in the mood to ask. Meantime, with all the commotion, I've run a stop sign and once again, check my mirrors—this time for cops, though it's a little late for remedial measures. What I do see: that lunatic crazy-faced-mother getting into a De Soto cab, if I'm not mistaken. That is, into the driver's seat. It's a good time to make a quick right turn, a sharp left and another right. I crank the gas up a steep hill for another abrupt left turn. That should make it difficult enough for the crazy cabbie to track us down.

"You don't happen to know whether the restaurant called a De Soto cab?" I query.

"Dakota? Yeah, maybe. That sounds familiar, Dakota." The husband thinks aloud. "Why's that?"

"Well…" Unsure whether I should tell them; but maybe it's better they understand people are not just randomly banging on cars and threatening bodily harm without, in fact, some provocation. This city is **CIVILIZED**.

"I think actually, that may have been the cab driver, the one on your call."

"I told you, honey," responds the husband without a pause. "There's a bunch of goofballs in this town."

And in what town do you folks live? Go visit Finland. I've taken offense now. I don't know why—I mean, this poor guy's unsuspecting wife gets sideswiped by some freak-a-zoid who resembles Yoda on steroids after an all-night meth binge—he has some right to be a little put off.

"I don't think I'd want to be in HIS cab," says the wife. "Yes," she continues with a dead pan delivery, "I don't think so. He shouldn't be driving a car, not so agitated." She concludes the intellectual analysis. "I'm glad we're riding with you instead."

I think she's offering a compliment—to offset the husband?

"Well, you know," I offer, "there's fierce competition out there among taxi drivers." I figure they're from the Midwest; maybe they can relate to job market competitiveness—the struggle for which only the most fit will survive. Me? I double-check to make sure the meter is working properly and that De Soto isn't on our tail.

It's all clear.

Winding my way through the final few blocks of Noe Valley, traffic becomes heavier. Making our way to Market I decide that, in taking Bush Street, we might avoid the backed-up traffic headed downtown for the Bay Bridge and the ball game. Traveling north on Franklin Street, we swiftly make it past the Opera House and Davies Hall. After a hard right at Bush, speeding through the yellow-about-to-turn-red signal at Van Ness, we get stopped at a light a few blocks down.

"Hey, Mr. Cab Man, hey Mr. Cab Man! How ARE you?"

Tilting my head to the left, I spot her. It's Cat Woman, screaming in our direction, leg wrapped around a pole, in her familiar attire: bright red earrings, black fishnet stockings, low-cut bikini top, whip, cape, high heeled boots.

"Are you still lonely?" Cat Woman snaps her whip at us. "Hungry for some burgers? Meooooo-ooow!" she croons.

"Do you know her?" asks the inquisitive wife.

"How 'bout some hot buns?" Cat Woman adds, smacking his rear end, swirling his hip and his whip in the air.

"I don't know 'em—I don't know her," I interject.

"She seems to know YOU," counters the wife.

"I've seen her before," I admit.

"Why does she find it necessary to dress up in that, in that odd costume?"

"She's a prostitute, Elaine," explains the disgusted husband. "A hooker."

He only knows the half of it, and probably suspects I'm a customer.

I had rolled down my window because of the fog impression left by the crazy De Soto driver. I decide now to roll the window back up. The fog impression of his face is long gone; that tiny bit of food remnant, however, still clings by a strand to the window. There are no cars approaching the intersection as I spot the light turning yellow for the cross traffic. I step on the gas, just in front of the light turning back to green for our direction hoping my passengers don't notice that I've slightly jumped the red light.

"A bunch of freaks, Elaine," says the husband, reiterating his commentary. "The city's full of a bunch of freaks."

We soon arrive at the front entrance of the giant hotel lobby.

"Hello folks!" The doorman greets them, helping the couple from the cab's back seat. "Welcome back!" He throws me a knowing wink, as if he knew they were not quite mentally or psychologically prepared for their excursion to the hors d'oeuvres hot spot for homosexuals.

A second doorman blows his whistle for me to remain stopped. It's another couple, a husband and wife, best I can tell, needing a ride to North Beach. They get into the back seat. The woman is dressed warmly and is quite adequately perfumed.

"This is a great town," comments the man. "I haven't been here in ages. And how is YOUR night going?"

"Very fine, thank you." I restart the meter, pause to insure the monolithic hotel has not transformed itself into a hospital, check my seat belt, and make the inquiry....

"HOW HAS YOUR DAY BEEN?"

FAKIN' IT
THE SICK, THE DYING, AND THE WOUNDED
Will the real fake please stand up?

Cabs are taken by folks from all walks of life; and by folks who can barely walk. There's a good share of slow-moving people who have leg trouble, the disabled, the crippled. Some folks use canes, crutches or walkers, while others are confined to wheelchairs.

"It's differently-abled, not crippled," the man corrects me. He has literally pushed himself into my cab, cutting in front of a limping blind man holding a red and white cane. "I was waiting long before him," the pushy guy excuses himself.

From the driver's seat with the passenger side window open, I can hear the "differently-abled" man tapping his cane in a polyrhythmic Morse code on the sidewalk. He knows that a vehicle has pulled over.

"They wanna be treated equal?" Pushy Guy responds to my look of disbelief, "I'm treatin' 'em equal."

"Blue Byrd Cab?" questions the blind man in an unsteady, shaky, hoarse voice.

"No sir, this is a Yellow," I break the news.

"Hey! His cab's on the way," proclaims Pushy. "This is *my* cab. Fourth and Mission please."

Many folks depend on cabs for transportation even though some of them don't have much money. Some folks don't have any money. Some just *pretend* not to have money.

I get a call for a pickup at a Market Street movie theater. A skinny black man emerges from the theater lobby, rolling himself out in a wheelchair. He stops. He locks the wheels, casually rises from the chair, bends over, unlocks the wheels, positions himself behind the chair and smoothly pushes it to my waiting cab. I pop the trunk and get out to help, but he has already placed the brown leather and aluminum chair into place, slamming the trunk shut. He climbs into the back seat carrying assorted begging-for-money paraphernalia: a cup, a sign and a stack of the STREET SHEET newspapers (sometimes "sold" by street people, the homeless, or just folks who have somehow secured a stack of them). He can walk just fine and isn't trying to hide the fact. Why should he? Working hours are over.

"Ellis and Van Ness," he requests. "How much is it?"

"Depends on traffic."

"Less than five dollars?"

"Ohhh, yeah."

I slow for a yellow light at a busy intersection. It turns red and we stop.

"Man, you could-a made that light. You drive like we're in New York," he accuses.

I think he means he WANTS me to drive like we're in New York, and now establishing the foundation for not leaving a tip. I turn right onto Van Ness, taking the corner a little on the sharp side. Perhaps a little low on air pressure, the tires emit a quiet squeal. Maybe that'll make him happy. It doesn't.

"Man, you cab drivers," he complains.

I ignore the comment. Regardless, there's no tip coming here. Another incident reinforcing **MY CAB POLICY**: when people in wheelchairs or with groceries order a cab, I get out to help. But right before that, the meter goes on. Why not at least get paid for the time it takes to load the passengers and their straggling items? Those who conjure up complaints about the meter having started too early or that the fare is three dollars and we haven't yet moved, invariably don't tip anyway.

With some people I'll fight over seventy-five cents. It depends on whether I think they're trying to take advantage. If I determine they're severely mentally incapable I'll let it slide. Sometimes that's a hard one to call. Scammers, criminal types, people who are drunk—I've gone the distance with most of them: pay up. I chased one guy down the street and caught him. I didn't get my money but I highly doubt he will ever ditch a cab again. The look on the faces of the two crack dealers hanging on the corner watching this cab driver charge out of his cab at the midnight hour—yelling obscenities, proceeding to kick a guy in his ass while scolding him for not paying his six-dollar cab fare—must have been a minor but possibly memorable event for them. They certainly looked amused. Afterwards, I waved a friendly hello, got back into the cab and completed my shift. It's good to maintain friendly relations with the local business owners and area merchants.

Then of course, you have some older people operating on the 1930s valuation of the dollar.

A very elderly man gingerly flags me down at 1:30 in the morning on Twenty-Fourth Street. I exit, open his door and wait for him to make his way to the car. He literally can walk only about six inches at a time. It's possible that he's 100 years old. His destination is less than two blocks down the street. At his age and with his mobility, what else can the guy do but take a cab? He wasn't drunk; maybe he was just out for a walk. Whatever the reason, it's impressive that he's out and about at all. I'm glad to assist. We arrive at his destination and I lend a hand to pull him from the back seat of the car. The meter ends up at $2.90. He gives me three singles.

"Keep the change," he proudly tells me.

Some people want you to move their legs for them or handle personal items such as the wheelchair pillows they sit on during most of their waking hours. After sweating or peeing their pants they want to bring this damp pillow into the cab, and have it placed just so.

One woman claiming severe leg problems requested to be carried up the driveway to the side door of her house. Carried! She vehemently claims other drivers ALWAYS carry her to the door. She only weighed about ninety pounds. But I don't care what precedent has been set; My Cab Policy: I don't carry people. It's one rule I've managed NOT to break, *so* far.

"I'll help you up the driveway. You can lean on me."

"Okay," she says. "Thank you." She grabs my arm. Maybe the carrying thing was just a negotiation tactic.

Several minutes later we successfully scale the slightly uphill pitched driveway, slowly move through the garage and up three stairs to the entryway door to the home located inside the garage, where I position myself behind her in case she falls down. Catching someone falling over is different from carrying them—acceptable under current My Cab Policy guidelines. She hasn't the strength to knock on the door and actually asks me to knock for her.

I knock.

No one answers.

"Hello?" she shouts.

I knock again. She shouts. Then she produces a key. I don't know why she didn't get the key out in the first place. She fumbles with it and can't get the key to unlock the door mechanism.

I figure she's also having problems with her hands. She gives me the key.

Turns out it's one of those deals where in order for the key to actually unlock the door, it requires specialized maneuvers: you must push it in (while pushing out while pushing sideways) but not all the way in, and then jiggle it ever so gently. I try it once. I try it twice.

She tells me I'm not jiggling correctly. Anyone have an axe? This goes on—two, three minutes. It seems longer. The cab gods return from their coffee break and finally the key retracts the bolt. We're in.

It's a modest home built about fifty-five years ago, decorated with its original furniture from fifty-five years ago. From the looks and smell of it, the last time any of it was moved was about fifty-five years ago.

She instructs me to follow her into the house. I haven't been paid. I follow her.

"I'll just be a minute," she says. "Is that okay?"

"That's fine." Not.

There's dark blue short-pile commercial carpet in the hallway. She holds her arm out along the wall as she methodically slides along a narrow hallway to a darkened bedroom.

Then I hear the husband (I presume) talking (now loudly) on the phone. He is comfortably seated at the (comparably modern) kitchen table (a speckled early 1960s Formica model). He completely ignored the commotion of the ritual to get the wife into the house. He is still ignoring it. He wouldn't answer the door, has not acknowledged his wife's presence or her bedroom pilgrimage.

This could be an exception to My Cab Policy—I wouldn't mind carrying the husband to the cab, throwing him in the trunk and testing out the shocks on a pothole-challenged road.

The wife returns with cash; his back turned to us, the husband is still yapping away on the phone. I thank the wife and interrupt the husband.

"And thank YOU, sir."

He finally turns and offers a lost, puzzled look. I quickly exit, anxious to breathe fresh air. Once back in the cab, I am sorry to see that the zone I booked into had a fare waiting, but I was booked off and lost it for not responding.

Some people are sick, some people pretend to be sick; some people are sick and pretend not to be. I've picked up quite a few people suffering with AIDS. These folks are usually quite open about their condition and maintain a surprisingly pleasant and even positive attitude toward life despite suffering various and terrible afflictions, muscle problems, even broken and crumbling bones. They're always generous tippers. They tell stories about their own illnesses, and the deaths of friends and loved ones. Sometimes, they're returning from a visit, sometimes from a funeral or a memorial.

Slowly ascending the hill on Castro Street headed towards Twentieth, one man begins telling me that he has just returned from Minnesota—a rare family visit.

"I'm really glad to be back here," he tells me, "back to my home. It was sad, sometimes. And being out of town can get kind-a tough."

I agree.

"I'm from Detroit," I tell him. "How was Minnesota?"

"Well," he hesitates. "I got to see my sister. That was nice. The weather wasn't too bad. My parents wouldn't use any of the silverware I touched." He clears his throat and touches his forehead. "That was hard. I don't think I'll be going back there again."

PSYCHOS, PSYCHICS
AND SUNDAY DRIVERS

Dealing with the habits of drivers "sharing the road" for a ten-hour shift and trying to remain calm while I do so, truly challenges my patience. For some reason, it's been a day of pesky pedestrians jaywalking against red lights and stunned tourists (driving unfamiliar roads with those puzzling traffic signals that alternate between shades of yellow, red and bewildering green). Then there are the folks on foot either aimlessly or purposely impeding traffic flow by loitering in the middle of the street. They would seem relatively easy targets to hit, but this does not appear a serious deterrent for them.

Once again, a woman is up ahead dawdling in the midst of two lanes of opposing traffic. She is possibly a Haight-Ashbury 1960s drug casualty, perhaps schizophrenic. As I approach she holds out her hand. Now, she's waving her arms and moving her shoulders in a rather nonconformist fashion. I realize she's actually signaling for me to stop, I think. Usually this is done from the curb rather than from between lanes of traffic. Nothing wrong with that, except that if a driver thinks you're practicing *Tai Chi* in the middle of the road rather than flagging for a cab, you might have trouble scoring a ride. There also seems to be some additional commotion up ahead.

I beckon her closer to the vehicle. She's not bleeding from the head. This is good. She's maybe twenty-four years of age, has a kind of hippie Haight Street musty second-hand store fashion style going for her. She's wearing several layers of clothing: a coat, a thin sweater, a paisley vest, a white shirt, red scarves, bracelets, earrings, orange beads and some other stuff—hanging and dangling, carrying a large baggy green and brown purse. It goes well with her long, straight, blond-highlighted hair. It's early in my shift, about 4:43 in the afternoon. Maybe she's been drinking.

"I'm not going far," she says. "Is that all right?"

"Of course. No problem." I get out, opening the door for her.

There's also a De Soto cab stopped in the middle of the street, driver's side door swung wide open. The animated operator of the vehicle is screaming at a man, who sits double-parked in a maroon two-door sedan, blocking traffic. Though he has obviously not completed his homage to this late afternoon traffic impeder, the unshaven De Soto driver suddenly turns and faces me. He has a strong resemblance to the crazy guy from outside the Noe Valley restaurant; the one who hung off the side of my cab, face pressed against the window scaring my passengers. (Okay, I found him a little scary also.) He points at me, then turns his attention once again to the illegal double-parker.

"This is a BUSINESS district, damn it. YOU are blocking traffic. You are BLOCKING traffic. You are BLOCKING TRAFFIC. How did YOU ever get a driver's license? How DID you ever get a driver's license?"

Yes, it's him. He seems a little taller than I remember, but his linguistic style gives him away. It appears that neither comb nor shampoo has breached his scraggly hair's security system since our last encounter, and this definitely increases my motivation to steering well clear of him. Who knows what pesky vermin might jump from his body onto my own? Adding several obscenities to his diatribe and a little dance while waving both hands in the air, crazy De Soto smacks his palms together with a loud crack, comments on the opposing driver's family lineage, stomps the pavement with his foot, then returns to his own cab where a passenger in the back seat patiently awaits his return. Before he positions himself in the driver's seat, he turns once again to face my cab and my lady passenger-to-be.

"Gotta keep these folks in line, you know." He calmly smiles at me, winks at the lady, apologizes to his passenger for the delay, and drives off.

She gets in and I turn on the meter.

"He seemed odd," she says and directs me to her nearby destination.

"Yes, a bit odd."

"Sorry for the short ride," she apologizes. "One driver wouldn't take me because he said I wasn't going far enough to make it worth his while."

"Well, that's illegal unless he thinks you're dangerous—that is, unless he suspects you have intentions of going places you shouldn't." That did not come out right. I attempt to correct my imprecise little witticism. "Ya know, if you're going to ride the cab driver illegally." WHAT? I turn to her. "I mean, intentions for the cab driver, that you say you want him to go somewhere, but you have criminal, um." I already said intentions, but can't think of another word. "Criminal intentions." I have myself tongue tied, but she politely nods as if she has understood exactly and that I have not thrown out some kind of weird sexual innuendo. What she probably understands is that I'm the schizophrenic.

"The driver kicked me out of the cab. I was so pissed."

She has a nice smile. I'm surprised someone would refuse her a ride. Attractive, articulate, non-threatening; she seems fine to me. Too bad she's probably thinking I can't put a sentence together, or perhaps simply that I'm just another run of the mill sexual predator. "You should have reported him."

"It didn't occur to me," she says. "I'll know the next time. Is it busy today?"

"Not really, but typical for Sunday. Only nine hours and fifteen minutes to go." I'm not complaining, just making conversation. But again that phrase, the precursor to a robbery that raises my attention level no matter who is asking. She doesn't seem the robber type.

The computer makes a five-second-long sustained beep. It reads: *ANYONE SEEING CAB #294 - TELL HIM TO RETURN TO THE GARAGE—THAT DOESN'T MEAN THE AIRPORT GARAGE.*

A guy with a shopping cart full of bottles, trash, clothes and wood comes dashing across the street in front of us. He hits uneven pavement, the cart tips over, and his belongings spill onto the road. I slam on the brakes to avoid hitting him and two of his bulging green plastic bags—mandatory items for all shopping-cart people.

"That's pathetic," I comment. "Sometimes I think these people are trying to get hit on purpose." I have a recurring fear of accidentally slamming into a jaywalking shopping-cart person, getting sued in court and having to support him for the rest of his life and mine.

"The cab company has insurance doesn't it?" she asks.

"Yeah, some company in the Bahamas."

"Sounds sleazy...."

"This state auditor guy told me there's some big lawsuit going on."

"Do many drivers have accidents?"

"The insurance adjustor has an office *inside* the cab company's building." That's efficiency. "So I guess the answer would be yes. You make an accident report and then go downstairs to get your cab and start your next shift."

"I saw two cabs crash into each other a few months ago," she tells.

Poetic justice? We both watch as the street person gathers his belongings and carefully places them back into the cart. I slowly maneuver around him.

"These cart people have no regard for other traffic."

"They have nothing to lose," she says, sounding very serious.

Somewhat cynical for a young hipster; or am I the one who started it? I don't know.

"A truck driver told me about being stopped at a red light," I tell her. "His truck is so big pedestrians disappear from his view when they cross in front. So two guys are crossing the street while he waits for the light to turn green, but he notices only one guy has crossed out to the other side. He gets out of the truck and the second guy is lying down in the street, under the axle of his truck—to stage a scam accident."

"What people will do for money."

"How's the guy gonna collect insurance after a ten-ton truck flattens him?"

"You never know what's in a person's mind." She continues to direct me to her destination to a section of town with which I'm not very familiar. A few blocks down, another person commandeering a shiny new cart almost runs down two people walking on the sidewalk.

"They should issue driver's licenses for these carts. It must be impossible to maneuver with all that stuff in it."

"I can't get one to steer in a grocery store," she says.

I like this woman. I turn on the headlights. Maybe the street people are hogging the new carts and return them only after damaging the wheels. We shoppers end up with these secondhand carts no longer capable of traveling a straight line in the food aisles, no wonder, with hundreds of city miles on 'em. I'm outraged.

Meanwhile the guy with the cart has recovered and is almost across the intersection when a car making a right turn on a red light nearly runs him over. He doesn't flinch. It's dog-eat-dog out there—or maybe car-eat-cart-eat-pedestrian.

The computer interrupts with a buzz: *LAST CHANCE FOR #294! I WANT TO KNOW WHERE THE F HE IS!?!*

"So how's your day been?" I ask my passenger.

"Okay." She adjusts one of her scarves. "How about yours?"

"Fine, except for people driving exceptionally badly and it isn't even dark yet."

"Is it true about Sunday drivers?" she asks. "People out joy-riding?"

"Not that I ever see," I kid.

"I thought people do weird things on Sundays," she says.

There's a short silence. I glance back at her. She's fiddling with something in her coat pocket.

"I wish the weird were limited to Sundays."

"They're always bad, huh?"

The computer beeps again: *FIRE EQUIPMENT @ UNION STREET BETWEEN LARKIN AND HYDE—AVOID.*

We're traveling at the speed limit as the light ahead turns green. There's a dull colored Toyota in front of us and it begins to slow.

"Maybe they should give actual driving tests more than once in a lifetime," I suggest. "Not only when you turn sixteen." I doubt my passenger has much to do with it.

I can't help noticing the water swishing back and forth inside both of the Toyota's rear taillights. I'm personally very familiar with the feature. The Toyota's rear brake lights brighten and the car comes to a dead stop. The light is still green. Perhaps the driver has forgotten which pedal is for the gas? Foot pedals can be very confusing, especially if there are three.

"Why have they stopped?" she asks. "Blast 'em."

Maybe she's from New York.

But wait. In less than twenty-five seconds the light is going to turn from green to red. Perhaps the driver of the Toyota is a psychic—

having trouble discerning the future from the present. This theory would also explain the habits of many other (psychic) drivers in the city. Rather than Dr. Phil or Oprah, this might be more fitting of Maury Povich:

PSYCHIC DRIVERS: ARE THEY REALLY PSYCHIC? OR ARE THEY JUST… BAD DRIVERS?

…find out next week.

And why do you need to make appointments with psychics? Shouldn't they know you're coming to see them?

I'd like to get my passenger to her destination before the Monday morning rush. I blast the Toyota with my horn. It immediately moves.

"Turn right at that street before the light," she directs.

We're heading through the outskirts of an industrial area that is no longer used for industry; really, it's no longer used for much of anything. It's an area of town I consciously avoid. Just last week a woman was convicted of slashing the throat of a cab driver. She needed five dollars to buy crack. The incident took place somewhere on this same street my passenger is now asking to travel.

We travel it anyway. Then she directs us to a street I've never heard of—and it worries me. I've lived in the city off and on for twenty years. I don't like where we're going.

"Do you need a special license and stuff to drive a cab?"

"No. The police department and the cab company give you separate tests."

"Do they ask where different streets are?"

"Yeah. How would you get from Geary to Lombard Street?"

"You have to know the city pretty good, huh?"

"It's not exactly a grueling test. I think it's more for English comprehension, frankly. Of course, no one would ever say that publicly."

"I hate driving in the city. That's why I take cabs."

"I don't like driving either." We have that in common.

"Turn left here," she says.

It didn't look like one could make a left turn. I didn't know this area even existed.

"Make a left at the pole."

"Here?"

"Right," she says. "I mean, yes, a left."

It's an old dusty road through a deserted area. I think it's a road. There are scraps of steel strewn about and old tires lying around. It feels like we're miles from any residential area. I can't believe anyone would ever drive through here. At least it's not my car. We're kicking up a huge swirling trail of dust—prime FLAT TIRE country. I hate changing tires and there are no phones in sight for calling a tow truck. I think I left Bob's phone in my sock drawer, this time. It wouldn't seem out of place for some homicidal maniac to come running out from behind one of these aluminum shacks we're passing. My passenger seems a very nice person, not someone who would hang out with a bunch of psychos. But hey, the psychos couldn't do psycho stuff if people could tell right off they're psycho. They need to appear normal, right? What do I know? I know I don't like where we're going.

It's getting darker and I drive right into a giant pothole. The car takes an unexpected dip and hits hard with a loud, painfully unpleasant bang, bouncing us around. I'm going four miles per hour. I can't go much slower. And she can't be going much farther, I think. She has me make another turn. We're nowhere. To the right are three big black oil drums about four feet high. Just to the left are some piles of rusted car parts, a large engine block, a car door, three tires and part of a back seat. There's a pile of grayish-brown, rotted two-by-fours lying next to an abandoned shell of a stripped Volkswagen van, its axle broken in half. It probably got that way from driving through here. It's a junkyard obstacle course.

For any other person, I wouldn't have driven any farther, thinking I was being taken out to be killed and, no doubt, dumped into one of these empty steel drums (or into a steel drum that contained other dead bodies). No one would ever know. It's five o'clock in the afternoon, yet I'm becoming a bit scared. I can't figure out what the hell she would be doing over here. Visiting her boyfriend? If so, she should get a new boyfriend.

"Stop here," she says without warning.

It's a deserted-looking rusty metal corrugated building surrounded by other vacant buildings. It's a step below an abandoned railroad yard. There are no tracks. This place is too far out of the way even for a railroad.

There is no one around. She's wearing loose clothing. My hand develops a sudden nervous twitch.

"This is IT," she says.

Turning my head to face her, I have a bad premonition involving a gun.

Her hand reaches wrist-deep into her purse. In a flash, our small talk and conversation no longer seem so innocent. "...the cab driver kicked me out...I was pissed. Busy today? Some people have nothing to lose. What people will do for money. Know the city pretty good, huh?"

I quickly hit four buttons on the computer: *destination— six—eight—send*, to show my general position.

The computer beeps back at me: *PRESS SEND.*

I press the "send" button. I'm not getting anything. Dispatch is not picking up my radio signal. Pressing the *"send"* button again, I turn to watch her hand. The computer beeps registering my position. I turn to check it. It reads: *TEMPORARY ZONE.*

I hit the *code* button, then the *zero* button, and the *five*. The police emergency code. Pressing the *"send"* button again will signal dispatch for immediate police assistance. Immediately to where? We do **not** have GPS.

"Seven dollars forty cents," I announce to her.

She looks me in the eye, then down into her purse, then over to the metal building on the left, like she's expecting someone, or some thing. She shifts toward me, pushing her hand deeper into the large baggy purse, seemingly using her other hand to support the bag from underneath. The muscles in her arm tighten. She pulls out a black object.

It's her wallet.

She hands me a twenty-dollar bill.

"Keep two dollars for yourself."

My heart is racing. I'm not sure I really need the adrenalin that this job has to offer.

"Thanks," I mutter because my throat has completely dried up. She takes her change.

What is she doing over here anyway? I won't embarrass her by asking. And I don't want to embarrass myself by divulging the chain of events on my emotional roller coaster over here in the driver's seat. The police emergency code is still up on the computer poised and ready for action. I hit the *clear* button and turn off the meter.

Maybe I should move back to Detroit and start my own business—get some funding to manufacture a new type of automobile with the steering wheel in the back seat. The passengers would sit in the front where the driver can keep an eye on them. We'd have a built-in security scanner—keep the guns, the knives and the screwdrivers at bay. I'd market them to cab companies.

I get out in time to open the door for her as she fumbles with the oversized shoulder bag. She gets out, gently sways across the dusty road and quickly disappears through a surprisingly silent doorway in a metal building. There's no sound—no sign of life anywhere.

I want to get the hell out of here. Fast is not an option. Hoping I remember all the turns, I slowly maneuver my way back through the potholes, the dust, and the mangled steel.

YOU'RE NOT IN KANSAS ANYMORE

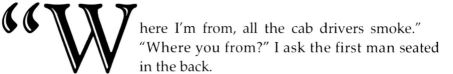

"here I'm from, all the cab drivers smoke."
"Where you from?" I ask the first man seated in the back.
"Kansas City."
"You're not in Kansas anymore." I start the meter.
"I'm sick of hearin' that shit. It's not funny."
"Ohhh please," sighs the man seated next to the first. "Then stop tellin' people you're from Kansas City, bitch."
"Your momma."
"Better from where your momma's from."
"Fuck you, honey, I got a boner."
"You can take care of your own boner tonight."
"No, we gonna do it tonight."
"Do it to yourself."
The smell of sulfur fills the air.
"Put that cigarette out. He told you not to smoke."
"No cigarette and a big boner. That's what I got."
"Ohhhh, shut-uh-uppp."
"Kansas City here I come."

CHIN-UPS,
CHIN MUSIC
AND CHINASKI

Slightly wavering at the curb, motioning me to roll down the window, he's dressed in a forlorn-looking jacket and a flannel shirt. It's hard to tell from just the dim light on the street, but he either has a complexion problem, or someone punched him in the face. Maybe both.

"The name is Chinaski," he explains. Receiving a formal introduction like this, as a precursor to a ride, is a first for me. "Here's five dollars," he says, as he waves Abe Lincoln in the air. "Would you just take me down the block? Frankly, I may have had a little too much to drink."

He then takes half a jab at me with Abe, still flagging with his other arm. "I can usually make it home, but tonight? Shit." He looks wasted but, at the same time, managing in his own way. He's being extremely polite.

I let him in. He hands me the five and mounts the front seat; he rubs his jawbone with three fingers, pulls at the gray whiskers of his goatee and hoarsely clears his throat. I don't want him puking in the front. Of course, I wouldn't want him puking in the back either. Telling him that he must sit in the back, that passengers are not allowed in the front seat,

Chinaski

would take longer and require more effort than the entire ride is going to last. Forget it. I quickly and very smoothly deliver him down the block. It takes 25 seconds.

"There ya go, sir," I pronounce, in case he doesn't realize we've already arrived at his destination. The odds that favor his stomach contents rising are themselves rising exponentially. "You're a nice young man," he says, as his eyes squint and his face appears to stiffen. His arms appear oddly muscular, almost misshapen—maybe from pushups or just the family gene pool. We're at a dead stop but, nevertheless, his body jerks slightly forward and his mouth gapes open. From where he's sitting, there's no way I would be able to completely avoid projectile vomit. Again, he juts his jaw forward. His bottom teeth could well benefit from a dentist's attention, although it might be too little too late for even the most talented technician.

"That monstrosity of a building," he condemns. It's not simply an architectural appraisal; it's the address he requested.

"Yes sir, I know. We have arrived at your destination."

His head wobbles as he turns to face me and his eyes lock onto mine. Somehow, he doesn't blink. The alcohol on his breath would cause a horse to stagger. "YOU should get out. Get OUT! Get OUTTA this business, 'fore you get hurt."

It's almost as though he is personally threatening me. I don't think that's the intention obviously. He stares at me again. I check the computer and hit a button.

"You're a nice young man and thank you for the ride," he recites calmly. "Have a good evening. Have a wonderful evening." Now, he's even sounding a little sarcastic. I figure it's the drink in him.

He pushes himself from the front seat. Once outside he positions himself just so at the side of the cab and, with a dramatic Juan Marichal wind-up, slams the door shut. He nearly tips over in the process, falters to his left, and regains his balance only to then slightly tip to the right. He manages to stand upright, strides as best he's able to the side of the white building, and pukes on the sidewalk. He reaches into his coat pocket, pulls out a bottle of whiskey with about an inch of liquid left, pulls out a wad of tissues, wipes his mouth, takes a long swig of the drink and disappears into the building. I lock the doors, pocket the five dollars and hit the gas.

His warning lands in a place of discomfort, both with my superstitious side and my gut. I don't like hearing premonitions from people that ring true. It's another hour until I need to turn in the cab. But I'm tired, business is slow and now I'm spooked. The bars have closed early and the night is quiet, other than the sound of a bus engine chugging up a nearby hill.

It was just an old drunk man talking gibberish. But maybe he felt something in this chilly night air. I take one lap around the Castro and then decide to call it a night.

Traveling down Duboce underneath the freeway, two men walking along spot my approach. One nudges the other, prompting both to flag and whistle for me to stop. The concrete amplifies their whistles. I don't like their location; I don't like their whistling; don't like the numb feeling on both sides of my head. I check that the doors are locked. I slow the cab, thinking I shouldn't turn down the fare. Superstition and paranoia don't pay the rent. I gently hit the brakes. Our eyes meet. My gut says don't stop. I don't like their looks. I imagine myself safe at home in my apartment with its quiet view of the city's lights, shoes off, bowl of cereal in hand. I imagine them stuffing a body into one of those old rusty oil drums on my not-so-psycho hippie girl's dusty deserted street.

"Hey, hey, yellow!" I hear them shouting. I lift my foot from the brake pedal and I hear the old man's voice, like he's still sitting next to me: "GET OUT!" I gently touch the accelerator.

The two men continue to shout as pass I them. And I just keep drivin'.

BEHIND ENEMY LINES

NEWS ITEM: *"Earlier today, police were summoned to Dolores Park, where a man was stabbing himself with a knife…one officer shot him in the chest. Doctors pronounced the man dead on arrival at San Francisco General Hospital."*

I usually keep the radio off when I have passengers in the cab. I'll turn it on at their request. This particular afternoon I have turned on the radio and it's one weird news item after another—like they save them up for Friday or something.

A young kid babysitting his even younger brother stuffs him into the microwave in an attempt to cook him—or maybe just dry him off really well. I switch to an AM talk-radio station.

"Robert in San Jose," says the moderator with enthusiasm.

"You're on the air. Hello, Robert? Looks like we've lost Robert. Let's go to line two. Rick in Contra Costa, you're ON the air."

"Yeah, I just want to say that the Raiders are a bunch of cocksuckers and when the front office can't…."

The show host cuts off the caller immediately, but not immediately enough. There are still a few words that I've never heard on the radio. This word is one of them. I thought these shows were on seven-second delays?

Of course, an elderly passenger is seated in the back of my cab. There *is* the possibility that she didn't hear it.

"What *are* you listening to?" she asks.

So much for Plan A. My stomach sinks. She's not elderly enough that she doesn't hear cuss words coming over car speakers in *surround-sound-stereo.*

"It's KGO," I tell her, figuring this will also absolve me of any fault in the matter. It doesn't get any more mainstream than KGO.

She says she listens to that station all the time. Good.

"It can't be," she insists. "That's not KGO!" She's convinced it's one of those vulgar FM stations.

"It's the AM radio," I insist, attempting to save face.

"I don't think so." She knows what she heard. Her station does not broadcast filth.

My Cab Policy: do not argue with passengers over 80 years old.

I gradually fade down the volume and turn the radio off, thinking I'll keep it that way for the rest of the evening.

Up ahead, a bicyclist travels towards us. As we pass, he turns his head toward the cab and SPITS. My window is down. It's a direct hit on the left lens of my eyeglasses—one advantage of NOT wearing contact lenses on the job. I don't think my passenger noticed what happened. I'm embarrassed and I'm pissed. The guy on the bike is way down the road already. It's not like I can turn and go after him. I'm already on thin ice with my passenger after the radio incident. Under the circumstances, I don't think she would appreciate my turning the cab in the opposite direction and running down the bicyclist. Even if she didn't notice my turning the cab around and traveling in the opposite direction, there's no way she wouldn't hear this guy on his bicycle violently banging his way underneath the axle of the car.

"Oh my, what's that terrible noise? You ran over that nice young man on the bicycle."

"I didn't hear anything."

I wipe the spit from my glasses; a completely unprovoked attack. Perhaps it's just one of those days. Full moon, maybe? Not to worry, I've only got eight-and-a-half hours left on my shift.

I drop the woman off in North Beach. Immediately I'm flagged by a man and woman, Midwest tourists, fresh from Fisherman's Wharf. Two bags of sweatshirts and souvenir clothing pile into the back seat. The husband and wife team follow close behind, smelling strongly of garlic.

"You look like the last driver we had," says the woman.

"It wasn't me."

"Your hair looks so much like the other driver's." She turns to her husband. "David, doesn't he look like that other driver we had?"

I'll do the husband a favor and resolve the issue.

"We're all issued hair when we leave the yard," I inform her.

We proceed through a green light as a pedestrian suddenly runs across the street jaywalking in front of the cab. I stop to keep from hitting him.

"Some of these people are amazing," says the awe-struck Midwesterner hubby. "Have you ever hit anyone?"

"Not by accident."

"The pedestrians here are very aggressive."

"There should be one day a year when it's legal to run them over if they're jaywalking like that," I comment.

"Bit of an unfair advantage, car versus pedestrian," reasons the husband in his deep Chicago (I'm sure of it) drawl.

"True," I agree. "They could publicize the thing, give people some warning—if they go darting through traffic against a red light, it's at their own risk."

There is no response. I assume they view this idea with skepticism. A white limousine passes in the opposite direction, followed by another one, a black stretch.

"There are a lot of limos in this town," comments the woman.

"The Canadian Navy is here this week."

I feel like I'm on this woman's case. I'm not. It's a joke. They don't laugh. Maybe they have close relatives in Canada. At least I restrained myself from confessing my true desire to run down tourists loitering in crosswalks and on sidewalks. They probably wouldn't think that's funny either.

"Oh, how nice. Is that good for business? The Canadian Navy?"

Now what do I say?

"Very good for business," I finally react, after an awkward pause. The husband whispers into her ear. Probably telling her it's a joke. Great. Now there's no question that I am making fun of his wife. Maybe I do have it in for them. It's those Chicago accents. Why don't they just carry along a little chalkboard so they can scratch their nails on it and save themselves the trouble of talking? The thought of my once similar Detroit accent bothers me even more. No more wisecracks.

I drop them at a posh downtown hotel. They leave a twenty percent tip. I guess I didn't offend them after all—or maybe he doesn't like his wife either.

Continuing down Geary, I unhappily swerve around another group of tourists loitering in a crosswalk, slamming on my brakes to stop for two women and a young man waving their arms above their heads. The cab tailgating me honks his horn—like he has never blocked traffic to pick up a fare.

MY CAB POLICY: do not give De Soto Cab Company drivers the finger while potential customers are in the immediate vicinity.

The two women duck their heads and hurry into the back seat while their male travel companion takes his time getting in, then slams the door shut. The cab behind us blasts us once again.

"Shut up and quit honking," he yells out the window.

"Yeah," I agree. This guy's not so bad. I also double-check to make sure it's not the crazy wild man Yoda mutant from the Noe Valley restaurant and all. It's not.

These three are locals, probably in their mid-20s, not quite old enough to have completely lost that fraternity-sorority scent. Among the three of them they have two different destinations. The guy is eating pretzels.

"We're making two stops," says the better-looking woman.

What I'd really like to know is how she gets her hair to look so perfect.

"Sacramento and Octavia," she says. "We're dropping you first, right?"

"Yeah," says the guy.

"Steve," asks the second woman, "so, how is your new roommate?"

"Anal," answers nasal Steve. "He's so anal."

Steve sounds like he just learned the word a few nights ago.

"He cleans the bottom of his shoes," Steve continues. "He has the Felix Unger medicine cabinet stockpile—four shelves of medicine. I come home; all the messages are from Walgreen's pharmacy." Steve changes his voice to an even higher-pitched whine, "Your prescription is ready to be picked up."

"I thought you liked him."

"He's a nerd."

"Didn't you go to Mike's party last night?"

"Yeah, it wasn't that great; mostly a bunch of randoms," says Steve. "After midnight, Mike didn't even know anyone there."

Steve offers me a pretzel.

"No thanks. Too much salt. Then I have to get a drink; then I've got to find some place to…." I pause. Should I say "pee?" Could that be offensive? They're so stiff looking. "Some place to stop," I restrain myself. "It's one thing after another." I finish.

"Too much for you to handle, huh?" says sarcastic Steve.

Yeah, my digestive tract can't handle such sophisticated food, Steve. He's getting out in a minute. I'll let it slide. "Yeah, I can't handle it," I blandly agree. Don't be *messin'* with *me*, Steve.

"How can you eat those?" asks the second woman. "They're junk."

"It's all protein," he argues.

"They are not. They're all carbohydrates."

"Don't be ridiculous. It's a protein," he counters with a trace of doubt.

"What I've heard," I interrupt, "is that it's a separate food group altogether…."

The two women laugh. Steve doesn't think it's funny. I don't care what he thinks. Steve's getting out first. The women are going to be the last ones out—they will determine the tip.

"I know my food," says Steve. "These are MAJOR protein."

We drop "Protein Pretzel Man" off at his apartment.

"My mother has been after me about him," the second woman tells her friend. "She thinks he's dumb. That I'm wasting my time with him."

"Hmmm," says her friend.

"Driver," she asks me, "what do you think?"

"Sometimes, even mothers can be right."

I drop them both off in Twin Peaks. I'm a couple of blocks from my apartment, so I drive home to grab a quick bite to eat, clean my glasses of any remnants of spit and pick up Bob's cell phone which I have left behind, this time on the kitchen table. Meanwhile, I dial the girlfriend.

"Hey, it's me."

"Aren't you working?"

"Yeah, I had a drop-off down the street, so I stopped to get a bowl of cereal."

"There was another cab driver who got hijacked in San Leandro. Did you hear about that?"

"No. I quit listening to the news. It's been pretty constant rides."

"That stuff freaks me out. They barely give any details, I'm just thinking, would he be in San Leandro? I don't think so. What company is it? Who is the driver?"

"I think San Leandro is a lot more dangerous than San Francisco," I offer.

"And I don't think you've had a good night's sleep in three months."

"I know, I know. I gotta go though. It's been real busy. But I'll call you a little later."

We hang up.

I make another call—this time on the cell phone, to check messages. Bob called exactly one hour ago. "I'm still laid up, but I've got a bunch of stuff you can really help me out with," he excitedly explains. "You're my driver. You're my number one guy."

That's great. I disconnect the message center and wind my way down the stairs to the street below, cell phone in one hand, munching Cheerios with the other. A fare is up from Laguna Honda Hospital. My current policy is to reject calls from hospitals unless I'm essentially already on hospital property or if I'm at Potrero and Twenty-Third Street for example (that's less than 100 yards from the Emergency Room at San Francisco General). Wasting twenty minutes of a shift looking for invisible folks can make a notable difference in the night's profits. Laguna Honda is less than two minutes down the road—Portola to Woodside Avenue. Two days ago I had a Laguna Honda Hospital call that was a no-show. I'll give it one more try.

The exact time of a call is only disclosed to a driver when a customer calls for the second time. The second request for this cab was twenty minutes ago. That means the original request was probably phoned in forty minutes ago. That's good because they went to the trouble of calling a second time—they still want the cab; and that's bad because they're probably calling another company as well for backup. Whatever cab shows up first gets the fare.

Maybe these folks are old or crippled. Either way, they are going to be upset for having to wait so long (I would be) and the reward for the driver who risks showing up for this stale order will be a good piece of their mind and no tip.

Accepting the call, I jab the accelerator cursing all the people remotely connected to wasting my time with this phantom order (including myself). In a record eighty-five seconds, I speed into the deserted hospital parking lot, and circle the area. Nobody. What a surprise. I radio a *no show* and park. I could go in and search the place. Taking that first step through the doors of the hospital entrance marks the beginning of a pointless exhausting hunt through a frustrating maze.

I slowly get out of the cab, mentally preparing for the ordeal ahead when a guy on crutches hobbles out from the hospital entrance. There are two brown paper bags and two small boxes of belongings next to the door, along with a shiny pair of boots. I'm impressed. For whatever reason, he's still there—if this is the same person who has been calling.

"Did you want a cab?"

"Yeah, I've been waiting an hour-and-a-half."

This guy is my hero. Not only that, he's going across town—a good fare despite the boxes, the bags and the crutches.

"I'm sorry about having all of this stuff."

"Not a problem," I tell him.

He's about twenty-five years old, thin and frail. I quickly load his things into the cab. He can't carry anything heavy. I help him into the back seat and we're off.

"The doctors have been cutting out the muscle tissue in my legs," he tells me. "They were going to amputate, but instead they've been removing little sections, piece by piece."

I'm glad that I'm sitting down. "It sounds awful," I cringe.

"The doctors thought I wouldn't make it. I was in fuckin' bad shape, man."

I didn't ask him how his day was going; perhaps word is out regarding my **DO NOT ASK** policy and passengers have developed their own counter meausures to circumvent my procedures. I might as well finish off the conversation.

"What is it that you have?"

"Some rare disease, I can't even pronounce it. It's amazing how fast your body can deteriorate. One day completely healthy, next day I'm connected to tubes. I've lived in San Francisco four months, in a hospital bed for three of 'em. Be glad you're not in a hospital."

"Believe me; I appreciate the ailments I *don't* have."

I pull out of the winding road leading from the hospital to Laguna Honda Boulevard and Woodside Avenue. Traffic is heavy. We make a left on Woodside, uphill, to where Clipper meets Portola Avenue.

"I'm glad to be out of there alive. They told me I'm one out of a hundred. Ever been on morphine?" he asks.

"No, not really. Demerol a few times, but that's about it for hospitals."

"Shit. They kept bringing this priest to my room while I'm in this, this umm, drugged out HAZE. Whenever I had pain, I hit a button and the nurses were right there givin' me shots of morphine. Man, no questions asked. They were great."

The nurses, the hospital, the morphine shots?

"Eight hundred seventy five dollars for the morphine, I saw the bill."

Sounds almost cheap considering the price of an aspirin. I only respond with a "Hmmph."

"And that priest always askin', 'Do you know what month it is? You know what day it is?' Shit, I never knew. I thought it was January in April, I thought it was Saturday on a Monday."

"I'm not sure what difference that makes."

"Yeah," he agrees. "And I wasn't askin' for no priest either."

"Well, I guess that's a bad sign, huh?"

"The nurse comin' in and out of my room with tables full of needles; that morphine fog would lift and there's the priest at the side of my bed. He'd say the same thing whenever he'd leave: 'You're doing well, my son. See you tomorrow.'"

A government agency is paying for his new residence. "It's a kind of halfway house," he describes. "They gave me the choice of a couple of different places, but one sounded same as the next."

The computer buzzes.

"What's that?"

"It's the computer. We use it instead of the radio although there's a radio too. There's another APB out on a stolen cab."

"Stolen?" This seems to concern him more than I would have thought. "That happen very often?"

"Occasionally." It's an epidemic of late, five in the last three weeks. I'm losing track.

"Does it give you directions on how to get places?"

"No, only the address."

"I didn't think a cab was ever gonna show."

Maybe he thinks I was lost—that's why he waited so long. It wouldn't be tactful to tell him that no one wants to make a pain-in-the-ass hospital pickup.

"Sorry for your wait." I apologize. "I'm glad you were still there."

"Oh, I didn't mind waiting. It's the first time I've been outside. You like driving a cab?"

"It wouldn't be so bad if it weren't for all of the driving and having to pick up strangers."

Maybe he could use a touch of humor. We wade through traffic at Clipper and head downhill through Noe Valley.

"This city seems kind of dangerous," he observes. "I'm thinking of going back to Indiana."

Hearing about people returning to live in the Midwest is more depressing than hearing their accents.

"It's more like a big city than it used to be," I rationalize.

"Damn," Indiana comments. "There's a lot of those homeless people. I don't wanna end up like one of them."

"Some are homeless, some are criminals. Some are schizophrenics. Back when Reagan cut mental health funding these people got dumped into the street. It's been like this ever since."

"Do you ever have trouble with people?" he asks. "Like gettin' robbed? You ever throw anyone out?"

"The first month driving, I was throwing someone out of the cab every week."

"Really? Why?"

"One guy didn't have ENOUGH money. Another guy had NO money. One guy was asking ME for money; stuff like that; mostly people I picked up from bus stops." My average has been slowly steadily improving ever since.

As we cross the bumpy streetcar tracks at 24th and Church, the computer buzzes with another message: *ANYONE SEE CAB #294, TELL HIM HIS SHIFT IS OVER!*

"California doesn't have mosquitoes does it?"

"We get stowaways on tourists."

"Is it safe to walk around at night?"

"It depends on the area but you just never know."

"It's okay in the day, isn't it?"

"I picked up this attorney visiting from St. Thomas. He had lived in San Francisco for twenty years and he was back in town visiting his son. Some Chinese guy drives into him—shatters his kneecaps. So, he stays in town recuperating; had those metal bar polio-type crutches. A few days later, a man and woman push him down over on Market and steal his wallet."

"I'm from a small town," he says. "That just wouldn't happen there."

"Well, I thought people on crutches are like, off limits. You leave 'em alone."

"Yeah," says Indiana, "where I'm from, people kinda watch out for each other."

"That guy told me he had some kind of City Hall connections—got a permit to carry a gun and now straps a pistol to his leg. People bother him; he points to the gun and gives it a pat."

"I hope that isn't the same area where I'm staying."

"No. Where you're staying is a worse neighborhood."

"They didn't say it was a bad area. Shit!"

"I don't mean to scare you, but you might not want to walk around there at night."

"Well, I'd rather know than find out the hard way."

"There's heroin dealing, gang activity, ya know, the usual share of muggings and violence. I hear lots of stories, more than most people, probably. I see lots of stuff, driving around."

"In my hometown, if some robber attacks you, shit, cops and everyone else would be right there."

"It's turf wars over drug territory," I tell him, making a right turn onto South Van Ness. "If these drugs were legal, kids wouldn't be carrying around automatic weapons shootin' the place up." I almost add "and knocking off the occasional cab driver" but I don't.

"Legalize the drugs?" he says. "You can't just legalize 'em. There'd be all kinds of trouble."

"Well, whatever." There's already trouble, haven't you noticed?

I change the subject while picturing the last guy who was shot driving during the night shift. "I'm from Michigan, made a couple of trips to your state when I was a teenager," I disclose to Indiana.

"California's a lot different than Indiana, that's for sure."

"True." When making these trips to Indiana, I thought that I was visiting a neighboring northern state of the Union, but parts of Indiana are farther "south" than Alabama. Even though it wasn't a slave state, it must have been a borderline decision for them not to secede from the Union.

"I could live real cheap back there," Indiana recounts. "Cost of living's cheap, get a nice quiet place, heal up; fish on the lake, relax."

It's sounding pretty good to him. Doesn't sound that bad to me either, except I hate fishing.

Obviously unhappy about his crutch confinement, he has a likeable demeanor and a cheerful attitude. He seems relaxed with me. I feel for the guy with his sudden disabling health trauma and all. However, it turns out that he doesn't do much for improving the image of his esteemed home state—not with me. I guess that in an effort to solidify our newfound friendly kinship, Indiana enthusiastically embarks upon a tirade and analysis of today's urban crime:

"It's all the niggers," he confides. "It's the fuckin' niggers."

Silence. And I've got a white sheet and a wooden cross in my trunk. I'm not sure what I should say, and don't even know where to start. Maybe he didn't realize that Michigan is north of Indiana, but does it matter? Silence is not a dramatic form of disapproval. If you're not part of the solution you're part of the problem, but I'm not going to change this guy's attitude in a twenty-minute cab ride. I have supposedly given up trying to change the world.

Many years ago, my best friend's brother got in an argument regarding black people and racism. It was during the Nixon administration—Black Panthers and all. One guy made some bigoted remark and my friend's brother told the guy to apologize. The guy refused.

"I won't have that language in my house," said the brother.

"Don't tell me you're another asshole nigger-lover...."

A fistfight ensued. Correction, there was a beating. There were no black people there, just a bunch of white guys—General Motors executives, no less. The bigot ended up in the hospital with a broken jaw and his mouth wired shut; more poetic justice? The couch was history, completely soaked with his blood. Now, did that change anything? Once he could start eating solid food again he likely thought twice about making "nigger" comments, even while in the apparent safety of a group of white-collar executives. I'm certainly not saying white people go around breaking jaws every time the word comes out of someone's mouth. If they did, we'd be building many new hospitals.

After a notable silence, Indiana changes the subject back to his ailing health. We turn off South Van Ness to the Sixteenth Street "hotel" address where he will be staying.

"I see what you mean," he says. "I've never been in this area before. It looks pretty bad."

I help him out of the cab and carry one of the boxes to the building's entrance. The wooden front door is locked and there is a second locked door with steel bars in front of it. The place is a real dump, completely run down, the obligatory paint peeling off the building, except for the graffiti of course, and there's garbage on the sidewalk. A wino eyes us with bad intent and so do a couple of other folks. I'm concerned someone might try to steal this guy's stuff in the time it takes to go back to the cab's trunk and return to the doorway. It's a good ten feet.

Indiana rings the hotel's doorbell. I retrieve the remaining possessions as an attendant appears from the bowels of the building to assist. We succeed in getting his belongings to safety. Indiana hands me fifteen dollars in taxi scrip. PROBLEM: it's DE SOTO SCRIP.

I break the news to him, "This taxi scrip is for another company."

"The nurse said 'call a taxi.' I just called you guys."

"We don't accept this." I'm very not-happy; and annoyed.

"I don't have any money. The nurse, she didn't say it had to be a specific company."

I could return to the hospital and seek out the nurse's throat. This guy's hero status was long ago flushed down the toilet. What can I do? Cut the muscle tissue out of his legs, little by little? The doctors beat me to that one. If I take the scrip, how will I get rid of it? I could use it to take a De Soto cab, but I generally don't take cabs. They smell. Ever see how those guys drive? I radio dispatch.

"I've got De Soto cab scrip from a passenger, a hospital patient. Do we accept this stuff?"

"No," she says.

"I didn't think so."

"You can probably exchange it with a De Soto driver," she suggests. "But that's at your own risk."

Yeah, where's a slobbering De Soto driver when you need one?

Indiana offers no viable alternative.

"Maybe you can talk to the nurse at the hospital," he says.

I guess there's still some morphine in his system. I smell something burning. It's me—from this deal. If it's not one stupid thing, it's some other stupid thing. Always sneaks up on you too, when you least expect it, out of some innocent situation. Many people completely avoid hospitals. So what the hell is wrong with me? It doesn't matter if you're not deathly ill—you go in with a cut, you come out with a disease. Look at Andy Warhol. The guy goes in for a routine operation and comes out a dead man. He never knew what happened to him. You'd think someone might be saying, "Hey folks, it's Andy Warhol, let's take a little extra care here." No. No one is safe.

I need a new policy and the name of the nurse. "I'll try to get someone to exchange it for me," I tell my now ex-passenger.

"You should be able to do that," he says with complete assurance. I'll give him the benefit of the doubt—it's the morphine.

"Pay more attention when you're using taxi scrip, okay?"

Later that night—about seven hours later—I'm in North Beach. Business has significantly slowed down. Cabs are parked and waiting on every corner near Broadway and Columbus; several are De Soto cabs. I reluctantly drive over to one of them, get out and ask the driver if he would kindly exchange cash for his company's vouchers.

"I'm ending my shift," he says, "otherwise I would."

I try three different drivers. You'd think I was a child pornographer or something. These drivers have great answers:

"I just started working so I can't."

"Can't help ya," says another guy, "but you shouldn't have any trouble getting someone to exchange it for you. Ask that driver over there."

"I already did. Thanks."

Another guy pretends he doesn't speak English—very original. I give it up.

At the end of the night, I turn in the cab, making a valiant try to get our own cashier to take this fake money. He's been in the business for a long time. Doesn't he have any connections? No.

"You don't know any De Soto drivers?" I ask.

"You're gonna have to find one so you can exchange it."

"I've tried that."

You'd think these cab companies would have some kind of exchange system going. Haven't they heard of multinational capitalism?

"You might need to call their office," he says. "I don't see why they wouldn't exchange it."

Yeah, right. I turn to walk away.

"They don't have to if they don't feel like it," he adds.

That's a real surprise. Okay, here's the new policy: anyone coming from a hospital has to show proof of cash on hand. One supposed benefit of this job is that it's over when it's over. You never really have to spend time at home preparing for the people you will be picking up on your following shift. Sure, you double-check the pepper spray and make sure you have enough singles, but there's not much more you can do. I certainly don't want to spend my time trying to collect money I've already made. *You've just been released from the hospital? Give me your wallet and let's see some ID.*

Two days later I still have the fake money. From my Twin Peaks apartment I walk downhill, take the underground to downtown and walk from there over to the rival cab company's headquarters, past the vagrants, two hookers, then the transvestite prostitutes and finally to the main garage and headquarters just off Larkin Street.

I walk through the main entrance. The corridor narrows leading to another corridor lined with fluorescent lighting, all of it on the blink. There are a few closed doors and no windows. I accost a man dressed in dark clothing sporting a rough two-day beard on his face. He's wearing a badge on his shirt. He's a driver.

"I'm looking for the cashier."

He looks at me suspiciously. "Down-there-left-through-the-garage-over-by-the-window go straight passing the pumps right-at-the-pumps-then-go-to-the-right-take-a-left-and right-there," he says with disgust.

Well, I'm just as disgusted with his directions. Do I turn to the right at the pumps or is it straight and on the right? He said something about the garage. I should be able to find that. I amble forward with little confidence.

Another musty passageway leads to a hallway into the garage. Dozens of people are hanging around, looking me up and down. It's dark, it's dirty and it's unfamiliar. I've crossed into hostile territory while trying to look like I know where I'm going hoping nobody figures out I'm from the competition. I'm also double-checking for the short crazy bearded guy with the multiple personalities. Who knows which one is in control today? Otherwise, it seems like a good idea to keep a low profile behind enemy lines.

Sitting on a bench, I spot him. It's the crazy guy, or should I say the crazy-acting guy? On closer examination—it's not him. Then I hear one of the drivers in conversation—repeating his sentences—but that's not him either. I'm getting strange looks from folks and being watched for any suspicious behavior. They can sense my tentative demeanor and my "I'm looking for something" manner.

This guy is on our turf. Does he have clearance? Are his papers in order? Interrogate the son-of-a-bitch. Hook up the electrodes. Two men scurry past me as if their outstanding warrants are on the verge of disclosure. But, I also need to face reality. I'm lost.

I approach a guy who seems *NOT* to have a scowl on his face.

"I'm looking for the cashier."

"Who are you?"

A robber, asshole.

"I drive for Yellow. I have some scrip to exchange."

"They won't do that."

"Well I'm going to try anyway. I'm a sado-masochist."

"It's that way." He points his trigger finger through my gut.

"Thanks."

Wandering back through the dark hallway this time leads to a large office with a large glass window. About a dozen drivers are milling about. I've probably given several of them the finger, just in the last week. Approaching the window, I try not to look at anyone too directly. I state my case and my desired business to the gentleman behind the partition, handing him the scrip. He whispers to another guy. The second guy confers with a third. These people KNOW that I'm not to be trusted. A fourth guy from behind the glass motions to me.

"How did you end up with our scrip?" asks Mr. Prosecutor.

Okay. I CONFESS!! I'm counterfeiting it in my basement. What's more valuable than old Benjamin Franklin? Why, De Soto scrip, of course.

"I got it from a hospital patient."

Now, it's back to the second guy who carefully looks over the scrip. There's more shuffling around and another conference with a bald guy on perpetual coffee break leaning back in his chair and drinking a soda. This is taking way too long. I'm expecting bad news. The first guy steps back up to the window, slowly and deliberately filling out a form.

What is it already? The wrong color? Expired? Maybe I have to come back on the second Tuesday of the Leap Year? This guy is an ass. He thinks I don't know that? He's waiting for me to say something incriminating so he can run me out of there. I'm not talking without my lawyer present.

He counts out fifteen dollars and lays it on the counter. He wants me to grab it so he can cuff me when I stick my wrist out. He abruptly picks the money back up and rearranges it. He slowly counts it again. I let the bills sit. I don't want to seem too anxious.

"We don't normally do this," he says.

Fuck you, too.

I thank him and smile. He suspects I might not be completely sincere. He squints at me with disdain.

I carefully make my way from the office, back through the garage, down the dark passageway—and out to freedom.

PILOT TO COPILOT
The Co-Driver:
"May I see your financial statement, please?"

The cab driver needs to know and verify whether a customer has the five or ten dollars required to pay the fare (either in American dollars or the correct company's taxi-scrip). The implementation of a "co-driver" would be useful and fruitful. This person would ride "shotgun" for the official cab driver. Passengers would be required to check all firearms, weapons and large metal objects with the co-driver (not including those lodged in the passengers' faces). The co-driver would also be responsible for reviewing submitted financial information to determine ability to pay and assist in providing services other than the actual transportation of the passenger. The co-driver would assist with language translation, personal and crisis counseling and suggest destination alternatives to the Hard Rock Cafe.

It would be the duty of the co-driver to explain to all French, English and German tourists the concept and computation of *tipping*. (Oh yeah, let's include the squeamish and the Finnish also.) To hold down costs, these co-drivers could be recruited from University work/study programs or other vocational services. All psychology majors would be required to spend 120 hours as a taxicab co-driver.

FRIENDS LIKE THAT

A call with an unusual address comes up on the computer, an even eighteen hundred located in the Sunset on an Avenue. I was looking for some giant apartment building, a store or hotel or small business, but it turns out to be a residence resembling a miniature Southern mansion with ornate pillars out front, curtains on each of the tall windows facing the street and a small balcony jutting out from the second floor. A bright porch light illuminates the black metal numbers next to the front door.

I pull up into the driveway, park, get out and follow a narrow dirt path to the porch. I ring the doorbell and wait as I scan the property grounds. I knock.

"Coming."

Good. Walking back to the cab I can hear voices from inside the home. I look behind me. A burly, broad-shouldered, unshaven man with a paunch and a rounded face has emerged from the house. He looks to be in his late forties, maybe fifties. He is wearing tight black leather pants and a black leather motorcycle jacket with lots of zippers. I expect the jacket to read HELLS ANGELS. It doesn't. I'm glad. Do Hells Angels wear pink shirts with little orange flowers? I think they wear whatever they feel like. His pink and orange is partly tucked into his pants, partly hanging out the front of his black jacket. As he approaches the cab, he struggles to zip a compartment on the upper left front of the jacket. Zippers are cool. I once bought a pair of hundred-dollar sneakers because they had zippers. He's transporting a half-empty beer bottle in one hand and a six-pack in the other.

"You don't mind me suckin' a beer while you drive, do ya?" he says with a mechanical delivery, attempting to disguise his far from sober condition and not doing a very good job of it.

"No problem." I open the door for him. I notice he has a slight overbite.

"I've had a *bit* to drink," he slurs, stinking of alcohol.

"So have I," I tell him. If he takes me seriously, I figure he probably won't care or at least won't remember.

"Huh?" He pauses and his jaw drops. "Ohhh. We'll get along fine," he chuckles.

I close the door and go around to the driver's side. He seems okay. If I stay friendly with him, I don't think he'll try to kill me. If I kiss up, he might even tip.

"There's one other person. You mind waiting?"

"Not at all." It's a slow night.

He takes a swig from his bottle and burps, attempting to keep his mouth shut. He does not succeed and I'm on the receving end of a fresh dose of that all-too-familiar garlic-and-alcohol effervescence.

"Geez, excuse me," he says, as he straightens his posture for the moment.

"How's your night?" I ask.

"I don't know what's with her. We had a great dinner, but," he sounds agitated and pauses. "I've had this friendship for twenty years. There's a certain bond you have with someone after so long. Ya know what I mean?"

"Uh-huh, sure."

"Twenty years is a long time."

"True."

"Where the hell is he? You can start the meter."

Good! "Okay." I slowly reach over and turn it on.

"I can't take it any more. Ya know what I mean? Friends are friends but I don't have to take abuse. Do I?"

"Ummm, no. You shouldn't have to do that."

"Oh, where is he? Honk the horn would you?"

I offer two short bursts on the horn.

"Damn it, hurry up. I'm gonna drink all the beer before he even gets his ass into the cab."

He tries to clear his throat of mucus. Very lovely.

"Things aren't going too well," he continues.

"I'm sorry to hear that."

"Well, I'm sorry to say it. It's sad to see a friendship turn like this, for the worse" he says. "Do you mind if I smoke?" He has a cigarette out.

"Sorry, it's a no-smoking cab."

"Oh, that's okay. I can smoke when I get out."

Danger, danger; the tip has become endangered!

"I just quit," I tell him.

"How long ago?"

"Uhhh, it's been a week." I tap my fingers on the steering wheel. "A very long week."

"I wish I could quit," he says.

"I've saved $35 on cigarettes." Now, I'm the one clearing my throat. "But I spent $40 on gum and candy." I congratulate myself on the great line. I think I'll add that to the permanent routine.

"I like smoking." He gulps down more beer. "I like a cigarette after dinner and when I wake up."

"Yeah, the first cigarette of the day, that's the best," I agree.

I've been learning quite a bit about the cigarette habit. Everyone I've talked to has tried to quit. Everyone. I've even started having pangs of sympathy for these nicotine slaves. I hear all kinds of confessions now that I'm a professed reformed smoker. Prior to that, as simply a non-smoking antichrist never-addicted adversary, I was met with hostility, resentment and rebellion.

"I like smoking after sex," he adds, "and BEFORE sex." He sounds very willing to furnish the details.

I definitely don't want to hear about it. The computer beeps providing some distraction: *SFO TO FAIRMONT HOTEL—WHO JUST HAD THE FARE?*

"What was that?"

"It's the dispatcher. It's the computer."

"That's really irrill-irritating."

"Yes it is." I glance back at him and he's picking at something on his face. It doesn't slow his jabbering.

"Twenty years of friendship and I've had it. This woman's so frustrating; am I repeating myself?"

"Uhhhh…no."

"Sorry. I'm *really* drunk. WHERE THE FUCK IS HE?"

Is this twenty-year relationship with a girlfriend, a platonic thing or is it a woman at all? Maybe he's gay. Is he an ex-hood or just a drunk? I like to know these things.

"Excuse my French," he says. "I don't need this shit. Ya know?"

"No one needs shit," I agree.

"Yeahhh. No one needs SHIT. Who needs friends like that? Honk again, damn it. Honk it again."

I honk.

I'm slightly concerned that he is becoming agitated. He may just be excited to talk about his problem. I'm not sure. I turn for another look to evaluate the stability of his mental state. Though his skin-tight leather outfit is slightly trendy and expensive-looking, in my humble estimation he's a little too old (and a little too fat) to be wearing it.

"Am I a bad person because I'm not going to take any more BULLSHIT? Am I?"

"No, not at all. Have you talked to her about it?" I ask.

"There's no talkin' to her. She inherited this house and she doesn't do anything."

I nod my head in agreement. "Oh, that's terrible." Where's his friend already? And where's some fresh oxygen? He's the one who has been drinking, but I'm the one starting to feel nauseous. And a little faint.

"She's just lazy." He opens another bottle. I crack the window further. "Where does she get off? Tell ME how to LIVE? She has nerve, really some kinda nerve. All these years of friendship, ya know? Down the drain; I'm just sick about it."

He's a big guy and he drinks fast. The meter hits $4.10.

"Honk again," he asks.

I give it a good hard blast. The front door opens.

"There he is. What the *fuck*?"

He's a big guy and I don't want him throwing up. He could have two or three days food stored up. Seeing that revisit the light of day would just not be a good thing. The tickling nausea in my stomach has moved up to just below my throat as his friend appears at the front door, strutting deliberately and leisurely toward the cab, directed by a pair of black pointy shoes.

"LOOK at him. Can he walk any slower? Honk again."

Instead, I reach over the seat and open the back door. I don't know who's paying—I'd rather try and keep the peace. Mr. Pointy Shoes looks in his mid-20's, shorter than my passenger, thin, with a "James Dean" styled haircut, exuding a "James Dean" tough attitude. He's smoking a cigarette. He gets into the car.

"You can't smoke," says the leather guy.

"Oh," says James Dean, unimpressed. An annoyance but he will obey. He hits the silver automatic button and flicks the butt out the window.

The computer beeps again: *THE DRIVER THAT STUTTERS HAD THE FARE FROM SFO UNITED TO FAIRMONT. CHECK IN PLEASE. NOW!*

"This is costing," says Leather, "just sitting here."

"It was Madelyn. I don't know what's with her."

I detect what might be a slight Southern drawl, very slight. One thing for certain, it's important he keep an air of invulnerability about himself, a type of inaccessibility—like the way he walked over to the cab, an aloof *confidence*, a calm but serious intensity. Charisma. My concern, however, is that this attitude might lead to some kind of trouble.

"Oh," says Leather. "Don't let Madelyn get to you."

"She really doesn't like me," says James.

"Where are you heading?" I ask.

"The Haight," says Leather.

I put the car in reverse and pull out of the driveway.

"She's jealous," says Leather. "Doesn't like you hanging around."

"It's a very uncomfortable situation," James propounds seriously.

"Oh, ple-ease. Ignore her." Leather noisily takes another swig of beer. "Madelyn has her own problems, believe me."

"What did I do to her?"

"She's upset because you're taking my time. You won't have to deal with it anymore," guarantees Leather. "That's a promise."

"I'm nice to her." James plays dumb. "I just can't figure out why she has such an attitude."

He knows exactly why. I don't, but I'm certain that he does. I don't like him either. And what it's been, about thirty-seven seconds?

"You got the booze?" asks James.

"Yeah, yeah I got it."

"We're going to have to stop and get some more."

"Don't worry. We'll get more."

"Where are we going to stay?"

"On Lombard, or we can go down to Market. There's a place on Sixth or Seventh Street. Driver, you know that place?"

"The Holiday Inn?"

"No, it's a little motel. Never mind, I'll tell you where to go."

"We gotta make a stop first," says James. "I need to make that call."

I hear the clinking of Leather's beer bottles.

"After twenty years that woman treats me like this. Ya know? I'm through," Leather proclaims hoping for a rewarding pat on his back or whatever.

"I've bent over backwards for Madelyn," says James. "I mean, we can all be friends. I told her that."

He's carefully manipulating the situation. I can tell by his voice he hates her guts and wants her out of the picture. Between James and I, we're both playing Leather—me for a three-dollar tip, and James for who knows how much.

"Ya see how she treats me," James pleads his case.

"I'm sorry to say it." Leather opens up another bottle and quietly belches. "She's screwed up. She's my good friend but the truth is the truth, right, driver?"

"The truth is the truth," I once again lend my support.

"I'm thinking of just telling her, you know, put it all up front and just say to her, 'look Madelyn, you know that I care about you, but you're lucky to have any friends at all.' The rate she is going…" Leather interrupts himself, adjusting his pants and coat. "You know what? I don't have to take that shit."

"No, you don't," says smug James. "We need some more booze."

I'm not even sure James is drinking or if he's simply interested in Leather remaining wasted and incapacitated.

"This is the end. I'm telling you. This is the end," warrants Leather.

"Let's stop at the store," says James.

"Let's go downtown instead," Leather says. "She's gone too far. Have I just had too much to drink?"

"No, you're right," says cool James, collected and distant. "But I don't want to say anything. You need to make up your own mind"

Yeah, right. He doesn't want to say anything? He's thoroughly enjoying the ragging session. It's security insurance. At Seventh Avenue, I take a right on Lincoln Boulevard.

"You saw what happened. You see how she's acting."

"I don't want to be in the middle."

"She's never going to get a man. She's gotta lose some weight. Doesn't she realize that?" Leather exasperates.

"We gotta stop at a store."

"There's one on Divisadero," I volunteer.

"Anywhere is fine," says James.

"Take Seventeenth," directs Leather. "Stanyan to Seventeenth Street."

We're driving in circles now. Stanyan to Seventeenth is backtracking. I learned early on that arguing with the inebriated about directions is fruitless. They don't remember whether they've been driven in a circle but they do remember that you were arguing with them.

"Now, I want you to remember this," James reminds his memory-challenged pants-bulging dupe. "I'm gonna call my friend and I can't guarantee he will meet you, but I'll do my best. Okay?"

"That's fine." Leather sucks at another beer.

"I'll talk to him. I'll ask him about it, but I don't want you to be upset if he says he can't meet you. Okay?"

"Yeah, yeah, okay. I know, I know."

"I don't have control over him."

"I'm cool. That's cool. Just call and see what he says."

"I just don't want you upset. I know how you get."

There are several seconds of silence. Leather breaks it. "What's she gonna do about the house? Madelyn's got easy sailing," says envious Leather. "She'll screw it up. She hasn't got a pair of nylons without runs. And her teeth? My god."

"It's a nice house," says James. "Really nice."

"She should shave her legs," slurs Leather. "Lose weight and shave those legs. The house is a mess; her life's a mess. Clean the god-damn place up! PLEASE. She can't get laid with the place stinkin' like cat piss."

The computer breaks in again with a message: *WHO JUST HAD THE FARE FROM CLAY/VAN NESS TO 22ND NOE. JUST NOW.*

"Can't you disconnect that thing?" Leather complains.

"Those animals walkin' all over the kitchen table," says James.

Madelyn this and Madelyn that—they continue running her down, item by item. It's fairly brutal. As an innocent bystander, I figure it's all bravado, exaggeration and hot air. Leather's so drunk, he can't remember anything from the last forty-five seconds. James Dean though seems in full and sharp control of his faculties, to insure being able to take advantage of any opportunity that arises.

"I can't let her bring me down," burps Leather.

"Oh no," says James. "You shouldn't have to take abuse."

"All I've done for her—she treats me like this. Who needs *friends like* THAT?"

"Yeah, yeah," says the gasoline-throwing empathetic James. "I know. I know what you mean."

"Where are her friends?" asks Leather, and then he answers himself. "She hasn't got any."

"It's really kind of sad," says James.

"No, no, she deserves it all."

"Driver, we need a hotel room for a couple of days," says James. "Can you recommend something cheap?"

"I know a good place," says Leather. "Don't worry."

I take a left onto Seventeenth Street heading down the hill. It's a clear night, a gorgeous view. The headlights of cars traveling the Bay Bridge are visible all the way to Treasure Island.

"Now remember, I don't want you to be upset about this if it doesn't work out," says James. "I'm going to do my best but he may have other things to do, I don't know."

"That's okay," says Leather. "Don't worry."

"I don't want you to be upset. Okay?"

"Either way, I'm okay."

At Castro and Market we stop at a red light, right next to a group of men walking along the sidewalk minding their own business.

"Oh, wow," says Leather. "Look at that guy."

One is wearing blue jean cutoffs. Another guy's wearing chaps, black leather pants with the rear end cut out.

"Look at the butt on him!" says Leather. "Owwww!!" He sticks his head out the window and starts hooting. "Hey, baby. Hey! Lookin' good!"

Heads are turning, people are stopping to stare.

I look back at James. He has an uncomfortable look on his face as Leather shakes and points his beer bottle out the window now at a group of hefty women walking into the corner bar.

"Slow down," Leather says to me. A tall thin blond man is briskly walking along the sidewalk toward a corner bar.

"I got somethin' in my pants for you!" yells Leather.

I continue driving; Leather continues screaming out the window as we drive from Castro Street all the way down to Noe, when he finally reins in his head from outside the window. "This town is GREAT!!!" Leather is pumped. "We'll get some vodka, like the other night. It's gonna be all right."

"I don't think the cab driver here wants to hear any more about our personal business," says James.

"I'm just saying the last couple of days...."

"I don't feel like talking about it here in public. These are things between you and me."

Maybe James thinks I might call the police. Of course, Leather might attract them by himself if he keeps screaming at everyone on the street.

"I didn't...I mean...." Leather stutters. "You were the one upset the other night for...."

"Later, okay?" James abruptly cuts him off. "We can talk about it later in the room."

"If you need more money, you don't gotta worry about it."

I wait for him to add "sweetie" at the end of his sentence. He doesn't.

"We should really talk about this later." James speaks softer, tactful but agitated and manipulative.

So, here's the situation. James is a hired gun, maybe not your stereotypical one-night stand/hourly-rate male prostitute who charges a set rate. Or at least at this point in the relationship they're working on some sort of longer-term basis. I guess it's an easier route than going from one trick to the next trying to eke out paying for meals, a place to stay, drinking money, etc. Who knows? Maybe it's just a straight ahead bilking scheme. Apparently Leather has been paying the guy's food, expenses, everything. Certainly James likes to be in control. He doesn't seem well educated, but I sense he's a good hustler with above average street smarts. And he's got his hooks (among other things) in Leather.

"I'm just looking forward to spending the night," Leather coos.

"Me too," says the hireling. "Let's talk about something else."

The computer beeps twice. It reads: *ANYONE SEE CAB #775 TELL HIM TO CALL IN IMMEDIATELY.*

"What is that noise anyway?" asks James.

"Just the computer. We use it instead of a radio."

"That's bothersome. It's annoying," he mutters. "Fucking annoying."

"Sorry. I hear it all night long. I've blocked it out." Maybe he thinks it has to do with calling the cops.

"Is this place very far?" asks James.

"We're close," says Leather. "Make a left on Franklin. There's a liquor store over there."

We get to the liquor store. We stop.

"Can you wait while I make a phone call?" asks James.

"That's fine," I tell them.

"Now, remember," says James to Leather, "I can't guarantee he's gonna want to meet you. I don't want you to be disappointed or upset. Promise me. If he doesn't want to do it, there's nothing I can do. I can only ask him."

"Okay, I know. I'm okay." Leather slurps and slurs.

How much is this whole shebang going to cost Leather? While James walks to the phone booth at the side of the store, Leather enters the store. I get out and stretch, staying in proximity to the phone, feigning a nonchalant disinterest while still within earshot. James dials and waits. He hangs up and buttons again; waits; hangs up and walks into the store.

Five minutes later, we're all back in the car.

"We'll try him from the hotel," says James.

On Market Street between Eighth and Ninth Streets we pull to the curb in front of the lobby door of the National Motel. It looks closed.

"I hope this is nice," says James.

I have grave doubts about that. It looks like a no-frills Bed & Breakfast retreat for winos. "They better have a TV," says James.

"I'll go in and check it," says Leather.

He gets out of the cab and walks up to the door. There's a cardboard sign reading "*ONLY THE NATIONAL HAS FREE F&C!*"

I have no idea what that is. Fleas and cockroaches?

Leather goes in. Two minutes later he returns.

"Keep driving," he says. "Fifth Street."

We drive three blocks and take a right.

"Stop at the blue car," says Leather.

This place looks no better groomed than THE NATIONAL.

"I don't wanna be stuck with no TV," says James. He senses a problem. "Is this a nice place?"

"It's fine," assures Leather. "Don't worry."

Still, it looks like a total dump from the outside. "Did you want to go in and check first?" I encourage. This has turned into a pretty good fare. Maybe they want to keep the meter going.

"That's okay. How much is it?"

Oh well. "$17.80."

Leather digs for his wallet.

"Thanks for your patience," he says.

"Have a good night." I check the computer. There's a fare up in the zone. If I clear the meter I have a chance to get it. But, if I clear the meter, he might forget what the fare was.

"Let's see." He's paging through scraps of paper and various bills. "How much?" He looks at me. "$17.80?"

"Yes."

Hurry up. I'm watching the computer screen: *FARE AVAILABLE ZONE 13.*

A car pulls up behind me and honks.

"I hope it has cable," says James getting out of the cab.

"They do," says Leather handing me a twenty. "Keep it."

The car behind honks again.

"Just go around!" says Leather. "Some people." He waves his hand at them.

I clear the meter as the **FARE AVAILABLE** on the computer is gone. I press the "send" button. A car alarm sounds off on a BMW parked in the alley next to the hotel. Standing adjacent to the Beemer, a guy drinking from a bottle in a brown paper bag lowers the bottle from his mouth and stares at the vehicle.

"Hey, man!" yells a guy from across the street. "Get away from my car."

The man with the bottle slowly backs away. The guy across the street yells again and shoves a hand into the front coat pocket of his coat.

"I said, GET THE FUCK AWAY FROM MY CAR!"

The man with the bottle hurries down the alley and out of sight.

The computer beeps back at me: *ZONE 13—PLACE 3.*

I'm now third in line for a fare in Zone Thirteen, the area between Third and Seventh Streets from Harrison to Market Streets. When drivers see an available fare in a zone, they often book into it. They want to be booked-in where there is action, hoping there will be more calls—maybe it's a big party. Even a small party will do tonight.

"Thanks," I tell Leather.

"Oh, here." He hands me two more dollars.

"Thank you."

I watch as they both disappear through the doorway with large white letters reading ROGERS MOTEL. It's an older building with paint peeling from the cement facade. I put the cab into drive.

"Are you available?" It's a clean-cut, short, stout man wearing horn-rimmed glasses, carrying a red backpack and a green umbrella. "I'm just going to the Castro."

"Sure," I answer as I complete my waybill by writing the drop-off point of my last two passengers.

He opens the back door and gets in. The same car behind me honks again.

"What's wrong with that guy?" says my passenger. "Why doesn't he just go around us?"

"I don't know."

I punch the meter and step on the gas.

THE PAINTER

"**O**h," she says in a gently compassionate tone. "You're an artist!"

"Well, I don't think I've ever referred to myself as an *artist*; da Vinci was an artist, or Dali."

"Well, I mean you're a creative person!"

"I suppose."

"There are not many places to go these days for creativity; for the creative person. It's not a real value these days."

"Tell me about it."

"Trying to make it in music is hard." She pulls her very beautiful long clean silky straight blond hair to one side of her forehead, gathering it into a tight bun atop her head. "I'm a painter."

She tugs hard at the bun, and pulls upward to reveal a black bob—her true hair style and color beneath this lavish wig. The unexpected transformation is slightly startling. The long blond hair remains lifeless, lumped on the seat next to her thigh.

"That's as tough as it gets."

"What do you mean?" She tries to make the connection.

"That's got to be about the toughest way to make a living these days, unless you're already famous," I add, "and dead; seems the camera put a pretty good dent in the painting business." The brakes make a high-pitched squeak as I stop for a jaywalking pedestrian dressed with strips of blue, red and white cloth hanging from his shirt sleeves. "Well, there's always sculpting, that would be harder." Maybe she's makin' millions.

"Pretty soon machines will do all the creating." She pronounces her words using a wonderfully soft-spoken accent of some sort, slightly European—slightly FAKE-ish European.

"That leaves the serious creating to the individual," I sarcastically comment following her lead, "punching buttons and inputting calculations."

"Yeah," she accents.

"Is that your painting?" I ask.

"Would you like to see it?"

"Sure."

I hear her unwrapping the paper from the frame as we approach the Market Street BART station. We come to a red light as she invites me to look. But the light turns green and people are already honking. Traveling the rest of the short distance to her destination, we come to a halt and she once again invites me to look. This time I do.

Four red stick figures stand in the foreground on an off-white background. Globs of brightly-colored water droplet figures of blue and puke orange sprawl across the canvas. It's hideous awful. There's a yellow object on the right resembling a broken up A-frame building or something. Maybe it's a broken swing set—perhaps some symbolic childhood nostalgia theme. I certainly don't know.

An electric Muni bus pulls up behind us and lets out several passengers, then goes around us to the left. We (including the painting) seem to have attracted the attention of a few of the passengers and some passers-by.

"I still have some touching up to do," she says, as if expecting to hear an objection from me regarding her own "harsh" criticism.

How about touching it up with kerosene and putting a match to it?

"Oh," I nod instead, pursing my lips tightly. I can feel my face go sour and stiffen, completely against my will. I try several anecdotal psychological measures—thinking about chocolate, thinking about a tip, thinking about her naked. Nothing is working.

We're in front of the BART Station now. I stop the meter and turn around, obligated to examine the artwork carefully. "That's, ahh...." grotesque, repulsive, should be burned. Just a nominal dysfunctional description, that's all I need, but instead, an awkward silence has been created while my brain attempts to recover from involuntary spasmodic activity to avoid offering an actual and honest observation of this repulsive conglomeration of random paint swabs. Meanwhile, the blond hair blob lays on the seat, appearing as if it's all that's left of dear Cousin It after an untimely vaporization.

"You don't like it, do you? I can tell."

My gaze of artistic evaluation is not fooling her. "What? Oh no, I'm just taking it all in." She's really very attractive although she should lose the hair cut. I don't want to hurt her feelings and she probably deserves more than just stunned silence.

"The, ahhh," I stumble, "different *levels* you have there. The colors and," (pause) "the ummm, CONTRASTS. The concept, the um, your use of color and form are very bold." Should I tell her that I adhere to the belief that art is in the eye of the beholder (and would she mind plucking mine out)? Silence is probably better than some cliché. If I knew some art jargon, I could fake my way out, maybe. She's being very quiet. HELP!

My face begins a series of contortions that generally only occur when I've consumed a high volume of chewable Acerola vitamin C. Perhaps ignoring the painting's details, focusing instead on the "total effect" of the painting will help. It doesn't. And the longer I say nothing, the more she probably expects some profound creative observation. I pretend to cough. If she thinks I've got the plague, maybe she'll ease up and let me go on my merry way. Instead, her eyes widen, waiting for a compliment. How about: "You know, you're a very attractive woman. Have you considered a modeling career?"

"That's really in-ter-est-ing," I finally blunder, desperately drawing out each syllable as if I'm offering some rare visionary insight. The brightest alternative is a myriad of insulting euphemisms and witty sarcasm. She seems a completely lovely person, with beautiful eyes and a poise that's very artistic (one thing the painting lacks).

"Interesting? That's a terrible thing to say," she pauses to scoff. "You hate it, you don't like it all."

You're right. It sucks.

"If you don't like it, you should just say so." Now she sounds hurt AND thinks I'm an ass. She grabs the hair piece, looking as though her next act will be to instruct it to attack me.

"No, I DO like it," emphasizing the do, making sure to avoid a Freudian slip by saying "don't." My facial muscles have relaxed, able to maintain a simple and neutral expression.

I still have some touching up to do.

"It's a *modern* look," I bamboozle. "You know, at the same time a statement."

A statement? What statement would that be? That art supply stores should have a waiting period just like gun stores?

There must be something good about the painting. I scan left to right, right to left, up and down, as she studies my own expression. I try left to right one more time. What if I were blind and had, at this moment, miraculously regained my sight?

"Your use of color…is so *vibrant*. There's a vibrant childhood vibration about it, ahhhh happening." I'm faltering and repeating myself.

"I'm experimenting a lot with color. Colors can really evoke emotional intensity."

She succeeds there—

"My theme is the force of technology, the repression of society and the perversion of our natural development; the suppression of our true selves; technology as the antithesis of passion." It's a noble thought, but I don't see it in her globs of finger paint. How many school credits is she getting for her attempt? Are my tax dollars paying for this?

"It looks like so much work," I sympathize. I think that's complimentary. Don't say it's pretty, nice or pleasant. "Very sophisticated...." Sophisticated what? Loosen up those stomach muscles, relax and breathe deeply. Making faces gives you wrinkles. The tip, the tip!

"Well," she says, "of course, the circular imagery is a cluster representation of abstraction. I mean, that's what I'm trying to do."

Is this art lingo, or stuff she's just making up? She might be from Oklahoma; she just talks funny—that accent.

"It's a *unique* style," I tell her. "I like it." She knows I hate it. Who am I kidding?

"I'm on my way to a show."

"Your show?" I hope I don't sound too incredulous.

"Mine and a few other artists."

"You're selling it, or it's on display?" I ask, hoping this also passes for a question of interest and not of disbelief.

"Both. It's my friend's gallery. There's a client who has been very interested in my work. I'm hoping to sell this too."

Interested in her work? But has the guy actually bought a painting? Tracy and Gina have clients interested in their work too. She's either very naïve or a great businesswoman. Maybe I'm the naïve one and she can't get to the bank fast enough.

"It would be hard for me to sell something like that," I clamor. "Ya know, hard to let go after putting so much work into it." YES!! I did it. That's flattering, right?

"I sell one and paint another."

"Well, good luck," I tell her with enthusiasm, relieved to have made it past the "how do you like my painting" phase of our little dialogue.

"You have an honest way of looking at art," she says.

Now SHE is bullshitting ME. Wouldn't it be great if it weren't her painting? It's someone else's and she hates it too.

"Some people," she taps the seat, "they don't know anything about art and try to get all deep and analytical. Ya know?"

"Hmmm," I nod. Oh yeah? I think she just insulted me. Listen lady, I'll give you analytical. Throw the thing in the trash, see if it burns.

"You have a refreshing outlook," she says with sincerity.

"Well, you either like it or you don't. There's no absolute standard that exists. Same with music, there's no right or wrong."

"Yes, people don't realize that. I just love to paint."

"It's great you can make your living doing that." UNBELIEVABLE, actually. The rendering gets worse the more I look at it; it's slop, an imprecise rush job.

"I can tell you take a lot of time with your work." I imagine a laser-guided lightning bolt coming down from the sky, striking me dead.

"I think I'm fortunate. I feel lucky," she says.

Tell me about it. I can't draw a concentric circle, but I could paint crap like that for days. I'm not sure if it's more astounding that she's painting this stuff, or that people are buying it.

"I've been doing this now for three years," she says. "How much is the fare?"

"It's five dollars."

She hands me six and fumbles with the door.

"Do you need some help?" I start to get out.

"Oh no. I've got it."

Forbid something should happen to the painting while she's getting out of the cab. If she were to ruin it because of my not helping her, would I be eligible for some award? Is there a "spare the world from hideous art" Nobel Peace Prize? Maybe she really does know that I hate it. She doesn't want me getting any closer to it.

Mozart and Beethoven, Edgar Allen Poe—starving or unappreciated castigated artists of their time—and this woman, cruising along with her brightly colored blobs of oil colors. Galileo was thrown in prison for less.

She slams the door shut and disappears through the entrance to the BART Station. Well, it's nice she can make a couple of bucks. And the people who buy it? That's their punishment.

AND MADELYN TOO

Caught in a zone in the Avenues, a call comes up to rescue me. The address is 1800, 1800 even. Very unusual for a residential address. I know the exact location of the cross street beeping on the computer screen and judging from that, it's not a business. I must be mistaken that the address seems familiar. Dealing with a hundred addresses in a week, I cannot possibly distinguish one address from another. It's my imagination.

I take a left, drive three familiar blocks uphill and turn right. I reach the destination and sure enough, I've been there before. It's where I picked up Leather—the chunky guy squeezed into his black motorcycle outfit, and James, his enterprising parasitic young companion who was being handsomely paid (I assume) for his companionship. Will this be another escapade with Leather hanging his drunken face out the window, screaming at all the boys? Or maybe he has a new companion for the month or evening; perhaps the mysterious "third" guy will be with them this time.

Pulling into the familiar driveway, I honk lightly, pull myself out of the cab and walk the long path towards the door. I knock. No one answers. I ring the bell. I knock again. No answer, no sound from inside, nothing.

Disgusted, I retrace my steps back to the cab, when an ear piercing screeching voice pierces the evening fog: "I'll be right there."

As the vibration clears from the deep recesses of my ear canals, the front porch light comes on. And out walks: *MADELYN!*

It's the woman who was the subject of James' and Leather's brutal ragging session. This *could* be interesting. Am I bored, have no life, or just easily entertained? Surely, they must have exaggerated the description of this poor woman. At the least, it's a sorely needed fare for a painfully slow night.

Madelyn shakily staggers and zip-zags, following the path to where I'm parked in the driveway. She's dressed in a light blue nightgown-thing. Luckily you can't see through it. She is a bit overweight, as the boys described. Okay. She's obese, and there's a large rip in her nylon stockings leading down to her bright white fuzzy slippers marred with dirt and coffee stains.

I'm holding the passenger side door open as she slowly approaches. Her teeth are brown-stained and a few are noticeably crooked. She can barely balance herself and half-falls into the rear seat. Her nose is swollen red; her face is puffy. Her breath smells of alcohol. A lower tooth on the left side is missing. James and Leather were not exaggerating.

While she adjusts herself in the back seat, the alcohol stench momentarily subsides and I suddenly smell a strong pungent cat odor—no, it's dog turds, the smell of freshly smooshed dog droppings. I've stepped in it. I look down at the ground. It's about eight o'clock in the evening, twilight, difficult to see with only a bit of reflecting sunlight remaining to fight the incoming fog. I examine the bottom of each of my shoes and scan the immediate area. There's nothing out of the ordinary except that recognizable fresh smell lingering in the air, an almost steamy aroma. I shut her door, check the area and the bottom of my shoes once again. Nothing. I can definitely smell it, I just can't see it. And it's very upsetting.

"Driver," announces my anxious and sauced passenger, "let's go!"

"Okay," I answer, while I imagine this turd, lurking and evasive, dodging my detection, somehow finding its way between the fake leather seats and my pants where the unsmooshed portions will release more of those stored-up odor molecules, until all possible combinations have been exhausted—like a dog-turd Rubik's cube. Every different squish formation must be realized until the smell is exhausted and finally subsides. It's one thing to step in it. It's another thing to get it smeared all around on the accelerator, the brake pedal, the floor mat, my clothes, the steering wheel... AHHHHHHHHHHHHHHHHHHHHH. Essentially, the best offensive strategy would be a firm defensive position: turn the cab in, call it a night, and hit the shower ASAP.

"What's wrong?" she senses.

"Oh, nothing."

One more attempt. I check the cement; inspect my right shoe and then the left, squinting my eyes examining every square centimeter for foreign matter. There it is!

No. Nothing there, false alarm. I check my left shoe once more. Alas, there is no excrement of any kind.

"Can we go?"

"Sure." Before putting my feet back into the cab, I again examine the bottom of my shoes. Nothing there. Something stinks, but my shoes look clean.

I carefully sink back into the driver's seat, as if this is going to somehow help the situation. I'm no longer sure I even smell anything. Maybe it was a bush on the other side of the cab; some eucalyptus transplanted from the Golden Gate Park panhandle.

I scoot my legs into the car and shut the door. Glancing to the left, I notice the front door of her house is still cracked open. She failed to shut it all the way. Maybe someone else is home or maybe she's lost her keys. I can't rationally justify it, but I am reasonably sure that if I tell her she has left the door ajar, this will lead to some kind of trouble that I will come to strongly regret. More superstition? Gut feeling? I'm not going to tell her. Besides, the dog poop is out there. Somewhere. The door is not my problem.

"I'm not going very far," she says with precision. "Just to the Safeway."

"No problem."

"Oh, no. Did I bring my money?"

Great. I start the meter.

"I'd like you to wait for me while I shop."

Wow, her breath is strong. She's talking slowly, slurring her words. Just then, another hit on my reeling sinus cavities. It's definitely a bad cat odor. It's her. She smells like a cat box. And now I have it figured out. The dog smell is more from outside, I think. The cat smell is from her and the body odor smell, that's a eucalyptus tree, also from outside. But I don't see a eucalyptus tree. Maybe this is the onset of an epileptic seizure? Don't you start smelling weird stuff right before the onset?

"How much is it gonna cost?" she snorts.

"It depends on how long you take."

"I don't have that much money."

"It's thirty cents a minute, a dollar-eighty a mile." I put the car in reverse. "Do you need a bank machine?"

"I have enough." She starts coughing uncontrollably.

This is going to be a fantastic ride. After counting out their nickels and dimes (hopefully no pennies), people this drunk rarely tip. You're lucky if they have enough for the fare; lucky if they remember you're the cab driver. You have to keep them in the car with the fare showing, keeping the doors closed to reinforce the reality that, yes, they are in a cab, there's an amount owing and the cab driver needs to be paid. If they get out of the cab prior to paying the fare, it may take some convincing that they actually were driven someplace. And, again, arguing with the alcohol-challenged is not going to streamline the evening or contribute much to the night's positive cash flow.

She gets her coughing under control. I only hope she doesn't puke.

The front door of her house is still cracked open. No one has shut it. No animals have run out. Someone could walk in and rob her blind, but I know what will happen if I tell her. "Would you mind shutting it?" No way will she drag her own drunk ass over there. She'll beg and plead for me to do it. I'm not trekking through that dog-doo minefield to close the damn door.

Maybe she left it open on purpose. It's none of my business. I'm not her guardian, I'm here to give her a ride; the front door is not my problem. If I tell her and she goes to shut the door, what if she doesn't have her keys? Or, she could lose the keys in the store and wind up locked out. There are endless possibilities and they all mean trouble. It's a smart thing she did, leaving the door open.

I'm already exhausted from the ride and we haven't even pulled out of the driveway.

I roll down both front windows and turn on the heat. Maybe her slippers are full of crap. Maybe it's on her robe. Maybe her house smells and she does too.

"Go down to the Safeway," she directs. "It's close."

"I know."

"You go down to Nineteenth Avenue," she squeaks.

"Yes, I know. Don't worry, I know where it is."

"Thank you. Then I want to come back here."

"You got it. How is your evening?"

"What?"

"How—has—your—night—been?"

"My night? My night is…my night is horrible baaaad. Things are very *bad*."

"I'm sorry to hear that," I sympathize.

Wait 'til she gets home and finds out she's been robbed.

She readjusts her position, slamming into the front seat causing me to lurch forward slightly.

"I don't know what to do." She coughs. "I'm in a real *funk*. My father died a few weeks ago."

"That's terrible. Was it sudden?"

"It's been the worst month of my life."

"Well, I'm sure things will get better."

"Have you ever been in a funk?" she asks.

"Yes, I think I have."

"I'm in a funk. I'm depressed. That's what it is, I'm depressed. I don't know what to do with my life." She rustles around in the back seat. "Do you have a light?"

"I'm sorry, it's a no-smoking cab."

"Just one cigarette?"

"I just quit, two weeks ago. Sorry."

"I should quit smoking. My doctor says I should quit."

"I'm on a nicotine patch," I explain, doubtful it will do any good. "I can't be breathing smoke."

"I quit drinking," she says.

I don't think she heard me at all.

"How many things should I have to quit at once?" she says opening up her purse. "Ya gotta live a little, right?"

"Definitely."

"I haven't had a drink in two-and-a-half months. I've been totally…sober. I've *wanted* to have a drink, but I *haven't* had a drink. Gone to A.A., and I've been really good. No drinking. No drugs, straightened out my act. No pills; nothing."

"Well, that's really good."

She starts coughing again.

"Are you okay?"

"I just need a drink, one drink. I can't take it anymore. I haven't had a drink...it's been weeks. Totally sober; whaddaya think of that?"

"That's great. It's hard to quit. There's nothing I'd like more than a cigarette."

"Have one of mine."

"Oh no, I really shouldn't. I've got this patch..."

"I'm a miserable wreck," she interrupts. "I'm sorry."

Thankfully, we drive in silence for the next block.

"I wonder if I'll ever see my father again," she says. In my rearview mirror I can see her swivel her head from left to right. "Where are we?" She offers a jittery high-pitch cackle.

"We'll be there in a minute," I reassure her.

"Do you think I'll see him again? I mean, what happens when you die?"

"I can't really say."

"What happens when you're dead? What happens?"

"Uhh, I don't really have sufficient information on that."

"Well, do you live again? Are you up in heaven or something? Will I see him if I die?" Her voice trails off.

"I don't really know."

"I don't think anything happens. It's all a bunch of crap. Those priests, they're no help at all, stupid idiots. I don't know what to do." She starts coughing again.

Maybe I need to start requesting a shield. The thing is: they're installed in such a manner that you can't pull the driver's seat back far enough and after a ten-hour shift, you feel like you've been driving with your knees jammed into your own face. It's very uncomfortable, but perhaps a more advantageous alternative than tuberculosis or some unpronounceable rare disease incubated by some cab-riding-alcoholic-dog-turd-laden-nightgown-toting....

"How am I going to pull myself together?" she interrupts. "I've never lost anyone close."

"Well, it's something that takes time to get over."

We arrive at the Safeway. There are billows of fog in the parking lot. I pull into a space about thirty feet from the entrance. There are only three other cars parked in the entire lot.

"Please wait for me. I won't be very long. I just got to get a drink, just something to drink. I won't be long."

"Okay."

"You're gonna wait, right?"

"Right. Don't worry about it."

"I'll be right back."

"Take your time. I'll be right here."

She gets out of the car, barely able to stand up. I watch as she zigzags her way into the store. I imagine this major scene, with her waddling up and down the aisles. I could be waiting a long time—a long, long time. She could pass out, or fall down. . . I only hope that if they carry her out they do it through the front door, so I know she's not getting back into the cab. I get out of the car and walk to one end of the parking lot and then the other. The temperature has dropped about twenty degrees. It's cold. Once again, I've left Bob's cell phone at home. There's a bank of pay phones at one end of the store. I walk over to them pulling a quarter from my pocket; I deposit the money into the phone. The girlfriend should still be awake. She should get a kick out of this one. I turn to watch the store exit, and figure I'll also be able to notice any emergency vehicles called to the scene. Suddenly, Madelyn staggers back out of the store. I hang up the phone, grab up my coins and hurry back over to the cab just barely in time to open the door for her.

"They won't let me buy any liquor."

"Really?" I'm glad.

"They won't let me buy any." She's very upset. "Fucking assholes, they're a bunch of assholes. I'll *never* shop *here* again. *NEVER*. That's no way to treat a cussss-tomer! *I'M A CUSSSS-TOMER!*"

I've never heard of someone being thrown out of Safeway before, but she has managed it. I hold the door for her as she makes her way into the back seat, her loosely-fitting nightgown riding far up her massive thighs and exposing lots of skin. I think I'm staring.

"We have to find a store that's open," she says. "Okay?"

"There's not much open on a Sunday night."

"Where's the closest liquor store?" She's fumbling with her wallet. I'm hoping she has enough money to go driving around town looking for a bottle of booze, not to mention for the booze itself. The liquor budget is going to have priority over the fare. I get into the driver's seat and pull out of the parking lot. We drive to one street, up another street and down another. All the shops are dark; the stores are closed.

"Please hurry," she says. "We've got to find something. I'm feeling sick."

"Maybe you should go home. Make dinner, get some sleep."

"No! I need a drink. Something has to be open, somewhere."

I'm not familiar with the store hours in this neighborhood. We keep driving. Returning to Irving Street there's an open liquor store, finally. I park in front.

"I can't go in that place," she says.

"Not much else is open."

"Let's go somewhere else."

"There *is* nowhere else. We've been everywhere around."

"Would you go in for me?"

"I really can't do that."

"Please, here's the money." She panics, holding out a twenty and a ten. "Get me vodka and a blackberry liqueur."

"I think it would be better if you bought it."

"Please, would you get it? I'll tip you, don't worry."

What are the consequences of this? It doesn't sound good to me. The last thing she needs is more to drink. What if she goes into some kind of an alcoholic coma? Worse yet, what if she goes into a coma and then comes out of it? Of course, she will remember me.

"Well, Your Honor, I bought the booze for her because she was way too drunk to buy it herself...." I can see it now. A relatively short, but UNPLEASANT jail term while becoming pals with Bubba. I could probably get probation on a first offense—which would be what offense, exactly? Could they hit me with some kind of minor public nuisance violation? Or create something with a felony charge attached; make an example out of me?

> *He took advantage of a*
> *poor unfortunate woman,*
> *drove her in circles, inflated the fare*
> *and allowed her to drink herself into a stupor,*
> *only to drive her in more circles.*
> *Meanwhile, her home is ransacked.*

"I just can't go in there," she whines. "Please...please."

"Well, I don't think I'm allowed to do that."

"I'll give you extra money." She starts rummaging through her purse.

"I don't think I'm allowed to buy alcohol while I'm working. The police wouldn't like it."

"Are you under age?" she sneers. "It's not illegal!"

What is this anyway? Suddenly she's Perry Mason? I ponder the situation. Could I be suspended from driving? I don't know.

She is stubborn like a mule. I don't have the stamina, time or patience to outlast her in this argument and I can tell you this, there's no way in this lifetime that I could force her out of the back seat. She outweighs me by at least 135 pounds, and most of it is cemented into the seat cushion.

"Okay." I'm very unhappy. "I'll go in for you."

"I want the blackberry liqueur and a pint of vodka."

The bottom line is she certainly doesn't need it. But she's not going to get out of the car without it, or without me at least showing her a valiant effort. And I'd better hurry up before she starts puking up her guts. I'm sure she would find some other way to get it anyway.

"Thank you," she says, "I really feel too sick to go in."

Oh no. I turn off the engine and grab the keys from the ignition.

"A pint of vodka and a blackberry or cherry liqueur," she requests.

Gross. She gives me the thirty dollars.

"Vodka and a blackberry liqueur," she repeats.

"I know, I know."

"Bring me back the change," she chimes as I shut the door. I go into the store. I buy the booze, no questions asked. Getting back behind the wheel in the cab, I hand her the change, the vodka, and the blackberry liqueur—yecchhh.

"How much was it?"

"There's a receipt in the bag, twenty-two something."

"I don't understand. There should be more change."

"Believe me; I gave you all the change."

"No, it shouldn't be that much."

"The vodka was four dollars; the blackberry was seventeen dollars plus tax. I gave you seven dollars and some change."

"How much did I give you?" She's still going through her purse.

"You gave me thirty dollars." I start the engine.

"I gave you forty. I had two twenties."

"I don't know what you had. You gave me thirty dollars."

"I don't understand how much I paid. I had forty dollars."

"You have all the change. Now, where do you want to go?"

"Take me back home."

I drive her back home quickly and smoothly. Please don't puke. We make it to the driveway of her house. The front door is still cracked open as before.

I stop the meter and check the computer. There's another fare up in the zone. I can only get the fare if the meter is off. But, worried she'll forget the amount, I don't want to turn the meter off until she pays.

"That's ten dollars and seventy cents," I tell her.

"I can't see it. How much?"

"Eleven dollars."

The computer reads: *FARE AVAILABLE ZONE 75.*

My eyes stay fixed on the available fare in my zone.

She is slowly counting to herself. She hands me twelve dollars. I turn off the meter. The computer makes a clicking sound and buzzes.

Waiting to see if I get the fare is like waiting for a Las Vegas one-armed bandit to stop; pathetic, seemingly desperate people, eyes transfixed, standing in front of shiny silver machines with quite limited capacity, nevertheless, waiting to see if they have hit the jackpot; a sea of casino zombies pulling, watching and waiting again. Folks jammed into smoke-filled rooms with no windows and no clocks while scantily clad women scurry about delivering liquids to all amidst the hum of machines and the chinking of coins in buckets.

I hear choking noises. I turn around. Madelyn has her head out the window. She's puking.

She stops puking.

She helps herself out of the cab's back seat and slams the door shut.

I can still smell the cat odor. Only now I smell the puke AND the dog-turd-infested surroundings. I still smell that phantom eucalyptus tree. Madelyn staggers away, headed for her home's porch. I'm sure she is going to fall over. I should probably make sure she doesn't kill herself before reaching the front door.

"Do you need some help?" That may require touching her.

"No, I'm fine."

GOOD. Perhaps surgical gloves would be a reasonable addition to my arsenal of cab accoutrements? Having only a medallion, lots of singles and the pepper spray seems to leave me ill-prepared.

She stumbles, then gently swaggers up the driveway and across the long pathway and eventually makes it to the porch. She bends over a bush and throws up again. She straightens back up, wipes her mouth with her sleeve and teeters to her right.

She's setting me up for when she falls, headfirst into the bushes and causes me to trek through the dog-doo minefield and pull her back to her feet by the sleeve of her blouse, her *wet* sleeve.

Madelyn reaches out with her left arm and steadies herself on the doorjamb, pauses, looks back at me, looks away, pushes open the already ajar door and goes inside the house.

The porch light flips off. She closes the door.

The night is dark, quiet and still.

POPEYE'S BITTER HALF-BROTHER

Late Saturday afternoon I receive a call for a fare that borders on the Tenderloin. I push the "accept" button; the computer beeps and commits the fare. I double-park across from 670 Eddy Street, a rundown, deserted, dirty, drab-looking apartment building. There's a sign above the entryway that reads **ELK HOTEL.** I'm not sure if that means the whole building or just one of the floors. I guess it's the whole place. At the side of the building is a parking lot with multi-colored graffiti that runs from one end of the parking lot to the other. Although it's still light out, there's not much foot traffic. But there are a lot of doorways, nooks and crannies where people are or could be hanging or waiting: to make a drug deal; for an unsuspecting tourist to mistakenly walk down this momentarily quiet street; for an opportunity to accost that person who needs an item from the corner store. I grab my pepper spray from above the sun visor, lock up the cab and walk up to the building. My thumb pushes hard on the protruding black buzzer. No sound at all. The bell is broken. I move closer to the row of steel bars to get a better look into the building. It's dark inside and looks vacant.

"Damn."

In times like these I suspect radio dispatch has a "bad addresses" list to punish drivers who don't tip them or to provide a good laugh when they're bored and things are slow. Meanwhile, the "good" fares are saved for those drivers who tip the radio dispatchers, properly kiss ass or simply supply a good fat joint of Hawaiian. Maybe it's disgruntled customers trying to muck up the system—or De Soto drivers calling in fake street numbers, addresses of vacant lots and abandoned buildings.

I go back to the cab to check for any additional instructions on the Tenderloin fare that I may have missed. Of course, there are none—no apartment number, only an address. Not even an addendum to the message, reading: **SUCKER**.

There's movement in the shadow of the apartment doorway. I get back out of the cab. Two men have appeared inside the lobby, one man standing at attention while blankly staring out, the other in a wheelchair.

"Did you call a cab?" I ask.

The guy standing continues to stare without expression or acknowledgement. The guy in the wheelchair wheels himself out the door and past me. I walk over to him.

"Did you want a cab?"

"Can you get closer?" he says.

"Sure." I take that to mean "yes." Getting back into the cab I make a U-turn, pulling around in front of the building and get back out of the cab. A row of parked cars separates the cab from the wheelchair on the sidewalk.

"I'm going to the corner," he says. "There's no curb over there."

The corner is a half-block away.

"Why don't you try the driveway?" I point in the opposite direction. It is only a quarter-of-a-block away. "I think it's closer than the corner."

Why aren't they sending a wheelchair-access van to pick this guy up?

"Hell, I don't care," he says, slowly wheeling himself to the driveway, past an unshaven wino and his drinking partner sharing a paper bag.

Somehow I missed this pair when I first arrived. I put the cab in reverse, turn the meter on, pop the trunk, get back out, walk back around the cab and open the back door.

He lines up the wheelchair with the passenger side back door and shakily stands up. He steadies himself on the cab door. I'm holding the door open with one arm, holding the wheelchair steady with my other arm. Brown age spots cover his large hands and long fingers. There are black marks on his pants. There's part of an anchor tattoo on his arm peeking out from his shirtsleeve. I notice newspaper on the seat of the wheelchair. I don't know if it's for padding, peeing, or reading.

"Would the front seat be easier for you?" I ask.

"Makes no difference to me." He scowls, turns, and then half gets in, but mostly falls into the back seat. Newspapers go flying everywhere.

"Shit," he says.

"Are you okay?"

"Fine." He pulls at his leg to place it in front of him.

I fold up the wheelchair while keeping an eye on the winos and a couple of crack dealer types walking slowly and taking notice of us. I'm always thankful when a wheelchair folds easily and fits right into the trunk. This one does. I'm not touching the newspapers. A guy with loose-fitting pants and a plaid flannel shirt approaches me from behind.

"Got a quarter?" he asks in a gravelly voice. "I'm trying to get some bread."

"So am I." I slam the trunk shut and open the driver's side door. The guy follows me.

"Got a cigarette?" he asks.

"No. Sorry."

I get in the cab, lock the doors and address my no-longer-wheelchair-bound passenger.

"Where are you going?"

"Nowhere."

"What?"

"I don't give a *shit*."

"Is there some place you want to go?"

"Hell. Makes no difference to me."

I hit a button on the computer and request voice. I don't have time for this. The computer beeps: *GO TO CHANNEL TWO.*

I switch channels.

"Yes, six-nine-six."

"Do you know," I try keeping my voice low, "if this passenger has a destination?"

"What do you mean?"

"He says he's not going anywhere; over."

"Go back to data and I'll give you another fare."

"Thanks."

I switch back to the data channel.

"Take me to the water," says my passenger.

"Which water?"

"I wanna see the water."

The computer buzzes. It reads: *660 PINE STREET #302 TO SFO.*

A fare to the airport? Is this a joke? It's very uncharacteristic for the dispatcher to show pity. Maybe what some drivers say is true: there's a list of airport orders they somehow hoard and use at their own discretion. I assume this is one of those urban myths. I don't believe in myths, nor do I believe the list does NOT exist. Do they make bets on the amount of time it takes for a distressed, frustrated driver to call in and request assistance on phantom orders? It's like the over/under on a Las Vegas parlay card:

"How long 'till we hear from 696 on that wheelchair fiasco?"

"I'm in for five."

"I'm in for twenty."

"I'm in...."

The dispatcher will think I'm a total flake if I send the airport order back to him. It will be the last time he does me a favor. I'll be sent every grocery store order that ever comes up. I can drive this man to his $3.25 cent destination and then pick up the (forty dollar plus) SFO fare afterwards. Sometimes that approach works; often it does not. And tonight I should drop the dispatcher a five-dollar tip after my shift ends for sending me the airport. I'm under the impression, that unlike David, they are mercenaries and expect a quid pro quo exchange.

"Where exactly do you want to go?" I ask Popeye's half-brother.

"It's all the same to me, the water."

"You want a view of the water?"

"Yeah."

"From where?"

"I don't give a damn."

"Do you want the ocean or the bay?"

"Makes no difference. Anywhere."

Now I understand. A great view of the bay is within minutes. Traffic is light. A quick drive, look at the view, take him back home. I'll be to Pine Street in ten minutes.

The computer beeps twice. It reads: *ANYONE SEEING CAB #386 - TELL HIM TO RETURN TO THE GARAGE—THIS IS URGENT.*

"We can drive for a view of the bay. How's that?"

"You got a better suggestion?"

Would the front seat be easier for you?

I have all kinds of suggestions. "No," I answer, driving west to Franklin and making a right turn which places us facing down the steep hill. "There's a great view at Fillmore and Broadway."

"Sounds good as anything else," his raspy voice cracks. "It's just goddamn good to get the fuck outta there."

Now, I wonder if he has "escaped," if he's not even supposed to be going out of his room. He never actually answered whether he called a cab or not; ten-to-one he has no money. We stop at a light on Franklin.

"You can see the bay up ahead."

"Yeah, I see it," he says.

"I'll drive closer for a better view."

"I've got taxi scrip. Is that okay?"

Yesss. He has money, unless it's De Soto. "Oh yeah," I politely answer, "that's fine."

"You one of those guys who likes men?"

"You mean, gay?"

"Yeah. Are you gay?"

"No, I'm not."

"Ever seen a man kissin' another man?"

"Well, yes I have."

"It's disgusting; fuckin' disgusting." He pauses. "You should get a hair cut."

"I am a little overdue for a trim," I confide.

"If I were younger," he growls, "I'd knock yer head off."

Listen, you old codger, I'm at risk to lose an airport 'cause of you.

"Knock yer head right off," he repeats.

I should ignore him, but I don't. "Anyone bothers me about my hair," I inform him with matter-of-fact precision, "I kick the SHIT out of 'em." Well, no tip on this ride.

"Oh, you do?"

"I studied karate," I continue. "I don't take crap about my hair."

I can't tell whether he's impressed or doesn't believe me. He's got taxi scrip anyway. People pretend it's against the law to tip with it. Maybe that's the case, I don't even know. And the time it would take to check which company's scrip he's carrying, we could have already completed the ride. So, I'm just trying to get this over with as soon as possible.

"Are you Irish?" he questions.

"No, I'm not."

"Yer parents Irish?"

"Nope."

"Really? Hmmmm." He rustles around in the seat. His rustle sounds perplexed.

"Are you Irish?" I ask.

"My mother was from Waterford," he says proudly. "My father was from Kilkenny. He worked on the docks."

Is that a "yes" or a "no?" It sounds like a yes.

"You get many Irish?" he asks.

"Yeah, there's a lot of Irish in the city."

"What do you think of the Irish?"

"They seem fine to me." Number one tippers actually, although I'm not sure about the ones over ninety years old whom I've threatened with bodily harm. By far, the Irish have the highest class-consciousness of those who have occupied the back seat of my cab.

I take a right at the top of Fillmore from Broadway and stop. It's a clear view out to Marin County. Even the San Rafael Bridge is visible in the distance, past Angel Island.

"Can you see from the back seat?"

"I can see everything."

The Golden Gate Bridge is to the left; it's a few minutes after sunset and a dozen or so sailboats dot the dark blue waters.

"The bay is beautiful," he says.

"Yes, it is."

"It's the most beautiful thing ya can ever see."

Two cars pull behind us; I slowly continue down the steep grade of the Fillmore hill.

"Nice and clear today."

"Perfect," he says. "It's exactly what I wanted to see."

If he hadn't been so much trouble to begin with, I could see driving him around for fifteen or twenty minutes. But now, I've got my fare to SFO waiting.

"That's Alcatraz to the right," I point.

"The prison?"

"They closed it. It's a tourist attraction now."

"What?" He doesn't understand. "Alcatraz the prison."

"Yeah," I agree, "the prison."

"Lucky I didn't end up there."

"You wanna see more?"

"Ehh, I've taken enough of your time. Take me back."

I turn right on Green Street, five blocks away from my very first apartment from when I initially moved to the city. Once I drop him I can quickly make it to Pine Street for the SFO pickup.

"Came here when I was eighteen," he says. "I didn't appreciate it."

"I moved here when I was eighteen, too."

"You're not Irish?"

"No." Still not Irish.

"Do you smoke?" he asks.

"No, I don't smoke."

"Do you drink?"

"Once in a while."

"So you drink," he pauses, again perplexed, "but you don't smoke?"

I try to think of an explanation he might understand. "You can drink more if you don't smoke," I tell him.

"Hrmph. I don't want to go back yet."

Damn. My airport fare is slipping away.

"Where do you want to go?"

"I wanna drink."

"Where to?" A stupid question.

"Fuck, I don't care."

"Close to where I picked you up?" His neighborhood's a total dive.

"Don't take me to one of those men places."

"You mean a gay bar?"

"Gay bar? Yeah, don't take me to one of those."

"Okay."

"A good place."

"Okay, somewhere good," I repeat.

"I don't give a shit. I just wanna drink."

Of course, it immediately occurs to me that I *should* drop him at a gay bar. He'd never realize it 'til I was long gone. They would be nice to him, right up to the time they knock him out of his chair for being so obnoxious.

We drive a few more blocks. "You know a place?" he asks.

"Yeah, I know a place."

"Not some SHIT-HOLE."

I guess he's saying not to drop him back in his own neighborhood. It's a depressing thought, his neighborhood, dropping him there, the whole thing.

"No, not some shit-hole." I assure him, "Don't worry."

I need to quickly get him to some kind of a destination and hope that my airport fare waiting is one of those last-minute packers and running late. Here I am with two orders, so often seems like a feast or famine deal. I get a flag when there's a fare waiting or someone's already in the back seat. Otherwise, I can drive around empty for an hour and no one wants a cab. Once a confirmed order comes up on the computer, all of a sudden everyone on the street starts waving their arms like wild baboons.

"I got two sons in the Pacific," he blurts.

"Oh?"

"They was just like me; they were gonna be *punks*."

I guess they were killed in battle. Judging from his melancholy tone of voice, an interesting mix with his previous purely bitter attitude, I think they must be history. So, what do I say now? I'm sorry they're not punks? Or, I'm sorry they're dead, but I'm not sorry they're not punks? I'm having trouble here. Maybe they're not even dead at all. But the way he phrased "in the Pacific" it pretty much sounded like they are not stationed in the Pacific, they are, exactly, *in the Pacific*, like, without a boat.

"You're not takin' me to one of those men places," he perks up.

I flash on a small inconspicuous bar on the corner of Broadway, conveniently close. I quickly turn the cab around and backtrack a couple of blocks. "You'll like this place," I assure him.

"Where is it?"

"Well, it's sort of an Irish bar, a couple blocks from here. How's that sound?"

"I don't give a shit."

I think he does.

"It's a nice clean place, friendly people."

I pull up to the doorway, pop the trunk, open my door and proceed to remove the wheelchair from where it's lodged in the trunk. Narrowly able to avoid touching the pillow and the newspapers, I then line the chair up with the cab's back door.

"Here." He hands me a book of Yellow taxi scrip. "Ya don't smoke, eh?"

"No, I don't smoke." I tear out the coupons that add up to the fare.

"Well, you're a fine lad. You should just get a haircut."

I allow a smile. "You have a good night, all right?"

"Take two dollars for yourself," he says.

I tear off two dollars, thank him and hand him back the book of scrip.

He rises from the back seat, gets into the wheelchair and maneuvers himself away from the cab. Stained glass decorates the center of the bar's heavy oak front door. I prop it open for his entrance. There's a small group inside. They take little notice of him. They'll be taking lots of notice pretty soon.

Getting back into the cab I spot him wheeling his way into the bowels of the bar as two fraternity types approach the cab.

"Are you available?"

"Sorry, I'm on a call."

"Can you call us a cab?"

At the same time, his buddy is already waving his arms in the crosswalk trying to hail a passing taxi.

"Sure," I say. Can I also order some takeout food for you and your friend?

"That would be awesome," he says.

I pull out in front of oncoming traffic and speed over to Pine Street. It's a large shiny state-of-the-art apartment complex with a fancy walkway, trees with conforming shapes and an expensive ornate iron gate. I get out and dial the apartment number.

The phone picks up. It's the answering machine. I ring again: answering machine. I walk back out to the street and wait a few minutes. My Pine Street SFO folks are history. Maybe they never existed or walked out and flagged the first cab that passed. I'm not even upset about it. Fridays and Sundays are good days at the airport, not Saturdays. People don't fly as much on Saturdays. A cab can be stuck for hours trying to get a fare back to the city.

It's a crisp clear San Francisco evening. The air feels fresh. I look past the traffic and out over the hills. It's another beautiful day. I love this city. I book into Zone 25 and just keep drivin'.

A SMELLY GUY

An older gentleman in his sixties flags me down in front of a dumpy downtown bar in the Tenderloin on Ellis Street. I'm not far from the ELK HOTEL, Popeye's bitter half-brother's digs. It's 1:32 a.m. The man is casually dressed and wearing a Willie Brown styled cream-colored hat. I slow down and stop.

"Can I get a ride?" he asks.

When people ask in that manner, I don't know if they mean for free. Sometimes they do and sometimes they don't. If I have any doubt at all, I ask. Oddly, experience indicates that many people who don't have enough to pay a full fare often make comments such as "I'm not sure I have enough." Then, I want to *see* the money and, of course, this generally creates further problems.

Upon examination, this gentleman is doing some slow but serious staggering: steps forward, steps back, then grabs for the back door-handle on the cab to steady his legs, orient his position and plan his next move. He attempts to align his torso with his legs. It's turning out to be a difficult maneuver.

"I'm just going down-a street," he says.

"Do you have any money?"

"What do you mean, do I have any money? Do you ask all the black people who want a cab if they have any money?"

"No, I don't." But sometimes I ask people who are staggering drunk if they have any money.

"I can pay for the ride; you just drive."

That's what I need to know. He fumbles with the door trying to make his way into the back seat. The cab is not moving, but everything else is—the street, his feet, his head—as he continues to have a very rough time.

After I quickly check my waybill and punch the coordinates into the cab computer, I start to get out to assist, but realize he has already fallen into the cab.

"Where you goin'?" he inquires.

"I was going to help you with the door."

"I don't need no help. I look that old?"

"I help all kinds of people into the cab—young, old, whatever."

I get back into the driver's seat. There's a strong odor of alcohol on his breath and it fills the cab.

"You're prejudiced. THAT'S yo' problem."

"What?"

"You a racist. You don't like drivin' black people."

"No." I'm at a loss for words. "I like black people. That has nothin' to do with it."

"Your attitude—that's yo' problem."

"I think you're misunderstanding...."

"You cab drivers don't like pickin' up black folks."

"What other cab drivers do, I don't...."

"Had trouble gettin' a cab yesterday, too."

"What kind of trouble?" I start the meter and drive forward.

"Couldn't get no one to stop. They just drive on by."

"Well, I'm sorry about that."

"Yeah, 'cause I'm black. A white man gets picked right up."

"You're right, I see it happen."

"You're just the same; asking me if I can pay."

"When people ask me...."

"I don't wanna hear no mo'. Just get me home. Pierce Street and Fulton. You know where it is. That's where I'm goin'."

I drive, silently. I can hear him rustling around a bit but he is not saying anything. After a couple of minutes I smell a foul, foul odor. It is unusually strong, like someone took a dump on the seat, right next to me. I'm not sure it's coming from inside the cab or from the outside. Maybe he's in the process. I look back at him. He's sitting there minding his own business.

I keep driving. The smell worsens. I look back again. He isn't moving. He's looking out the window. I drive a couple of blocks, look left, look right and quickly look back at him again.

"What?" he asks with a harrumph. He sees that I'm distracted.

"What?" I answer.

"Keep going, to Pierce; Pierce and Fulton."

"I know."

"You know where you're going?"

"Yes, it's just a few blocks."

We get to a stop sign. Again, I slowly peek back at him.

"PIERCE!" he says. "I'll tell ya when to stop."

I drive another block. Stoplight. Again, I take a quick look back at him.

"*What* are you looking at?"

"Nothing." I glance left and right as if I'm looking for traffic.

Maybe the smell is from the outside air. I'm not going to say anything about it. We keep driving. It still smells.

After two more blocks, I decide this smell is originating from inside the cab. I look back at him again, then crack open the front passenger's side window and hope he doesn't notice.

"Why do you keep looking at me? I got money; I'm going to pay you."

"I'm not looking at anything."

The smell lingers heavily in the air. I crack my own window open this time and sneak a look back again. I turn the heater on low.

"Stop looking back here. What's the matter with you?"

By the time we get to his house, he's as irritated as anyone could ever be. It's cold out, but now I have the window rolled halfway down. I look over my shoulder. The smell just keeps coming. It's really bad.

"I got the money. Stop looking at me like that."

I haven't been looking at him, I've been scanning the seats. It's too dark. The seats are black and I can't tell whether there is anything back there or not.

We arrive at his home. I get out of the cab and open the back door on the driver's side, trying to get a better look. If he "did something" back there, I want him to clean it up.

"I'm getting out the other side," he says agitated. He looks very unhappy, slowly getting out of the back seat, passenger's side. Keeping his eye on me, he walks around the cab to where I am standing.

I scan the back seat again. It definitely smells like someone took a dump back there. He's the prime suspect.

"Over here," he says. "I'm over here."

"I know." I see nothing on the seat. I squint. Nothing.

"I'm gonna pay. What you worryin' about?"

"I'm not worried." I had another sleepless night; maybe things smell more when you're tired. This time I dreamt of driving off the Golden Gate bridge with my brother, mother and grandmother screaming at me about something. My sister might have been in the car too. The dream was extremely vivid. I'm not sure it could be considered cab-related. I *was* driving and there *were* people yelling. It's one of the only times in my life where I jumped up from my sleep, actually thinking I had been screaming out loud.

"Stop looking around like that!" says the Smelly Guy.

I keep thinking I'm going to see a pile of crap. I don't see anything.

"How much is it?"

"Um. . . " I look at the meter and then down at the back seat again. "It's four-fifty."

"Worst service ever." He hands me a $5 bill.

I dig in my pocket for change and hold out two quarters. "Here's your change."

"I don't want no *change*," he scoffs.

"Have a good night, all right?"

"Something's wrong with *you*." He turns and walks up the driveway toward his apartment.

If he made a mess I want him to clean it up. I squat down and look into the back. Nothing. I shake my head and stand up, then lean forward to get into the back seat. I change my mind. I don't want to find something that way. He's in the apartment doorway waving at me.

"Don't wait for me," he says, impatiently. "I'm okay."

"All right." I raise my hand and acknowledge.

I get behind the wheel. It still stinks. I drive down Pierce, turn right on Eddy and left on Steiner, rolling down all the windows and dialing up the heat, full blast. A few blocks away, on Post Street, I stop the cab. It still smells. I can't be driving around town with a pile of crap in the car. I don't have a flashlight and the street is dark. I still can't see anything, can't really be sure if anything is back there that shouldn't be. I get out of the cab, open up the back door and take another look. It's still reeking like crazy but I can't see anything. I get back in the cab and hope the stench goes away. I keep driving.

It's not the first time that I've had to air out the cab and, unfortunately, it probably won't be the last. It's another slow night and no one is out on the streets; no fares are coming up on the computer. Driving to Pine and Van Ness there's the Holiday Inn: a clean, well-lit place to look for a stink. There are lights from the street and the hotel. I pull into the driveway, place the cab into park, get out and open the back door. I look on the seat, I look on the floor and I look at the back-rest. Still nothing. I go around to the other back door and open it. Same routine. There's nothing on the floor and I can't make out anything on the seat. I step back a few feet to get a different angle and not to block the light.

"Are you available?"

Startled, I jump back a half-step as my body involuntarily jerks. A guy wearing a striped sport jacket, dress slacks, a yellow shirt and a loose-fitting tie stands next to me. His stomach juts out over the top of his pants. I figure he has come out of the Holiday Inn.

"Yeah," I answer. "You surprised me. I'm not supposed to let that happen."

"Can't get caught off-guard," he chuckles and I notice his belly shift. "Not in the big city." His distinctive southern drawl suggests Atlanta, maybe Texas.

I picture him getting in and sliding across the seat through a turd.

"Looks like yer concentratin' on somethin'," he says.

"No, just takin' a break." Now I'm not sure what is bothering me more, the phantom (or not so) phantom doo-doo or my lack of attentiveness. Being startled by a passenger is not good.

"I'm going to the Travel Lodge? On Polk Street?"

"Sure, get in." And hope for the best, sir. You may want to slip into a heavy duty plastic bag before you sit down.

"I think it's pretty close to here, yeah, pretty close."

Tourists are always trying to pretend they know where they are and where they're going. Those evil cab drivers will zigzag you around the block four times and drive you by the airport if they think you're lost.

One elderly woman, accompanied by a distinguished escort, challenged my knowledge regarding the direction to the Broadway Tunnel.

"I've been in San Francisco forty years," she says.

Her hair is a bright grayish-blue and she has no eyebrows—well, she has those penciled eyebrows (like my grandmother's. Her explanation was that they were scorched off from working too close to the ovens in her father's bakery).

"The Broadway Tunnel is the other way!" screeches the refined lady in her knowing high-pitched voice.

"Not unless they moved it in the last twenty minutes." I stubbornly continue our direction of travel.

"Where are you taking us?" she queries accusingly. "We're not a couple of dumb tourists!"

"I'd be glad to turn around, ma'am," though first I'd like to make a check of their cash on hand. "If you're that certain."

"I think maybe it is in this direction," pipes in her male companion finally sensing a directional malfunction. I hope, for his sake, he isn't married to her.

"No," she insists, "this street doesn't look familiar."

"We're parallel to Broadway," I say. "I can turn around, if you want. I don't think you'll be happy about it."

She shuts up. At least they didn't smell.

On another occasion I DID turn the cab around and proceeded to go the wrong way at the insistence of a drunken German tourist. She wanted Fisherman's Wharf and began yelling out orders. I tried to disagree, tactfully. She threatened to take over at the wheel. I held out until we hit Pacific Avenue when she was about to jump over the seat and start pounding me in the head. Deciding that my physical well-being was of greater value than saving her four dollars, I surrendered, made a U-turn and headed south on Van Ness toward the beautiful town of Los Angeles. When the San Luis Obispo exit appears, maybe she will realize that silence can, on rare occasions, actually be golden. She realized her mistake when City Hall came looming into view. It turned from a $4.00 fare to a $10.00 fare and she (sheepishly) paid it. She started out so adamant and so *GERMAN*. It was great.

Meanwhile, back at the Holiday Inn, I consider offering my cowboy tourist with the protruding stomach a seat in the front, that's plan A. Plan B, make a disclaimer to Mr. Texas/Atlanta: "Listen, the last guy in here may have taken a dump, so be careful where you sit." What should he do at that point? Feel around with his hand first?

Plan C, feign ignorance.

I step aside, offer a silent prayer to the cab gods, motion him to enter the violated vehicle and shut the door.

"Thank ya," he says.

Don't thank me yet. I walk around to the driver's seat.

What if he sits in it? It smells like an outhouse and I haven't noticed? A pile of what? Oh, yes, that's to make passengers who are throwing up feel more comfortable. No extra charge.

Plan D, I have a sinus infection; I haven't smelled anything in two weeks.

Before I have a chance to offer him the front seat, he scoots into the back; plan C and D go into effect. I get into the cab. The heater is roaring at full blast. I turn it down to a low rumble. We proceed on Van Ness. I can hear him telling his good ol' buddies, back home: "Ah get into this taxi an' this psycho-sicko-cab-driver…"

"Hey," Bobby Joe slaps him on the back, "we warned ya 'bout that San Francisco."

I turn right on California Street. He coughs and clears his throat.

"Canna roll up this wind-dah?" he asks.

You'll be sorry. "Sure," I answer.

He rolls up the window on his side; I roll up the other back window and the front passenger side window. I keep mine down. The smell lingers.

"Is this NORMAL?" he asks.

"What's that?" I ask, feigning ignorance.

"Is it always so cold here?"

"You can get sunburned and frostbitten in the same day."

"I flew out this mornin'," he says. "Was ninety-six degrees in Atlanta, plus the humidity; man!"

"We had pretty good weather today, a little smoggy."

"Not as bad as New York," he says.

That's it, New York.

"It's getting to be like New York," I tell him. "Crowded, traffic jams, broken glass in the streets, noisy, smelly."

"Yeah," he drawls. "I noticed a funny smell in the air…"

TO THE HIGHEST BIDDER

Dispatchers are instructed not to laugh at a customer requesting a cab from a grocery store late on a Friday afternoon. Rare is the driver who will go out of his way braving rush-hour traffic to pick up someone with twenty bags of groceries who's going around the block—it's a time-consuming short ride with a small tip. Shoppers can end up waiting and waiting. After depleting several aisles of food, these shoppers will go four blocks, take ten minutes to load and unload themselves and their groceries, take more time to carefully count out two dollars and sixty-five cents in nickels and leave a twenty-five-cent tip.

"Have I counted right?" asks the cautious passenger.

Who cares? I need to return the cab this evening. Would you get out of the car, please?

"Yes, it's fine," I'll answer, without bothering to check.

Meanwhile, the frozen dinners are thawing while melted ice cream leaks out of the grocery bag and onto the street. On Nineteenth Avenue, a main boulevard at the edge of town plagued with severe traffic backups, Stonestown Mall sports a large grocery store. Three strikes are already against those with bags full of perishable goods wishing to get home for dinner or for that matter, before the next sighting of Halley's Comet.

Today, I'm driving in circles giving people short rides. It's bad, but better than no rides at all. Scouring the area for desperate folks who need a cab, I'm already in the parking lot when I accept a call for a pickup at the grocery store. My Cab Policy regarding grocery stores and hospitals are about the same: if I'm right there, I'll take the call. I won't drive more than two blocks out of the way. The no-shows at grocery stores are a higher percentage than the hospital no shows.

An older woman gestures toward the cab. She only has three bags of groceries. This is encouraging. I stop and get out.

"Would you like those in the trunk?" I ask.

"Yes," she decides.

I begin to load the bags into the trunk, anxious to move on when I notice another woman struggling with two grocery bags and determined to avert further action.

"Hey wait," she yells. "That's mine. That's my cab!"

She's using a cane, now raised in the air, walking slowly but as fast as she can. She is not happy about this "other woman" taking *her* cab.

"I'm the one who called," she forcefully insists. "I've been waiting a long time."

The first woman doesn't allow this to slow her a bit. "I called too and I've been waiting just as long." She hurries into the back seat. "I'm 86 years old and I'm taking this cab." She shuts the door.

Eighty-six years old? This closes the deal. Possession is nine-tenths of the law. Besides, I can't see trying to pry her out of there.

The second woman isn't giving up so easily. "I'm 91 years old. I called an hour ago."

Section 512.72 of the Taxi Ordinance and Vehicle Code:

RIDE GOES TO THE HIGHEST BIDDER.

Do I hear one hundred?

Ninety-one walks over to the open car window. "This is my cab," she repeats, knocks atop the roof of the cab, paces alongside the vehicle and begins a stare down with 86 who then averts the piercing eyes of her elder potential assailant.

I'm quite astounded. The 86 year-old is less impressed.

"My feet are tired," says 86. "I'm going home." Nothing is going to move her. They've attempted to pull rank on one another and the situation can only get uglier. What am I going to do? I can't very well throw the young one out and take the old(er) one? I can see the headlines now:

91-YEAR-OLD WOMAN FOUND
EXPIRED IN PARKING LOT
Cabby Sought For Questioning

I'm 86 years old and I'm taking this cab.

The elder stateswoman comes up with a brilliant but risky all or nothing counter-move. She doesn't have much to lose at this point.

"Who are you here to pick up?"

She's stressing me out now. Where is senility when you need it? She must have been the cause of the husband's premature death.

I reluctantly get back into the cab to check if there is a name associated with the call. It's trouble either way. I'm going to be attacked by one of the two. The 91-year-old has a small build, but seems alert, agile and spry. The 86-year-old is nearly twice her size and also has an ominous cane that she could wield around if she chooses. It's a toss-up between who can probably inflict the most damage.

Brace yourself, kids; the cab computer beeps. "I'm here for…"

We all look back and forth at each other.

"Mrs. Matelski," I announce with cautious bravado. Well?

Neither of them is Mrs. Matelski.

Perfect. If I can just find Mrs. Matelski, I'll leave these two behind to fight it out and I'm out of here.

Mrs. Matelski is nowhere to be found.

The fighting resumes. Soon, they'll be pulling each other's wigs off.

"Where are you going?" I ask 91.

"Home," she says. "I'm not going to wait any longer."

"What street are you going to?"

"Ninth Avenue and Irving."

"Okay." I turn to 86. "Where are you heading?"

"Darien Way. I was here first."

"Where's that?"

"Near Cerritos Avenue."

Darien? Cerritos? I've never heard of either of the streets.

"How come there's never a cab when you need one?" asks 91.

"Yesss," squeaks 86. "Never a cab when you need one!"

"It cuts both ways," I say. "Cabs get stuck out here with no fares, too."

"The damn town needs more cabs," says 91.

"Yeah," says 86. "Like in New York."

"Where no driver speaks English and they make four dollars an hour. You want Darren Way?" I ask 86.

She points east. "One, two, nine Darien Way," she says impatiently. "You take Ocean Avenue. It's not far."

They're both going in the same relative direction, sort of.

"What if I take both of you?" I propose. "You can split the fare."

Hoping they co-operate, I patiently watch them pondering the proposition. Each one seems both leery and suspicious of the other's motive and veracity and they are equally unconvinced that this proposal will not have more advantage for the other than herself. Eyeing each other with bad intent, I know what's going through their minds: "If it's okay with her that means I'M GETTING SCREWED."

But, let's face it, this is probably the most fun they've had all week.

I propound an offer for additional incentive. "You will BOTH save money. I will make sure of it."

The magic words. They agree. Relieved, I lend a hand and an arm to 91 helping her into the front seat and walk back around to get into the driver's seat. Before I do, however, lurks one more subject of contention.

"Who is going to go home first?" whines one woman.

What next? They go at it again. They're on their own. I'm not getting involved in this one. I'm not even listening any more. I get into the cab and flip on the meter.

The computer beeps: *POSSIBLE FARES WAITING AT 19TH AVENUE.*

I noticed.

Somehow the brief stand-off resolves and the ladies miraculously work it out.

"Okay," says 86. "You take me first."

"Excellent."

They're both happy and are actually now conversing with each other quite civilly about the trials and tribulations of shopping for the lowest-priced carton of eggs. "Those 'Farm Laid' aren't as fresh as they say," comments 86.

"And what else is new?" asks 91.

We finally begin to pull away from the curb.

"Oh look," I excitedly point. "It's Mrs. Matelski!!"

They stop mid-sentence. A look of horror comes over their faces.

I turn and smile. "Just kidding, ladies. Just kidding...."

THE END GAME

“**A**lways wanted to drive a cab,” he says.

“It’s interesting,” I tell him. “But then, I’m easily entertained.”

“You must know the city really well.”

“Some areas better than others.”

“I never go anywhere. Drivin’ a cab, I’d go everyplace in town,” he laments. “Are you packin’ heat?”

I look back at him discerningly. Is *he* packing heat? Or is he just curious? He has a less-than-ordinary, National Nerd Convention-Peoria look; clean-shaven, with greased-back, brownish-blond hair. He’s wearing a wrinkled white shirt, brand new black slacks that are way too big (not deliberately hip-hop baggy) and thick brown-rimmed glasses that suggest he comes equipped with a plastic pocket protector for his pens. If he were hanging with Napoleon Dynamite, it would be a giant step upward on the social ladder. He can’t weigh more than 125 pounds.

“No,” I sadly admit, “I’m not…packin’ *heat*.”

“Oh,” he’s disappointed. “You just don’t pick up anyone who’s bigger than you?”

So he’s a smart ass, too? I’m really not in the mood today.

“That can work. But there’s not a size requirement for buying a gun. Do WE have a destination today?” I imagine him implementing the “*I won’t pick up anyone bigger than me*” policy; he’d make about five bucks.

“Yeah,” he responds. “I have the address here somewhere.”

He’s now straddling the line of simply being a dumb-ass.

“How about downtown? No, make that North Beach.”

He was no doubt constantly picked on throughout his junior and senior high school career. How many times did another student try to stuff this guy into a hallway locker? With him, one is only to wonder whether the goofy gene is located on the nerd chromosome and if they are sex-linked traits.

He again expresses his disappointment that I'm not carrying a gun. This would normally concern me. With him, it just doesn't. I'm sure he's quite harmless.

"Do the women drivers have guns?" he persists.

"I don't know. It's illegal for a driver to carry a gun, but it's good to make people think you do. It's not a subject drivers like to discuss," I reprimand him and make a right turn onto Bush. Moments later, I have the odd sensation that I'm being watched. Turning my head to the side, I almost knock into my passenger's head. He has leaned forward from the back seat and is apparently studying the computer, the meter and the dash.

"This is just like a police car, isn't it?"

"Well, the police drive the same make of car."

"Yeah," he says breathlessly. "That's what I thought."

I will say a Crown Victoria stands up to a beating. At 100,000 miles, it's still considered a new car. Of course, the company also has a repair facility located at the yard.

"What's that?" He points above my sun visor. "Mace? Cool."

"It's pepper spray." Maybe I'll save face a little bit; or maybe I'll try it out on HIM. I make a left on Larkin. Actually, I think it is illegal to carry the pepper spray too. Checking back on him as we stop for Caltrans road construction, he's deep in thought.

"You could get one," he says.

"One what?"

"Permit to carry. You know, to carry a gun."

"Oh, are you selling them?" I highly doubt.

"Oh no," he says, defending my sarcasm with a matter-of-fact tone. "You could make an *arrangement*."

"*Arrangement*? You with the Family or something?" I doubt that too.

"I've just…heard stuff. Ever use the pepper spray on anyone?"

"Yeah, on one guy, a couple weeks ago."

"What happened?"

"Nothing. No, I take that back. He got very upset and threw his skateboard at me."

"Oh?"

"I still have the bruise on my arm. The cops came, booked him and his girlfriend into jail."

"Wow."

"You wanna buy a skateboard?"

"I don't skateboard."

"Neither do I, but now I have one."

"What else do you do?" he asks.

"About what?"

"Like, when you're not driving?"

"I'm finishing a manuscript." Why am I telling him?

"What's it about?"

"About three hundred pages—cab driving, sort of; the cab is just...a *vehicle for the writing*."

"Oh, hah-huhh," he laughs. "A play on words, yeah-huh-huhh."

I hope he has money, probably has taxi scrip. These people seem normal at first, graduate to "highly eccentric" after thirty-eight seconds of conversation and then turn out to be on disability or something.

The computer buzzes with a message: WHOEVER THAT WAS WHO JUST CALLED IN—YOU'RE A COWARD! CALL AND IDENTIFY YOURSELF YOU MAGGOT.

As we are about to enter the Broadway Tunnel, a man holding a small dog darts across the street against a red light. I slam on the brakes.

"In New York, you run 'em down," he confides.

"Yep. But I just washed the cab." I blast the horn as the pedestrian/dog owner passes the bumper.

The dog owner stops and turns his head. "Asshole!" he snarls, shifts his runt-excuse-for-an-animal under his left arm and gives us the finger with his right.

"Thank you," I wave back at him and smile. "Mahalo."

"I hate little dogs," says my passenger.

"I grew up with two yapping *Poodles*. They would lunch in the cat box and then, of course, want to lick you." We had a large dog, too. My mother made a huge roast beef one night. We left the room for a few seconds, came back in, and the dog had hopped on a chair, jumped onto the kitchen table and taken several hurried bite-size portions from the slab of meat, like the dog hadn't seen food in three days. **TEMPTATION.** You can't blame the dog that much. It certainly makes more sense than eating out of a cat box.

Emerging from the Broadway Tunnel, we hit the light at Powell Street. An old wrinkled Chinese woman wearing thick glasses, using a silver walker and carrying a large grocery bag, slowly crosses in front of us. She bears a strong resemblance to the woman Bob and I encountered in Chinatown. The one he thought was an innocent bystander, who I suspected was not innocent and not a bystander. The light turns green for us, but she's still crossing. A Blue Byrd cab next to us blasts his horn. The woman looks over at him. She continues slowly and steadily. The driver honks again. The woman stops in front of his cab, shifts the grocery bag slightly to her left, raises the walker with her right arm and bashes the thing against the front grill of the taxi while loudly swearing in ear-piercing Chinese. Okay, I don't know if she was swearing, but I don't think she was opining on the unseasonably warm weather. We can hear the cab driver commenting back in *his* native language. Now, I'm pretty sure this is the same Chinese woman from over near Waverly Street (who orchestrated Bob's welcoming committee). Or maybe it's her sister. Blue Byrd should be careful. This woman will send her hirelings to the guy's home and for starters, beat the living crap out of him and any other family members found lounging or otherwise. I take the opportunity to give our vehicle gas and proceed through the green light turning yellow.

"Yesss." My passenger expresses his approval of the unfolding drama. At Stockton, we still hear honking and a check of the rear-view mirror reveals the woman's steadfast position in front of the blue cab's recently dented hood.

"How much of yer book is done?" asks my curious passenger.

"I'm working on the ending. I hate books with weak ones, so mine doesn't have one."

"There's a bunch-a Hemmingway hopefuls in San Francisco. But, I'm sort of a writer, too," he confesses.

In L.A., everyone's an actor *and* a musician while they wait tables. Here, they're writers. "What do you write?" I ask.

"Comic books. I do all the art."

"That sounds *in-tristing.*"

I say "intristing" when I'm interested. I say "interesting" when I'm not.

I met another starving comic artist years and years ago. I was renovating a Victorian house I picked up for cheap and hired this guy who literally dug ditches for me. He brought over this project he was working on, the adventures of some hero guy. I mean, I don't know much about comic books, well, *NOTHING* about them, really. But it looked great; professional and clean. He had an *investor* backing him. He might already be famous, I wouldn't know. I can't remember his name. Or he could still be digging ditches. I don't think comic books are exactly a big money-making career path. He was a hulk of a guy, though, a hard worker, and man could he dig. Thinking back about the comic book ditch digger begets a fond feeling for this boob.

"Marvel likes my stuff," he reports. "But, I'm no salesman. I'm just happy doin' the work."

"I've seen some great art—stored in closets."

"That's my closet," he says.

"Everything is politics. I used to think it was only the government and the music business."

"I was thinking to try cab driving. A friend of mine drives. He tells me stories."

"Don't you need some kind of a superhero for a comic? Supercabman," I suggest. "Cab driver by day, superhero by night."

"I like that," he says. "But, I wanna drive at night, superhero by *day*. Or how 'bout TWENTY-FIRST CENTURY DEATH CAB. Can't be stopped; blood on the hood; wreaking terror and havoc throughout the city; pedestrians: stay off the sidewalk. And it never stops for gas."

"I like that gas idea." What's an ending anyway? A change, a death, redemption? A *true* ending is a solution.

"Kill some people off," he recommends. "The cabbie, or some passengers; kill everyone off."

"I'm rather superstitious about that." Next he's going to go off about the gun thing again. I turn left at the alley, next to a strip joint on Columbus where a couple of scantily-clad women barkers employ their charms to lure a couple of sailors dressed in their "whites" inside their establishment for an eyeful and a drink.

"The only place on the strip serving alcohol," touts the tall woman. "Come and have a free look! No obligation to come and take a look!"

The sailors are sold.

"Are you serious about driving?" I ask.

"Yeah. Oh yeah."

"You wanna drive tonight?" I ask.

"Drive a cab?"

"Yeah. This one."

"That would be…" He stops.

I look back at him. His face is frozen in wonder. I could see how this guy would be writing comic books, definitely comic books.

"That'd be fantastic," he says. "Could I?"

"You know the city?"

"Some…."

"Do you know Market Street cuts diagonal across town?"

"Yeah."

"You know how to get to the Hilton?"

"Yeah."

I make another left turn down an alley and come out at Grant Street next to THE SALOON, one of several blues bars on the street. It's quiet. The band hasn't started playing yet.

"Can you recognize a French tourist from a distance?"

"What?"

"Never mind. We'll drive around, pick up some people; if you get the hang of it, I'll give you the cab."

"You're kidding."

"I don't think so. Were you going somewhere important tonight?"

"No, not really."

We continue down Grant, a street with a lot of character and a lot of *characters*. There are restaurants, coffee shops, pubs, music, gourmet desserts, pizza joints, corner stores. There are yuppies, students, beggars, winos and tourists. On a busy weekend, cars parked on both sides of the narrow street, it's a place to dazzle your senses. I knocked a side view mirror off the cab one night trying to squeeze through one of these streets. It cost me a hundred dollars.

I slow to a stop in front of the Savoy Tivoli as a young couple ambles across the street daring the cab to do them bodily harm. We continue down Grant Street as it narrows even more. I turn left on Lombard, make another left on Columbus and pull to the right into a bus zone.

"My shift ends at three in the morning. You wanna work the rest of the night?"

"And then what?"

"Then you drop the cab at the yard and go home."

After explaining some routine details, I unbuckle my seat belt, get out, walk around to the passenger's side and open the door for him. He stares at me. I motion to him with my hand. He rises from his position, walks around to the driver's side, gets behind the wheel and shuts the door. I take a seat on the passenger's side in the front.

"Wow," he says. "Cool." He looks at the meter, rubs his finger up and down the computer and gazes, open-mouthed at the brightly colored blue, red and white controls displayed on the dash. The meter reads $6.20. I punch the second button on the left to stop it.

"You *have* driven a car before, right?" I ask.

"Oh yeah." He pulls out and hands me his California license.

He's actually quite photogenic, Matthew Alan Gleason, twenty-seven years old, lives on Powell Street, license expires in a year and a half. A Pisces, I think. Hopefully he doesn't drive like another good friend of mine, also a Pisces. Very mellow, but keep him out of the driver's seat. I hit another button, shutting the meter off.

"Can I try it?" he asks. "I know how it works."

Matthew hits one button and the meter drops to $1.70, hits the second button twice and it goes blank. He seems very *attracted* to it. Meanwhile, jotting down his driver's license number, I hand back the ID.

"I'm Larry." I extend my hand.

"I'm Matt, or Matthew, that's what my Mom calls me when I get in trouble."

"Hmmmm. Well, Matthew, don't get us in any trouble."

"Okay," he meekly responds.

"How's your driving record? Moving violations, speeding tickets?"

"Got a parking ticket last week."

"That's fine. Let's go."

"Shouldn't I have a test or something?"

"You just had it." Should I ask if he's prone to nightmares and sleeping difficulties?

"That's all?"

"Well, what do you want?" A physical? "Okay. What do Gough, Pine and Franklin Streets have in common?" Boys and girls? Are we back in the first grade?

"Uhhh, they're all…one-way streets?" He pauses. "The lights are timed, some of them; along with Bush Street."

"Very impressive, Bush Street. Have you met Cat Woman?"

"From Batman? Do you know her?"

"No, no, never mind. So what part of town is going to be profitable tonight?"

"Right here; North Beach, people finishing dinner and stuff."

"Good choice."

"WOW, COOL!"

I can't help but laugh to myself. He slowly pulls to the left. Traffic is light. We make a smooth descent down Columbus and make a left on Pacific. He's already driving much better than *my* Pisces friend, very cautious and mindful of the road. A bit slow, but I'm sure the speedometer will pick up once he gets a little more comfortable.

A man flags us, puts his head forward and squints as he realizes our cab has a passenger in the front seat, *me*.

"Pull over and get that guy," I tell my driver.

We pull over next to the man flagging.

"Get in," I order.

"Isn't the cab taken?" questions the uncertain man.

"No," I tell him curtly. "We're in training here. He's a new driver."

"I'm really in a hurry," he says.

"You got money?" I ask.

"Of course."

"You goin' to Berkeley?"

"I'm going to Fillmore and Union," he quickly responds.

"Approved." Reaching back from the front seat, I pop the back door open. Berkeley-ites don't tip. Some don't even have enough to pay the meter, plus you're stuck in Berkeley. You're out the fare, the bridge toll, the twenty-minute drive, the gas; once in Berkeley it's illegal for a San Francisco cab to pick up Berkeley passengers. Unless you get a call, you drive back to the city, empty. People in Berkeley don't call a San Francisco cab for a ride. Capeesh?

"Matthew, when they're in a hurry," I whisper, "ask them if they have money. And if they're going to Berkeley, that's a bad sign too."

Matthew scrunches his lips and nods his head. "Yeah, cool. Berkeley."

Our new passenger positions himself for the ride. He smells good, like bubble gum; and we're off.

"I'm Larry and this is Matt," I tell the passenger. "You're his first fare."

"Oh," says the flustered passenger. "Umm, my name is Thomas."

"Hello Thomas," says Matt.

"Is this a smoking cab?" asks Thomas, already with a cigarette and lighter in hand. I look at my driver and he looks at me with concern. I point at Matthew.

"Oh no," says Matthew. "I can't have smoking in my cab."

Yeah. I like his approach. "Matthew just quit smoking," I reveal.

"I did?" questions Matthew.

"What?" Thomas follows up.

"Well, it's been three weeks. Having smokers around makes him want a cigarette. And I've got a nicotine patch." I point to my arm.

"Oh?" Matthew still fails to mask his expression of wonder.

"Oh," repeats Thomas, sounding mystified.

"Oh yeah, that's on behalf of the two addicts here in the front seat. Ya know, I figure in another two weeks, we'll both be smoking again; might not even last two more weeks."

More bewildered than convinced, Thomas packs the cigarette away. No tip.

We get to Fillmore Street. Matthew stops the meter, turns it off and the computer beeps. "What's buzzing," asks Thomas.

"The brakes went out," I say.

"Ha hah. What if the brakes *do* go out?" asks Thomas, obviously new in town.

"Only drive uphill," I advise.

The fare is six dollars. Thomas holds out a ten.

"Keep the change."

"Thank you," I tell him. "Sorry about the cigarettes. We owe you one."

"Have a good evening," Matthew tells him.

I hand Matthew the ten. "That's yours. You're gonna need it to pay the gate."

"Thanks." He pockets it. Thomas bails out, almost burns his hand lighting up his cigarette in waiting. Three seconds later, two rambunctious young women in their twenties, one blonde, the other brunette, both wearing tight blue jeans and high heels, get into the cab as they are in the midst of a discussion. Their destination: Greenwich and Larkin. They comfortably settle into the back seat.

"Did he stay over?" asks the brunette.

"Well…yes," says the hesitant blonde. "It got late and we…we had a couple drinks."

"Are you like, gonna see him again?"

"I don't know."

"C'mon Marci," the brunette wisps. "Did ya close the deal?"

"Yes. It was a big mistake. He's really a nice guy."

The curse of death—being a nice guy. Passengers don't realize it, but it's no use whispering in a cab. The driver hears everything.

"The problem was," says Marci, "he went on for like…two hours. It was ridiculous."

"Well did he…uhhh, I mean, what did you do?"

"I told him he was killin' me. I'm still sore."

"How come there's two of you?" asks the brunette.

"Cabs are so scarce in this town," I explain, "it's two drivers to a cab. We split everything, gas, the gate, tips, the driving; when we get to Van Ness, I'm gonna take the wheel."

"I'm in training," Matthew counters. "This is my first night."

"You're his second fare," I add. "Ever."

"Oooo-oooh," says the brunette, intrigued. "I like those inexperienced ones. Hold 'em, *mold* 'em and fold 'em."

"Fold him?" I ask. "Now you be nice to him."

"Oh, we will," says the blonde.

Matthew enjoys the attention, straightens his driving posture and proceeds in a most businesslike manner. At Greenwich, the women get out and tip him two dollars on the four-dollar fare. I watch them as they climb the stairs of a large white apartment building.

"Look," says Matt holding up one of the five dollar bills as we drive off. "There's a phone number on here. I think it was the brunette, I saw her writing on something with a green pen."

"You're not supposed to be collecting women's phone numbers," I scold.

"Oh. I'd never call her. I like a more…substantial woman."

"What? Like a career woman?"

"No, no. A *larger* woman."

"Bigger breasts?"

"Bigger EVERYTHING!"

"Fat," I say. "You like *fat* women?"

"I like *zaftig* women," he corrects. "A warm soft place to nestle in for the night."

Matthew begins to relate his romantic woes to me, when we are interrupted by a tall skinny man wearing a dark blue sweat suit, matching blue socks and a gold watch, flagging us at Union and Larkin. We stop.

"Are you available?" he asks.

"Yes," I tell him. "I'm just along for the ride."

The man appears unhappy. He grimaces and gets into the back seat. "Van Ness and Golden Gate; please hurry."

Matthew hits the meter and continues down Union Street.

"Make a left onto Polk Street," the man curtly directs. "Make a right turn when you get to Pacific. Don't go down Broadway with all that traffic. And when you get to Van Ness, make a left turn, go straight to Golden Gate Avenue. On the right hand corner at Golden Gate you can drop me there at the news stand."

Matthew looks over at me. Our eyes meet in acknowledgement of our—odd passenger.

"How is your evening, sir?" Matthew tactfully and professionally queries.

"I'm very late," he answers.

"You ever make love to a *big* woman, Larry?" asks Matthew, in a low, quiet voice, as if our passenger is not going to hear.

"How big? Actually…no."

"You don't know what you're missing. They have a different attitude; more approachable; appreciative."

"Hard up," interjects our passenger.

"No," Matthew scolds. "Well…maybe. No," he corrects himself, "horny; but in a good way."

We drive in silence past Broadway. Matthew makes the right turn on Pacific as precisely requested by our guest. We travel one block to Van Ness and get stopped behind three cars making a left turn. We miss the light.

"Damn," says the passenger.

"So anyway," Matthew says to me. "I just ended a relationship. She ended it." His voice trails off momentarily.

"Was she…what, overweight?"

"Weight-challenged," he corrects.

"Fat," our passenger offers.

"In water, like a hot tub, it's a whole other deal." Matthew primes us on the details, more than I really need to hear.

"Making love with a big woman is exhilarating, it's…." Matthew's voice trails off again, whether from lacking an appropriate metaphor or from overwhelming emotion, I couldn't say. But the light has turned green and his foot is cemented to the brake.

"So ya hang out at restaurants, see who eats the most food, and ask the winner out for a date?" I ask.

"No, there has to be an attraction," Matthew corrects.

"Carry wine, cheese and crackers," chimes in our blue friend. "But, excuse me, Casanova, the light's goddamn green!"

"There's a car in front of me, sir," says Matthew.

"Well blow yer horn or something. I don't have all night to sit here."

"There's a pedestrian crossing the street, sir."

Our passenger hrrumphhs, letting out a heavy breath of air doused with garlic—or it could be tuna salad. As we finally make our left turn we meet bumper-to-bumper traffic on Van Ness.

"I met her in a restaurant," Matthew pines. "I was waiting tables. She came in for dinner. I'd never seen her before. She had soup and a large Caesar salad with anchovies. Then she had an appetizer off the bar menu and after that, ordered a chicken entree, vegetables, rice pilaf and a baked potato. None of this 'I'm embarrassed to eat in front of people' crap or that low-carb diet bullshit. Excuse me," he says sheepishly. "I didn't mean to swear. And, she orders a virgin Bloody Mary. Very sexy. Just the name turns me on."

I'm not sure who needs more help, our blue passenger or our green driver.

"So then she asks, 'Could we have more bread?'" Matthew beams. "That was awesome."

"She was there with a girlfriend?"

"No, by herself."

"Oh, isn't that, ahh, Raymond Carver or a Nabokov novel or something? A gigantic fat guy in a restaurant?"

"Yeah. That's what got us talking. We had so many things in common."

"Are you just going to stay on here with all this traffic?" asks our irritated passenger.

"You were very exact, sir," says Matthew. "You wanted to travel this street."

"Not at this speed. Hellfire, can't you take another street?"

"How about Gough?" asks Matthew.

"That's *way* out there," groans our passenger. "I know my way around."

"Sir, it's two blocks over."

We turn right on Clay, travel up-hill to Gough, turn left and make it downhill to Golden Gate, clear sailing and not a single red light. The fare reads $4.80.

"I don't have any change," excuses the man, throwing down a five-dollar bill as he darts across the street into the corner building.

"Don't let the assholes get you down," I tell Matthew. "That's the main challenge of the job; that and keeping people from throwing up in the cab. Get 'em outside the car, at a tree or in a bush or something.

Worst case scenario: with their heads completely out the window; when you're at a stop. Trouble is, you get these folks with the far-away look in their eyes (not from being in love, but from drinking seven Heinekens in two hours). Or they complain of a headache, say they're thirsty or want you to open a window when it's forty degrees outside. You can offer to pull over for them, but they will ALWAYS insist they're fine; whether it's before, during or after they're revisited their breakfast, lunch and evening snack. Or maybe it's simply denial of the obvious projectile vomit warning signals (never mind the 'one last beer,' several rum and cokes, two Long Island Iced Teas, a Planters Punch, four bowls of pretzels, two orders of nachos and a handful of pistachios). And finally, they decide to CATCH the vomit in their hands which never works. It's important to be able to detect the pertinent warning signals that identify those people who started drinking at 5:30 in the afternoon and didn't stop until half past midnight.

"You don't want them vomiting when the cab's moving. There's gonna be barf splashed all over the seats and you will be the one left to clean it up. Pukers don't clean up after themselves. You don't wanna be conducting business with the car smelling like puke."

We make a left turn onto Van Ness. At Pine Street, we lose out to a competing hack on the pickup of a group of European tourists with Hard Rock Café shopping bags. We drive to California Street where the cable car has stopped, unloading a handfull of passengers but none of them wants a cab. We drive east to Polk Street and make a right. The computer beeps: *ZONE 26—PLACE 1.*

"We're first up in the zone," I point. "Ya see?"

Matthew looks at the display. I again explain how the computer works, dividing the city into zones. He figures it will be easier to cruise and pick up fares off the street once he's on his own for the night.

"So what happened with your *zaftig* love?" I ask.

"Jean was her name. She played the violin. Well, she had a violin. I don't even remember if I ever heard her play. Oh, well. Jean the queen. What a wardrobe, bright and glossy colors. The neighbors upstairs thought she was a female impersonator. She wanted to lose weight, but I liked her the way she was. She had this huge vibrator, biggest I've ever seen. And very noisy."

"Don't they usually have, like, a quiet hum?"

"Not the vibrator...her. She was loud; ya know, a screamer. She would moan and I mean, just very enthusiastic. But, the downstairs neighbors, they complained to the landlord. Very vindictive. They called the police on Valentine's Day and we weren't even home that night."

"So...how much did she weigh?"

"Oh, three-twenty-five, three-fifty. She fluctuated; she hit two-ninety-seven on her diet. And I told her, 'Diets don't work.' She gained it back."

"Ya gotta exercise." I point to our left. "There's a guy flagging."

"No, he's just talking with his hands."

"I hate that."

As we travel down Polk Street, the computer beeps again with a message: *FARE WAITING. 870 HYDE STREET O'FARRELL/GEARY.*

"We got one!" says Matt. We make a left on Post (transvestite prostitute turf) and travel past the MOTHER LODE. It looks quiet there tonight. There are three people standing at the entrance to the club, speaking to the security guard posted at the door. The guard I assume is to prevent gay bashers from causing trouble.

I ask Matthew to drop me at Jones and California, after we pick up and drop the Hyde Street fare.

"You goin' to Grace Cathedral?"

"Yeah, to pray you don't get into an accident."

"I'm drivin' okay. Aren't I?"

"I'm kidding. I'm going to Vanessi's. The minestrone soup should be good and thick about now. You feeling comfortable?"

"I like this."

"So, do you still talk to your ex, Jean?" I ask.

"She met some *fuckin' FAT* guy at this weight control seminar. They got married last month."

"Ohhh." I nod my condolences. "Well, I'm sorry. That's bad, right?"

"You should see him. He's bigger than she is."

It sounds lovely. Then he said something under his breath I couldn't make out. It didn't seem appropriate to ask what it was.

"A big woman offers certain things ya can't get other places," says Matthew, taking a right turn on Hyde Street. "I mean, unique qualities of love-making."

"Oh yeah?" I don't want to hear his details.

"There's a tremendous outpouring of love, ya know, of fluid."

"You're makin' me sick."

"Ahhh, you're a prude. You haven't lived yet."

"If *not* wanting to hear about Jean's gushing sexual juices make me a prude, then I'm a prude."

"I just can't figure it out. Ya know what I mean?"

"It sounds like you miss her."

"What she sees in that fat fuck she married...."

We pull up in front of 870 Hyde.

"Take the car keys and the pepper spray in this neighborhood," I caution him.

I reach over and grab the canister tucked between the ceiling and the driver's side visor. He turns off the motor and pulls out the keys. We both get out of the cab and walk up to the black metal bars on the doorway. There's a bank of 12 buttons to the side of the steel entryway, one for each apartment.

"There wasn't an apartment number on that order, was there?"

"Nope," says Matthew.

"Didn't think so."

We go back to the cab and I contact the dispatcher. They have no apartment number either. They cancel the order. We honk lightly on the horn to see if anyone responds from the second or third-story windows. Nothing. We wait another minute, get back in the car and keep driving, cutting over to Polk Street and heading north.

A huge lesbian wearing a leather hat and black leather pants, pierced lip, a pierced chin, a stud pierced into the bridge of her nose and keys dangling from her belt loop, flags us from the doorway of a donut shop across the street. Matthew pulls to the right. She struts across the lanes of traffic, deliberate and confident. Even though she's moving slowly, her whole body shifts twice with each step she takes resembling a walking gigantic mold of Jell-O, if you could fit something that large into a refrigerator.

"The woman must weigh four hundred pounds!" he says excitedly. "Should I open the door for her?"

"That's your call."

She already has the door open and is *crawling* into the cab. Her hands are stretched out in front of her, groping the back seat, while she uses the back of my seat rest for leverage, pushing forward with her leg wedged on the floor of the cab.

"I'm goin' to that Thai place over on Market," she shouts out. "Near the Mexican restaurant." She rolls herself upright onto the seat and shuts the door. Very smooth maneuvering.

"Do you know the cross street?" I ask. Market Street is five miles long. And why is she yelling?

"I know which one. I know where it is," says Matthew.

I look at him askew; one of those head-tilted-sideways dog stares.

"Sanchez and Market," he says.

"Yeah that's it," she nods.

Very impressive. "Okay," I say, "that's going to be Zone 37 or you can book into Zone 41." I punch in the destination. The computer beeps and a car alarm goes off on a blue Oldsmobile parked next to us.

"How's your day?" asks the woman.

"Good," says Matthew.

"Who the hell are you?" she asks. She's not talking so loudly anymore.

"You talkin' to me?" I turn to her and stare at the piece of steel piercing her chin. I try not to, but I can't help it.

"Yeah," she says. There's the scent of alcohol on her breath.

"It's the new company training program," I tell her. "Every new driver gets a co-driver, to help the new driver and help the passengers."

"Shit," she says. "You didn't even know where the fuck I was goin'. Driver, he ain't helpin' ya. You should trade him in."

"No, he's been really good," Matthew defends.

"Dump him. Dump his raggedy ass in the river."

River? What river? What the hell is she talking about now? I figure it's some kind of lesbian code. I'm sure Matthew knows what she's talkin' about.

"So what's happenin', brand new driver?" She locks onto his shoulder with a firm hand.

"We were just talkin' about the virtues of love-making with a large woman."

I can barely believe what I definitely heard. But I understand everything now, with perfect clarity. He has some sort of a death wish; some not-so-subconscious, self-destructive suicide mission he's on and he has somehow dragged ME along. He's not going to crash the car. We are going to be crushed IN the car, by a hulking, very unhappy woman. First, our brains will be squeezed from our heads, and then....

"Yeah?" she sounds amused and releases her grip on his shoulder.

"My ex wasn't quite your size," he explains. "But she WAS a big girl."

We *ARE* going to be killed.

"No one *enjoys* love-makin' like a BIGGGG woman," says the lesbian, rocking back and forth. "*No one* makes love BETTER than a full-size woman."

"We broke up," says Matthew. "We ate at that restaurant every Wednesday night; curry and Pad Thai for dinner, margaritas at the Mexican place. Sometimes we'd order pasta at the Italian place across the street, walk around Market, hit the hot tubs, sauna and a *sex-travaganza*, as she'd call it. I will never forget our love-making," he pouts.

"On a cold San Francisco night, you grab a warm spot and hold on tight," she says. "Don't worry, kid, there's other big fish in the sea."

Or whatever. Matt stops the meter at eight dollars, gets out of the cab and circles around to open her door. While he's circling around the cab, she taps me on the shoulder.

"Hey," she jabs her finger into me. "I wanna know if he's just goofy, or if he's goofy and wants to fuck me?"

I shake my head and shrug my shoulders. Matt opens the door as she laughs and gives me a "playful" shove. If my seatbelt had not been taut, I would have been body-slammed into the dash.

"See ya later," she says to me, hands Matt thirteen dollars, telling him "keep it" and then crawls out of the car the same way she entered, only in reverse. Where she had pulled to get in, she pushes off to get out. Once outside, she slams the door shut and has a few words with Matt; they both laugh, then he goes around to the driver's side and gets in. I watch her from behind as she methodically makes her way to the front door of the restaurant where an enthusiastic slender man wearing a white shirt and a black bow tie stands to greet her. Matt offers to split the money with me. I refuse.

"You did the flirting, you get the dough."

"She's a *sexy* woman," he says.

"Did you get her phone number?" I ask.

"Naw, but I know where to find her. You know," he informs me, "she's a lesbian."

"Really?" I raise my eyebrows. "I didn't know. Maybe you could turn her."

"She's not really my type." He appears melancholy. "It might be fun."

We make a U-turn on Market and once again head toward my destination at California and Jones. Matthew is in deep concentration. About the lesbian? Driving? The old flame? Whatever. There's a lot of time for thinking on this job. It's what drives some people nuts. If you're gonna do lots of thinking, you gotta have a good mind set; you need something good to think about.

We descend down Market to Franklin. I brief him on dealing with passengers, traffic and **MY CAB POLICY,** not that he needed it, but he was asking.

"You're gonna do fine. Just don't crash the car."

"This is great," he says. "You gonna get in trouble for this?"

"How much trouble can I get in? I *QUIT!*"

Matthew takes a left on Franklin going just a little too fast.

"I thought you were going to get us killed," I say.

"Sorry about that turn."

"No, I'm talking about the bull-dyke."

"Ahhh, she's harmless. Like a kitten."

"A four-hundred-pound kitten. You wanna be careful about testing people, Matthew. You put yourself at risk."

At Franklin and Turk the cell phone rings, just as three Japanese men in pinstripe suits flag us from the southwest corner. I check the flashing caller ID. It's Bob. I don't answer. "Is that a company phone?" Matthew asks.

"No, no it's not. "Pick em' up," I point to the immaculate business-suited men.

"Aren't you hungry?" asks Matthew.

"They're probably going to the Nikko or the Hilton. I can wait. And I want you to make my gate."

He pulls to the left.

"Are you available?" asks the younger man.

"Yes." Matthew reaches back to open the passenger door.

They converse in Japanese as a City Cab pulls in behind us and honks. The men get into the back seat.

"Hilton Tower," says one of them.

The City Cab driver honks again to no avail and then lays on the horn, shakes his waybill at us, jerks his vehicle in front of oncoming traffic and speeds off down Franklin.

"What's with him?" asks Matthew.

"Probably upset you've got a passenger in the front and now an additional group in the back and he's driving around empty. Or maybe we stole his order."

"Why-ah they two cab drivah?" inquires one.

"He's in training. Same price though, two for one."

"Twoofer-one," repeats the other man. They converse. I know ten words in Japanese, five of which I've forgotten. But they like the two for one.

"Ya know," says Matthew patiently waiting for traffic to clear, "this image thing with bull-dykes is blown way out of proportion." He carefully merges to the right. "Jean was friends with a couple. They were nice people."

"I don't doubt that."

"There should be a more *neutral* word," says Matthew, slowing to a stop for a yellow light.

"I imagine some people are offended by 'bull-dyke' and others are proud of it."

"Probably, it's acceptable if you are one," says astute Matthew.

"Excuse me please," interrupts the youngest Japanese man from the back seat. "What is bull-dyke?"

I look at Matthew and he looks at me. He shrugs.

"Kind of like…like a female samurai," I attempt to explain.

"Ahhh so-ooo," he nods, turning to his two companions and says a few words in Japanese. The man next to him asks a question. The third man volunteers an answer and they continue their discussion. Usually when the younger guy speaks, there is nodding of heads, oohs and ahs. I figure he is the one responsible for showing them around town, educating them on the eccentricities of American culture.

At O'Farrell we make a measured and cautious right turn. As we cross Polk Street, one passenger comments in an over-exaggerated accent, "Meetchell-Brotha-sex-tee-a-tar." Their conversation excitedly heats up.

We drop them at the Hilton, drive past the Nikko and make a left on Powell Street. At California Street I look downtown admiring the view of the Bay and the Bridge. Matthew is about to take a left.

"There's no left turn here."

"What? Isn't that for other drivers?"

"No. A cop pulled me over once for honking my horn. You have to obey the traffic signs."

He is disappointed, but proceeds down Powell, turns left onto Sacramento and circles back to California to patiently follow behind a cable car traveling from Mason across to Taylor. He gently jogs to the right, checks his mirrors twice and smoothly pulls around an empty tour bus. We glide left into the courtyard entrance of Vanessi's restaurant.

"Remember," I tell him. "Get into the gas line at the yard first thing. Just follow the rest of the cabs. The attendant tops off the tank. Give him the waybill so he can write down the gasoline charge. Park the cab in the sixth row toward the back; the medallion, the waybill and the money go to the cashier."

"Yeah," Matthew confirms. "And that shortcut, Sixth Street onto 280, then the Army Street exit, a left turn and two right turns gets me into the yard. What if I forget something?"

"Just ask a driver. They're all pretty nice until you're competing for a fare or telling them not to smoke cigarettes while waiting in line. Oh, and tip the cashier a buck or two."

"Won't *he* ask questions?"

"He'll wonder who the hell you are. Tell him hello for me, or good-bye. No, don't say anything unless he asks. Actually, here." I hand him a five dollar bill. "Give him five bucks, so he's not any trouble."

Matthew looks doubtful.

"Just bring back the cab and the medallion. That's what the company cares about; you don't want the cops putting an APB on your ass. And paying the gate, they want their money."

"I'm just nervous."

"You should be. Tell passengers it's your first night. You can make wrong turns, roll through stop signs, and they'll still tip you." My final parting words: "Just don't get into an accident. It'll cost me $500." That's the deductible.

I unbuckle my seat belt, jump out and slam the door, before better sense takes over. I watch him signal, cautiously back out of the courtyard, politely merge into traffic and coast down California Street toward the Mark Hopkins. As good as it feels to stand up, I'm exhausted; I had another night of anxious dreams. Usually can't remember details; but this time, one minute I'm driving and the next second I'm lost, navigating on foot through gang-controlled neighborhoods where a beating is the punishment for being on the wrong side of the street. They never catch me, but there's a lot of running through people's yards and across unfamiliar streets.

And now, what if he steals the cab? Hopefully the APB comment will make him think twice about that. Why steal it when he's got semi-legitimate use of it? I check my pocket for the scrap of paper with his license number. I've got it.

As I stride into Vanessi's, there's a stylin' middle-aged man wearing an obvious toupee, crouched atop the piano bench and violating a Steinway grand while molesting the unsuspecting chord structure of

Strawberry Fields with an abusive battery of awkward staccato arpeggios. It's god-awful. At least he's not singing. After all, people *are* eating.

I make my way down the carpeted stairs to a bank of pay phones. I put in a quarter and dial the girlfriend. No answer.

I'm feeling nauseous. Maybe it's from too much caffeine. I call her cell phone. No answer.

She was supposed to be home tonight. Maybe I'm just hungry. Or perhaps the realization has set in that I just gave my cab to a total stranger. Or it might just be the friggin' piano player who has completed the Strawberry Fields butchery, moving on to his next selection and now he IS singing: *"Feelings. Nothing more than* FEEEELINGS...."

I strongly consider a stop at the men's room but instead I double back up the multi-colored carpeted stairway in time to hear a portly and generous gentleman offer the pianist a proposal.

"I'll give ya ten bucks to play Take Five, but ya gotta do it, now. Right NOW."

The pleasant good-looking hostess wearing a sleek black mini-dress and sparkling gold high-heels, seats me in a booth. I order minestrone, meat lasagna and a shot of whiskey. If Matthew runs over any pedestrians, a shot of whiskey won't ease my troubles. Gut feeling: everything will work out just fine. More whiskey. As the hot sensation engulfs my forehead, the ability to distinguish gut feelings from wishful ones is lost.

I finish off the thick soup, request additional French bread and the cell phone rings—unknown caller. This time I answer.

"What are you, in a bar?"

"No, I'm grabbing a bite to eat." It's Michelle. I sip at the whiskey, but can still recognize the piano player's crooning. Should I ask her to join me for soup?

"I was calling for a ride to the airport. I'm going back east to visit family."

So much for the soup. I down the remains of the next shot.

"Sorry." Should I tell her I quit? What if it's only temporary? Then I'll feel like a real goofball. "I'd love to do that, but I already turned in the cab."

"Well, I'll call you when I get back, if that's alright."

"Yes." Please. My head is overheating. I hope I wasn't slurring my words. "Call when you get back." Was that too anxious?

"I will." She hangs up.

I think I handled this wrong. But my mind is too fuzzed to figure an alternative. I finish off the meal and another whiskey. I successfully flag a De Soto for the ride back to my apartment. The driver is somewhat normal. I'm glad and possibly drunk.

Later that night, in the midst of a troubled sleep, I get up, pace, then get dressed and make my way back to the company yard. It's 4:30 in the morning. The cab is quietly parked right where I told him to park it. There are no dents, no blood, safely in the yard. And the police have not come looking for me, so far. I return home atop Twin Peaks and sleep soundly through what's left of the night.

•

Several months later, as they say, on a beautiful, warm, sunny day, I'm purchasing a grape juice from the corner store at Market and Sixteenth in the Castro. There's a tap on my shoulder. Someone hitting on me? Someone asking for spare change INSIDE a store?

It's Matthew. He's buying salted peanuts, bottled water and a chocolate bar. Standard issue cab driver provisions, but I don't see a cab.

"How's it goin'?"

"Excellent," he tells me. "I went back a week later after you gave me the cab and got hired on the weekend day shift."

I'm happy for him. And I'm happy for me. I'm well rested, but miss the income, now living solely on student loans. "That can be tough," I reminisce, walking out of the store with him and into the sunlight. "Money-wise."

"It's great," he cheers, raising his peanuts to the sky and attracting the attention of several folks. "I haven't seen you around." He cracks open the package of nuts and pops one into his mouth. "I kinda owe you."

"You don't owe me. Just be careful out here."

"Yeah," he nods. "How's yer book?"

"Good. I think I have an ending, at least for now. How's the comic book stuff?"

"Cool. I've got a publisher interested. Hey," he points at my gut, "you need a ride?"

"Naw. I'm walkin' today."

"I'm parked around the corner," he points. "I even have my own regular assigned cab. No more spares! You should check it out."

I take a swig of my grape juice as he pops one peanut after another into his mouth. I follow him as he happily struts to the waiting vehicle.

"These hours though, they get weird. My girlfriend's been stressin'." He gets in, shuts the door and rolls down the window.

"A new girlfriend? Congratulations."

"Yeah. She wants to buy a pet 'cause I'm gone so much."

"Better than shopping for a new boyfriend."

"The 5:30 a.m. shift is getting to her. I told her it's only temporary." He crinkles his forehead and rubs his eyebrow. "She wants this pet *pig*. I don't know what's wrong with her." He produces a picture of the two of them—him and her, no pig. Judging from the picture, she's a little taller than he and about three times his size.

"Hmmm," I nod my head. That's when I look down and notice the side of his bright yellow vehicle, curiously numbered—294.

He barely has the key in the ignition when the vehicle's motor starts up with a loud roar.

"You sure I can't give you a ride?" he cheerily offers. The engine races twice. "Anywhere you wanna go. No charge."

"Thanks," I answer, still distracted by my discovery.

"Hey," he shouts, "I'll buy a couple copies of yer book."

"That's a deal," I say.

I step to the sidewalk. The engine guns once again, gas pedal to the floor, transmission in neutral. The headlights flash on, off, then on again. The cab jerks uneasily into gear, out from the parking space and into the lane of traffic. Seconds later, the right turn signal flips on as the yellow four-wheeled craft makes a screeching left turn, abruptly cutting off a spankin' new red 1½-ton pickup truck, prompting suggestions from its two occupants on additional maneuvers Matthew might employ; this amidst a long stream of obscenities, punctuated by loud blasts from their horn. Matthew's cab jerks to a stop, then burns rubber, making its own erratic path across the Market Street six-way intersection, somehow avoiding pedestrians, a double-parked cart of groceries and two small dogs. There's a near collision with a green Honda civic driven by a young Chinese woman. She slams on her brakes, shakes her fist and "blasts" her meek horn in unison with the red pickup, while attempting to follow Matthew's blazing trail. Taxi number 294 accelerates and switches lanes cutting in front of a De Soto Cab rightfully about to pick up two people hailing for a ride from a crowded bus stop. De Soto blasts his horn, presents Matthew a middle finger and a not-so-friendly (Italian) double-pump salute.

"That's my fare," yells furious De Soto.

Two oblivious passengers pile into the bright yellow cab. Paying absolutely no mind to road courtesy or De Soto's arguable first right of refusal, Matt returns De Soto's offerings with a friendly wave of his open hand. De Soto is still fingering. Number 294 engulfs the formerly impatient bus-waiting folk (barely seated), accelerates ahead of oncoming traffic, makes a dangerously illegal U-turn and veers out of sight. The Honda, the now forlorn pickup and a host of people still waiting for the bus are left behind.

"Hey," I yell. "Hey, De Soto!"

De Soto looks over at me from across the six lanes of traffic, peering out from behind a palm tree planted in the cement divider. I give *him* the finger. De Soto jerks to a stop. Perplexed, now realizing I'm not interested in a ride, he backs up and almost collides with a Muni bus closing in on his rear. The car shifts out of reverse, makes a screeching sharp right turn onto Sanchez and disappears into the distance.

It's a fine day.

I cross the street and walk west on the upward-sloping side of Market, where another man and his female companion deliriously attempt to attract the attention of an oncoming cab. One taxi passes them without even slowing down. Then another drives past, this one already filled with passengers. A third cab without passengers also drives past them.

"Damn, damn," cusses the man to the equally frustrated woman. I walk by, offering a friendly smile, finish off the last swig of my drink and toss the bottle in the trash.

"Ya know?" I say to them. "There's never a cab in this town when you need one."

And I just keep walking.

CAB DRIVING GLOSSARY

Blurtation: an inadvertent admission; to say something better left unsaid.

Book in the zone: registering your cab in position located in a certain area of the city which places the cab into line for the orders phoned into dispatch; same as booking into the zone. Some mistake the phrase to mean the cabbie is driving fast in the zone – this would be redundant.

Booked off: when the computer knocks the driver out from his turn in line to get a fare in his zone of choice. When a driver does not respond to (accept) the message FARE WAITING within one minute, the computer books you off. A driver can also get "booked off" because the computer crashes, from signal interference, by being out of range of the home base signal, or simply because the driver has not appropriately tipped the radio room folks in three weeks.

Brakes: standard auto equipment treated as optional accessory.

Butterfly: a serious wound; deep gash; cumbersome insect.

Computer: method of communication between the radio dispatcher and the driver used in lieu of the radio.

Danglings: clothing accoutrements with no particular purpose or practical function.

Dead Head to the Airport: when a driver decides to drive to the airport "empty" (without passengers) in hopes that the airport is moving and that he can quickly (within one hour) pickup a passenger; no connection related to Grateful Dead fans headed to the airport.

DeSoto: rival cab company; the enemy.

Dispatcher (cab dispatcher): bitter person who distributes cabs and their corresponding medallions to drivers for the start of their shift. He determines when and whether or not a driver ever gets on the road.

Dispatcher (radio dispatchers): the sarcastic radio room dispatchers answer and handle calls from customers requesting taxi services. Drivers show appreciation for the dispatchers after their shift with small talk, tips, and good drugs. The dispatcher shows appreciation by sending drivers an airport order, traffic tips, and addresses that have never and will never exist.

Fare Waiting: the message a driver receives over the computer when a fare becomes available in his Zone; synonym: the enemy.

Gas pedal: item often removed from vehicles rented to tourists.

Gate: cost of a cab for a shift. Friday and Saturday nights are the most expensive nights of the week. Gate fees will range from $80 to $130 per shift.

Hills (traveling up hill): gas is an out-of pocket expense. Drivers will avoid traveling up hill at every opportunity. Also, tourists rarely scare when traveling up hill. Traveling down hill is the preferred route.

Hills: (traveling down hill): a chance for cab driver to express his gratitude to passengers.

Horn: mandatory cab equipment; if not working, get the vehicle to the shop immediately.

Lights (red, green, yellow): residents of Los Angeles, green means go, yellow means go, and red means go faster. **San Francisco's Chinatown**, red means stop, yellow means stop and green means drive 10 feet; then stop. **Taxicab drivers**: meanings vary depending upon road conditions.

Juan Marichal: famous San Francisco Giants pitcher—had an exaggerated wind up featuring an above the head kick of the front foot that confused hitters who already couldn't hit him in the first place.

Medallion: metal bicycle size license plate that makes the cab legal to be on the street.

No Money: common traits of those persons traveling to Berkeley or flagging from bus stops.

Murgles: sound emanating from the throat when one's speech pattern has been altered as a result of a severe beating about the head and body.

Nina Oord: again, c'mon, look her up on the internet

No soap radio: dilemma often encountered by two lions sharing a bath tub together.

No-Show: when a driver shows up on a call for a pickup, but no one shows up. Synonymous with a call from a hospital or grocery store.

Scrip: vouchers sold primarily to seniors and persons with disabilities, usually on a discount, whose value is recognized only by the taxi company issuing them. De Soto scrip must be used for a De Soto cab; Yellow scrip must be used for a Yellow cab.

Short-Shift: on a busy evening, the cab dispatcher will offer up the opportunity for drivers to cut their standard 10-hour shift "short" and bring the cab in early, requiring pro-rated payment only for the hours worked. This opportunity arises on Friday and Saturday nights, New Years Eve, St. Patrick's Day, and Halloween.

Spare cab: an "older" cab with over 300,000 miles used as a replacement for regularly assigned cabs; vehicle assigned as a convenient form of punishment meated out by the cab dispatcher; synonyms: stink mobile; jalopy; banger; junk heap.

Tip: chance for passengers and tourists to express their gratitude to the cab driver; a word not yet found in French or German dictionaries.

Tourist: the enemy, but usually good for business; often recognized from a distance—generally confined to the Fisherman's Wharf area; those wearing shorts.

Toss the Cookies: ralph up; blow grits; not a baking term.

Transgender: a person considering (if not already a done deal) surgical options to distance one's membership from a designated sexual group (male, female, etc.). A politically correct term only found in this glossary; if you're looking for politically correct, buy some other book.

Transsexual: a person (usually a man) who employs surgical procedures to obtain components traditionally furnished as original equipment possessed by the opposite sexual persuasion.

Transite: type of pipe manufactured from asbestos and cement; nothing to do with this book.

Transvestite: a person (usually a man) utilizing old socks, tissue paper, make-up and thrift stores to masquerade as the opposite sex for sexual gratification and a chance to try out new hair styles; cross-dresser.

Warren Spahn: my favorite pitcher whose solo appearance is in this glossary.

Way bill: the paper that the drivers record and track their pickup and drop off of passengers.

Whisps: when a person unsuccessfully whispers confidential information from the back seat of a cab.

Zones: areas of the city divided by numbers.

Zip-zag: walking style inadvertently employed by the zealously inebriated.

ABOUT THE AUTHOR

Larry Sager's work has been published in journals, literary publications, textbooks, and newspapers. This is his first published novel. It was primarily penned in the early morning hours between 2:30 and 6 am following a ten-hour night shift of picking up strangers and sordid sorts from street corners and city haunts. He would then return to his mundane pursuit of a Bachelors Degree from the San Francisco State University Creative Writing Department. The nocturnal writing ritual lends a cogent immediacy and detail to the events described. He has a J.D. from the University of Michigan, having previously endeavored as a radio talk show host, producer of several short amateur films, professional musician, and White House Intern.